RETURN TO DEAD HORSE CANYON

Grandfather Spirits

A Novel by
Marcha Fox & Pete Risingsun

Kalliope Rising Press
Burnet, Texas

Kalliope Rising Press
P.O. Box 23
Burnet, Texas 78611

Dead-Horse-Canyon.com

First Printing 2021

Printed in U.S.A.

Cover and interior design by Marcha Fox

Stock photos copyright license
Cover Photo Credit: www.123rf.com/profile_jozefklopacka

PRINT: ISBN-13: 978-1-7334186-2-1
ELECTRONIC: ISBN-13: 978-1-7334186-3-8

BISAC: FIC059000, FIC024000, FIC039000

Quotes attributed to George Bird Grinnell excerpted from "The Cheyenne: Their History and Lifeways" used with permission from World Wisdom Inc. worldwisdom.com

Sequel to Award Winning Book 1

The Curse of Dead Horse Canyon:
Cheyenne Spirits

Dead-Horse-Canyon.com

Electronic Version:
https://books2read.com/deadhorsecanyon

Print Version:
Ingram & Amazon.com

DEDICATIONS

To my granddaughter, Sierra Star Sioux
—Pete Risingsun

To Mike Skaggs, without whose work and dedication to the Northern Cheyenne people Pete and I would never have met.
—Marcha Fox

ACKNOWLEDGEMENTS

Authoring this story and its predecessor, "The Curse of Dead Horse Canyon: Cheyenne Spirits" has been a bold and exciting adventure for both of us. Our own personal experience, research, and the help of friends who are experts in many fields of study have helped us bring this story alive.

Pete wishes to thank his friends Pastor Scott Shreffler and his Northern Cheyenne wife, Suzette Shreffler.

Marcha wishes to thank her many writing friends who slogged through earlier drafts of this story and especially the one who offered constructive criticism that pointed out a glaring inaccuracy that required a major rewrite. That's what friends are for! ;-)

OTHER TITLES
by Marcha Fox

This Series with Pete Risingsun
The Curse of Dead Horse Canyon: Cheyenne Spirits
(Book 1)
Revenge of Dead Horse Canyon: Sweet Medicine
Spirits
(Book 3 forthcoming)

Science Fiction
*Beyond the Hidden Sky**
*A Dark of Endless Days**
*A Psilent Place Below**
*Refractions of Frozen Time**
The Star Trails Compendium
*The Sapphiran Agenda (Short Story)**
*The Terra Debacle: Prisoners at Area 51**

*Available as audiobooks

Family History
The Family History Fun Factor

Astrology
Whobeda's Guide to Basic Astrology

"I will tie another one to it."
—*Old Cheyenne saying for when there's more to the story.*

BOOK II

An Indian Prayer

O Great Spirit, whose voice I hear in the winds and whose breath gives life to all the world, hear me! I am small and weak, I need your strength and wisdom.

Let me walk in beauty, and make my eyes ever behold the red and purple sunset.

Make my hands respect the things you have made and my ears sharp to hear your voice.

Make me wise so that I may understand the things you have taught my people.

Let me learn the lessons you have hidden in every leaf and rock.

I seek strength, not to be greater than my brother, but to fight my greatest enemy—myself.

Make me always ready to come to you with clean hands and straight eyes. So when life fades, as the fading sunset, my spirit may come to you without shame.

DRAMATIS PERSONAE

Bryan Reynolds - Systems Administrator, Denver Employees Federal Credit Union (Deceased)
Sara Reynolds - Bryan's wife
Charlie Littlewolf - Bryan's closest friend
Will Montgomery - Sara's father
Connie Montgomery - Will's wife, Sara's step-mother
Jason LaGrange - NSA Cyber Unit
Bernard Keller - Owner, BK Security Services LLC
Eddie Johannsen - BKSS Task Force Lead
Eaglefeathers - Charlie's grandfather (Deceased)
Liz Hudson - Sara's neighbor
Bob Bentley - U.S. Fed. Dist. Judge
Gerald Bentley - Bob's brother; CEO, Lone Star Operations
Myron Bentley - Lobbyist; Bob & Gerald's father
Ida Schwartz - Marina/RV park owner
Mike Fernandez - Falcon Ridge P.D.
Kyle Bishop, M.D. - Belton Reg. Med. Ctr.
Steve Urbanowsky - Captain, Falcon Ridge P.D.
Patrice Renard - Proprietor, Cosmic Portals
Dick Duncan - LSO Toolpusher
Trey Maguire - LSO General Mgr
Phil Stafford, PhD - LSO geologist
Kenneth Carlson - attorney-at-law
Joe Whitewolf - Cheyenne Medicine Man
Winston Ellsworth - CIA
Nigel Muller - Denver P.D.

He who is present at a wrongdoing and lifts not a hand to prevent it, is as guilty as the wrongdoers.
—*Omaha Proverb*

PROLOGUE

OLD EBBITT GRILL
WASHINGTON, D.C.
June 20, Thursday
8:04 p.m.

The collective mood in the downstairs Cabinet Room was glum. In spite of the promise of epicurean delights in one of Washington D.C.'s most highly-rated restaurants, the assembly of carefully selected individuals shifted restlessly in their chairs, conversations limited. Myron Bentley sulked at the head of the table, staring into the depths of his Pinot Grigio while the waiter noted his fellow lobbyists' respective orders.

They knew, as did he.

Mahogany cloaked walls consumed the soft light, complementing his thoughts. He sipped his wine, perusing the invitees. Only those in the elite innermost circle even knew the facility existed.

PURF would house but a fraction of his fellows, who'd be identified via lottery. Those privileged to occupy Phase One had already been chosen by the powers-that-be.

He was not among them.

Some would get in through the proverbial backdoor, one way or another.

Especially former Congressmen.

1

His own position, however, along with thousands of others, was tenuous.

Few present were union fans, but everyone understood the principle. When people were treated unfairly, banding together could wield influential power.

The waiter headed for the stairs.

Myron signaled his colleague, Calvin Nielsen, to close the door. Like himself, Calvin didn't make the first cut.

Even more egregious given the facility was his idea in the first place.

They exchanged knowing looks as the man resumed his seat.

Wine glass in hand, Myron arose from the head of the table and stepped behind the dais. His spoon kissed the crystal's rim.

The din grew still.

"Your attention, please, gentlemen," he stated. "We're gathered here this evening to consider a proposal. It will secure our positions as influencers, increase our status among the citizenry at large, and most important, provide resources to protect us, our livelihood, and earned benefits, should the need arise."

"Hear, hear!" someone called, to which all raised their glasses in a spontaneous toast.

As the din diminished Calvin prompted, "Okay, Myron, old boy. Let's hear it. What are you up to now?"

A hint of a smile teased Myron's thin lips.

"I'll get right to the point. As you all know, it will take several budget cycles before PURF is complete. As long as it remains buried in the black budget we're relatively safe. But nothing in this world is static. Without military or national security justification, sooner or later its existence will leak out. When it does, public opinion will not be in our favor."

The room rumbled as attendees murmured agreement. Crystal sang, demanding silence.

"It's essential to protect our interests," Myron went on. "To do so, I propose the creation of a nonprofit. Its charter will reflect the official purpose of training new lobbyists in existing law. It will also support a public relations sector to solicit public opinion and promote the service we provide by informing lawmakers of their diverse wishes. When we convince the citizenry we're on their side, future funding problems should disappear."

Muffled laughter cast a knowing shadow. In the majority of cases, lobbyists represented multibillion dollar corporations. The few human rights and environmental groups who conducted such activities not only depended on donations for survival, but were noticeably absent.

Myron's smile likewise defied containment. Thus, he allowed the chuckles to continue while he mustered the appropriate level of solemnity to finish his speech.

Everyone present had been carefully picked, then required to show government-issue photo ID for admittance. However unlikely it might be that anyone would foolishly record the proceedings for subsequent upload on YouTube, the façade needed to be maintained.

The room grew still.

Myron continued, "I propose annual dues of a thousand dollars per member. If five thousand join, which is roughly half our ranks, we'll have the needed resources." He battled another conspiratorial smile, then added, "Come what may."

The Lobbyist Opportunity League would have their back. Even those who'd already secured a comfortable place in PURF's luxury accommodations couldn't argue the benefits.

The organization's acronym had likewise been carefully selected to reflect what went on behind closed doors.

LOL.

Seek the ways of the eagle, not the wren.
—*Omaha Saying*

1. DECISIONS

BELTON COUNTY PARK
LAKE WILSON RECREATION AREA
COLORADO ROCKIES
June 24, Sunday
12:23 p.m.

Pine needles whispered in the stiff summer breeze, Lake Wilson dancing with waves that teased the shore. For Sara Reynolds, however, the view from that picnic table evoked far less pleasant memories. Goosebumps slithered down her arms at the instant replay of Bryan's mangled Silverado at the bottom of Dead Horse Canyon.

Connie, scooted onto the bench beside her, her father, Will Montgomery, facing them from the opposite side.

He cleared his throat. "Sara? Are you okay?"

Her distant focus shifted from somewhere beyond the rugged mountains flanking the public recreational area.

"Yes, Dad. I'm fine."

"If you're having second thoughts, that's good."

"Actually, no. Quite the opposite." She held his gaze long enough to make a point. "This is where Charlie and I first watched the dashcam videos."

"Oh, honey," Connie said, slipping her arm around her waist. "Maybe we should go somewhere else."

"No. It's good motivation."

4

Paternal eyes infused with sodium pentothal fixed on hers with that look she'd dreaded since her teens.

"Is this your decision? Or did Bryan force it on you?" he asked. "He's dead, Sara. They tried to kill you, too. More than once. Does he want you dead, too?"

Her eyes didn't waver. "Dad. We've been through this. It's not just Bryan. This information needs to be released. What they did to me is even more reason. People deserve to know."

He scoffed. "C'mon, Sara. Voting records show people couldn't care less. Do you think they approve of the billions sent overseas? The cost of wars? The outrageous million dollar pork barrel projects and legislative favors that keep Congress critters in office? The average person doesn't even know the names of their Congressional reps, much less give a damn."

"Well, *I* care," she retorted. "And I think they would, too, if they knew."

"That's pretty idealistic, don't you think?"

"Maybe. But I can't let Bryan's work, much less his life, go to waste. If no one cares, then nothing will happen. At least I'll know I did what I could."

"Then will you let this insanity go?" Will persisted, words clipped by the roar of a jet ski bumping across the waves.

She watched its carefree rider skim the water until the racket faded, its wake slapping the shore. Her eyes reconnected with his.

"He didn't want them to get away with it. Neither do I. But I have no control over that. All I can do is release the information." She straightened with resolve. "If you don't want any part of it, Dad, I get that. I'll just do it myself."

Will rolled his eyes. "I just think you're making a huge mistake." He shook his head in apparent defeat. "You're so stubborn sometimes, Sara."

Connie burst out laughing, bobbed hair dancing in the breeze as her hands covered her mouth.

His gaze shifted to his wife. "What's so funny?"

"Stubborn? Really, Will? I wonder where she got that?"

The corner of his mouth twitched. "You're right. I never won an argument with her mother, either."

"Haha," she replied. "You know *exactly* what I mean."

"Whatever," he mumbled, blue eyes back on Sara. "Listen. I can't let you do this by yourself. They'll eat you alive."

"Thank you."

"Doesn't mean I approve. I just want to keep you safe. Okay?"

"Okay."

Her defenses relaxed. Now maybe they could get somewhere.

"We know they're tapping our phones, which is why we left them at the cabin," he said. "So using them for internet access is out. We may have to do this the old-fashioned way. Do you have a printer up here?"

"I do. But we're talking thousands of pages. Snail mail, FedEx, or whatever could be intercepted. Delivering it in person is possible, I suppose. Except WikiLeaks is in Sweden."

"With good reason. Their laws protect journalists from revealing confidential sources. Considering we're on the government's radar, I doubt we could leave the country. Any place around here with public Wi-Fi?"

"There's a cafe in that little shopping center, next to the grocery store. But they're closed. Both today and tomorrow."

He peered over the top of his bifocals. "Doesn't mean their Wi-Fi isn't working."

Her eyes widened. "True."

"Okay. Let's do it. Is everything on your laptop?"

"Yes."

"You still have a backup somewhere, just in case?"

She lowered her chin and mirrored his condescending look. "You're kidding, right?"

"No. I'm not. When we get back make another one. You never know." He removed a tiny USB drive from an innocuous looking card in his wallet and handed it over. Sara slipped it in her purse.

"So that's the plan?" Connie asked, hand shading her eyes from the pine-filtered midday sun.

His tone was firm. "We're under surveillance. We can never be sure we disabled everything. Knowing their tactics, driving is risky. Taking both cars might help."

Sara tucked a gust-driven wall of chestnut curls behind her ear. "You know, since that raid the other night, those commandos haven't been back. I don't think they know we found it. Charlie and I were careful what we said and hopefully found all the bugs. With luck, maybe they actually believe I'm moving on with my life, like I told them. Acting normal might be our best bet."

She paused when Connie visibly winced. "What?"

"This is far from normal, honey. Do you really want to depend on luck?" She turned to her husband. "I'm sure you won't agree, Will, but maybe we should check with Patrice. See what she says."

Sara's eyebrows shot up while her father's dove in the opposite direction. "Really, Connie? Do you honestly think this astrologer friend of yours is accurate enough for a potentially lethal situation?"

Connie shrugged. "She's been spot-on so far."

Sara's mind drifted to the elegant woman with waist-length platinum hair and the many things she helped reveal the past few months. "What other options are there, Dad?"

His objections caved. "What the hell? I've heard worse ideas."

"How should I call her? My phone's back at the cabin and probably bugged."

Will pulled a burner from his jacket's inside pocket. "Here. One call before they find it. Out here, maybe not."

Sara stared at the keypad, then Connie, who fought a smile. "Give me the phone."

Will grunted. "You talk to this woman enough you memorized her number?"

Connie tapped it in, handed the phone back to Sara, then reached across the table to pat his cheek.

"I've been consulting Patrice since before we were married."

"Oh, yeah? How long?"

Her smile vanished. "A few months before Ellen died."

"Oh." He gnawed his lip. "Did it help?"

"Actually, yes. You can't argue with something that works."

"Amen to that," Sara agreed, then turned her attention to the call. "Patrice! Hi! It's Sara Reynolds. Are you busy?"

"Not particularly, sweetie. What can I do for you?"

"We want to, uh, take care of some of that, well—you know—old business. But we need to know if we're being watched. Can you see that?"

"It should show up. Where are you?"

"A few miles outside Falcon Ridge."

"Got it. Hold on."

Sara gave the others a thumbs-up, then watched splashes of sunlight do a table dance while she waited.

"Okay, here's what it looks like," Patrice said. "Right now, you're fine. Judging by the Moon, I'd say you have, oh, about a three or four hour window. You're doing this covertly, right?"

"That's the idea."

"They might be aware, but I don't see anything that'll stop you. My guess is it'll go public in three or four days."

"Perfect! Thanks, Patrice."

She hung up, then relayed the information.

"If we hustle, that's enough to get back to Denver or even Boulder," Will said. "Go somewhere public. It might be best if we're somewhere far away three days from now."

"I don't know, Dad. Maybe we should be in touch with Fox News or someone instead. Might be safer. What do you think?"

"Possibly. During that delay you should talk to an attorney. At least before going public yourself. I'd hate to see you wind up in prison."

"I wonder if Patrice can see that?" she said, then took back the phone and pressed redial.

"No, sweetie," Patrice replied. "They'll make a lot of noise, but you'll have enough public support they won't contribute to it by arresting you. You're likely to be seen as some sort of folk heroine. Other enemies are out there, though. You need to be careful. *Very* careful."

The warning wasn't a surprise, much less anything new. "Right. No prison is good news. Thanks again, Patrice."

"I have another idea," Will said. "There's a group called Judicial Guardian. They investigate government ethics violations, then take them to court. They've sued on behalf of whistleblowers in the past. If you agree, I'd be happy to contact them."

"Sounds perfect, Dad. We can send them the data, too. And a big donation, if it'll help."

"Usually does."

"There's a bunch of Bryan's personal stuff in that bench seat," Sara mused. "Legal documents, photos—things I'd hate to lose. Maybe I should take them with me, just in case."

"If you leave things as-is, they might not mess with it, assuming there's nothing of value," Will suggested. "They were pretty selective when they raided your condo."

"True. They found our guns and the server without turning the place upside down. It'd be a hassle to move everything, which might arouse suspicion in itself. I guess I should leave it."

"On the other hand, Sara, maybe you *should* bring anything of value along," Connie added. "They might torch the place to make sure anything they missed is destroyed."

Sara's nose wrinkled at the ugly possibility. "You're right. Shouldn't be that hard. Most of it's already in boxes. I'll check upstairs for anything I can't replace."

"While you do that, we'll start moving the other stuff," Connie volunteered.

"C'mon, let's go," Will stated, swinging his legs over the bench. "Time's a-wasting."

They are not dead who live in the hearts of those they left behind.
—*Tuscarora Proverb*

2. STARBUCKS

SARA'S CABIN
RURAL FALCON RIDGE
COLORADO ROCKIES
June 24, Sunday
1:03 p.m.

Back at the cabin, each pursued their respective tasks. Sara climbed the stairs to the A-frame's loft-style bedroom, twinges in her neck and hip unpleasant reminders of the two wrecks she'd suffered in as many months.

Both intended to kill her.

Gradually, her brain was becoming less addled from the concussion. At least for the most part. Anything too demanding still prompted confusion, anxiety, and frustration, often crowned by a nausea-inducing headache.

Nonetheless, her body was healing.

Heart, not so much.

Upon reaching the landing she paused, struck by nostalgia before thoughtful steps steered her to Bryan's side of the bed. She sat down, picked up his pillow, and hugged it to her chest.

Ignoring his death by staying busy had its limitations. In quieter moments her aching heart issued unwelcome reminders—her husband was *not* TDY.

The comforter's orange, red, yellow, and green floral pattern elicited a kaleidoscope of memories. It originally belonged to her mother—the last thing she bought before becoming too incapacitated with ALS to shop ever again. Connie was with her, the two women best friends dating back to college.

Three years after her mother passed away, Connie married Sara's father. She told Sara the bedspread made her feel guilty, as if she were sleeping with her best friend's husband. Thus, she asked Sara if she'd like to have it.

Its colors fit the cabin perfectly, where it became part of Bryan, too.

Joyful, carefree moments spent in their idyllic mountain retreat. Skiing, hiking, stargazing, making love before a roaring fireplace—all in a world that was theirs alone.

Now two of the people she loved the most were gone, the spread's soft touch a sentimental link to them both.

Whom did she miss more?

Her mom?

Or her husband?

She buried her face in his pillow, inhaling the scent that would always remind her of him, consumed by an unhappy flux of melancholy she didn't have time for right now.

"Sara? Do you need some help, honey?"

She sniffed hard and cleared her throat.

"No, I'm fine. Be right down."

She ducked into the bathroom to rinse her face and blow her nose.

Hopefully the cabin would be okay. Bryan's soul still resided there, his ashes scattered along their favorite hiking trail.

Everything, inside and out, had sentimental value—*everything*.

But for now, practicality had to reign.

Pushing back the mushy thoughts, she opened the closet. Ski equipment. That could be replaced in the unlikely event she decided to go again. The telescope in its bulky box in back could, too.

She smiled at what her father would say if she came trucking down the stairs with the telescope swaddled in the comforter.

That doused the temptation with enough logic she returned downstairs empty handed, Connie waiting at the bottom.

"Are you okay, honey?"

She nodded, but had always been a lousy liar. She bit her lip, unwelcome tears staging an encore. Connie wrapped her arms around her and held her tight.

"Everything's going to be fine. If you don't feel up to doing this, you don't have to. The only problem is how happy it'll make your father if you back out now."

A shaky laugh joined the renegade sniffles. "You're right. But it's not that." Her throat tightened, choking off the words. "It's just sometimes I really miss Bryan. And Mom."

Connie's eyes teared up as well while they embraced. Sara took a deep breath, then broke free to grab some toilet paper from the bathroom for them both. By the time Will stepped through the door, both were suitably composed.

He gave them a look as he swiped sweat from his brow. In the past few months, more of his thinning brown hair had yielded to grey.

Something she'd undoubtedly contributed to.

"What are you two doing, anyway?" he grumbled. "Everything's in the back of your car. Are you ready? C'mon. What are we waiting for?"

"We're ready," Connie said, winking at Sara. "Let's go."

Sara paused, paralyzed by another wave of nostalgia. "No. There's one more thing."

Ignoring their puzzled looks she went back upstairs, dragged the telescope out of the closet, wrapped it in the comforter, and made it halfway down before her father took it off her hands, looking more puzzled than critical.

"I'm sorry, Dad. Too many memories."

Ready at last, she locked the back door as the others went out the front. She glanced around one final time, then stepped outside and secured the front deadbolt with her key.

She reached her car part way down the gravel-strewn incline as Will closed the rear hatch. Memory flared with the Lakewood wreck, when that eighteen-wheeler loaded with logs ran her off the road.

"Hey, Dad. Question: If they put a tracker on my car, how difficult would it be to find?"

He pouted thoughtfully. "It'd be easy to tell on a lift. But they didn't do that to install one, so we should be able to see if there's anything there. Pop the hood. We'll need a flashlight to check the wheel wells and underneath. Inside, too. There could be microphones."

Sure enough.

Multiple bugs and a tracking device lurked inside and out, now a heap of intrusive electronics reposing on the ground by the passenger-side door.

She fumed as Will guided her a few yards away, thanking heaven they'd taken his car to that lakeside park.

"Did you or Connie say anything after we got home?" she whispered.

"No. She got everything out of the bench seat, handed it to me, and I took it out to your car."

She growled. "I can't stand those awful people! Every time I turn around I understand what Bryan did better than ever. I say we stomp them into the ground."

He snagged her arm as she stepped in that direction.

"Don't. A lost signal will tip them off. Leave them there. They'll think you're still at the cabin."

"Won't they hear me drive away?"

"It's a fairly steep grade. Put it in neutral and coast back before starting the engine. If they hear anything they'll think it's another car. Like ours."

"What about the telematics? Can they hack that?"

Deep lines accented his proud smile. "Good thinking, Sara. I trained you well. I'll disconnect it."

He reopened the cargo door and shoved the boxes aside to access the signal box and pull the wires.

"There. All set," he said, brushing his hands together.

"I want to stop by Charlie's and let him know the plan," Sara said, then they climbed inside their respective vehicles.

Gear shift in neutral, the tires crept backward until it rolled to a stop several dozen feet from the sensors.

The engine purred to life. She backed the car around, took one final glance at the cabin, then led the way to Charlie's.

CHARLIE'S CABIN
RURAL FALCON RIDGE
COLORADO ROCKIES
June 24, Sunday
1:38 p.m.

Charlie Littlewolf leaned against his aging Ford Ranger, waiting. Moments later the forest-muted sound of vehicles coming down the makeshift dirt road announced their arrival, confirming his intuition.

Sara's SUV stopped a few feet away, her father's Mercedes behind it. She got out, finger to her lips, and directed him several feet away.

"The car was infested with bugs," she explained. "We think we got them all, but just in case."

His eyes connected with hers. All they'd experienced together the past few months swirled in their doe-like depths.

"Good luck, Sara."

"Thanks. You, too. Be careful."

His response was a dark-eyed indigenous glare. "Watching out for treacherous white men is in my blood." He reached over and squeezed her hand. "You be careful, too."

"I will. According to Patrice, watch for something on the news in three or four days."

"I'm sure I'll hear at work. If nothing else, I have internet there. What are you releasing?"

"Everything in the Canopus file. We're going back to Denver to use public Wi-Fi somewhere. More anonymous than here, even though they're sure to know where it came from." She bit her lip, showing she wasn't as confident as she appeared to be. "So, we better go. Just wanted to let you know."

Back at her car, he noticed an array of boxes filled the rear cargo compartment. His breath caught in his throat.

Was she leaving for good?

He pointed.

"Oh, that," she replied. "That's all the stuff from the bench seat. Bryan's old photos, property records, that kind of stuff. I need to go through it, see what's there."

"Makes sense," he agreed, still wondering when she'd return.

He squeezed her hand again, then stepped back as she got back inside the car. Both vehicles turned around, then disappeared among the brush, whatever consequences awaited gathering as storm clouds on the western horizon.

DENVER, COLORADO
June 24, Sunday
4:15 p.m.

When they arrived in Denver, Sara led the way to the Starbucks on East Colfax, one of Denver's main drags, and a few doors down from the credit union where Bryan used to work. It felt right, as if the place that brewed his morning coffee would be where he'd do the deed himself.

She selected a place in the sparsely populated parking lot, her father pulling in beside her. They filed inside, welcomed by the aroma of freshly brewed coffee. Sara did her best to act casual, though adrenaline pulsed through her as if her foe were behind her in line.

They ordered. She removed her debit card from the zipper compartment in her purse. Will grasped her wrist.

Her eyes met his, confused. "It's okay, Dad. I've got it."

"No, Sara. I've got cash." His eyes drilled into hers.

Oh. . .

Beverages in hand, they looked around for a place to sit. "Should we go outside?" Connie suggested. "No one else is out there."

While Sara debated, Will noted, "It's too sunny. Lots of glare."

"True," Sara agreed, pointing to a table near the back window. After opening her laptop she laughed, afternoon sunshine obscuring the screen. She and Connie switched places.

She connected to Wi-Fi. As Firefox loaded Will's stiff posture reeked one final statement of disapproval. They held hands a moment, said a silent prayer. When she opened her eyes, it felt as if the coffee shop's new-age logo were leering at her from the opposing wall.

Her hands trembled as she typed in the WikiLeaks URL. The page loaded. The link for submissions beckoned. She entered the necessary information, then selected the huge file from the hard drive. She paused a single heartbeat, held her breath then clicked *send*.

Even as a zip file it took a few minutes to upload. She bit her lip, eyes locked on the progress bar. *Submission accepted* popped up on the screen.

After sharing a collective sigh, they raised their drinks in a solemn toast. Paper cups touched amid expressions saturated with unknowns.

As Sara drained her Cappuccino she noticed a thirty-something man with brown curly hair and a neatly trimmed beard watching from a single's table near the front.

He looked vaguely familiar.

Someone from Bryan's work perhaps?

"I think we're being watched," she whispered.

"Was he here when we arrived?" Will asked.

"I don't know. Maybe."

"You need to start paying attention to things like that, Sara. Let's go. See if anyone follows us."

"Why would he? There's not much he can do about it now."

"You'd be surprised."

As they pushed open the door and exited Connie said in a low voice, "Why don't I drive the Benz and you go with Sara?"

"Good plan. I'll help her go through the condo for any new listening devices. Meet us there. Keep a close eye on the rearview mirror."

Even before he recognized the brunette at the back table, NSA IT specialist Jason LaGrange's Spidey-sense told him that trio was up to no good.

In spite of the afternoon glare from the window beside her, when she'd glanced in his direction he remembered.

That picture. The one in Reynolds's personal belongings. In the box he picked up at the credit union.

That was her.

Apparently oblivious to his scrutiny, he casually picked up his iPhone, zoomed in, and snapped a surreptitious photo while they got settled at the table.

She opened a laptop.

What the hell were they doing holding hands? Praying?

Instincts fired.

Already into the establishment's Wi-Fi, a few keystrokes networked her computer to his own.

Firefox appeared.

She typed a URL.

Or tried to, correcting a few typos before getting it right.

When the website came up a bitter cocktail of emotions sailed through him.

This was *exactly* what that Cracker Jack ops team was supposed to prevent.

He hit *Cancel* too late to stop the file transfer, but snagged a copy, its size identical to the one on the thumb-drive recovered from Reynolds's place of employment.

He ground his teeth.

That incompetent bunch of wannabes had done nothing but screw up since Day One.

He texted Keller.

Heads-up. Target female just uploaded huge file to WikiLeaks.

The response was instantaneous.

WTF? Last report showed no movement or audio activity for several hours.

LaGrange attached the photo.

Then explain this.

3. NO BIG DEAL

BERNARD KELLER SECURITY SERVICES, LLC (BKSS)
ALBUQUERQUE, NEW MEXICO
June 24, Sunday
4:28 p.m.

Bernie Keller stared out the dusty window of his Spartan office, flexing his fists. If Johannsen were there, he'd rip off his ear and hand it to him. Then, while he gaped at it in shock, he'd use the heel of his hand to jam his nose cartilage into his brain and drop him like a sack of shit.

He picked up the cigarette smoldering in a tuna can on his desk. Took a drag, then exhaled through clenched teeth. Something stronger than nicotine would be needed damn soon.

He picked up the receiver of his landline and speed-dialed his ops lead.

"Hey, boss. Wazzup?"

"I don't know, Johannsen. Why don't you tell me?"

"Well, there hasn't been anything to report. Been real quiet the past day or so."

"Really. Do the words *'too quiet'* mean anything to you?"

"Well, yeah. It usually means someone's up to something."

"R-r-r-right. Did that ever occur to you, numbnuts? That the target might be, as you say, *'up to something'?"*

19

"Uh, no. Not really. Last time we saw that bitch she told us she was moving on with her life. We've been listening, but it's been real quiet. I assume she's chillin' out, doing just that. Moving on."

"I'm sending you something I just got from LaGrange. Look real close. Then tell me if that's what she's doin'."

He picked up his cell and forwarded the text and photo.

He waited.

"Got it..." The man's gasp was audible. "What the fuck?"

"We've had that discussion about assuming before. Do you remember, numbnuts?"

"How in the...? Wow. Hell, boss, I have no idea how this happened. We've been tuned in, listening, 24/7. Both residences, her car. I have no idea..."

"That's blatantly obvious. Where are you?"

"Home. In Lakewood."

"Get your sorry ass out to where you *think* she is right now, understand? Boots on ground. Find out what's going on and report back PDQ. Got it?"

"Roger that. On my way."

Figuring it would take an hour and a half or more for him to reach that damn cabin, he grabbed what was left of a doob from his top desk drawer. He dropped it in his shirt pocket with a clip, slipped on his prosthetic leg, then stood up and lifted Terminator's leash off the nail in the door.

His service dog scrambled to all fours, tail slapping the wall, while Bernie clipped the leash to the dog's collar.

The Rottweiler's nails clicked down the linoleum hallway in concert with Bernie's stealthy, albeit uneven, gait to the back door where man and his best friend stepped outside. The afternoon breeze was typically hot and dry, but stiffer than usual, forcing him to step around the corner to light up.

He took his usual series of baby hits, closed his eyes, and paused, waiting.

The canine whimpered, eyes fixed on something rustling the grass near the chain-link fence that separated the desolate property from the Albuquerque airport.

He walked a dozen yards into the vacant lot, unleashing the dog when he saw the ears of a jack rabbit. He clasped his hands together over his head and stretched, trying to release the tension while Mary Jane got to work.

Certainly more dependable than his idiot team lead.

What the hell was the matter with that asshole, anyway? He wasn't stupid, not as a rule. He was good at taking orders, at least. Following protocol. Like cleaning out Reynolds's truck. At the time they didn't even realize he was intentionally spying on the PURF site. Without that evidence, there would have been hell to pay for using lethal force on a couple cross-country skiers.

Johannsen came up with clever ideas from time to time, proving he was capable of original thought. He just made too many goddamn assumptions. Yet, for some reason, he had this unexplainable lucky streak, usually landing on his feet instead of his ass.

It probably related to all that down time, back in the beginning. Time he could have spent training those assholes. Like how to think. Guide them through what-if scenarios. How to determine anything that could cause a job to go off the rails.

Before the fact, not after.

His stomach clenched whenever he considered what went on while parole restrictions shackled him to New Mexico.

This PURF job was cursed from the beginning. A regular Class-A cluster fuck. At least when it was officially over, the pay should make up for it.

Maybe.

All this unexpected data security work had really eaten into their potential profits.

Would there be a penalty for missing this? Exactly what they'd been charged to prevent? No payment at all?

He finished the joint, ground the stub out with his heel, and pocketed the clip. He whistled, Rottie at his side moments later.

Slipped him a doggie treat.

Went back inside.

Checked his watch.

Still another hour before Johannsen would get there. He locked up his office and drove home to his efficiency apartment on Coal Avenue a few blocks away. Opened some Hormel chili, ate it out of the can, then brought up YouTube on his phone and watched some redneck reloading pistol shells until it rang.

"Yeah," he answered.

"Alright, here's the deal, boss. You know how the chick's old man's former FBI? Well, apparently he helped her get rid of all the mics and GPS. They're sitting here on the ground, right outside the cabin. Hold on, I'll send a picture."

"Don't bother. Just bring 'em back. You realize what this means, right?"

Silence.

"Let me give you a hint, numbnuts. This is what they call a failed mission. Which in this case involves a contract."

"Holy shit, boss. You mean we might not get paid?"

"It's a distinct possibility."

"So we're fucked."

"Yup."

The next morning at 0800 an email flagged *Urgent* arrived in Bernie's inbox from Elite Management Partners, Inc. He set his jaw and clicked, braced for the worst.

PURF government and contractor personnel:

Inside sources have reported an expansive quantity of classified data is expected to be released to the news media within a few days through the organization known as WikiLeaks. This is sensitive, potentially damaging Top Secret information with massive national security implications. All parties are hereby instructed to do the following, due in this office NLT COB today.

1. Assess and document all sensitive issues related to your organization.
2. Provide a list of expected repercussions.
3. Include a comprehensive description for remediation and damage control.
4. List of potential redactions related to National Security.

All contact with the media of any size, shape, or form is forbidden. An official response will be handled through government public affairs resources.

It was signed by the acting program manager, some guy from the Army Corps of Engineers assigned to see the project to completion following Steinbrenner's demise.

At least there was no mention BKSS was responsible. He leaned back in his chair as relief yielded to hope. EMPI, the project management firm overseeing the project, was the one originally responsible for data security.

Which was where Reynolds found one-stop shopping plus a road map to the originals.

His team's assignment was to protect the facility's perimeter.

Physical perimeter.

Somehow the rest fell into their lap, then went sideways from there with the discovery Reynolds's actions were not by chance.

His frown deepened, thoughts a whirlwind.

He'd been played.

Big time.

BENTLEY RESIDENCE
RURAL FALCON RIDGE
June 28, Thursday
12:03 p.m.

Bob Bentley glared at the television, fingernails impaling the padded arms of his burgundy recliner. Well-worn leather squeaked as he shifted his weight, as if past ruminations resided in its cushioned depths.

None of which were more serious than what lay before him now.

His worst nightmare since Lone Star Operations subcontracted on PURF was becoming the lead story on CNN. As a federal officer of the court, association with a company involved in this debacle would land on his porch like dog shit in a flaming bag.

He shuddered, picturing himself naked before a hostile jury.

A shaky hand raked his reluctant comb-over. He scowled at the grandfather clock beside the stone fireplace.

Too early for a drink.

If Angela caught him, there'd be hell to pay.

He picked up his phone from the teak table beside him to call his brother.

"Are you watching this, Gerald? Do you know what this means?"

"Yeah, yeah, I know, Bob. So it made it up the food chain to the White House. What did you expect? At least we had a few days warning. Gave legal some prep time. This isn't our fault, you know. We're only a sub. The ethics of the facility itself are not, I repeat, NOT our goddamn problem."

"What about that casing leak? The one that contaminated the local water system? That could come back and bite us, hard."

"Fixed and holding. We've done nothing wrong. Fu'thermore, we have federal protection. Liability's on the water company. As usual, Bob, you're worried about nothing. Why don't you know this? You're the one with a law degree."

"*Hmmmph.* Maybe I know too much, seen too much. Especially when a jury's involved. You never know what they'll come back with. Especially in a civil suit for personal injury or wrongful death. My involvement is bad, no matter what."

"Why? Can't judges have investments? Especially an inherited family business?"

"I know, I know. You're right."

"For a change," Gerald quipped, laughing.

He sunk deeper into the chair. "Look. I just don't want my name in lights headlining the next scandal."

"Just lay low. Don't paint a bullseye on your back, Bob. This will pass, like every other flap. I talked to Dad earlier. He's working on a solution if things get out of hand. Washington's got far bigger problems than we do."

"Hey, it's starting. Hopefully this will help. Later, Gerald."

"Bye, Bro."

MONTGOMERY RESIDENCE
BOULDER
June 28, Thursday
12:05 p.m.

Sara sat in her father's book-lined den staring at the big screen TV with him and Connie. After getting back from the cabin she'd stayed there, condo again sullied with surveillance devices. Depending on the reaction to the news, she might stay awhile.

She and Connie exchanged a knowing look, trying not to gloat that Patrice's timing was correct. The morning news broke the story, government response quicker and coming from a higher source than expected.

What would the president say? The blatant use of taxpayer money for a multi-billion dollar boondoggle was inexcusable.

What was said could also have strong bearing on her legal status. WikiLeaks protected its sources, but it wasn't like the government didn't know exactly where that data came from.

Bryan did the hacking and data mining, but she released it. As classified information, laws had been broken.

Which could put her in the line of fire.

She crossed her fingers Patrice was right about prison, too.

The president looked confident, almost bored, maybe amused. He wasn't easy to read sometimes and this was one of them. She glowered at the screen. Another shifty-eyed, career politician.

He eyed those in the press room, then favored them with a condescending simper.

"My fellow Americans. I realize many of you are troubled by information pertaining to the construction of a secure site for certain individuals who support government operations.

"First of all, I want to assure you that the process by which the Pearson Underground Residential Facility was created was within the bounds of our legal system and Constitution. The legislation was introduced by Congressman Pearson, a member of the House of Representatives, which is where all funding-related bills must originate.

"A fact you should know, if you were awake during your high school civics class.

"It was duly considered by the appropriate committees, then passed by the House, and later the Senate, modifications for phased construction periods negotiated between them.

"I signed this bill into law because I believe it's appropriately considered a matter of national security. The interface between lawmakers, the people, and their numerous advisors is an integral hub in our system of government.

"In many cases, this involves corporations. Corporations and jobs are essential to our economy. If our country should suffer a catastrophe—apocalypse, if you will—it would be essential for us to rebuild. Surviving corporations and lawmakers would have to work together to re-establish stability. Without knowledgeable advisors, this would be impossible.

"These advisors, who represent a variety of causes, are often referred to as 'special interests.' These cover everything from civil rights concerns to the environment. I'm sure that each of you support a few, either financially or philosophically. These will also be included.

"Upon completion the facility will only house twenty percent of those who work in this capacity. It has not yet been decided how this subgroup will be selected.

"We've set up a survey on the White House website where voters can express their views regarding which industries and causes will be represented. After that, a lottery will decide the individuals chosen for inclusion in the facility.

"I assure you that these actions have been taken in the best interest of our country's well-being in the event of a cataclysmic event. It's our responsibility as a government to assure continuity of our way of life. It was to that end that this project was introduced and built."

Sara's mouth hung open. Whatever she'd expected, it wasn't this. Denying the project's existence or defending it, perhaps. But the country's Chief Executive just explained it away as if it were no big deal. Government business as usual.

"Why do I feel like Bryan died in vain? Is this okay, what they did?"

Will shook his head.

"Most transparent crock of crap I've ever heard, even from him. If it was legal, then why'd they hide it in the Black Budget? The location could fall under National Security, I suppose. But you know damn well those selected will be based on the size of their campaign donations, not some survey."

"That's for sure," Sara muttered.

"No. This isn't right," Will went on. "While there's a modicum of truth to what he said, there's still something fundamentally wrong with corporations running the country. Corporatism is no better than socialism. Neither serves the public interest.

"On the positive side, this vindicates you, even if it squashes Bryan's intentions. If the process was legal, nothing can be done."

Her hopes crumbled, consumed by soul-crushing disappointment. Her dead husband's sacrifice, to say nothing of what she'd been through herself—nearly killed in two wrecks, the love of her life murdered, searching frantically for the data, being stalked and threatened by a black ops team—all for naught.

Her energy drained as all her efforts to fulfill Bryan's last request evaporated in futility.

Her father reached over to pat her hand. "You did your best, Sara. It's over."

The room blurred behind a veil of tears. "I would have rather gone to prison than fail him like this," she said, voice modulated with the devastation of defeat.

Oh, Bryan, I'm so sorry...

LONE STAR OPERATIONS (LSO) DRILLING SITE
June 28, Thursday
12:20 p.m.

Just before noon, site-wide intercom issued a raspy pre-emptive click in LSO's portable lab at the drilling site. Busy preparing a core sample for the mass spectrometer, Charlie froze in his tracks.

Seconds later, Trey Maguire's booming voice stated, "Alright, y'all. Listen up. Except all ya'll working the rig, get to the office ASAP. The president's giving an unscheduled State of the Union. Could be important. Ride's on the way."

The roustabout made six trips with the 8-wheel ATV, Charlie and his geologist boss, Dr. Phil, in the last teeth-rattling run. As always, the office trailer smelled like stale cigar smoke with a hint of scorched coffee. When he was pretty sure what the speech was about, his first reaction was a satisfied grin.

Sara pulled it off. Good for her.

Multiple bored faces indicated no one was impressed, most more interested in their phones. Roughnecks weren't exactly news hounds, most more concerned with beer and lotto tickets.

It surprised him the president got involved so quickly, but not his response. By glossing over the issue, people would go back to their daily grind without a second thought.

He stared at the big screen from his folding chair, stewing. As a Native American the denial of wrong-doing was exactly what he expected.

The U.S. government made its own rules.

Broken as necessity arose.

Anyone or anything that got in its way was eliminated.

The dream he had after the raid at Sara's teased his mind. Something building up for generations. At least as far back as Black Cloud's curse, maybe before. He was supposed to do something.

But what?

He needed another sweat. That would bring the required inspiration. After helping white men violate the Earth Mother for a living he needed to purify himself, body and soul,.

But what choice did he have? He needed a job. He took Bob Bentley out fishing, next thing he knew he was trying to remember college chemistry classes.

His first paycheck replenished his savings enough to catch up his child support. The next one provided a much overdue oil change, new battery, and tires for his truck, plus enough to pay back Sara.

Which he forgot to give her when she stopped by earlier in the week.

By the end of July he could afford to quit. Then he could get serious figuring out what he was supposed to be doing as far as *Maheo* was concerned.

His ponderings ended with the broadcast. As he stood up, the drilling site's prematurely grey general manager caught his eye. Maguire pointed to his private office on the far end of the double-wide trailer.

He swallowed hard.

Now what?

Maybe he'd be leaving this job sooner than expected.

When he stepped inside, the man motioned to shut the door. He complied, then sat facing his desk, braced for some sort of complaint.

PhD Phil didn't say much. For all he knew, he'd messed something up. Maybe the geologist was afraid to say something directly. From those side-long looks he got, he was probably worried about being scalped—a practice that originated with French Canadian bounty hunters, *not* indigenous people.

Maguire's white mustache twitched as he perused him with probing blue eyes

"Y'all told me this area's familiar. That you knows your way around. Is that right?"

He nodded. "Yes, sir. I do. Know it well."

"If I tell y'all what we's looking for, say a certain geological profile, do y'all think you could find it?"

"If one exists around here, it shouldn't be a problem."

An enigmatic smile crinkled the corners of the man's eyes. "Great. I reckon that's pretty much what I wanted to hear."

Charlie's gaze met his expectantly. Maguire's mouth sagged, mood shifting.

"Okey dokey. Here's the deal, Littlewolf. I'll be honest with y'all. We haven't had a strike since Dr. Phil's been telling us where to dig. Fu'thermore, he's got us pullin' too much core."

He grabbed a tall roll of paper from behind him and unfurled it across his desk. "Does y'all know what this here is?"

The paper had four columns, multiple line graphs taking up three, the last one broken up according to a color-coded legend defined at the top. The data looked familiar, like what he'd seen in his work study job in college.

"Looks like seismic data. Density. Resistivity, maybe. That last column, probably what type of rock is at a certain depth."

He jumped when Maguire's fist struck the desk. "Y'all gots it, son! Not exactly rocket science, now, is it?"

He braced himself when the man's body language switched to one of disgust.

"Well, from what I's seen, it is for Dr. Phil. We do as much as possible using LWD—you know, loggin' while drillin'—to eliminate the hassle of core samplin'. But he seems to have a bunch o' trouble readin' telemetry, which is what y'all's lookin' at here. I'm thinkin' that man's as useless as teats on a boar hog."

He leaned forward, forearms on the print out. "If we finds somethin' good, we'll set up a perm'nent-like operation and might not bother doin' any more exploration. Which means he'd get shit-canned. Either he's milkin' us, or he flat-out don't know shit from Shinola."

He reached into a side drawer and pulled out a cigar. He licked it end to end, then struck a match to light up, belching out a cloud of pungent smoke as he continued.

"He's supposed to be doin' a basin analysis. Simple stuff. Seismic work's done, which should tell him what any decent geologist needs to know. But he keeps wantin' samples. Like he gets off playin' in the dirt or somethin'. He spends too damn much time messin' with the internet. For all I know, he's lookin' at porn. Or worse yet, figurin' stuff out."

Charlie silently agreed. What he'd seen so far implied exactly that.

Maguire gave him a long, speculative look, then removed a thick binder from the shelf behind him. It hit the desk with a *thump*, then he opened it up, rotating it toward Charlie. A stubby finger stabbed the page, even more emphatic with its tip missing.

"This is what we's lookin' for. We found a few other nice deposits 'round here and there's gotta be more. If we can find one more before we wraps up for the season, it'd be great."

The diagram described a basic oil shale profile.

An image appeared in his mind of a location shadowed by Eagles Peak. The surface topology matched, plus he was relatively sure there was a fault through the area.

The impression was so strong it startled him. Words spilled unbidden from his mouth.

"I know where you can find just that. There's tar leakage around there, too."

The man's eyebrows shot up, eyes wide. "Tar? Or oil?"

He paused, memory unclear. "Not sure. Black stuff, some more liquid than others."

"No shit? Even if it's tar sands, which is kinda dirty and a bit different to deal with, that's better 'n nothing. It'd be great, if it's a big enough strike. We could lease it out, if nothing else. Wow, Littlewolf. If y'all nails it, there's a hefty bonus waiting for y'all, believe me."

Charlie suppressed a smirk as *White man talk with forked tongue* flitted through his mind.

"If it's okay with you, sir, I'll scout it out tomorrow, before I come in. Take a closer look, make sure it's how I remember."

"We's gotta drone, if y'all wanna use that. Save youself the hike."

"Thanks, but no. I'd rather check in person. Make sure it's like I remember."

A huge grin beamed behind another puff of smoke. "Y'all's right. Nothing beats boots-on-ground. I knew I should've put y'all on the scouting team, right off the bat. I'm more convinced than ever Dr. Phil don't know diddly squat 'bout petro-gee-olo-gee."

Charlie's eyes blinked in silent agreement. "I'll check with you first thing when I get back. It's quite a hike, so it'll probably be afternoon. If you want, I'll text some pictures. Assuming there's a signal. It's pretty high up, so should be."

Maguire agreed enthusiastically, then they exchanged cell numbers.

"Do you want to tell my, uh, supervisor? Or should I?"

The man gripped the cigar in his teeth while he spit out an expletive.

"I'll tell Big Dick. As toolpusher, he needs to know. But let's leave that other asshole hangin'. I'm sure he'll be bitchin' and whinin'. Which, near as I can tell, is the one thing he's good at."

The man extended his hand. Charlie reciprocated and received a hearty shake. "Knock 'em dead, Littlewolf."

"Hopefully not, sir."

"No shit. Last thing we needs is OSHA up our asses with a flashlight. And how's about y'all ditches this *sir* and *mister* crap? The name's Trey. I'll see y'all tomorrow."

Charlie waved as he left, then hailed the roustie, a young redneck named Tommy, to take him back to the drilling site.

When he got to the lab, Dr. Phil was outside cutting into the plastic sheath of another core sample. He looked up, glasses perched in their usual place on the tip of his nose, staring at him in his usual pinched, disapproving manner.

He ignored the silent reproach, climbed back inside the trailer, and resumed where he left off before Maguire's impromptu meeting.

The old woman untied the feathers the young men had on their heads and threw them on the fire. She painted each man with red paint, and on each one painted the sun and the moon, in yellow.
—*Legend of Sweet Medicine as told by George Bird Grinnell in "The Cheyenne Indians: Their History and Lifeways"*

4. MORALS

MONTGOMERY RESIDENCE
BOULDER
June 28, Thursday
12:50 p.m.

Sara stared at the distant traffic along Boulder's Diagonal Highway from the bedroom where she'd spent her growing-up years.

It never failed to remind her that some things never change.

Did anyone care? Or had this sort of thing become so commonplace it wasn't worth a second thought?

Bryan's request was specific: *"Don't let them get away with this."*

By all appearances, they just did.

Even journalists didn't express disapproval. Bryan always said the media were controlled, if not owned, by the government. It had never been more apparent.

The commentary after the president's address centered around the facility's legality.

Not a word about ethics or morals.

Using taxpayer funds to house corporate lobbyists.

Wrong was hardly the word.

34

With it now public knowledge, would those responsible for its inception encounter any problems? Maybe a few hands would be slapped behind closed doors, that was it.

More likely high-fives.

Government fashioned the laws and bent them at will. Congressmen elected to represent the people only looked after themselves and high dollar campaign contributors.

Her cell rang. She sighed, not in the mood to talk.

Its screen bore the name *Liz Hudson*. A neighbor out by the cabin with whom she played *Mah Jongg* on occasion. Her husband was a retired Air Force colonel Bryan knew when he was stationed at Colorado Springs.

The woman was good-hearted, a bit gossipy, but probably the closest thing to a friend she had these days, besides Charlie. She sighed, plopped down on the bed, and accepted the call.

"Hi! It's Liz. How are you doing, dear?"

"Okay, I guess. How are you?"

"Well, I've just been thinking about the President's speech. Do you by any chance know anything about that? Like, say, before the broadcast?"

She couldn't help smiling. Liz was no slouch when it came to putting things together. No wonder she won at *Mah Jongg*, more often than not.

"Yes. I do. Quite a bit, actually."

"I knew it! Good for you. What are you going to do now?"

"I don't know, Liz. I'm pretty disappointed at the reaction."

"Well, whatever you decide, I'm behind you one hundred percent. I think it's outrageous. If people knew what they did to you and your hubby, I think there'd be more of a reaction. Squandering taxpayer money is one thing, murder quite another."

"True. But no telling whether the public would see it that way."

"Well, I certainly do. Are you still at your cabin?"

"No. My dad's, in Boulder."

"Let me know when you get back. We'll do lunch. We missed you at *Mah Jongg* last time."

"Thanks. I'll let you know."

"Great. Hope to see you soon."

"Bye, Liz."

The *Tomb Raider* poster above her bed beckoned. Placed there in her teens, she never took it down. Her favorite movie *ever*.

Lara Croft was indomitable.

Afraid of no one.

Stopped at nothing short of victory.

Tough against the bad guys, compassionate to the underdogs.

Her heroine whispered, *You're not going to take this, are you?*

She folded her arms.

No. Absolutely not.

Discouragement morphed to outrage.

The White House response was unethical, immoral, and fundamentally wrong.

Period.

But what could she possibly do to make a difference?

Her father would tell her to leave it alone. However, she could count on Charlie. His dedication to Bryan's legacy was as strong as hers, to say nothing of his opinion of the government.

Connie's voice issued from below. "Sara? C'mon down, honey. Lunch is ready."

She inhaled deeply, then plodded downstairs. The trio sat around the kitchen table munching fried chicken and Cole slaw until her father broke the silence between bites.

"Something's changed since you retreated upstairs to your lair. You're not planning to do anything stupid, are you?"

She met his signature paternal gaze, then broke into a mischievous grin. "And why exactly would you say that, Daddy?"

"Because I know how much this meant to you. Something tells me you're not going to let it go."

She exhaled through her nose as she squeezed a lemon wedge into her iced tea. "You're right. I can't. But I don't know what to do. And Dad? It may be stupid, but I promise it'll be the right thing—the moral thing—whatever it is."

He set down his fork. "You're a grown woman, Sara. So, even though I think you should leave it alone, I know you won't. Like I said before, I can't let you go into this blind. Let me know what you plan to do and I'll see if there's some way I can help."

He turned to Connie. "Is that okay with you? I don't want supporting one woman in my life to cause friction with the one I sleep with."

"Of course it's all right with me." Connie's response bordered on indignant. "I'm totally on her side with this one. I'd be more likely to cut you off if you told her to leave it alone."

"*Hmmph.* Should have known. You females stick together in some secret sisterhood." He lowered his chin and peered over the top of his glasses. "So what's your plan? Or making it up as you go along?"

"A little of both. I'm going back to the cabin tomorrow. I want to talk to Charlie. I'm curious what his reaction was. I'll call him tonight, after he gets home from work."

His eyes widened. "Work? He got a job? That's great! What's he doing?"

She chuckled. "Working for an oil company."

He nearly choked on his drink. "You can't be serious."

"No. He hates it. But he needs the money."

"What do they have him doing? Working a rig?"

"I'm not sure. He said something about a lab."

He picked up his fork and used it to emphasize his words. "He needs to stay away from those rigs. Dangerous as hell. Furthermore, those roughnecks won't be too keen on having a Native American on their crew."

She took a thoughtful sip of her iced tea. "He tends to get along pretty well with everyone. He's an educated man, Dad, with a bachelor's degree. He can't help it if he's Cheyenne."

"Maybe so, but those roughnecks aren't usually the brightest lights in the harbor. They're typically racist. Brutally racist. Oil is traditionally a white man's game. He needs to watch his back."

COLORADO ROCKIES
June 29, Friday
6:18 a.m.

Early the next morning, Charlie set out for the location he saw in his mind's eye. An old rutted mining road only went so far through the rough before his truck refused to climb any further. He got out and pocketed the keys, hoping there wouldn't be any surprises when he returned.

Like when he canoed down Tomahawk Creek to check out Bryan's wrecked truck and got arrested for trespassing. The most humiliating experience of his adult life.

His mind wandered as he began his upward trek through the brush. The pine-scented mountain air enlivened his soul, unlike the stale atmosphere of the lab.

His steps led him through a stand of lodge pole pine intermingled with aspens, heart-shaped leaves singing in the summer breeze.

Something rustled in the brush to his left.

His eyes met those of a bighorn sheep.

He hadn't seen a single animal, even a bird, at the work site. It wasn't above the tree line, which large predators avoided as mostly devoid of prey. Was it LSO's presence with all that equipment? Noise and odors, perhaps? Or was he simply not paying attention? There wasn't much to see from that windowless trailer.

Charlie softened his stance as he studied the majestic animal. No wonder it was chosen to represent the state. Lambs and young sheep served as prey to many predators. A bighorn ram was another story. It would take a cougar, pack of wolves, or bear to take this one down.

Or an armed man.

This one had survived many seasons and would possess quite a harem of ewes. Lambs would be frisky and active this time of year, not yet weaned and vulnerable. No harm would come to any with this patriarch around.

Curled horns framed its head like a war bonnet. They could inflict serious damage, either directly or by butting him on an uncomfortable tumble down the side of the mountain.

His eyes narrowed with thought. As a spirit animal, what message did he bear?

Protection.

Defense of one's own life as well as those for whom he was responsible.

The ram wouldn't attack unless threatened. Once he did, however, it would be at full-force.

The first person who came to mind was Sara. Danger undoubtedly lurked in shadows. There wasn't much he could do while she was in Denver, other than watch for any suspicious activity around her cabin.

The animal gave him one final look, then ambled off with sure steps.

Teddy Roosevelt's words, "Walk softly but carry a big stick," often quoted by Bryan, flitted through his mind, reminding him he needed one before the ground grew any steeper. A sturdy branch lay up ahead. He picked it up and thanked the tree that shed it for his benefit.

With nothing to use as an offering, he left a blessing instead, then sat on a downed Ponderosa pine to shear off the branch fragments with his knife. He examined it for any signs of rotting or vulnerable knots. Finding none, he set out again, remote sensing, Indian style.

He continued to the next rise, beyond which sprawled a bowl-shaped indentation, known in geological terms as an amphitheater. Shadowed by Eagles Peak looming above, the temperature dropped, evoking a chill.

The real question was whether it constituted the typical basin where hydrocarbons resided, trapped between layers of shale or limestone. Using the stick for leverage, he descended into the concave formation, rocky ground covered in a variety of grasses and succulents with a few yellow wildflowers.

Flat shale-like slabs were distributed throughout. Its texture matched Maguire's diagram, along with a noticeable uplift indicative of a fault. He approached the demarcation, stepping slowly along its downward side.

A distinct energy change rippled through him.

While the Earth always felt alive, here it emitted a higher frequency. The rocks were marred with a black, sticky substance.

Tar.

A substance his people used anciently to seal canoes and water jugs. He followed the trail it left, coming to a small pool of brownish liquid.

A subtle rainbow danced within.

This wasn't tar.

A prophetic flash teased his mind. The entire amphitheater presided over by an imposing rig, two functioning wells, a conglomeration of pipes, tanks, and a lengthy tributary to a commercial pipeline several miles away.

Unbidden fear fell upon him. *Was he betraying the Earth Mother?* To do so would be a very serious, potentially unforgivable mistake.

He proceeded upward, berating himself for not having any tobacco to make an offering or, better yet, the sacred red pipe to petition *Maheo* in the proper manner.

Trees thinned out, the last conifers a few subalpine firs distended by countless battles with drifted snow. Upon reaching the usual brush and grasses found at high elevations, he paused, breathless again, assessing the terrain.

Increased energy tingled through him.

Like the Sacred Mountain back home on the Northern Cheyenne reservation, known to the uninitiated as Bear Butte.

With all evidence of man and technology left behind, his thoughts shifted. People sometimes vanished from such areas, perhaps happening upon an interdimensional portal or star people. In the past he didn't always respect such places as he should.

He sat on a boulder facing the rock-strewn ground that led to the summit. His entire situation, especially how this job fell into his lap, remained an enigma. The past few months had been full of surprises, some bad, some good. His white brother's death was definitely bad, yet this job coming out of the blue was—good?

Putting his education to work and earning a paycheck were great. His confidence and self-worth were higher than they'd ever been. What he was supposed to accomplish, however, was an enigma.

Was its purpose no more profound than to haul him from the claws of debt? Help him achieve the joy, happiness, confidence, and peace promised to those who lived a good life?

Maybe that's all it was.

A means to an end.

He got up, brushed his hands off on his jeans, and assumed the challenge of climbing upward over several dozen yards of scree. The rocky incline was typical of the southern face where freeze/thaw cycles fractured rock into small, sharp edged shards.

One that would be perfect for an arrowhead caught his eye. Smiling, he picked it up.

Nothing happened by chance.

What was its message?

Was he evolving into a warrior at last? Only need a few hard blows to sharpen him into what he was supposed to become?

He dropped it in his pocket, then continued on.

Jagged towers of naked stone reached for the sky, Earth's original skyscrapers. Going any higher would be foolish without climbing equipment or at least a partner.

Upon reaching an outcropping, he ended his ascent. He made his way to where it jutted out over his ascent path and sat down to absorb the majestic view. Some mountains still wore a crown of snow, craggy peaks as far as he could see.

The stark contrast to the lab trailer drove his thoughts to the red and white ponies, always running in the background.

Were they converging at last?

Having a job, especially one that paid well—*really* well—inflated his self-image with confidence and pride. A sense of purpose, satisfaction, and control he hadn't felt since. . .

41

Since when?

Probably as a little kid, helping *amasani*.

Sitting in his Earth Mother's figurative lap enveloped him in a warmth that filled his soul, not unlike his maternal grandmother. His indigenous blood bound him to the Earth. His mother, in many ways literally. To harm her in any capacity grated against everything he knew to be right.

He felt her life force through the ground beneath his feet, sensed her personality and moods. The ram he happened upon was a distant cousin, not a wild animal. The box elders, lodge pole pine, even wildflowers, spoke to his soul, connecting him with *Maheo*.

Yet, the panorama before him presented a different perspective. Up close, corruption was more evident. "America the Beautiful" was quietly being eaten away, literally and figuratively, like an influx of spruce bark beetles feasting on old growth. His stomach issued an uncomfortable reminder that he was contributing to just that by helping greedy white men violate the Earth.

If *Maheo* told him to quit, he would.

So far no such prompting had come.

What would he tell Maguire if *Maheo* said no? That he changed his mind?

Or lie and say the geology wasn't as he remembered?

He closed his eyes and offered a vocal prayer, first apologizing for not doing so in the prescribed manner with an offering, then seeking guidance.

He waited for a response.

No words of counsel entered his mind.

No spirit animal appeared.

Even the breeze grew still.

Yet, he felt peace.

As if he were doing the right thing, whether or not it defied logic. Earth could heal, even rid herself of the parasitic human infestation on her surface.

Perhaps oil was another resource the Earth Mother offered for her children to use.

Were modern conveniences wrong?

What would he do without his truck? His phone? Was this no different than drilling a well for water?

No one looked upon that as a violation.

Was that the answer?

He listened a little longer to no avail, then got up and started his descent. Back at the amphitheater he took out his phone, surprised it had a signal. He scrutinized the surrounding peaks, finding no less than five towers within line-of-sight range.

Were he and his culture no more than misplaced anachronisms?

He snapped several photos from different angles, a few of the seepage. Maguire could send in his drone to take aerial shots and determine the easiest route to bring in the equipment for a seismic survey.

He held his breath, took one more apologetic look around, then sent the pictures.

The sticky substance puddled along the fault's seam drew his attention.

He needed a sample.

His pockets were mostly empty except for his keys, wallet, and LSO site badge—which was in a plastic sleeve attached to a lanyard.

He removed the ID card, dropped it in his shirt pocket, and hunkered down, urging as much of the liquid as possible into the holder. He coaxed it inside, for some reason reminded of catching night crawlers for bait.

By the time the makeshift container was full it was all over his hands. It smelled like oil. High viscosity, slippery, and slightly gritty, probably sand.

Like dirty crankcase oil.

Definitely not sticky, like tar.

He wrapped the lanyard firmly around his wrist, allowing the sample to hang freely.

The wound-up cord resembled a battle bracelet.

He paused, wondering at the similarity.

If geologists are right, it would mean that fault lines are far more sensitive to human activity than previously thought.
—*Columbia University's Earth Institute*

5. INSIGHTS

COLORADO ROCKIES
SARA'S CABIN
June 29, Friday
2:14 p.m.

The day after the president's demoralizing speech Sara returned to the cabin where she sat at the breakfast bar sipping a mug of green tea. She hadn't been publicly identified as the informant so felt safe.

Those insidious people who'd been stalking her knew, but now that the government's dirty deeds were public knowledge—which the president said was just fine and dandy—maybe they'd leave her alone. Nonetheless, she still kept her Glock in her purse, just in case.

However, there was another side to anonymity. Like Liz suggested, maybe public response was lacking because the story was faceless. No personal touch. No harm done. Government business as usual.

Her and Bryan's role, much less circumstances, were not released to WikiLeaks. Only the documentation he'd gathered detailing PURF's funding, purpose, and existence.

Money versus murder.

The more she thought about it, the more she realized this couldn't be done quietly. To honor Bryan's last request she had to take it to the next level. Writing letters and staying behind the scenes wouldn't do it.

Being blatantly suicidal about it, however, didn't make sense, either.

Determined to make an informed decision, she called the one person who might be able to help.

Patrice's cheerful voice was comfort in itself. "Hey, sweetie. How are you doing? May I assume that recent media flap was your doing?"

"You could say that. But it's already yesterday's news."

"It's definitely been quiet following the initial blast. Do you plan to let it fade into the sunset?"

"Actually, that's why I called. I'm furious they blew it off. But I promised Dad I wouldn't do anything blatantly stupid. So, I figured I'd check with you."

The astrologer responded with a hearty laugh. "Yes, my dear, that's in my job description. Hold on while I bring up your solar return. It can tell us what's in store this coming year."

While she awaited the verdict, Sara grabbed an apple from the basket on the counter. As its sweetness caressed her tastebuds, she gazed beyond one of the A-frames triangular windows, watching a lone cloud in the cobalt sky

Moments later, Patrice was back.

"Okay, sweetie, here's the deal. There's definitely some risk involved, both physical and emotional. This coming year will bring changes. Lots of them. Things will not turn out as expected. This is not to say they'll be bad, only different. Unpredictable. Awkward or disruptive. You'll have to change course or make some sort of adjustment, perhaps encounter a Catch-22."

"Catch-22?" Sara asked.

"*Damned if you do, damned if you don't.* Getting public attention and speaking your mind will come easily, but with mixed results. Going after what you want will foster some disturbing situations, some of which could be dangerous, maybe even life-threatening. While some people will be receptive, others, especially specific groups or those with some level of authority, will be upset. *Ha*—according to Pluto, *very* upset. Livid, even. When all is said and done, you'll be a different person by the time your next birthday rolls around."

That prognosis not what she'd hoped to hear.

"That bad, huh?"

"Well, let me put it this way. Your life's going to be bumpy this year, sweetie, whatever you decide. That's just the prevailing energy. How you choose to use it, that's up to you. You always have free will."

More undecided than ever, she shifted her focus to the everlasting mountains. "So if I back off, everything will be fine?"

"Not necessarily. There's a chance that even if you don't take action you'll encounter serious, soul-stretching issues. After all, you're a new widow getting over a series of traumatic events. Maybe a sense of purpose is what you need."

"That makes sense. When I stay busy I don't have time to feel sorry for myself."

"True. It's also a matter of whether you do so passively or assertively. In other words, you can start some trouble and perhaps make a real difference. Or just sit there, and still have problems. If you don't do anything, you may make yourself miserable feeling guilty. Or fall into a major depression over losing your hubby, then letting him down. Considering what you've been through already, perhaps even a case of PTSD."

Her thoughts raced, trying to process the influx of information. "So you're saying I have nothing to lose by making some noise?"

"Yes and no. A tenth house Sun brings public attention and Mercury there, too, implies speaking out. The fact you could be working at something you care about is clear with Venus ruling the second house and in the house of goals. It's going to be a life-changing time, no matter what. You need to keep your ideas realistic, though. With Jupiter driving your thoughts while trining Neptune, if you're too idealistic or think too big, you'll set yourself up for disappointment. Or trouble."

"So I need to take it slow."

"Changing the world in a day simply isn't gonna happen, sweetie. But you're a smart gal, and already know that. Scorpio on the third house will infuse your thoughts with passion. Your intuition will be strong. Accomplishing what you set out to do will bring growth, but require getting out of your comfort zone."

Sara clenched her teeth, weighing the options. "Okay, thanks so much, Patrice. As always, put this on the credit card you have on file. I'm sure I'll be back for more advice along the way."

"Good luck, Sara. You've got this, sweetie."

"I hope so. I'll keep you posted."

She ended the call, mouth pressed in a decisive line.

Then, before she lost her nerve, she brought up the website for Fox31 News in Denver. As expected, she found a form to submit news tips and feature story ideas.

ELITE MANAGEMENT PARTNERS INC. (EMPI)
DOWNTOWN DENVER
June 29, Friday
2:51 p.m.

Jason LaGrange hung up the phone, mental gears grinding as he punched in the extension of EMPI's temporary program manager. His admin answered.

"This is LaGrange. I need a copy of BKSS's contract."

"Of course, Mr. LaGrange. I'll send you a link."

Moments later it popped into his inbox. After reading it through—twice—he leaned back in his chair, mouth agape.

The verbiage backed up everything Keller claimed.

Site perimeter security only.

He swiveled his chair to gaze out his nineteenth storey window at the top-heavy Marriott City Center, one of Denver's iconic monoliths.

Half its forty-two floors jutted out farther than the lower ones, making it look top-heavy. More like an afterthought than intentional design. As if the architect, or perhaps his client, changed his mind after construction began.

Like Keller's contract.

The man was right.

They weren't at fault.

To the contrary, BKSS went above and beyond.

If anything, they deserved a bonus.

He threw back his head and laughed.

While they'd certainly screwed up, in reality it wasn't in their task order, but dumped on them by the original program manager trying to cover his own incompetence.

Which meant—technically—BKSS was in the clear.

As Keller's IT liaison with the NSA, he'd kept an eye on the team in a general sense. Offered occasional advice and directed them to resources that supported their surveillance needs.

Tracking targets directly was not Jason's problem. He worked that side when he first hired on with the government. While he quickly grasped the techniques and electronics available, his eyes glazed over with monitoring and transcription duties, even though software handled most of it.

Fortunately, his talent for coding and designing innovative hardware allowed him to opt out and work in various capacities. Depending on the situation, he stepped in occasionally, but always remained undercover.

Like replacing Bryan Reynolds as system administrator at that credit union.

It continued to amuse him they didn't recognize him as the same guy who'd picked up Reynolds's belongings the week before.

A Bronco's baseball hat, sunglasses, and confidence truly were the ultimate disguise. Though he had an entire suite of them for when simply being nondescript wasn't enough.

The credit union employees were far too friendly, trusting, and naive. During his employ he conducted a forensic audit of the entire system, looking for the purloined data on the financial institution's server or evidence of his predecessor's cyber snooping.

He found nothing.

What he *did* find was a highly secured system with some of the cleanest and most clever coding he'd ever seen. Without a doubt, Reynolds knew what he was doing. Too bad talents honed during his military service were wasted in such a two-bit operation. No doubt he got bored, which ultimately led to his downfall.

That mission completed, Jason "hired on" at EMPI. Their IT system was the diametric opposite. Sloppy, outdated architecture any adolescent gamer could hack in minutes, mouse in one hand, Cheetos in the other.

Which was where this fiasco began.

Bryan Reynolds was initially a site security issue. Keller's team handled it badly, using lethal force on someone who should have been arrested for trespassing. They covered their asses for that *faux pas* when it turned out his presence was no accident.

Reynolds knew something.

And by proving that, albeit after the fact, BKSS justified killing him.

A lucky break.

Except for the fact his wife survived.

But the data breach was *not* their responsibility.

It was EMPI's.

As a black ops guy, Keller wasn't a businessman. Otherwise, he would have insisted on an amendment to their contract before doing anything that wasn't specified.

When all those IT support requests started rolling in to track Reynolds's widow and find where he'd stashed the data, Jason didn't question it, assuming it was in their service contract.

Apparently Keller was one of those people with an over-developed sense of responsibility. If something needed to be done, he didn't stop to ask questions. He jumped right in and took care of it, posthaste.

How you survived a war zone—

—not a government contract.

It was actually Keller who'd blown the whistle on EMPI's lack of cyber security, along with Steinbrenner's cavalier attitude that facilitated the breach. A useless excuse for a human being whose miniscule brains were now a dark spot on the brick plaza on South Bell in Crystal City.

So far, the released data wasn't causing much of a flap. After the president explained its legality, it was swept away like any other piece of government dirt.

If it went any further, the only ones with anything to lose were Congressmen and a handful of lobbyists.

LSO LOGISTICS OUTPOST
June 29, Friday
4:12 p.m.

Charlie climbed out of his truck, chuckling when he noticed Trey hustling over to meet him. The man slapped him on the back, grinning as if he'd won the lotto as they walked to the office trailer.

"Hoe-lee-shit, Littlewolf! Them pictures made me happier than a pig in shit! Location's perfect! Right square in the middle of our lease area. I don't suppose y'all got a sample of that stuff, eh?"

As the site's lab tech, it was a no-brainer. Playing dumb to tease the guy failed miserably. He held out his badge holder, dripping with thick, brown liquid.

Maguire took it from his hand, grinning, then picked up the radio to summon a ride up to the lab.

"Don't you think we need a better container? The ride up there's pretty rough."

Maguire set down the radio. "Y'all's right."

He handed back the sample, white mustache riding pursed lips while he searched for something suitable. A Styrofoam cup and lid from the stack flanking the coffee pot seemed the only option.

Charlie tipped the plastic sleeve. . .

"Wait!"

Crude halted millimeters from the edge.

"I've gotta bottle of aspirin in my desk."

He took it out of his side drawer, dumped the pills in the cup, then took it to the sink in the map room to rinse it out. After shaking it dry the best he could, he jammed a rolled up paper towel inside, trying to eliminate any extra water.

Satisfied, he held it out. Charlie lined up the corner with the bottle, poured the crude inside, and secured the lid. There wasn't much, barely an ounce.

"Okay, one more thing." Trey punched in a number on his speed dial.

"Yo. Dr. Phil. We's on our way up. I need y'all to test out a hydrocarbon sample." The crease between his brows deepened. "No. Listen to me. Now, not Monday. . .No, goddamn it. Y'all's not listening. I said *now*. I don't care if y'all's headin' out for the weekend, there's work to do. We's on our way. Be ready."

He slammed down the phone, muttered *asshole* under his breath, then gestured for the door. "C'mon. Let's see what we's got."

It was a good thing the sample was in a closed container. The ride was bumpier than usual, Tommy clearly unhappy being called into service right before quitting time, too, especially when he couldn't leave until he brought them back.

In spite of the bone-jolting ride, Maguire's grin persisted until he sprang out, not even waiting for the ATV to stop.

Charlie followed a few paces behind, anticipating the scene once Trey stormed the lab. Knowing the geologist, this would be good.

Dr. Phil sat at the mud log table, brought inside for the weekend, as he gave Maguire the simper-laced glare Charlie knew too well.

"Here." Trey held out the sample. "I want a full assay, ASAP."

"Such as?" The tone was defiant, but contradicted by grey eyes tinged with alarm.

Trey blinked, startled. "The usual. Content. Hydrogen, nitrogen, carbon. Acidity. If possible, asphaltenes, wax content, whether there's any H2S. API gravity."

"API?"

"Uh, yeah." Maguire exhaled through his nose. "American Petroleum Institute. Oil standard. Different than specific gravity."

His bristly white eyebrows lowered. "Tell me—honestly now, Phil—has y'all ever run these tests before? Or is this, uh, as we says in Texas, y'all's first rodeo?"

The man averted his eyes and cleared his throat. "I've run similar tests, many times. It'll just take a while."

Trey glared. "Well, then, y'all'd better quit actin' like someone pissed in y'all's Wheaties and get started, don't y'all think?"

Dr. Phil reached for the sample, scrunched-up features balanced between defiance and tears. He sloshed it around, glaring at it with narrowed eyes. "Is this all you got?"

"I'm afraid so," Charlie volunteered. "Listen, if you want, I can get the AGI started. We probably don't have enough for all the assays, but we can put it through the chromatograph for the CHN."

Dr. Phil's gaunt features shifted to a hostile mix of relief and enmity. "Fantastic. Have at it, Chuck." He stood up, brimming with indignation as he handed him the sample. "I hope your pet Indian works out for you, Maguire. I quit."

Charlie and Trey exchanged startled looks as the man grabbed his jacket from the back of his chair. He got as far as the door, then turned around, glare fixed on Charlie.

"I can't believe you, a full-blooded Indian, are helping these people," he snarled, then stormed outside.

Charlie sucked in a breath, ponies rearing with confusion.

Trey narrowed his eyes. "Damn blivit."

The ponies vanished, Charlie's attention diverted to the unfamiliar word.

"Yeah. Look it up, Littlewolf. That asshole's picture'll be right beside it."

His vocabulary was reasonably good, especially derisive labels of which he'd been the recipient far too often.

Some oil industry term for incompetence, perhaps?

His boss noted his mystified look, then laughed. "Blivit's a fancy word for an overstuffed sack of shit."

Charlie chuckled. "That's the same as the Indian name, Walking Eagle."

This time his boss wore the puzzled look.

"Too full of shit to fly."

Phil Stafford sat stewing in his Murano. From the minute that Indian walked through the door he smelled trouble.

How could someone from a culture that honored the planet and protested pipelines work in the oil business?

What a hypocrite.

The politics inherent to his USGS job drove him to walk away from what could have been a life-long civil service position with a hefty pension. Lying that earthquakes were naturally occurring rather than the result of fracking, however, got to be too much. The local government was making money off it, to say nothing of the jobs it created, so didn't want any negative press. It was getting more complicated to cover up and the confrontations were giving him ulcers.

Thus, after twenty-one years in a job he otherwise enjoyed, he quit.

He snorted.

Apparently, he was getting good at it.

And sadly, he'd gotten good at lying somewhere along the line, too.

He knew exactly where LSO could find oil.

The last thing he wanted so close to home was fracking, much less drilling, though the latter was probably safer. Thus, he deliberately misled them, hoping they'd give up. Go home to Texas where they belonged.

Then that damn Indian came along and ruined everything. Furthermore, now he was out of work.

Again.

Gladys would have another one of her Oscar-winning conniption fits.

He started the car, shaking his head in disgust, and headed for Belton, wondering what he'd tell her this time. Too bad he wasn't old enough to retire.

Maybe as a former civil servant he could get on with the EPA. Except they were as corrupt as everyone else, raking in fines instead of correcting environmental violations.

There were plenty of non-profits trying to protect the earth. Maybe that was where he'd try next. Or teaching at some college. Like the Colorado School of Mines.

Not that he liked mining any better.

No. Teaching Geology 101 at some junior college was his best bet. The pay would be abysmal, but his conscience clear.

After a high-five and another shared guffaw, Charlie got to work. The results were good. Medium to heavy oil—certainly better than tar sands or gas, much less nothing at all. By the time the tests were complete, it was well past seven o'clock.

Trey radioed Tommy he could leave after he got back from taking Dr. Phil to the compound. A smaller Yamaha ATV from the shed returned them to the main outpost a spine-jolting twenty minutes later.

At that point, the fact more oil patch injuries resulted from site transportation than rig accidents made more sense than ever.

As soon as they stowed the ATV, Trey went to his office and took the big book off his shelf. They went through it, scrutinizing geological profiles again.

"We could be dealing with a normal fault," Charlie said. "There was a minor earthquake a month or so back."

"I remember that." He chuckled. "We probably caused it, puttin' in that geo-thermal system. That woulda let gas and seepage leak out."

"Or it could be a thrust fault. Pretty common up here in the mountains. There could be reservoirs on both sides of the bedrock, forming a trap."

Maguire's bushy eyebrows knitted together. "That could cause complications. I reckon whatever's goin' on, we won't know what we's got on either side 'til we have a look-see at the seismic. Gettin' a site set up won't be simple."

"An old mining road goes part of the way, but that's it."

"Just how wooded is it up there, Littlewolf?"

"There's quite a few trees. Big ones. Mostly pine, and plenty of brush. It's steep and rocky, but a fairly flat basin, once you get there. It's up there a ways, though. Just past the tree line."

"The what?"

"Tree line. Where they quit growing. Too rocky."

"Could a bulldozer handle it? Or would we need something bigger?"

"Good question. How about your drone? There's still plenty of light. You can see for yourself."

"Hell, yeah!"

They retrieved the bird from the supply shed, then jumped in Trey's mud-splattered F-350 with its heavy gauge brush guard. Charlie directed him to the old mining road, the vehicle making it about fifty yards past where it ended when the truck came nose-to-nose with a boulder the size of a sweat lodge.

"Guess we ain't getting past that bad boy," Maguire said.

Trey set the drone's GPS based on the photos, and fired it up. It whirred to life, sounding like an over-sized hummingbird. The camera skimmed trees, which gradually thinned out, yielding to a mixture of rocks and scruffy vegetation.

Charlie frowned, wondering why Bryan hadn't used a drone to investigate the PURF site, which would have probably saved his life.

The bird reached the programmed location and hovered.

Trey pointed to the monitor. "Does that there look familiar?"

"That's it."

"Great. Looks flat enough for the seismic guys, once they gets up there. If it's too hilly, those trucks don't work too good. Then it would hafta be an aerial survey. They ain't nearly as accurate."

The drone took some photos, then Trey brought it back and they returned to the outpost.

Trey went straight to his office and picked up the phone.

"Well, crap," he muttered moments later. "LSO HQ in Irving's closed for the weekend. Them guys in white shirts don't have a clue what an honest day's work looks like."

"So we have to wait for Monday?"

"Hell, no. I'll call the ops guy at home," he said, lifting the receiver again.

"That's more like it," Trey said as he hung up. "He done told me to hire some local to bulldoze a way up to the site. They'll get the company's track-mounted driller on a flatbed first thing Monday. Meanwhile, I'll find a seismic survey team and tell 'em to get their asses up there ASAP."

6. STARGAZING

CHARLIE'S CABIN
June 30, Saturday
7:10 a.m.

The next morning Charlie sat outside his cabin on a bed of pine needles cradling a steaming cup of coffee. While he still missed his white brother, the worst of the grief had yielded to earning a good living plus eating better, thanks to LSO's gourmet chow hall.

He couldn't remember when he'd eaten so well. There were times in his life when dinner meant going fishing with a side of foraged greens. Weekends he was back to his usual fare. Driving back to the site to eat had no appeal. It was leftovers, anyway, most of the crew partying in Aspen or Denver.

He wasn't exercising much, either, hanging out in a lab. His jeans were actually getting a little tight. The thought of getting soft was as irritating as an early frost. He vowed to start working out each morning before driving to the site.

He got up, went inside, and turned on the single overhead lightbulb, thoughts still on work. Trey warned him that drilling at a new site meant Big Dick would be all over him and everyone else to make sure everything was good to go, on paper as well as logistically.

He'd only been there about a month, thus his initial training was up to date, except for some OSHA course he had to complete before they broke ground.

He still needed to give them an emergency contact for his personnel file. Would Sara think it weird to use her father? If anything happened, the last thing she needed was to be the first to know. On the other hand, chances of that were slim. He already had it, so he texted it to Big Dick.

One less thing on his mind.

His thoughts lingered on Sara. How did she react to the president's speech? Probably pretty let down. What would she do now?

It felt strange with her gone.

Empty.

While they were uncovering Bryan's secrets, their lives had been closely entangled. Now they'd gone their separate ways.

He exhaled hard, dismissing another loss.

Catching a glimpse of the mantle, he realized he hadn't conversed with his fetishes since taking the job. It still felt as if he were in a dream of sorts. Not quite himself, yet in some way more genuine.

He'd never been so entrenched in *vehoe's* world, yet never felt more like a warrior.

Had he finally found a way to ride both ponies?

Prior rationalizations aside, he was helping violate the Earth.

Dr. Phil's parting words stung like a yellow jacket, unexpected and painful.

Was working for LSO right?

Or greedy?

It was time for another chat at the medicine wheel. If he moved to the work site, he wouldn't be able to. He shuddered at how those roughnecks would react if he sat on the bunkhouse floor conversing with tiny stone animals.

Gathering them from the mantle, he settled down in front of the fireplace and set them in their respective positions. He lit a sweetgrass braid, used its sacred smoke to bless himself, the wheel, and fetishes. Eyes closed, he inhaled the fragrant vapors deeply, then tuned into their energies.

Oddly enough, Eagle, Black Bear, Badger, Mountain Lion, Mole, and Wolf were all silent.

Instead, the impression was that of a lizard.

His eyes lost their focus as he drifted back to his childhood.

Lizard.

The first spirit animal Eaglefeathers told him to ponder. He thought back to that evening before the fire as a young boy, creeping through the dust on his belly.

What message did lizard have?

Lizards were naturally camouflaged, blending with their environment, whether on the ground, a rock, or against the bark of a tree. Their tongue snapped insects from the air faster than the blink of an eye. They were silent, often unseen, wily at eluding predators, particularly as they got older.

Like immature members of all species, humans included, they were more vulnerable when young, naive, impulsive, and foolish.

Enemies—lots of them.

Birds of all kinds, especially birds of prey. Dogs and cats, domestic and wild. Snakes, possums, raccoons, toads and fish. Their own diet was less varied, mostly insects, arachnids, even scorpions.

Ironic, considering some scorpions could kill a man.

So what was lizard trying to say?

Its ability to blend with its environment was one. Unless he was actually looking for lizard, it was probably invisible—until it moved. That could be no more than a flicker in his peripheral vision, gone before he realized it was there.

Next, its keen senses—sight, hearing, smell, vibrations in the Earth. If lizard missed something, it could wind up in a predator's stomach. Threats could come from the air, like an eagle. From the ground, like a snake. From its own level. Anything from a small mammal or possum to a bigger lizard.

One defense it had was its tail. It broke off easily, but would grow back.

Sometimes he got a second chance.

Recognizing his vulnerability and maintaining sharp awareness in all directions struck him as the intended message.

He rubbed his chin, sobered by multiple implications.

That was a lot to watch for.

SARA'S CABIN
RURAL FALCON RIDGE
June 30, Saturday
9:38 a.m.

Sara glared at the comforter-wrapped telescope box in the GX's back seat. It had been easy to ignore, moving it back inside a hassle she preferred to avoid. The SUV's rental period was nearly up, however, and she wasn't sure she'd keep it. Perhaps something a little smaller, but still with four-wheel drive.

All the boxes from the bench seat remained in the cargo area, too. They were not as easy to ignore. The rustic scent of aging cardboard and old documents reminded her every time she got in the car, incongruent with the expected new car smell. Now that the evidence was public, any rationale to burn the place down was eliminated.

Everything had to go back inside.

Whoopee.

She gathered her mass of curls into a scrunchi and steeled herself for the work ahead. Not exactly what she wanted to do today, but it needed to be done.

She no sooner wrestled the telescope back inside and got the comforter back on the bed when her cell rang.

Welcome break or annoying interruption? A 50:50 chance, one way or another.

She returned downstairs as quickly as she dared.

Upon seeing who it was she smiled.

"Hey, Charlie. How's the big oil baron these days?"

He laughed. "Good. Real good. You sound out of breath. Are you okay?"

She plopped down in a kitchen chair, gratitude for the impromptu pause now at a hundred percent.

"I'm fine. Just unloading the car. All that stuff I hauled off when I left. I need to turn in the car soon, so figured I needed to get it done while I'm here."

"So you're back?"

"Yes."

"Great! Would you like some help?"

"That would be wonderful!"

"Don't touch another thing. I'll be right there."

"Awesome!"

Much to her surprise, minutes later he arrived.

She opened the door, the pair exchanging a friendly hug as he stepped inside. He smelled a little smoky, but in a pleasant way.

"That was quick." He usually walked, which took a while. Then she saw his truck. "You drove? *Ha!* You never do that. Getting lazy, now that you're working again?"

He grinned. "Exactly. Now I don't have to worry about gas money. And speaking of such things, I have something for you."

She watched, mystified, as he dug out his wallet. He pulled out an impressive wad of bills, then counted out seven hundreds, a fifty, and a ten.

"Here. $760."

He held it out and met her questioning stare. When she didn't respond, he took her hand, placed the money in her palm, then folded her fingers around it.

"I'm paying you back. For bailing me out and getting my truck from the impound lot. Thanks so much. I don't know what I would have done if you hadn't helped."

"Oh! I completely forgot about that. You were trying to help so I had no problem paying for it. Whatever happened with your arrest? Anything?"

"Not a thing. Charges were dropped. Still waiting on the bail refund, though."

"Ridiculous, all around. I'm glad nothing came of it, though. That would have been a real pain. Going to court, needing a lawyer. And seriously, what case did they have? You did nothing wrong, for heaven sake."

"If they knew I got the dashcam card that blew this thing out of the water they'd probably get me for stealing evidence or something."

"Except it was mine and Bryan's truck. But you're right. That was a definite breakthrough."

She gritted her teeth, remembering.

Their eyes locked for a long moment before he switched the subject.

"What are we waiting for? C'mon. Let's unload your car."

"Right. Let's do it."

It took several minutes to get everything back inside the house. While she returned the boxes to the bench seat, he crouched down and stared longingly at the telescope box at the foot of the stairs.

"You can open it up if you like," she called from the guest room. "In fact, would you like to take it out tonight? I'd love to hear about those constellations you and Bryan used to look at together. We should also set up Bryan's comparative astronomy website again as a memorial. Like we told those obnoxious commandos. You know, my father swore they were total amateurs, handling it like they did."

"I don't doubt that."

He dropped to the floor cross-legged and opened it up. "Yeah, let's do that website. Great idea. Those are happy memories."

When the last box was stowed, not quite as neatly as Bryan had them, but good enough, she knelt beside him on the floor, going through Bryan's observation notebook.

"Oh! I have the latest copy of *Sky and Telescope*, too. It was in the mail at the condo. Hold on, I'll get it from the car."

Back inside, she flipped to the observation tips for the month. "Listen to this: *Mercury and Venus in Leo will be evening stars, just after sunset; Jupiter in Scorpio will be visible to the southeast.*

Mars in Aquarius and Saturn in Capricorn will rise an hour or so later. According to the calendar, the Moon rises quite late. That means nice, dark skies."

"Perfect." He grew quiet. "It will seem odd without him."

"Yes. It will."

He laughed softly. "Sometimes I forget that he is gone. Like when I got this job. My first thought was to tell him, knowing how excited he'd be for me. Then I remember."

She gulped back the lump in her throat. "I know what you mean. I've done that myself, thinking when he gets home I need to tell him something. Like he's on TDY."

He remained pensive as he lifted the tripod out of the box and set it up with the tracker. She attached the mounting bracket to the telescope, then set it in place, followed by the counterweight.

"There," he said. "All ready to go."

She led him into the kitchen area to sit at the table. "Tell me about your job. What's it like?"

He took the chair across from her and proceeded to tell her about Dr. Phil, Trey calling the man a blivit, then got her laughing to the point of tears when he mentioned Big Dick.

"Surely you're not serious," she sputtered, wiping her eyes. "What civilized person has a name like that?"

"Who said they're civilized? Actually, it fits him rather well." His mouth quivered, not quite restraining a boyish grin. "Okay, I admit I don't know about *that*, but he's a big, stocky guy with a shaved head and no neck. Who doesn't mind being called *Dickhead*. Not exactly an honorable Indian name, either."

"I would think not!"

"Roughnecks are well-named, to say the least. But the job's good. The bosses like me because I found that seep. Except Dr. Phil. But he's gone now. If the site I found works out, Trey promised me a raise. Maybe even a bonus."

"Seriously? That's fantastic! So you don't feel, well, out of place or anything?"

His lips withdrew briefly in a tight line. "Yes and no. Mainly I don't like violating the Earth. But for some reason, this is where

I belong. While I was up there, I asked *Maheo* if I was doing the right thing."

"Did that help?"

"A little. I didn't get an actual answer, but had a peaceful feeling. After all, it's temporary. It's up there high enough they'll probably shut down when the snow comes. If that happens, I don't know whether they'll offer me a job in Texas or lay me off. Just have to wait and see."

She folded her hands in her lap. "Would you go to Texas?"

His eyes remained fixed on hers. "I don't know. I'd prefer New Mexico. Then I'd be closer to my kids. Just have to see how it works out. So enough about me. What have you been up to since the big data release? How'd you like that State of the Union?"

She groaned, disgust renewed. "At first I was depressed. Then I got mad. Dad made me promise not to do anything stupid."

"So...did you?" He grinned. "Wonder Woman."

She snickered, remembering when they'd defied the commandos a few weeks earlier. "I'm still not sure where *that* came from. Anyway, after the president's nonchalant admission, no one seems to care. A few pundits chatted about it for a day or two and that was it."

She threw up her hands. "Gone! *Poof!* Yesterday's news. It was like the nation gave one, huge, collective yawn. No one was impressed, business went on as usual. No stock market blips, nothing."

"Business as usual, alright."

"Yeah. So I got to thinking. Liz Hudson thinks it needs a personal touch. Like she said, it's not just about taxpayer money, it's about murder. So, I contacted Fox31. I haven't heard back, so they may think I'm another crazy in a tin-foil hat. Or its not newsworthy. I guess I'm in a position like you—waiting."

They talked and caught up until lunch time, when she fixed sandwiches. After that, she hooked up the computer so he could show her the drone pictures on LSO's website.

"Wow. It's pristine up there, isn't it?"

"That's what bothers me. But being isolated is in its favor, too. Few, if anyone will know the difference. Which makes it good and bad at the same time."

He cleared his throat, dismissing the subject. "Do you think Bryan expects you to do more than expose it?"

"He told me not to let them get away with it. But they *did* get away with it. If I don't hear back from Fox31, I could write a book or something. Maybe a blog or podcast. What about you?"

"My intuition says they'll pay, sooner or later. I made a vow to avenge his death, but don't know how."

"My main concern is whether I'll wind up dead or in prison if I pursue it."

"Did you check with Patrice?"

She wrinkled her nose. "Yes. She said it looked like a bumpy year. You know, speaking of her, I bet she'd love to come out and see the planets through the telescope. I'll have to invite her out sometime."

"I'd love to meet her. The fact I connected with her during that fast was pretty startling. I'd like to know if it actually happened, not an hallucination."

"I'll ask, if you like."

Smile lines crinkled the corners of his eyes. "Yes. Please do. I'm rather curious."

"I will. Do you feel like working on that website? Or are you busy this afternoon?"

"Sure, sounds great. No other plans."

She turned back to the computer, wiggled the mouse to wake it up, then went to WordPress and filled in the information for a new website. "What should we call it?"

"Did Bryan name it?"

"I don't remember. Let me check." She retrieved the binder from the bench seat. "He called it 'Navajo Star Tales.' I like it. How about you?"

He looked pleased. "Yes. That works."

They spent the rest of the afternoon choosing a layout template, which took longer than expected, then started entering the data.

The introduction on the home page described the winter stories.

She paused.

They were named such because *Diné* tradition dictated they only be told that time of year. She gave him a questioning look.

"Is this okay with you? It's about as far from winter as it gets. And no telling when people might see it. Or, I suppose we could take it down certain times of year."

He shook his head. "No. It's okay. For now, it's pretty close to the solstice, which was another time they're allowed. I think mentioning it is enough. But thanks for asking."

"No problem." She typed in that section, then set up the next, starting with its first constellation, *Náhookos Bi'ka'*, known more commonly as Ursa Major.

"I'm looking forward to seeing the stars tonight from a different perspective," she commented. "I love the relevance to life your constellations express. The Greek mythology angle is entertaining, but not nearly as personal."

"My people consider the sky as the home of the Creator. We watch it for answers and it speaks. There are places in the night sky that are so sacred only *Diné* elders know what they mean. The mountain tops are closest to the sky, which is one reason they're considered sacred ground."

"That's a beautiful way to see the earth," she replied. "I appreciate your holistic view of nature. That it's all connected and we're an integral part of it."

"Yes, we are. Everything is connected in spirit."

"There's no way to reconcile it with the white man's materialistic view, is there?"

"No."

He got real quiet after that, so she continued typing in the text of Bryan's Eagle project.

The illustrations would have to be scanned at her condo, the photos using her phone not clear enough. There was still quite a bit to do, but they could finish next time. A dedication to Bryan and brief story of how he and Charlie connected as teens would be written later as well.

The project consumed the afternoon, suppertime soon upon them. Charlie grilled chicken drumsticks and roasted veggies outside while Sara prepared a salad. They ate on the back deck, then cleaned up the kitchen together.

After that, they carried the telescope outside a few yards from the back deck. She adjusted the tripod to the uneven ground, then calibrated the finder scope with a distant cell tower. Charlie made sure it faced true north so the equatorial mount would be aligned properly with the ecliptic.

The Sun took its time descending behind the distant peaks. Mercury and Venus appeared as the sky lost its color, two distinct points of light hovering above the mountains. She swung the scope around and focused on them, then offered him the eyepiece.

He took a long look, profile silhouetted against the fading orange sky. "Did you know when Venus is the morning star that she becomes the goddess of war instead of the goddess of love? Many battles began under that sign." He chuckled. "Some on the prairie, some in tipis, I suppose."

"I didn't. But I can relate. There are times when defending those you love requires putting on your armor."

"Like the Wonder Woman thing."

She laughed. "That blew you away, didn't it?"

He abandoned the eyepiece to turn her way, features lost in shadow. "Yes. But in a good way. It's great to see a woman who's not all helpless and whiney. Who knows how to take care of herself."

She paused, pondering his words. "Maybe so. But that doesn't mean that's what I prefer."

"I can appreciate that. My culture has distinct gender roles, but that doesn't mean our women aren't tough. In *Diné Bikéyah*, they have a Miss Navajo pageant where contestants compete in such things as traditional dance and dressing out a deer. Other reservations have similar events."

"No kidding? Good for them!"

"I believe you'd fit in."

"Why is that? The Wonder Woman thing?"

"Partly. Speaking of which, do you still carry your Glock?"

"Not lately. I know where it is and in most cases it's close by, but it was uncomfortable having it on me all the time. Plus, things seem to have quieted down. So far, anyway."

The night deepened, planets and brightest stars gradually appearing on the celestial stage. They scoped out each of the visible planets—literally—swinging the telescope on its mount to their respective locations.

Having five visible planets was a rare sky-watching treat. Both marveled at Jupiter's spot, Saturn's rings, and the distinctive red hue of Mars.

Eventually, they dragged the bench over from the picnic table on the deck to watch as more stars became visible, filling the sky while the Milky Way reigned overhead.

The first time she saw the night sky from the cabin she was astonished. She never realized how brilliant stars could be. No wonder ancient people felt drawn to their mystery. City lights and industrial pollution hid the stars, sometimes even the brightest ones. There was nothing to see, except possibly the moon, if people even bothered to look up.

How much did losing that link contribute to the sad state of the world? City lights were pretty, but what was more humbling and awe inspiring than the infinite cosmos overhead?

"Tell me about your constellations," she said. "Are they all the same groupings or entirely different?"

"A little of both. Ours tend to be larger." He shifted enough to point toward the North Star. "For example, we consider the Big and Little Dippers as well as Cassiopeia one constellation. It revolves around the North Star, so it's always visible, but its orientation changes with the seasons."

"I can see how that would be handy, with no actual calendars."

"Yes. And more accurate. When the Pleiades, or what we call *Dilyéhé*, become visible in the early morning sky its planting time. Their name translates to *seed-like sparkles*."

"That's pretty. So what's your favorite story? That is, if you can share it. Other than the Coyote Star."

He chuckled. "Yes, the Coyote Star is my favorite. Bryan connected with it, too. I'm still amazed he named that file with all the data *Canopus*, your name for the same star. My people see it as a disrupter of plans. You, or I suppose the Greeks, saw it as a pathfinder. Bryan certainly tied them together, didn't he?"

"That he did. And sealed it with his life."

"Yes. Unfortunately, that was the case."

Silence fell upon them for several moments, until Charlie steered the conversation back to more pleasant topics.

"Okay, here's a funny star story. What you call Orion we call *Átsé Ets' ózí*. He and *Átsé Etsoh*, which is part of Scorpio, are never in the sky at the same time. We associate that with mother-in-laws and son-in-laws. Like those constellations, they shouldn't see one another in everyday life. Only certain celebrations or special times. Some traditional *Diné* women actually wear a bell as a warning that she's in the area."

Sara laughed, grateful for the lightened mood. "So mother-in-laws have a bad reputation in both cultures. I guess human nature doesn't change."

"I guess not. I must say, however, that Bryan liked your mother, Sara. He was greatly saddened when she died."

Her chest ached beneath another nostalgic glimpse of days gone by. "Yes. They were actually pretty close. I suppose they get to see each other now, while I'm down here missing them both."

"They are closer than we realize."

That thought combined with the evening chill evoked a shiver.

"I'll be right back," she said, then went inside to put on a sweater and bring out a blanket. He helped arrange the throw around their backs as they continued to gaze at the sky.

As the sky fully darkened, Moon not yet risen, the cosmic dome filled with stars, making it difficult to distinguish individual constellations.

Her neck still felt the evening chill, so she pulled the band out off her ponytail and freed the curly mass.

"Are you still cold?"

"A little."

He pulled the blanket over their heads, then slipped his arm around her shoulders. She snuggled closer, consumed by the wonders of celestial creation.

No river can return to its source, yet all rivers must have a beginning.
—*Pawnee Proverb*

7. PROGRESS

LSO LOGISTICS OUTPOST
July 2, Monday
8:32 a.m.

Trey sat at his computer watching the drone's live feed of two bulldozers grinding through trees and brush, pushing a road to the exploration site. Getting up there was a challenge. However, if they found what he hoped for, it could justify a play, which would mean a nice bonus.

Not only nice, but *real* nice. Potentially huge.

He liked Colorado and wouldn't mind relocating, snow notwithstanding. The blistering heat of Texas summers was no picnic, either. If it didn't work out, maybe he'd find a summer home up there, like Bentley.

Things looked good for finishing that day. That old mining road had conveniently taken them most the way. The Cats smoothed it out some, roughing in the rest. Sufficient to get the core driller and lab trailer up there, for a start.

He sniggered. Dr. Phil sure got pissed when his Indian minion stole the show. Didn't hurt his feelings one bit when that man up and quit. His brother-in-law produced more gas from a bowl of Texas chili than PhD Phil found in over two months.

Whether Littlewolf could handle LWD telemetry was another story. His quick grasp upon seeing some was promising. Big Dick had no doubts. Once they got settled, what he intended to do was

71

backfill Littlewolf's former position preparing lab samples and get him out there in the field, finding more sites.

He added another item to his to-do list—fill out the promotion paperwork—which would also give the man a substantial, well-deserved raise. If he hit the jackpot on this one, he'd have a serious future in the business.

The people at HQ might even want to move him to the company's exploration team. Pure luck Bentley found him. They needed to treat him right. If he quit, they were screwed.

Those native instincts were worth their weight in gold.

He grinned.

Or black gold.

Having a Cheyenne Indian scouting for oil seemed as likely as a hound dog with no fleas. But then, so was one with a college degree coupled with boots-on-ground knowledge of the area.

Best combination ever. The oil patch version of chips and guacamole.

SARA'S CABIN
Monday, July 2
11:54 a.m.

Mountain peaks and valleys hailed majestically beyond the cabin's wrap-around deck. Snow, which could still fall into June, persisted at the highest elevations, where it could return as early as August. Depending on how much gathered over the winter, some peaks, especially the *fourteeners*, never lost their crown before it arrived again.

The area directly around the cabin was mostly clear, other than a few boulders surrounded by late summer grasses and black-eyed Susans in front. In back, a small aspen grove and pines reached for the flawless, cerulean sky.

Sara soaked up the spectacular view from an Adirondack chair on the wrap-around deck.

She was barely coming out of a figurative valley herself.

Was she headed for a peak? Or only fooling herself? Escalating the issue as Bryan requested wasn't simple. If the media weren't interested, who would be?

Then again, the media weren't normal people. Most wouldn't care about her story unless it fit their agenda. If anything, they protected the government, quiet on some issues, spinning others. Maybe a few talk shows, depending on network policy and political leanings.

Her brow lowered. Would they view her as a threat?

How else could she reach everyday folks?

Give talks to anyone who'd listen.

Prepper groups, perhaps. Independents and Libertarians, maybe. Some were underground and not easy to find, but they were there, hidden away on various websites, videos, podcasts, and blogs.

Writing a book was another possibility. Could she find a publisher who'd take on something controversial? Then again, self-publishing wasn't difficult anymore. That presented the challenge of finding the needed publicity, taking it full circle.

Maybe a book with Bryan's research would generate interviews. It would certainly demonstrate she had documented proof.

Or maybe give it up entirely.

Her thoughts drifted to spending Saturday with Charlie.

It felt so natural, so comfortable.

She giggled, remembering what Connie said about them getting together, way back when. She'd never hear the end of it if that happened.

Then again, what would Bryan think? Actually, he'd probably be okay with it. Surely he didn't expect her to be alone forever. Live like a nun. Why not with his best friend? Better than a stranger. Like her father marrying Connie. No one had any doubts her mom approved.

She still couldn't imagine Charlie working for an oil company, but he seemed comfortable with it. True, having an income was a good thing.

Something she gratefully didn't have to worry about.

Bryan had always been a good planner. If he hadn't, she'd have no choice but to go back to work as a physical therapist. She liked her job and wouldn't have minded.

But it would have been difficult to do much about Bryan's request if she had a full-time job.

She gasped.

Which explained his three-million dollar insurance policy!

Her cell vibrated on the chair's wooden arm, Denver number unfamiliar.

"Hello?"

"Mrs. Reynolds?"

"Yes."

"This is Tiffany, Jose Perez's personal assistant at Fox31. We're calling about the follow-up story you suggested. I know it's short notice, but would you like to be our guest on the six o'clock news this Wednesday, July 4th?"

What?

They were inviting her to be on TV?

Someone was actually interested in her story?

Wow! Patrice was right again!

"I'd, uh. Yes. Wow. I'd be honored," she stammered.

"It's Independence Day, so we're focusing on personal freedom. We thought your story fit well as an example of how some of that's being lost."

"That's for sure."

"We need you here two hours early. I'll email directions, a studio pass, and anything else you need to know."

"Is there anything in particular you'd like me to mention?"

"Mainly how your experience relates to freedom. Any angle of that should be fine. Jose will guide the interview. One thing you might think about is what the Founding Fathers intended, versus how things are now. It's your story, Mrs. Reynolds. We think it's important for our viewers to hear, as you stated, the 'human interest' angle behind it."

"Great!" She grinned as shock ebbed to enthusiasm.

"If you have any questions, feel free to call back at this number. Have a great day, Mrs. Reynolds."

"Thank you! See you Wednesday."

The first thing she did was text Charlie: *OMG! TV people called! 6 pm news July 4!*

That's fantastic! he texted back.

RU at work?

Yes. Packing lab 4 move to new site.

Fun.

Right. Haha.

I'm going back this p.m. Will call after Wed.

Great. Smile pretty for camera.

LOL! Will do.

Take care.

U2!

Still grinning, she indulged in an excited giggle and a happy dance, then went upstairs to gather the few things she needed to take back, mainly toiletries and her computer.

It didn't take long before the doors were locked and everything turned off.

All settled in the car ready to go, she texted the news to her father and Connie, adding she'd be back that night. Her dad texted, *Hope you're doing the right thing,* and Connie said *Awesome!*

Covering her feelings exactly.

Winding through canyons to the Interstate she considered what to mention.

What would fit the concept of personal freedom? The legality of the project was not an issue. Legal, yes; moral, no.

There had never been any proof regarding what killed Edna Parker or caused Rhonda Wheeler to flip out. However, tests she had run detected contaminants in her water and she had the documentation to prove it.

But not with her.

Damn!

Fortunately, she hadn't gotten that far, so made a U-turn at the next available cutout. The fact the water's chemistry changed about the time the project's geothermal system was under construction was worth mentioning.

She went inside, got the file box out of the bench seat, and extracted the accordion folder with the well and water records.

She paused, sucking her lower lip. Was there anything else?

Satisfied there wasn't, she left again.

Back on the road, her ruminations continued. Bryan's death was a biggie and most important. Her second wreck was suspicious, but hard to prove, especially with no police report ever showing up. Except that, in itself, was evidence of wrong-doing. They'd have to take her word for it about bugging her homes, illegal search and seizure of property, plus the commando raid.

Hopefully they'd believe her.

Predicting the public's reaction to a whistleblower was tricky. Would she gain support? Or harassment and ridicule? Usually the government's first defense was to attack the person's credibility and sanity. Probably blame her head injury from the wreck.

Fine. Go for it.

They killed her husband and the world was going to know.

Right! The dashcam videos!

They hadn't been uploaded because they were too personal and didn't relate to the issue at hand. Her stomach lurched at the prospect of sharing them, so decided against it. The pictures of the wreck site her father and Charlie took were on her laptop, so she could use them. She glared out the windshield to the twisted road ahead.

Let's see what POTUS has to say about that.

LSO DRILLING SITE
July 3, Tuesday
8:42 a.m.

Trey hummed *Darth Vader's March* as five snub-nosed vibroseis trucks lumbered up the road like giant mastodons.

"Dum, dum, dum, dum de dum, dum de dum. Dum, dum, dum, dum de dum, dum de dum. . ."

He waved back at the team lead as she climbed into the seismic company's green and brown Expedition, joining the others who'd set up the geophones and recording equipment. A few of the guys went along to help, evoking a wave of jealousy.

There weren't many women out in the field, much less cute blond fillies with gorgeous legs. This one was a grad-student at the Colorado School of Mines who appeared to know what she was doing.

Howdy, sweet-cheeks, he thought, then indulged in a wistful sigh.

It was invigorating to see such a fine female specimen with intelligence to match, especially after being around nothing but roughnecks for too long.

He savored the vision of her climbing into their SUV in those snug khaki shorts, the idyllic scene accompanied by the purr of diesel engines as they headed out.

Best of both worlds.

Like he done died and went to heaven.

Oh, yeah.

The vibe buggies had big-ass tires that could handle rough terrain. Would they tear up the road? Hopefully not. Once they got to the site, it was flat enough to function properly. He loved watching them drop that huge block with the vibrator in the center section, like taking a gigantic mechanical dump.

When it thumped the earth it was like dinosaurs humping.

He got a woody, just thinking about it.

Heavy equipment, especially when decorated with pretty women, was so much more fun than sitting in a damn office.

When finished, the survey data had to be processed. The computer folks would have Wednesday off, thanks to the goddamn holiday. With luck they'd see the results Friday.

Okay.

He'd ogled enough.

There was too much to do.

Pulling up stakes wasn't simple. Like bug-outs in the Army. A royal pain in the ass, plain and simple, logistics the worst part of his job.

There was the immediate site move, plus setting up a well, both big deals. If there was one thing he learned in project management school it was to triple however much time you *think* it'll take.

Commuting from the current outpost wouldn't work. Big Dick did a great job as his right-hand man, but the operation as a whole was his responsibility.

If anything went wrong, he couldn't be miles away.

The trailer housed his office, map room, personnel files, conference area, and small kitchen. All that crap needed packin' up. Otherwise, it would be doin' the Texas two-step all over the damn place when it got hoisted up on a flatbed and hauled to the new site.

Barracks, shower facilities, chow hall, and all the other support equipment, like water tanks and porta-potties had to go. The maintenance shed needed to be emptied out, too.

A caravan of heavy-duty eighteen-wheelers and a medium size crane were required for the trailers. Driving those convoluted mountain roads would be the trucking equivalent of a bucking bronco. They'd keep one of the bulldozers around, or maybe a front-loader, for creating a retention pond for flowback and manage the tailings.

Before they could drill he needed a load of pipe, mud, and everything else, plus staffing up. Serious drilling required skilled personnel running 24/7.

Speaking of which, he called HQ to find out when the track rig would get there. The dispatcher was an old friend who dated back to his Oklahoma oil patch days.

"Hey, Maguire! How's all y'all doin' up there in them Rocky Mountains?"

"We's doin' mighty fine, Lucas. Gettin' ready for that new dig. When's that track rig s'posed to get here?"

"Says here it's leavin' HQ on the low-boy 'round noon."

"Noon? What the hell," he grumbled. "The goddamn thing ain't left yet? It shoulda been on the road by now."

"Sorry, pal. Holiday week. We's as short-handed as a one-armed cowboy at Essie's all-y'all-can eat buffet."

"Alrighty, pardner. *C'est la vie.*"

"Say the what?"

"Skip it, Lucas. Thanks."

He scowled as he hung up, picturing the trip's timeline.

Fort Worth to the site was at least fifteen hours in a big rig. With luck, it would make it to Amarillo, then stop for the night. That would put it there around quitting time the next day.

Double-time and a half would convince the crew that setting up a new dig on the 4th of July was better'n gettin' drunk and laid.

Then again, maybe not.

He chuckled to himself, picturing that red-hot filly on the seismic team. Still smiling, he forced his mind back to his to-do list, trying to ignore that trouble maker stirring up potential problems in his pants.

Maybe he could increase the guys' work incentive with a little celebration of their own.

Yeah.

Good idea.

He added a few dozen cases of Lone Star beer to his list, thinking fireworks would be fun, too. He hadn't seen any local stands, however. They were a dime a dozen in Texas that time of year.

He turned to his computer and googled Colorado law.

Anything non-exploding that doesn't leave the ground.

A full-blown, Texas guffaw exploded from his chest.

Seriously? They calls that fireworks?

What a bunch of pussies.

Well, hell.

The guys'll just have to settle for beer.

The cook was planning a barbecue. Something smelled awful good, like brisket smoking. With luck, he'd whip up some 'tater salad, BBQ beans, and Coleslaw to go with.

There was plenty to celebrate.

The men's attitude so far was great. No hits for so long got 'em down, himself included. When they was grumpy, they was more prone to gittin' all bowed up or indulgin' bad habits.

Right.

On top of everything else, it was time to send 'em all into town for drug testing. Every goddamn thing needed to be in order before startin' this new dig.

He paused, wondering why beneath the anticipation, his belly tightened.

Excitement? Or experience?·

This wasn't Big Dick's first rodeo, either. He could count on him to make sure everyone was up to date on their OSHA training, had a full suite of safety and first aid equipment, air monitors, and oxygen masks on-hand.

The man was a certified EMT, in case anything went wrong and so was Trey. Bigger teams had a full-time medic or nurse on the crew. But that was first aid only. Seriously injured personnel needed to get to a hospital, ASAP.

Which as far as he could reckon, was over thirty miles away.

Rescuing hikers and skiers had to happen enough to have medevac services, even out there in the boonies.

Back to Google, he found several. None were close by, but it wasn't like choppers were hampered by treacherous mountain roads.

He copied the numbers into his phone, just in case. He'd seen some ugly accidents in his time. Having one on his watch would be bad enough, even worse if he wasn't prepared.

That's when OSHA handed you your ass on a plate.

The prophecy made by the culture hero, Mot si i u, *warned them that only harm would come to them by association with the whites.*
—George Bird Grinnell in "The Cheyenne Indians: Their History and Lifeways"

8. BEGINNINGS

LSO DRILLING SITE
July 4, Wednesday
9:12 a.m.

Charlie climbed out of the ATV feeling as if he'd spent a long day breaking wild mustangs. The trip from the old outpost took nearly an hour over rough, rock-strewn terrain.

"Why drive up there in a pickup like a bunch of pussies when we has the eight-wheeler?" one of the roughnecks declared. "It's what these badass things is for!"

The response at the time was a wild chorus of cheers.

Now they were more subdued.

Four guys puked along the way, including the one who had the bright idea in the first place. Charlie would have rather walked. He'd had more satisfying rides falling off a horse.

He lifted his arms over his head and stretched the kinks out of his back, wincing as he looked around the site.

Last time he was there it was a pristine mountain landscape resplendent with the Earth Mother's glory.

Now it was defiled by equipment intended to violate her.

What have you done, Littlewolf?

In reality, until they confirmed his find, he was no better than Dr. Phil.

"So where's this oil y'all found, Littlewolf?"

81

He turned toward the voice, meeting the amber eyes of one of the roughnecks.

"Yeah! Where is it?" echoed the others.

He gritted his teeth.

Since when did he answer to them?

On the other hand, provoking them was the last thing he needed when they were already stoked up, to say nothing of being seriously out-numbered.

He looked around to get his bearings as well as avert his condescending look, then signaled them to follow.

Something about these *vehoes* struck him as descendants of those who'd settled the west and drove his people like cattle to desolate locations. People who claimed cultural and moral superiority. What colonization was all about, shoving indigenous people aside to make room for a civilization morally inferior to what they'd had for centuries, even millennia.

As he led the yammering entourage toward the find that assured their paychecks he ground his teeth as generations of righteous fury seared his veins.

Yeah, vehoes. *When's the last time the Earth Mother spoke to you?*

The fault was easy to find about a hundred yards away, offset by a few inches. He paced along it, again sensing its energy, slightly stronger on one side than the other. When he got to the seep he stepped back and pointed.

As expected, the roughnecks were impressed. They rubbed their hands in it, sniffed it, laughed and exchanged high-fives. Two guys smeared stripes on their cheeks, then started dancing around, whooping like Indians.

Charlie strode away, torn between shaking his head and some sarcastic remark, either of which was inflammatory.

Falling prey to Trey's zero tolerance *No Altercation* policy was the last thing he needed.

He made his way back to the center hub of activity, then to where they roughed in the road. He flinched when he saw the tangle of trees pushed aside in the process. Already the place had been transformed, no longer virgin ground.

The syncopated rumble of a diesel engine grew louder. Moments later, the fortified grille of Trey's F-350 appeared, lab trailer in tow.

Once that was in place, he'd have something to do and could quit standing around.

It bumped up the road, slow but steady. When it got to the top, Charlie led the way to where they'd decided to park it—far enough from future rigs to meet safety requirements, close enough to minimize steps.

Big Dick, hard hat covering his naked head, roared at some of the men to get their sorry asses over there to help. Once it was unhitched, they cranked up the jacks, then placed blocks beneath.

Charlie held his breath when they released the jacks on one side before the other.

It rocked precariously.

Moments later it settled on the piers with a *thud*.

Trey pulled far enough forward for a few others to get the ramps in place to unload the generator and hook it up.

After that, Big Dick joined him in the cab and the pair headed back to get the deuce-and-a-half mounted with the wildcat rig.

With the lab in place, Charlie went inside to get everything unpacked and ready to go. The results of the seismic survey were due to arrive in a few days.

Nonetheless, Maguire and Big Dick wanted to start drilling and trusted him to show them where.

The seep confirmed hydrocarbons were there, but now it was a matter of quality, quantity, and how deep. The initial tests performed the day Dr. Phil stomped out looked promising.

The oil took a twisted path to the surface. The reservoir's location was far more important. He had a good idea, but the real question his bosses wanted answered was whether enough was down there to justify a full-size exploration rig.

Once they started to drill, he'd step into his new role as the Dr. Phil Replacement Unit to monitor LWD data. Trey told him he'd been "sucking hind teat" long enough and would get a raise and promotion to fit his new role.

A low frequency hum vibrated beneath his feet.

Now what?

He stepped outside.

A far deeper and lower frequency vibration announced the deuce-and-a-half's arrival. The rig's derrick was folded over the cab and extended well beyond the hood. It plodded up the road at a snail's pace, cheered on by the crew.

Moments later, the accolades faded, followed by a chorus of groans when one of the truck's rear duelies hit a rut, then mocked Big Dick's attempts to move forward by sinking deeper.

Wheels spun in vain, spitting dirt and gravel, tires burrowing into soft ground until the vehicle listed to the right.

Big Dick cut the engine and flew out the cab, spewing the longest string of expletives Charlie had ever heard.

What if it tipped over completely? What then?

He watched long enough to convince himself it wouldn't, then went back inside. Getting it unstuck wasn't his problem.

MONTGOMERY RESIDENCE
BOULDER
July 4, Wednesday
6:11 p.m.

Will sat on the sofa holding Connie's hand as they waited for Sara's live interview on KDVR's six o'clock news. His right foot tapped the floor, chest swelling with parental pride and paternal protection, a combination as compatible as oil and water.

Messing with powerful entities like the government was a bad idea. The fact they'd appeared to back off didn't mean they wouldn't come back with a vengeance. Like a pneumonia relapse more deadly than the initial bout.

At least Sara moved back to Denver. In theory, she was less vulnerable at her condo versus that isolated cabin. If she screamed, someone would hear her.

Maybe.

What could he do to help? She probably wouldn't listen, but he had to do something.

Hire a bodyguard perhaps?

Depending on who was threatening her, it could make a difference. Once a person was on their radar, they could be taken out any number of ways.

He'd seen plenty in his day. Accidents were common, like Bryan's. Or more subtle means, such as exotic poisons or diseases. She needed to keep her vitamins locked up in the thumb-print activated gun case he gave her for her birthday.

Connie squeezed his hand. "What are you thinking?"

He met her questioning eyes. "That Sara should keep her vitamins in her gun case."

"Her gun case? Why?"

He held her gaze, questioning his own paranoia.

"It's easy to poison someone who takes vitamins or medications."

Her green eyes widened. "You actually think someone might do that?"

"If she infuriates them, next time they'll be more subtle than a car wreck or home invasion. Remember the Karen Silkwood case?"

"Not off hand."

"She went up against Kerr-McGee about worker safety. The facility manufactured fuel for nuclear power plants. She died in a very suspicious auto accident, plus had high levels of plutonium in her body. They never proved it, but some speculated they'd been poisoning her food."

"Good God, Will! That's horrible! Should we do something to stop her?"

His eyebrows lifted as he peered over the top of his glasses. "Good idea, woman. Let's see, how exactly should we do that? Restrict her to her room? Take away her phone?"

She wilted in defeat. "You're right. At least she and Bryan didn't have kids. Then it'd be an entirely different situation."

"After Sara was born I couldn't get Ellen back on a horse. She loved to ride when we first met. We even backpacked on donkeys in the Grand Canyon."

His wife laughed. "I remember that. She loved it. But afterward, I tried to get her to go, too. I think Sara was a toddler, two or three years old. She told me her worst nightmare was chasing her baby around all day on crutches. Much less in a wheelchair."

He squeezed her hand, fond memories of Sara's mother swimming through his mind.

Hopefully their only daughter wouldn't be joining her anytime soon.

Commercials ended, attention back on the television. Sara sat in the studio beside the station's anchorman.

She looked beautiful and very much at ease. Her long curls were swept up and back, cascading down her back. The navy blue business suit and ruffled white blouse were professional, yet feminine.

He was proud of her.

Really was.

A lot.

Whether he liked the circumstances or not.

The anchorman's interest looked genuine as he introduced her as a Denver resident with issues related to the PURF project, then plunged into the interview.

"So it's my understanding, Sara, that this recent information release by WikiLeaks and the president's subsequent statement affected you in a very personal way."

"Yes, Jose, it did," she replied. "My husband was the one who found all that information. He wanted to document it with photos to prove the project's existence, so we went cross-country skiing in the area to check it out."

"And you found such evidence?"

"Yes, we did."

A picture of her and Bryan on the slopes he'd taken that fateful day flashed on the screen, followed by the one of the towering rig.

"On the way home our truck was forced over a cliff by a black SUV. My husband was killed and I was in the hospital for two weeks. I now have enough hardware I'll never make it through an airport metal detector again. And that was just the beginning."

The twisted remains of their Silverado flashed on the screen. Connie gasped. Will tightened his grip on her hand.

"This is where our truck. . ."

Sara's voice broke.

She paused mid-sentence and looked away from the camera.

"I'm sorry," she said, shaking her head. "I promised myself I wouldn't do that."

Perez gave her a reassuring smile and cut to commercial.

Ironically, for Chevy pickups.

Back from the break, Sara resumed control. She expressed how her First, Second, and Fourth Amendment rights were violated, to say nothing of the death of her husband. Another picture of her and Bryan filled the screen.

She went on about the water issue, providing the toxic figures from her records, and added that the pollutants allegedly killed a local resident and compromised the health of another.

The picture of the tower flashed again followed by facility plans from the WikiLeaks files.

"PURF was set up with geothermal power. That involves a process similar to fracking. The chemicals in my water were identical to the ones oil companies use for that," she explained. "That seems a rather notable coincidence to me."

There was also mention of her subsequent eighteen-wheeler accident, the raid on her cabin, and illegal search of her condo where personal property was confiscated, all without a warrant.

At the conclusion, the station flashed the GoFundMe address she set up the day before to help continue her grassroots efforts to expose the corruption involved.

The interview lasted over eleven minutes, exceptionally long for a local newscast.

"We definitely wish you luck in your efforts, Mrs. Reynolds. Thank you for being with us today. This is Jose Perez for KDVR News at Six."

When the show switched to sports Will turned it off.

"Well, what do you think?" Connie asked. The crease between her eyebrows relayed sentiments similar to his own.

He pursed his lips. "One little local interview won't change the world. But if additional ones follow, especially if they make it to the network level, there's likely to be a quiet, but forceful response."

"Are you going to do anything?"

"I think I'll go ahead and hire a bodyguard."

"Good idea. Are you going to tell her?"

"If I don't she'll probably shoot him by mistake."

Only when the last tree has died and the last river has been poisoned and the
last fish been caught will we realize we cannot eat money.
— Indian Proverb

9. STRIKES

LSO DRILLING SITE
Wednesday, July 4
7:01 p.m.

C harlie got his first taste of wheelin' and dealin', Texas style, shortly after the track rig arrived from Fort Worth. Trey lost no time inviting the semi driver to join them for "some grub." While the guy shoveled in smoked brisket, beans, and potato salad Trey bribed him into bringing his tractor up the road to nudge the deuce-and-a-half out of the rut.

It cost Trey, or in all likelihood LSO, a huge tip and a case of beer, but the driver eventually agreed. After heaping up his plate a second time and gobbling it down, he dropped the lowboy trailer and crept up the dirt road to the stuck digger, which he skillfully nudged out of the hole.

After that, Big Dick rode back down with the driver to bring up the track rig. When he returned, everyone fussed over it as if it were a thoroughbred stallion.

Charlie stood back a ways, looking it over. Its complexity was impressive, not only the control panel with its multitude of gauges and levers for the drilling mechanism, but the tangle of hoses that delivered and returned drilling mud, plus hoists to lift the casing.

The plan was to use the wildcat rig for the seep, the new arrival for the main reservoir.

By then it was too late to set up and start drilling, plus everyone was already celebrating. While everyone else headed for the beer cooler, Charlie finished off the last of his barbequed beans, dumped his plate and plastic utensils in the trash, and headed for the lab trailer.

The Fourth of July was not appreciated by his people. After the colonies won independence, Native Americans were treated even worse. For the newly formed Union, expansion was what it was all about and indigenous inhabitants were in the way. Between broken treaties and being forced from land they'd occupied for millennia, celebrating was as inappropriate as it was for Columbus Day.

Discovered America? Really?

Gratefully, he had an excuse to avoid the festivities. He still had plenty of reading to do before he felt confident analyzing a core sample on his own. He'd barely gotten engrossed in the online material when the door opened.

The trailer moaned as Big Dick ambled inside, bulk looming beside him like a thundercloud.

"I see y'all texted me your emergency info. Great. But y'all needs to hurry up and finish that OSHA training, too. Before we starts this new dig, which should be next week, maybe sooner. Ya'll's only completed 'bout half."

"Right. Thanks for the reminder."

"Y'all needs to get your red ass movin', Chief, or y'all's gonna miss the fun. We cain't let y'all anywhere's near that rig without it. Playin' with Dr. Phil, it was optional. Now it ain't." He paused to emit a belch that smelled like beer-soaked barbeque. "If anything goes south and that ain't done," he went on, "OSHA will be on me and Trey like stink on shit. Comprenday?"

He held his gaze. "I understand."

Big Dick grunted, then left, trailer rocking as if celebrating his departure.

Following Dr. Phil's impromptu exit, he spent most his time studying the science of core analysis. The last thing he needed to do was check every test procedure on the internet like his predecessor.

Thus, he forgot that online OSHA stuff. Most of what he'd seen so far was little more than common sense.

But safety was one area where, when left on their own, most roughnecks came up short, that wild ATV ride a strong case in point.

One thing was clear—breaking ground at a new site was loaded with unknowns. Which was why they did seismic studies and pulled core samples. That was also why Big Dick was busy making sure all the necessary safety controls were in place, training being one of them.

The site sizzled with anticipation. The unspoken consensus was if they didn't find something good they'd pack up and head back to Texas.

That meant goodbye paychecks, so making a strike was in everyone's best interest.

His own included.

Or so he thought.

SARA'S CONDO OFFICE
DENVER
Wednesday, July 4
8:43 p.m.

Sara rocked back in her computer chair, leisurely checking her email.

The first message to arrive following the KDVR interview was from a lawyer.

She scoffed.

How typical.

She laughed out loud when dozens more followed.

First come, first served, she thought, and clicked.

Kenneth Carlson, attorney-at-law, wondered if she was pursuing a wrongful death suit.

Interesting.

Such had never entered her mind.

It wasn't like she needed money. The punitive aspect of it, however, reeked with appeal. If she won, it would bring more publicity and implicate them in a different way.

The President failed to mention they'd been killing people to maintain their dirty little secret.

She clicked the link to Carlson's website. The header was an accident scene, ambulance in the foreground surrounded by a cadre of police cars, all lit up like Christmas trees.

An ambulance chaser.

Big surprise.

On the other hand, maybe that was exactly what she needed.

Furthermore, in addition to the wreck at Dead Horse Canyon, there was the eighteen-wheeler incident. If this guy specialized in vehicular accidents, he knew liability laws inside out.

However, the defendants in her case weren't identified personally.

That could be a problem.

The only official record of the one where Bryan died was with the Falcon Ridge cops. There was no record of the second one, much less the phony Highway Patrolman who pulled her from the wreckage.

Where did her car end up, anyway?

No one knew.

Which made the insurance claim a real pain. The only way to resolve it was to say it was stolen, which was a bit of a stretch, but not exactly a lie.

How could she file a lawsuit against an unknown party? Or could she go after the government itself?

From what her father said, you couldn't sue the government without their permission.

As if!

Whistleblowers got their butts kicked and that was about it.

But there had to be some way.

The more she thought about it, the better it sounded.

But was this guy the right one for the job?

Maybe she needed someone familiar with dealing with the government. Situations where the responsibility went higher than individuals who simply carried out orders. Her eyebrows lowered again at the adage about fighting city hall.

Was it pointless?

No.

This battle needed to be waged on as many fronts as possible. This seemed a viable approach. Otherwise, all those lawyers wouldn't be yipping at her heels.

Did such a lawsuit require a different specialty?

Maybe not.

PURF was managed by EMPI, a private company. Going after them might be easier, even if it did involve a government contract. No doubt the management firm was responsible for all aspects, including security. At the least, they could point to the contractor, whether company or individual.

Like Bryan always said, "turds roll downhill."

Her mind wandered among the possible options. Maybe her father would have some ideas.

She picked up her phone.

Set it down again.

No.

This was her battle, not his.

He claimed to be behind her, but she could tell he wanted her to give it up. Plus, she didn't want to be a pest, much less drag him into it. If she needed his help, that was one thing. When other professionals could do the job, that was the course she should take.

Except he knew a lot of people.

Could he refer her to a more suitable attorney? Maybe this guy wasn't the most qualified. By the looks of her inbox, there were plenty to choose from.

As much as she hated to keep running to "daddy," it was downright foolish not to take advantage of his knowledge and experience.

He promised to support her efforts.

It was also an open invitation to tell her what to do.

Okay.

She'd ask.

In an email.

It was less intrusive and if he thought it was stupid, she wouldn't have to listen.

Avoid that condescending tone she knew too well.

With that, she forwarded Carlson's email with a note asking what he thought. Not necessarily with this guy, but the concept.

The more she thought about it, the more she liked it.

Sue the bastards.

They deserved it.

She'd barely hit "Send" when her phone rang. She laughed out loud. Her father tended toward strong feelings with opinions to match. Did she want to hear them?

Maybe, maybe not.

But she'd thrown it out there.

She answered with forced cheerfulness.

"Hi, Dad. That was quick."

"That's an excellent idea, Sara. Maybe not with this one, though. You need a major law firm with plenty of capital to support an in-depth investigation. Let me do some checking and get back to you."

"That's great! I wasn't sure what you'd think, but wanted your thoughts."

"Money talks. Hit people like that in the pocketbook and it gets attention. It would certainly be satisfying to put the people who did this out of business even if we can't put them behind bars."

"Amen to that. By the way, did you ever get in touch with those Judicial Guardian watchdog people?"

"Yes. They were sympathetic, agreed it was outrageous, and put it on their list. But like everything else these days, it's all about funding. They're understaffed, so they're not in a position to take on anything else. Needless to say anyone fighting corruption these days has a target-rich environment. So it's doubtful they'll do you any good."

"Oh. That's too bad. I could give them a pretty substantial donation if they decided to take it on."

"I mentioned that. I think being understaffed is their biggest issue. It speaks to their integrity not to take the money, then do nothing."

"So, what did you think of my interview?"

"Nice job. You presented yourself very well. But watch your back. Messing with people of this caliber is dangerous. And along those lines, I'm hiring you a bodyguard."

She jolted upright in the chair. "Wow! Isn't that expensive?"

"You're worth it. And the more noise you make, the more you'll need one. It's possible you'll become quite a celebrity. And there are all flavors of nut cakes out there."

"No argument there."

"I'm looking for recommendations from some people I know. I assume you'd like to sit in on the interviews."

"Absolutely. If I'm going to be around this person a lot he needs to be someone I can tolerate."

"Right. I'd hate for you to shoot him."

She laughed. "I might. Especially if he's annoying. Like some of those PIs on TV."

"I'll see if Thomas Magnum is available. How's that?"

"Now *that* I could handle."

"Figured as much. I'll keep you posted."

LSO DRILLING SITE
July 5, Thursday
8:20 a.m.

"Whoo-hoo!"

Charlie looked up from the gas chromatograph at Trey's booming whoop. They were sharing the lab trailer until they got his office and everything else moved, which would happen once they found enough crude to make it worth setting up a permanent site.

He got up and headed for the door. "FedEx just left a package at the gate. Should be the seismic. I's headin' down to git it."

A confident grin crept across Charlie's face. He knew *exactly* what he found. Now they'd have objective, scientific data to back it up.

Ten minutes later Trey was back, Big Dick in tow. "Alright, let's see what we's got."

He hooked his laptop up to the big screen in the conference area while Big Dick ripped open the envelope. He pulled out the thumb drive it contained and plugged it into a USB port.

The graphics section included a rendered 3D view of the site. Color-coded by density, it displayed a series of intermingled layers hinting at what lay below.

While interpreting it was tricky, the correct profile was there: A thrust fault surrounded by a variety of stratifications that favored one or more pockets of hydrocarbons.

The one that explained the seep was only a few hundred feet down. On the fault's opposite side, about eighteen hundred feet below, a void of similar color indicated potential for a reservoir— a huge one.

Trey pointed at it, then rubbed his hands together. "After we checks out the seep, I say we shoots for that. I seen similar ones spill their guts. With luck, it's oil, not gas, and won't take fracturing to git to. How's the rig coming?"

"We oughta be ready to pull core first thing Monday," Big Dick replied. "Then Littlewolf, here, can try his hand at some serious analysis. Y'all familiar with USCS?"

"Unified Soil Classification System? Yes, sir. Since college, actually."

"Good. In a way, it's kinda cheatin', 'cause we all knows somethin's down there, right Chief?"

Charlie winced. Not because it was insulting, but because he was far from worthy of the title.

Most likely it was intended as a compliment.

Someone who didn't mind being called *dickhead* wasn't likely to be sensitized to defamatory or inappropriate nicknames.

He turned his attention back to the graphic. He felt nothing. No impression or instinctive reaction regarding what, if anything, it was trying to say.

BKSS LLC
ALBUQUERQUE, NM
July 5, Thursday
9:43 a.m.

Bernie Keller stood beside the mail boxes in front of the dilapidated building that housed his office, pumping his fist in the air.

"Hoo-rah!"

There'd been nothing worth celebrating for a long time. But after getting that contract issue straightened out, life had taken a sharp turn to the right.

He kissed the check, hugged it to his chest, then flipped off a passing motorcyclist rubbernecking as he hobbled back to his office.

Getting paid $1.3M for seven months work when he didn't even get his hands dirty was pretty damn sweet. His plan was to pay each of his five team members $80K, with team lead, Eddie Johannsen quite a bit more at $150K, which left $750K.

In spite of their various screw-ups, of which there'd been too many, everything came out okay.

More than okay, even.

But like other battles he'd fought, things eventually worked out.

He knew from the start bidding a fixed price contract was risky. There were moments when he was scared shitless. If it had dragged on, especially with them covering the data security side, it would've been a freakin' disaster.

But that was moot since his initial gamble delivered.

Data security wasn't in their task order, so the NSA actually refunded what they'd paid for transcription services, all charges transferred to EMPI, where they belonged.

The original program manager, Virgil Steinbrenner, was such a prick. If he'd known he'd have to deal with the likes of him, he would have doubled the bid.

Fortunately, that asshole wouldn't make life a living hell for anyone ever again.

For two cents he would've taken the guy out himself.

He was a damn good sniper in his day.

After everything went public, the government called off the dogs. No charges would be filed. Reynolds was dead, his widow took no security oaths, and all was quiet following the initial release.

Once the construction equipment was gone, security was unnecessary. It wasn't military, no outside entrances, leaving nothing worth spying on.

Thus, his contract was fulfilled.

He'd barely gotten settled back at his desk, thinking he'd take off early and stop by *The Watering Hole* for a cool one, when his cell rang. He scrutinized the private number, a scramble of random digits, probably a burner, with a D.C. area code.

"Yeah," he answered, poised to hang up at the first mention of a car warranty.

"Keller Security?"

"Yeah. Who's this?"

"Doesn't matter. You interested in a job?"

"Maybe. Whatcha got?"

"Neutralize an annoyance. Discreetly."

"Oh, yeah? Who?"

"That bimbo, Sara Reynolds. I assume you've heard of her."

While the government seemed okay with the outcome, apparently someone else was not.

Assassinations were sensitive business. Working with the alphabet agencies included the benefit of their backup. Otherwise, they wound up in the crosshairs themselves if the government refused to turn its head. Though in this case they probably would.

Only one thing terrified him—going back to prison. He'd suck a pistol before doing time again, period.

Apparently reading his hesitation, the caller added, "Two million plus expenses. Take out that Indian, too, you get another $500K."

Which allowed plenty for payoffs.

Or attorney fees.

No doubt someone wanted to make an example of her, plus assure no one else took up the banner.

"It needs to be subtle. She's gone on TV, making the optics crucial. Nothing that could bring more publicity. I want it finished within a month."

It was sounding better and better. His guys could enjoy a couple weeks off. Blow off some steam, then come back refreshed to a familiar, relatively routine assignment, this time without the NSA.

Meanwhile, he could gather updated information. The chick moved back to her Denver condo, which was already familiar and convenient. He had to laugh that the Indian went to work for LSO.

"Well, Keller? Interested?"

"Yeah. I need a retainer. Half up front, remainder with delivery of the death certificate."

"No problem."

He provided the transfer information, grinning as he ended the call. He saved the number, though he doubted he'd ever see that one again.

> *"Great services are not canceled by one act or by one single error."*
> —*Benjamin Disraeli*

10. DÉJÀ-VU

MONTGOMERY RESIDENCE
BOULDER
July 5, Thursday
10:15 a.m.

Will kicked back in his leather office chair, feet propped on his desk. The two action items he accepted for Sara took turns weaving through his mind: First, a law firm for her wrongful death suit; second, a trustworthy bodyguard, preferably good-looking and charming.

Being a societal renegade was the ultimate risky business. The thought his only child had joined their ranks did not generate a warm feeling. Stopping her was out of the question, so the next best thing was to provide the best support and protection available.

Finding an attorney was simpler, so he'd tackle that first.

As he researched the issue, he discovered there were few differences between wrongful death and the typical personal injury or medical malpractice lawsuits.

The fact Bryan's death was intentional fit the former template. Seeing it as manslaughter in lieu of first degree murder, however brought his usually cool disposition to the boiling point.

He pondered the issues Sara mentioned regarding culpability, finally deciding that figuring out the particulars was why you retained an attorney.

Out of curiosity, he checked the ambulance chaser's trial record. The guy advertised on TV, which was expensive. If he could afford that, he was probably good.

Turned out his record with the American Bar Association was clean. After that, he scanned court records and found the guy did quite well. The fact he initiated contact gave her case credibility, too. He collected the relevant links and emailed them to Sara.

That done, he tackled the bodyguard issue. While he knew some retired FBI types who might be interested, he didn't trust any of them, especially with Sara preparing to sue the government.

A quick web search left his nose wrinkled with distaste.

He didn't like the looks of any of them, either, especially around his little girl.

For some strange reason, the Falcon Ridge cop who investigated Bryan's accident came to mind. The man hadn't been particularly friendly, but professional. Maybe he'd have some recommendations.

Extracting the guy's card from his wallet, he set his feet back on the floor and placed the call. When the desk sergeant picked up, he asked for Officer Fernandez.

"Who's calling please?"

"William Montgomery. I spoke with him a few months ago about an accident my daughter and son-in-law were involved in."

"Did you want to talk to him about that case?" the man responded.

"Not specifically. Is he not available?"

"Actually, no, he's not. He resigned a few weeks ago."

He straightened in the chair.

Cops didn't resign without good reason, though sometimes it was to avoid being fired.

"Oh. Is there some way I can get in touch with him?"

He wasn't sure what to think of the pause that followed.

"I can't give you that information," the man said at last. "But if you leave your number, we'll let him know you called."

"Okay, that works," he replied, and did as requested. "Thanks."

He ended the call, thoughts churning.

Why'd he leave?

Under pressure?

Do something wrong?

Find another position?

If they were willing to provide him with Will's number, his departure probably wasn't on bad terms.

Unless it was a blatant lie.

No telling.

Small town cops could tilt either way.

Speculating was pointless, so he blew it off. If the guy didn't call back, he'd be back to square one.

Before he could decide whether to get back to work or get a snack downstairs, his cell rang. The area code and number were unfamiliar.

"Will Montgomery," he said.

"Hello, Mr. Montgomery. This is Mike Fernandez. I hear you're trying to reach me."

Will blinked with pleasant surprise.

"Thanks for calling back. I have what may be a strange question, but thought you might be able to help. I talked to you a few months ago about my daughter's accident."

"The Reynolds case?"

"Yes. Was it ever closed?"

"I'm afraid it was. I'm not supposed to talk about it, though."

"I understand. And that's not why I'm calling. I'm looking to hire a bodyguard for my daughter. Do you know anyone you could recommend?"

"Huh," he replied. "I saw her on TV the other night. I can see why you'd be concerned for her safety."

His laugh was short and dry. "That's certainly an understatement. Does anyone come to mind?"

The ex-cop chuckled. "Actually, yes. I'd be interested. One of the reasons I quit FRPD was how that case was handled. I'm fed up with, well, the politics of law enforcement. I got my PI license and I'm looking for work. Anything short of security guard, if you know what I mean."

Will grinned. Being familiar with the case was a definite plus. In fact, he probably knew a few things he and Sara didn't, making it even better.

"Great. My daughter's living in Denver now, not her cabin. Is that a problem?"

"No, not at all. I'm living just outside Boulder myself."

"Perfect. Are you available tomorrow afternoon? I live in Boulder, so we could meet at my place. Say around three o'clock?"

"Sure. Give me your address and I'll be there."

He provided the information, then hung up, feeling duly satisfied as he called Sara.

"Hi, Dad. What's up?"

"You'll never guess who's interested in being your bodyguard."

"I have no idea, Dad. Who?"

"The cop who investigated your accident. How it was handled bothered him enough to quit the force. Now he's a PI."

"Oh."

His eyes narrowed at her reaction's insipid inflection. "What's wrong? You don't sound very enthusiastic."

"I'm not. He was pretty rude and obnoxious when I bailed out Charlie. If he treated me that way again, I probably would shoot him."

Will chuckled. "Do you think it was just the circumstances? He said he quit because of how your case was handled."

"It's possible, I suppose. I went by to tell him about a few things I remembered, like he asked me to do. Then I found out Charlie was there. He was pretty cold. As if I'd done something wrong."

"*Hmmmm.* He seemed okay when Connie and I talked to him. Not friendly, but professional. I asked him to come out to my place for an interview tomorrow at three. Should I cancel? Or are you willing to talk to him?"

"You think he's worth talking to?"

"I do. If you still don't like him, we'll keep looking."

"I suppose. He's sure no Thomas Magnum, looks *or* personality-wise. But nothing to lose, I guess."

"Okay, great. We'll see how it goes and take it from there. His familiarity with the case would be pretty handy. He probably knows plenty we don't."

"True. Change of subject, Dad. Did you get my email thanking you for checking out that attorney? I'll going to make an appointment."

He hesitated, not wanting to intrude, yet felt compelled to offer. "Do you want me to go with you? Or handle it solo?"

To his relief she laughed. "I'd love for you to go along, Dad. Just let me do the talking, okay?"

He grinned. "Point taken. Set something up and let me know time and place."

MIKE FERNANDEZ'S APARTMENT
BOULDER
July 5, Thursday
10:31 a.m.

Mike's mind tumbled like ice in a frozen margarita machine. With it approaching the "too good to be true" category, was it some sort of trick?

Was the call really from Montgomery or one of those goons at the wreck site? Had they gotten wind of his distaste for their tactics, so much so he walked away from a job he otherwise liked, a lot?

Dealing with those people was enough to make anyone paranoid. Cops were already suspicious by nature. Much less a case that involved a government agency, possible conspiracy, and black ops.

People who considered themselves judge and jury, then went around executing people. Pissed him off all over again, just thinking about it.

A reverse look-up on the address confirmed it was Montgomery's home.

So far so good.

He'd still be on alert.

With the man former FBI, there was no telling. Maybe he was in cahoots with them as well. Then again, he was former FBI himself, with no love lost there, either.

Something told him it was legit. His daughter was nearly killed twice. He knew what he'd do if anyone messed with one of his girls. That would be enough to make any man check his loyalties at the door.

This could be exactly what he was hoping for. A chance to make a real difference. The circumstances had gotten under his skin from day one.

No one was above the law.

No one.

He didn't care who it was, who a person represented, or was working for. Murder was murder, pure and simple. Even in the line of duty, he only used lethal force when required, when his, his partner's, or someone else's life hung in the balance.

Otherwise, his goal was to stop the suspect in his tracks. Inflict some pain on the bastard and let the courts do the rest. Knee shots required skill, but were effective—seldom fatal, assuming you missed the femoral artery, but always debilitating. They wouldn't be fleeing another crime scene on foot anytime soon.

The justice system often let him down, but his conscience was clear. Nonetheless, he had to admit there were a few suspects he later wished he'd taken out at the scene, consequences be damned.

Now that he knew more about why Reynolds was targeted, he was even more incensed.

Nothing pleased him more than when Sara Reynolds went public. When the media first picked up the story from WikiLeaks, he hadn't made the connection. When she showed up on Fox31 blowing the whistle, he was nothing short of shocked.

And cheering her on.

That took a lot of nerve.

Which he'd seen first hand, that time she came into the station and bailed out that Indian guy. Made that sarcastic comment that at least someone was looking into her husband's murder.

Which was true.

But pretty gutsy.

Would she be a pain in the butt to work for?

Those types couldn't take directions and made it more dangerous for all concerned. For that, as well as various other reasons, the risks were high.

It could also be the most important, at least from a moral standpoint.

In addition to being her bodyguard, he'd do some detective work as well. Anything he could do to help her kick some federal ass would be frosting on the cake.

So far it sounded good.

Unless Sara Reynolds turned out to be a psycho bitch from hell.

MONTGOMERY RESIDENCE
BOULDER
July 6, Friday
3:00 p.m.

Fernandez arrived, doorbell ringing exactly on the hour. Sara watched from the living room sofa while her father answered the door. Having met before, the two men skipped introductions, shook hands, then Will gestured toward the living room.

"Would you like some iced tea?" Will asked.

"That would be great," the man replied. "It's definitely hot out there today."

When he stepped into the parlor area he held out his hand. "Mike Fernandez," he said, taking hers in a firm grip.

"Sara Reynolds." She withdrew her hand. "But I'm sure you already know that."

His expression fell. "Right."

He settled into a wingback chair across from her. For some reason he looked different. Maybe because his black hair was a bit longer and he was out of uniform, wearing a navy blue jacket, white button-down shirt, and khakis, but no tie. Will returned moments later with their drinks.

"Okay," he said, taking a seat next to her. "Thank you for coming."

"My pleasure." He shifted his gaze to Sara. "It's good to see you've recovered so well. You were in pretty bad shape that first time I saw you."

"That's for sure." She blinked hard, remembering when she woke up in the hospital to see him standing there with a host of medical personnel. "Not exactly the best day of my life."

"So tell me about your experience," Will said, cutting to the chase. "How long were you in law enforcement?"

The ex-cop reached up toward his mouth, then stopped abruptly and folded his hands in his lap. "Most my life, actually. As soon as I graduated from the University of Minnesota with a degree in criminal justice I went to work for the FBI."

Will's eyebrows lifted. "No kidding? When? I worked for them awhile myself."

"I was there ten years." He reached into his inside pocket and pulled out a folded piece of letter-sized paper. "Here's my resume."

"Thanks." Will took it from him, then adjusted his glasses. "So you were an operative in the LA Field Office all of that time?"

"Yes."

"Then you left to work for the San Bernardino County Sheriff's office. Why'd you leave the Bureau?"

His chest heaved with a sigh. "I didn't like how they handled too many cases." His hand headed toward his mouth again. It stopped halfway as he smiled. "I used to have a mustache," he explained. "I didn't realize how important it was to my thought process until it was gone."

Sara smiled. That was why he looked different, his Poncho Villa look fallen victim to a razor.

"Maybe it was local leadership," he went on, "but there was too much emphasis on closing cases versus solving crimes, if you know what I mean. Their main focus was keeping the numbers up. Or down, depending on your point of view."

Will's response was grim agreement. "I saw some of that, too. I was an analyst, but the same deal. So how did it work out at the Sheriff's office? I see you were there for over five years."

"It was actually pretty good. I just got tired of the area in general. Too many people, too much pollution. Rat race environment. My wife and I had a couple teenage girls and wanted to move to a quieter area. She had a sister in Belton, so we wound up there.

"I got right on with Falcon Ridge PD. I enjoyed it quite a bit." His expression darkened as he took a swig of his iced tea. "Turns out the politics at any level get pretty abrasive, eventually. My wife died two years ago, the kids are grown, so I had the option of trying something new, out on my own. Got my PI license, and here I am." He held out his hands. "PI, bodyguard, detective—whatever the job requires."

Will leaned back and folded his arms. "You mentioned on the phone that my daughter's case was one of the things that drove you to leave. Can you elaborate on that?"

"Yeah." He shifted in the chair. "It was pretty clear something shady was going on. No sane person would approach that curve from either direction at a speed high enough to send that pickup over the edge. Long story short, we were instructed to investigate, yet told what to find."

"Told by whom?"

"The Feds. More specifically, their contractor."

"Indeed!" Will unfolded his arms and leaned forward. "What exactly did they say?"

For the first time, Fernandez looked uncomfortable. His hand lifted, then stopped, redirected to the armrest.. "This is all in confidence, right?"

"Of course."

Sara nodded as she, too, leaned forward.

Fernandez worked his jaw a moment, as if collecting his thoughts. Sara smiled to herself at how badly he missed that mustache.

"Okay. It was obviously not an accident, yet they wanted us to investigate as if we didn't know who was responsible. They were surprised when we showed up at the scene. They apparently didn't know the truck had that On-Star system. We stayed until your daughter and her husband were loaded into the ambulance. Then they told us to uh, you know, get lost."

Will glanced at Sara, then rubbed his forehead. "I can't bear to think how it would have ended if you hadn't shown up."

"True. When I went by the next day, the truck was in the ravine. It was pretty stable there on that ledge, so they must have shoved it over the side. They set up video surveillance so when your daughter's friend—the Indian guy—went there, sometime later, they insisted we arrest him for disturbing a crime scene. About then, I was done. Couldn't get away from the feds, no matter what."

No wonder he was in a bad mood that day, Sara thought. "You'd probably be interested in the dashcam videos Charlie recovered from our truck," she said.

His brown eyes lit up. "You bet I would! How much does it cover?"

"Right up until they removed it with a hammer. The SD card got knocked loose. The video includes a short glimpse of the guy's face."

"Wow. I'd definitely like to see it. There's a good chance the same people might threaten you again, depending on who's got a problem with your activities. Voices are helpful, but having a photographic record to compare to mug shots is priceless, especially with facial recognition capabilities."

"Did you ever hear about my second wreck? With a logging truck?" she asked.

"We heard about it when your car was totaled. We wouldn't have, except it was registered in Belton county."

The conversation continued, mostly filling him in about other events of which he had no knowledge. An hour later when the conversation paused, Will took advantage of the break. "Would you excuse us a moment, Mike?"

"No problem."

Sara and her father stepped far enough into the kitchen to be out of earshot.

"Well, what do you think?" Will asked.

She held his gaze, reservations mostly put to rest. "I think he'll be fine. That background knowledge is worth a lot. We'd have a lot of filling in to do with anyone else. Plus, his attitude matches mine toward the government. What about you?"

"I agree."

When they returned to the living room, Will apologized for the interruption, then added, "We agree you're the man for the job. When can you start?"

Fernandez grinned. "As soon as you like."

"How about now?" His smile widened. "Okay, Mike, you're on the clock."

They negotiated rates and per diem, then continued the debriefing process so he knew as much as they did about the situation.

Logistics were a critical component. They discussed having him stay at her condo, given she had a spare room. She stiffened, not thrilled at the prospect.

"My presence could be a deterrent and keep them away," Mike mused. "Which could conceivably put you in more danger elsewhere."

Her mind sifted the pros and cons. "Yes, but if they break into my condo, then what?"

"Maybe I can find a place close enough that I could get there fast. We'll wire your place for our benefit as well, so I'll know if your place is breached."

"It's a fairly large complex," Will noted. "I'm always in the market for investment property. If any units are for sale, I could buy it and set you up there."

"That sounds great, Dad. But even if any are available, it'll take weeks to close. What do we do in the meantime?"

"Let's see what's out there. Maybe we can find a rental. Or some sort of residence inn."

She copied several files as well as the dashcam videos to a flash drive for him to review later. Then, while Will checked real estate listings for within a block or so of her condo, she and Mike headed for Denver to assess the logistics.

The intellect has little to do on the road to discovery. There comes a leap in consciousness, call it intuition or what you will, and the solution comes to you and you don't know how or why.
—Albert Einstein

11. CONCERNS

LSO DRILLING SITE
July 6, Friday
4:40 p.m.

Charlie studied the seismic data until its scramble of colors resembled a poorly designed Navajo blanket. The reservoir where the seep originated wasn't as clear as he'd hoped. Technology was handy, but it didn't disclose everything. It indicated densities, not specifics. No algorithm declared, "X Marks the Spot."

Every two minutes, or so it seemed, Big Dick tromped in, asking where to set up. The pressure was eroding his confidence, to say nothing of distracting and irritating. Everyone was strung tighter than a hunting bow, himself included.

Having Trey underfoot didn't help, either. He was constantly on the phone, his booming voice repeatedly crashing his train of thought.

For the moment, both bosses were down at the old work site, shutting things down. With luck, he'd have an hour or so of peace.

He took a deep breath, determined to figure it out. The answer was there somewhere. Following a short, silent prayer, it dawned on him—his approach was all wrong.

Learning how to interpret seismic data, a skill that took years of training and experience, wasn't going to happen on demand.

He found the site intuitively.

There was no reason he couldn't figure out where to drill the same way.

He examined the graphic one more time to make sure he hadn't missed anything. Bedrock, porous rock, voids, sand, and petroleum reservoirs all showed up as different densities. A seep could have bypassed the porous rock completely, leaking through the fault. Its path would be that of least resistance and possibly convoluted, not anywhere near the source, depending on how much pressure was behind it.

His mind shifted to his red and white ponies, the latter of which had started to prevail. It felt good to be using his education, to feel intelligent, and especially the respect he received from his white bosses. Furthermore, knowing the geology of his Earth Mother increased his respect for her, much as medicine men benefited from knowledge of human physiology.

All that aside, sensing the energy inherent to either the earth or a person's body was what counted. Blending the white man's knowledge with his indigenous intuition resulted in powerful synergy.

But having exhausted the white pony, it was time to yield to the red.

Feeling grounded again, he tapped a soft rhythm on the table with his hand, and quietly sang an honor song to the Earth Mother. He thanked her for her abundance, marvelous structure, and revealing her secrets.

Following a prayer of gratitude, he stepped outside to visit the seep. It was still leaking when he got there, which was good. Closing his eyes, he concentrated on sensing what he felt originally.

Where was the deposit?

How deep?

Did the ground shift to release the pressure holding it in place?

The energy was there, but too general. He hunkered down, then flattened his hands on the edge of the uplift above the seep.

Using the same means of perception as connecting to spirit animals, his mind merged with the oil and followed its vibrations through a tortured path into the earth.

The surface directly above its perceived location was about five meters west, a little over a hundred meters down.

He stood up and wiped his hands on his jeans. A psychic twinge alerted him to being watched. Big Dick was twenty yards to his left, looking puzzled.

Less than thrilled they were back, Charlie strolled back to the lab, purposely slow, not wanting his body language to give away his revelation.

He chuckled to himself at using an OIT—Old Indian Trick— to throw off the white man.

Back inside, he examined the seismic data again in the context of what he sensed. Now he could see it, clear but subtle. It definitely didn't jump out like its energy had.

Seconds later, Big Dick stomped through the door with his usual finesse. Had the big redneck seen through the OIT? Or was it simply time for his next prompting?

"Has y'all earned yer pay yet today, cowboy? Oh! Wait. *I'm* the cowboy, *y'all's* the Indian!"

His attempt at humor was edged with impatience.

Charlie tapped the location on the big screen. "Yes, I believe I have. Let's drill here and see what's down there. Come outside, I'll show you where."

"Great. By the way, Chief. Has y'all finished up with OSHA yet?"

His grimaced at both statements. "Not yet. I'll finish this weekend."

"Y'all'd better, Littlewolf." His voice dropped a full notch below its usual pitch. "Or I reckon I'll hafta open up a can of whoop-ass. Comprenday?"

The veiled threat contradicted Maguire's *No Altercation* policy, though it quite possibly didn't apply to management.

"Comprenday, boss."

SARA'S CONDO
DENVER
Friday, July 6
7:38 p.m.

When they got to Sara's condo, Mike held his finger to his lips before they reached the front door. She stood aside after they entered while he went to work. His actions were confident and efficient. He wielded a handheld RF detector for wireless devices, then proceeded to check places she and her father missed.

When he found bugs in those locations she assumed they were from the previous time. But when he found them in places she knew they cleaned before, it was apparent they were watching her again.

What surprised her most was when he left them in place. She gave him a questioning look. He pointed toward the front door, then directed her out to the parking lot.

"Here's the deal. If I remove them, they'll know. That won't make you any safer. However, what I can do is set up an app on your phone so you can turn them off when you want some privacy. I still need to check for more cameras. There was one in the kitchen, and one in the rafters in the living room, pointed toward the front door."

"So they saw us come in?"

"Possibly. Not much we can do about that. I'll wire them in, too, so you can freeze the image when you want a private conversation. Just make sure you're not in visible range. If you freeze your own image it'll be a dead giveaway. For everyday stuff, just let them listen. Then they won't suspect anything."

"Okay, that makes sense. But what about our phones? It's been a real nuisance using burners and always worrying about them listening." She growled with disgust. "Sometimes I just feel like saying, 'Did you get all that, fellas?'"

"I get that. But if they know you know they're listening, then you're just playing spy games. Which don't usually end well."

At the sound of a car coming toward them, they moved to the other side of the parking lot, away from her building, then strolled along the sidewalk.

"Here's what we'll do," he went on. "I'll get us encrypted satellite phones. In the meantime, there's an app you can use to encrypt your conversations. Just make sure that anyone you talk to uses it, too. There are virtual private networks, or VPNs, you can use for anything on the web. They're not foolproof, but will slow them down."

The persistent tension stepped down a notch for the first time in weeks. "I wish we'd known about that encryption app before. All this IT stuff was Bryan's domain so I left it alone. I already have a VPN on my computer. What about an alarm? Should I contract with a commercial company?"

He shook his head and waved his hands. "No, no. Definitely not. Someone who knows what they're doing can disable one in about ten seconds. We'll set up our own. And I'll wire it to my phone, so if there's any sort of breach I'll know immediately. And so will you."

"How long will it take to set up?"

"I should be able to get it done in a day or two. Why don't you stay with your father until it's good to go? I'll just need you to let me in to set up some cameras. Inside and out for the doors, and outside for the windows. I'll dress like a window washer, carpet cleaner, or something like that."

"I can just give you a key." She frowned, not liking his troubled look. "What's wrong?"

His hand lifted toward his face, but this time he scratched his nose while it was in the neighborhood.

"There's only one problem. If it's a private security contractor stalking you, this should work. Especially if it's the same one you were dealing with before. But now that you've gone public, if the powers-that-be aren't happy, there's no telling what could happen.

In other words, if it's the NSA or FBI, working on behalf of high government authorities, I'm powerless.

"If they decide you're guilty of colluding with WikiLeaks, they'll come after you *en force* with half a platoon in battle armor, kick down your door, and probably notify the press beforehand."

"Seriously?"

"Definitely. They've done that before. Needless to say, their last concern is any sort of alarm system, much less being detected."

"So it would be far worse than the raid on my cabin?"

"Big time."

She puffed out a nervous breath. "Wow. Not good."

"Right. And if that's how this plays out, there's not a thing I can do about it."

LSO DRILLING SITE
Saturday, July 7
10:07 a.m.

Charlie stared at his laptop, determined to finish the OSHA training. His eyes were glazing over, which was slowing him down almost as much as distractions the day before. For now the site was quiet, everyone partying for the weekend or back at the old outpost. Monday they'd take their first core sample.

He'd much rather study up on that, but needed to finish this first to get Big Dick off his back. With no internet at his cabin, he had no choice but to do it there.

About the time he was ready to doze off, he reached the accident investigation section. It described several smaller incidents he never heard of before, but focused on the 2010 Deepwater Horizon catastrophe in the Gulf of Mexico off the coast of Florida.

When the blowout preventer failed, the ensuing explosion and inferno killed eleven workers and ultimately destroyed the gigantic offshore rig.

Videos captured the pure, visceral rage of a furious Earth Mother. Flames that reached three hundred feet high were visible from thirty-five miles away while nearly five million barrels of oil spewed into the Gulf. Needless to say, the environmental problems that ensued were what gave the industry its sordid reputation.

Shaken, he paused the video, staring open-mouthed at the frozen image of raging hell. His web search on how often BOPs failed was far from comforting. The complex devices were part of a conglomeration of valves known as a Christmas tree that resided beneath the rig floor. Checking the many causes of such disasters made it clear that various mistakes on his part could cause a similar disaster.

Rationalized doubts ricocheted, like coming nose to nose with a copperhead on a boulder intended as a hunting blind.

Would the Earth Mother display even more fury because he should know better?

Maybe Dr. Phil was right—he *was* a traitor.

More than ever he understood why he'd been told to stay out of the way during drilling operations. Specific procedures and terminology assured communications and safety while any deviations or misunderstandings could spell disaster.

Confidence yielded to humility.

Would his connection to the Earth keep him safe, given it led him to the deposit in the first place?

He pondered the timelessness of that sixth sense, how it alerted him to future events. It was a matter of listening and responding appropriately, never ignoring such a prompting.

It still felt as if *Maheo* wanted him there.

Why continued to elude him.

SARA'S CONDO
DENVER
July 7, Saturday
2:18 p.m.

Sara sat on her living room couch, eyeing the tiny camera Mike installed that morning. High among the rafters that criss-crossed the ceiling, it blended with the shadows, barely visible.

It was aimed at the door and triggered by a motion sensor, which would send a wireless notification to both hers and Mike's cell phones. If she responded, that indicated it was set off by her own comings and goings or an innocuous guest.

Mike spent the night in a Motel 6 on Hampton Boulevard, a few miles away, where he'd remain until they found something closer. It didn't make her feel any safer. For a break-in, seconds counted.

Even being next door didn't guarantee safety.

Furthermore, after what he said about the FBI, second thoughts loomed. Patrice warned her the year would be intense, but said she didn't see her going to prison. That helped a little.

Didn't mean she might not get arrested, though. Go through some big, ugly court battle.

And what if Patrice was wrong?

Should she invite more drama into her life?

If she didn't, then what?

Might it happen anyway?

How did cosmic energy work?

She had no idea.

She needed to talk it over with someone, but didn't know who. Could Patrice provide more information? Possibly.

What her father would say was obvious. She hated to admit it, but maybe he was right.

Then there was Charlie. He'd understand, better than anyone. Unless he thought she was omnipotent or something, after the Wonder Woman incident. She chuckled in spite of herself.

Did her behavior alone drive off the commandos?

Nah. Something else affected that outcome.

But what?

Charlie was a pretty imposing figure himself in all that body paint. Maybe they believed he could muster some supernatural power to zap them into next week.

Maybe he actually did!

But now she was on her own. Whom should she talk to? Connie?

Maybe.

The person she really needed to talk to was Bryan. But he was also the one who put her in this precarious position.

How far did he expect her to go? Did he understand how serious it would get, and fast?

Probably not. As smart as he was, he was naive at times. He'd been gone almost three months. In some ways, it felt like yesterday, in others, forever. The ache faded from time to time, but never disappeared.

Except, perhaps, that night stargazing with Charlie.

Whatever *that* was about. Why did it feel like a date? Was Bryan playing matchmaker, too? Weird, on both counts.

She bit her lip, no closer to a decision on that or anything else, when her cell went off.

She went into the kitchen and sat down at the table to get out of camera range, then used Mike's app to turn off the bugs.

"Hey, Dad."

"Is everything okay, Sara?"

"Yeah, it's fine. Why?"

"You sound a bit down."

"I guess I just have a lot on my mind."

"Depending on what that might be, I might have some good news."

"I could use some. What's up?"

"I've been checking real estate listings in your neighborhood. Guess what?"

Her spirits sagged, not in the mood for games. "I don't know, Dad. What?"

"The condo directly behind yours is up for sale."

Her shoulders straightened. "No kidding? That *is* good news!"

"It gets better. It's a fixer-upper, so the price is good. I gave them a rock-bottom bid—cash—to see what they'd counter with. And guess what?"

"Dad..."

"They accepted! We can probably close in ten days, maybe sooner."

"Wow! That's great!"

"We could actually put a door between the two units," Will went on. "That way he's not only next door, but literally only a door away. And no one will know except us. Pretty nifty, huh?"

She heaved a giant sigh of relief. "Yes. That makes me feel a lot better. He spooked me out a little when he was here last night."

"In what way? Is something wrong? Should we still hire him?"

"Oh, no, nothing like that. He definitely knows what he's doing. He said he was no protection if the feds came after me. For colluding with WikiLeaks, or some other bogus charge."

"It's probably not the feds watching you. If they wanted to go after you for that, no surveillance would be required. They'd just get a warrant from some federal judge and arrest you."

"Thanks, Dad," she said. "That really helps."

"Are you having second thoughts?"

She rolled her eyes, knowing his fingers were crossed. "A little. But now that I've gone on TV I can't undo *that*. Besides, my interview has gone viral on YouTube."

"If you want to garner public attention, to say nothing of sympathy and support, that's a good thing. Being a celebrity can provide a certain level of built-in protection. Unless you're dealing with the Clintons."

He chuckled, she didn't. "I can handle being a celebrity. I think. But I don't know how well I'd handle federal prison."

"Martha Stewart came out of it okay."

"Thanks, Dad. Maybe I can be a guest on her show to get some tips. Bake your way to cellblock popularity. Something like that."

"Wouldn't hurt."

"Haha. Very funny. So, back to the condo, that's great. But what do we do in the meantime? I don't feel any safer with him miles away."

"The condo's vacant. A mess, to be sure, not unusual for a foreclosure, but I'll see if I can work out an interim rental agreement for immediate access. For what I'm paying Mike, he can help clean the place up."

A multitude of muscles relaxed. "That would be great."

"I'll get right on it and let you know."

They'd no sooner hung up when her phone rang again. Did he forget something?

No—it was Liz.

"Hi, Liz. How are you?"

"Great. How about you? TV star that you are." She giggled.

Liz was old enough to be her mother but, similar to Connie, had a mischievous streak she loved. Her stylishly coifed hair fit her so well. Bryan always swore red hair on a woman was a genetic warning label.

"So what did you think?"

"I was interested to hear the whole story. I had no idea."

The inflection in her voice implied she was hurt she hadn't confided in her.

"It wasn't until we found the information that I understood what Bryan discovered," she explained. "Not that much has come back directly."

"It's okay, dear. I just feel badly you were going through that all by yourself."

"My family was a great help. So how are the *Mah Jongg* ladies?"

She smiled, recalling how images on the game's tiles helped her remember what she and Bryan had seen.

"They're fine. We miss you. Oh! Dang, I must be getting old. I meant to tell you last time. I saw an unfamiliar pickup heading up the road toward your place. Were you expecting anyone?"

The fine hairs on the back of her neck stood on end. "No! Not at all. What color was it?"

"Black. Shiny black. Dark, tinted windows, too. That's why it stood out. As far as I know, no one around here has one that color. Or that new, either."

"When?"

"A week or two ago. Before the president's speech. I was talking to Rhonda at the store and she said someone with a similar truck stayed at Ida's RV place for a few days. She said the guy gave her the creeps."

"Rhonda? Isn't she the crazy lady?"

"She was. She's a different person after having chelation therapy. She even apologized for the weird things she did."

"That's good to hear. Thanks for letting me know. If you see anything suspicious again, be sure to text or call. And see if you can get their license number."

"I will. So you're doing okay otherwise?"

"Yes, I am."

"Are you going to do any more TV shows?"

She laughed. "I haven't been invited to any so far. So we'll see."

"Let me know if you do so I can be sure to watch. And if you come out this way, stop by to say hello. I haven't seen you in ages."

"Thanks, Liz. Say hello to the girls for me."

"Will do. Toodle-oo, dear. Hope to see you soon."

"Bye, Liz."

She got up from the table and glared out the window over the sink. So those jerks went back to her cabin. Maybe she needed to check it out and make sure everything was okay.

Her facial muscles relaxed into a smile.

She could also see Charlie.

In nature there are neither rewards nor punishments—there are consequences.
—Robert G. Ingersoll

12. DRILLING

NEW LSO WORK SITE
RURAL FALCON RIDGE
July 9, Monday
7:08 a.m.

Charlie stood behind the truck outfitted with the wildcat rig, directing Big Dick to the drilling spot. The vehicle crept toward it with ease, showing the toolpusher was no stranger to precise maneuvers.

A sizable audience stood at the sidelines, several enjoying a cigarette with nothing better to do until it was up and running.

Except for their size, LSO's minions all looked the same, himself included: yellow flame-resistant coveralls, safety vests, hard hats with the LSO logo, goggles, gloves, ear protection, and steel-toed work boots. Everyone had mustard yellow head gear except Maguire, Big Dick and the driller, whose hardhats were red.

Charlie smiled to himself.

Like a tribe, suited up for war.

The truck's double-duelies crept toward him, an inch at a time, diesel engine purring, until he signaled *stop*. Brakes squeaked as it bumped to a halt. Big Dick got out to set the outriggers, front bumper settling in about a foot off the ground. The rig creaked as it elevated from its parked position over the cab.

The drilling apparatus was an impressive conglomeration of equipment snaked with cables and hoses on the back deck. Big Dick lowered the grated metal platform where the operator stood.

A water truck pulled up beside it, connected its hoses to the rig. A drilling hand checked the mud tank, contents chemically designed to lubricate the process.

"How deep do y'all think we need to go?" Big Dick asked.

Charlie measured its depth in his mind. "Around three hundred feet. That's where the seep's coming from. The seismic showed something in that area, too."

"Okay. A hundred yards. Nice shallow dig. Let's see what we's got."

Charlie watched from a short distance away, nervous about interpreting LWD data real-time. At least he was confident there was something down there. The lithology between the surface and reservoir didn't matter if they found what they were hoping for.

The shaft rotated slowly, allowing a drill hand to connect a spade-like bit about six inches in diameter. The huge plates around the shaft separated, then swung outward, allowing the bit to descend.

The drill hand yelled, "Wing bit goin' in the hole!"

The plates closed around the shaft, additional centering devices securing it in place. The drill head dropped, dirt spitting out around the deflector.

Charlie apologized silently to the Earth Mother, then went inside to monitor the telemetry. Reading it wasn't as bad as expected. The drilling process, and thus the data it returned, was relatively slow. About a half-hour later, the output changed and descent rate decreased, confirmed audibly by the rig's change in pitch and vibration, noticeable even inside the lab.

They'd hit rock, roughly thirty feet down.

He went back outside to watch as they extracted the shaft to remove the wing bit. The driller replaced it with a tricone rotating bit with a fluted shaft, the star performer of the petroleum industry. Originally invented by Howard Hughes, the clever design was a major contributor to his wealth.

People like the Bentleys got rich in the oil business.

Would he?

He chuckled to himself.

Probably not.

The Earth Mother would probably kill him first. He shivered amid flashes of the Deepwater Horizon.

The driller's voice rose above the din. "Star rotator, goin' in the hole!"

Drilling resumed at a steady pace, tailings mixed with mud belching from a pipe on the side of the shaft. From there, they were collected by the mud logger to determine what lurked below.

Charlie returned to the lab to continue monitoring telemetry, which he compared to the seismic data. So far, the two lined up.

A few hours later they reached three hundred feet.

They kept going.

Charlie watched a half-dozen lines snake their way down the graph, earth's stratification on the right. With the sensors at different depths on the shaft, the readings didn't line up.

According to the seismic data, they should be getting close.

A few minutes later the telemetry changed. Wiggly lines went straight, reporting a sudden drop.

Drill RPM bolted.

Resistivity decreased.

Someone started yelling.

Charlie stiffened.

Had they found it?

Or some sort of trouble?

He froze, undecided. Should he leave his post?

Maybe there was something wrong he should know about.

He stepped outside, finding quite the opposite. The mud logger was whoopin' and hollerin', hands dripping with tailings mixed with brown stuff, far different from drilling mud's shades of grey.

They kept drilling. Before long, the tailings were mostly brown ooze mixed with mud.

Big Dick signaled *Stop* and went over to see for himself.

"Wahl, butter my buns and call me a biscuit," he declared. "I reckon the Chief's done found us some crude!"

A huge, collective cheer echoed around the amphitheater's stone rim, notifying resident wildlife it was past time to move on.

Charlie stood on the lab trailer steps with his arms folded, unable to restrain a smug grin as Trey headed his way.

"Good job, Littlewolf. I'm impressed." He reached out and gave his hand a hearty shake. "We'll put in casing, do a flow check, measure the pressure and so on, but something this shallow, well, it's likely just a pool feeding the seep. We needs the main reservoir. Do y'all have any idea where that might be? Should we go deeper where we're at? Or somewhere else?"

"Let's check the seismic again."

Back inside, they brought it up on the computer. Charlie pointed to where they just drilled, then to a place on the opposite side of the thrust fault. Both areas were the same color, indicating similar density, but the other had far more volume.

"That's probably the reservoir. Looks like it's down there around, oh, two thousand feet or so."

"Great. I just need y'all to show me where to put the rig. But for now, the lunch wagon's here. Let's get us some grub."

They went outside to load up their plates. Charlie dressed his barbecue sandwich with chopped onion and pickles, grabbed a bottle of water, then the two of them returned to the lab.

His brain buzzed with success, excited to figure out where to drill next.

He couldn't remember when he'd been so elated.

Ever.

This was what education was all about. Success and respect from *vehoe* as well as income beyond his most inflated aspirations.

His thoughts drifted to Eaglefeathers. Would he congratulate him? Or poke holes in his pride with his unrelenting stare?

Trey wiped his mouth on his sleeve, slapped him on the back, then got up to leave.

"I hates to leave y'all to celebrate by youself, but I's got work to do. I needs to get on the horn and tell HQ the good news, that we needs to beef up the crew for 24/7 ops. They needs to send up a standard logistics run. We don't have enough on hand for no two thousand foot hole. Sure'd help if we had a water source. Just not too close. Bit our ass last time on that geothermal job. That means water trucks, too."

Charlie's brows pinched together. He could find water as easily, considering the abundance of mountain springs fed by snowmelt, but something held him back.

Water was sacred.

It was life.

To use it for this felt wrong.

More wrong than what he'd already done?

Thoughts cycled, deflating the euphoria.

"It'll take somewhere 'round thirty hours to reach that depth, if no problems arise," Trey went on. "Y'all do whatever magic it is y'all does to figger out the next site and tell Big Dick. Back-at-cha later. Oh, one more thing, Littlewolf."

Questioning eyes met Maguire's.

"Good job!"

He smiled, more humbly than before. "Thank you." To himself he said, *Néá eše,* thanking *Maheo* for the opportunity that brought him to this stellar moment.

Maguire no sooner left than Big Dick blew through the door, wanting to know where to set up the track rig as soon as it arrived.

He tossed his lunch plate in the trash, and gave the toolpusher a probing look. "I need to figure that out. And don't take this wrong, boss, but I can probably do it faster by myself."

"No problemo, Chief. The rest of the crew's gonna be occupied puttin' in casing and takin' measurements to figger out what's goin' on in the current hole. We don't need y'all for that."

"Okay, great. I'll see what I can find."

Big Dick left, leaving him alone. He was still running the edge of an adrenaline high, not the best mental condition for reading his instincts.

A series of deep breaths cleared the static.

After calm washed through him, he examined the seismic map. The thrust fault was obvious. He suspected the small pool was the result of a fracture and fault shift, allowing a limited quantity of hydrocarbons to escape from the main reservoir. With the seep fresh, it was likely the result from that tremor he felt at his cabin a month or so back.

If he was interpreting the map correctly, the center of the main reservoir was on the other side of the fault from the seep; about a hundred and fifty yards away, and just short of two thousand feet, like he told Trey. The area directly above was a different density—sand perhaps—which was missing from the pool feeding the seep.

He went outside and strolled over to where he suspected it would be, multiple eyes upon him. Undoubtedly they had no idea how he knew such things.

The real question was why didn't they?

All it took was tuning into the Earth Mother's energies. That required a relationship with her, however. One of love, honor, and respect, same as human relationships. With the right attitude, she'd talk of such things.

With the wrong attitude you got the Deepwater Horizon.

He uttered another silent prayer that she'd forgive him, hoping *Maheo* would stand up for him, come what may.

When he reached the place that corresponded with the map, he concentrated on what dwelt beneath his feet. If he removed his work boots, it would be easier. If he had to, he would, but preferred not to appear any weirder to his unwelcome audience than necessary. Furthermore, they were a real pain to put on and off.

Taking slow steps in various directions, eventually his instincts spiked, a subtle vibration tickling the bottoms of his feet, then landing in his heart. Picking up a rock the size of his fist, he marked the spot, then placed a few smaller ones around it to make it clear.

Its resemblance to a miniature medicine wheel motivated him to thank the Earth Mother again. He wiped his hands on his coveralls, confident a strong energy source lurked directly below.

Another impression blasted through him, its imprint far different.

SARA'S CONDO
DENVER
July 9, Monday
3:21 p.m.

Sara sorted the email invitations for public appearances into categories, each with its own folder:

Television appearances; radio talk shows; podcasts; journalists.

Being a celebrity was never on her bucket list, but it looked as if she were headed that way. Patrice told her going public would be easily accomplished and such was definitely the case.

She read and assessed each one. So far she hadn't replied to any. Some felt suspect, potentially hostile.

The "Legal Stuff" folder held messages from lawyers.

Lots of them.

Besides the wrongful death issue, she needed to find out if she was inviting criminal charges. She'd put it off long enough.

Furthermore, her GoFundMe campaign had amassed several thousand dollars. The response was encouraging. Setting up some sort of foundation or charitable organization needed to be done, too.

If Carlson didn't get involved in such things, he could recommend someone who did. She retrieved his phone number and made the call. A woman answered.

"Carlson and Associates. How may I help you?"

"Hi. My name is Sara Reynolds. I'd like to make an appointment with Mr. Carlson."

"Please hold while I'll transfer you."

She repeated her request when the next woman picked up. "Let me check his schedule, Mrs. Reynolds. How about this Friday, two o'clock?"

"That should be fine. Thank you."

"Very good. You know where we're located?"

"You're in the Chancery building on Lincoln, correct?"

"Yes. Lincoln and East Eleventh. Mr. Carlson's on the sixteenth floor."

"Thank you. See you then."

She brought up her calendar, then laughed—Friday the 13th. Good thing she wasn't superstitious.

Upon ending the call, she called her father.

"Hi, Dad. How's it going today?"

"Real good. I just signed the interim rental agreement. Mike can move in tonight."

"Fantastic! By the way, I just made an appointment with Carlson. Are you available Friday at two?"

"Let me check."

She bit her lip, debating. She loved him dearly, but he did have a tendency to take over.

"Sorry, Sara. I have a telecon with a new client on the East Coast that starts at noon. He wants quite an array of satellite images, but doesn't want to pay the going rate. No telling how long negotiations will last."

She couldn't contain her wry smile.

"No worries, Dad. If you can make it, great. If not, I'll let you know how it goes."

"Don't sign anything, okay? I know you're a big girl and this is your project, but don't get suckered into something."

"I understand, Dad. No problem. If he hands me a contract I'll bring it home."

"Good. Listen, I need to go. I have a potential client on hold. By the way, rental agreement for the condo is all set. Do you want to tell Mike?"

"Sure, no problem."

That call was likewise short. He'd meet her at her place around 6:30, the time her father expected to arrive to drop off the key.

That done, she returned to the cadre of invitations. She deleted the ones she didn't feel good about, then scrutinized the rest.

Maybe she should talk to Carlson before agreeing to any. Either way, she could start working on what she'd say as well as any visuals.

She'd already shown several of Charlie's pictures of the site.

That left the dashcam videos.

Dread sucked the air out of her lungs.

She hadn't watched, only listened, when she and Charlie played them at the park. Reliving the wreck, even through sound alone, was so terrifying she'd fainted.

Not a smooth move for a TV interview

However, showing them would have a strong impact. Put viewers right there, literally in the driver's seat. See what those monsters did to her and Bryan.

People loved reality shows, some of which were downright gory. Like that one with those alligators.

Ewwww.

But if anyone thought she was a cry baby, there was no stronger evidence to what she'd been through.

Charlie kept the original SD card, but the files were saved on her computer. She moused to the dated subfolders. Total video time was over a couple hours.

Her and Bryan's conversation on the way out to the cabin was irrelevant.

Too personal.

Besides, anything they discussed was covered by the data release.

She needed the wreck itself.

A shaky hand clicked the one dated 17 April. The second file contained the impact and rescue, followed by those insidious men cleaning out their truck.

If people actually saw what happened, they'd be on her side, for sure.

The cursor hovered over the relevant file.

Her heartrate spiked, nerves on fire, as a whirlwind of terrifying memories gripped her heart.

The coroner's report said Bryan died instantly.

Multiple blunt force trauma injuries.

Instantly.

That digital recording of screaming, traumatized metal contained the moment the love of her life drew his last breath.

The very moment.

Both hands covered her heart, as if to subdue its staccato beats.

How could she share this?

How?

This, too, was way too personal. Sacred, perhaps.

The exact moment. . .

She, too, was clinically dead when they removed her from their truck. The moment preserved forever.

Was having this recording a blessing or a curse?

So far, it had been a blessing. Otherwise, she would have forever wondered. Never found Bryan's cache of incriminating data. Her teeth seized her bottom lip as the debate raged, tilting toward logic.

Should she? Or not?

Such would be edited out of any reality show.

Except maybe the news.

Exactly what this was—*News.*

News of an entity so evil it took no pause at taking a life.

Her husband's life.

Liz was right. This was evidence the public needed to see, albeit with a viewer advisory:

The following program contains material of a graphic and disturbing nature and may not be suitable for some viewers. Viewer discretion is advised.

She took a deep breath, held it, then—

Click.

As soon as she heard Bryan's voice, the tears broke cover. When she listened with Charlie it seemed vaguely familiar.

This time she was there.

Memory synchronized with the recording, she relived the nightmare, one from which she'd never entirely awakened.

The grating screech of a violent collision exploded from the speakers. She jumped, startled. Hearing her own screams wracked her lungs with trauma-saturated sobs.

Then silence, followed by the notification from OnStar.

At least there wasn't much to see other than the truck's hood, the road, impact jolts, and subsequent plunge to the ledge overlooking the precipice. Nonetheless, the visual input slammed its affect into overdrive.

The EMTs conversing and raucous sounds of a saw as they removed them from the cab were surreal.

A long pause, then the recording shifted to the black ops team cleaning out the truck. People definitely needed to hear their cavalier attitude toward taking human life.

Tears still flowed, her breath ragged gasps, except now they were fueled by fury.

More determined than ever to honor Bryan's request, she opened the video editor and selected key scenes. Repeated impacts showcased the wreck's violence. Arrival of the ambulance. Then the final section with the commandos.

She added written transitions that indicated how much time elapsed between each clip. Date, time, and location stamps integral to the recording provided additional credibility. To fully drive the message home, she added a few of Charlie's photos she hadn't shown before of their decimated truck in the ravine, especially its blood-stained interior.

When she finished up, she played it through to check its continuity, noting it ran a little over three minutes.

She slid the time marker back from the still photos to the frozen image of the guy who whacked the dashcam to bits.

She snarled into his ice-cold eyes with vengeful satisfaction. *You're going to look just great on national TV.*

Grandfather, Great Spirit, once more behold me on earth and lean to hear my feeble voice. You lived first, and you are older than all need, older than all prayer. All things belong to you—the two-legged, the four-legged, the wings of the air and all green things that live.
You have set the powers of the four quarters of the earth to cross each other. You have made me cross the good road and the road of difficulties, and where they cross, the place is holy. Day in, day out, forevermore, you are the life of things.
—Black Elk, Holy Man of the Oglala Sioux

13. SETTLING IN

WILL'S RENTAL CONDO
DENVER
July 10, Tuesday
8:53 a.m.

The contents of Mike's storage unit fit the bed of his Toyota pickup. An old, grey metal desk that weighed a few hundred pounds with its matching chair, obtained from a government excess property sale. A gun safe that weighed even more. Eight boxes with family pictures, tax records and books. The dresser he'd had as a kid. And a double bed.

Everything else from his apartment, besides his couch and fairly new Lazy-boy, was already in boxes or the padlocked toolbox bolted to the truck. Fortunately, his previous apartment had a waiting list so breaking his lease was not a problem.

He needed to be out by the end of the month, giving him time to get the couch and clean the place so he could get his deposit back.

He didn't really need the money. It was the principle of the thing. He'd always been careful with his finances with no reason to stop now.

Having a roof over his head as part of his compensation was one of the best perks ever. If the unit had a garage, it would have been perfect.

Montgomery warned him the place was a wreck. That said, he was still unprepared for what awaited when he opened the door.

Wreck was hardly the word. That would require a major upgrade. This was a disaster.

That stench.

Even more offensive by its familiarity.

Nausea teased his throat.

Hints of toxic fumes permeated the unit, explaining the futility of cosmetic repairs such as paint and carpeting.

The previous occupant was cooking meth.

Thus, it was stripped down to the studs, even the insulation removed.

Maybe free rent wasn't so spectacular after all.

He opened the windows. As soon as Will closed the deal contractors would start rebuilding the interior. Offgassing from sheetrock, paint, and carpeting was toxic as well, but certainly better than this.

Being stripped down did have one advantage—creating the entryway to Sara's wouldn't attract attention. If anyone was watching, they'd think nothing of some noise or construction materials toted inside.

He unloaded what he could from his truck. The desk and gun cabinet could wait until he hired a couple beefy day laborers the following day. If anyone managed to steal them, more power to him. The gun chest was empty, so they'd be mighty disappointed. In his younger days he tried hauling those monsters around himself and had a tricky back and bad rotator cuff to remind him daily not to be a macho fool.

At a month short of fifty-one, he didn't need to prove anything anymore. Even with help, there was no way either item would be going upstairs. It was bad enough wrestling the double bed frame, mattress, and box springs up there alone.

The office chair squawked as he sat down to rest. He looked around at the surrounding chaos. Was it only him or were more and more people going down the crapper? Places like this were common in LA. Including plenty that hosted an explosion that burned it to the ground.

War on drugs, my ass.

How many complaints from neighbors and tenants were ignored?

Would the legalization of marijuana help?

One could always hope, though what he'd seen so far wasn't encouraging. Legal or not, would neighboring apartments want the smell permeating their place as well?

A free buzz or obnoxious olfactory annoyance?

Would nonsmoking policies suffice?

Or would a new law be required to cover the buzz element? What if someone got a DUI without realizing they were compromised by their neighbor's indulgence? Who'd be liable?

Oh, well. That's why he quit being a cop. His personal goal to have a positive impact on society's woes had been far too high.

He wasn't going to change the world. However, maybe he could influence one person's life.

Too bad it took decades to figure that out.

A refrigerator and stove wouldn't be delivered until work in the kitchen was finished. Sara offered him dinner at her place on a regular basis. That would have to wait until the units were connected, however, to allow discrete access.

Meanwhile, the open walls offered the opportunity to hardwire bugs for both units. That needed to be done before they brought in insulation and drywall. With a little over a week before that happened, he needed to design the system, order the components, and put it together.

Tradeoffs between wireless and hardwired technologies needed to be decided. Wireless was great if the power was cut, but required batteries, which needed to be replaced if the job dragged on. Their RF signal was also easily detected and hacked.

He promised Montgomery a draft proposal, then they'd refine it together. Between the two of them, they'd keep his daughter safe.

He smiled, grateful she hadn't turned out to be a psycho bitch from hell. A strong woman, no doubt, but thankfully sane.

Now that he was moved in, albeit not quite settled, he set up his computer to watch the dashcam videos.

He recoiled with every impact, eyes tearing up at Sara's screams. At its completion he just sat there, stunned, rattled far more than expected. The dashcam captured some of the most implicating evidence he'd ever seen. While he'd witnessed certain aspects of the accident in person, seeing it from that perspective cemented his determination to expose this travesty any way he could.

His thoughts wandered back to seeing Sara in the hospital back in April, shortly after the wreck. At the time, in his capacity as a cop, he'd felt badly at the extent of her injuries, but was emotionally unaffected. After seeing exactly what she'd been through, however, his respect for her and what she was trying to accomplish welded to his psyche.

While Falcon Ridge PD had a vague idea who the original perps were, the video combined with what he witnessed in person could identify the person behind the initial wreck. Unless they hired a different group of mercenaries, that would help hunt down the source of any continued threat.

But what they really needed to know was who he was working for.

LSO LOGISTICS OUTPOST
July 10, Tuesday
10:30 a.m.

Charlie, Trey, Big Dick, and the team's mud logger, a guy named Ben, sat in the conference area of the office trailer discussing the upcoming dig. Oddly enough, one of the action items Trey assigned to Charlie was to name the hole.

Name it?

Totally befuddled, a much appreciated reprieve came when Trey's phone went off with its usual raucous ring tone. The man excused himself and walked to the far end of the trailer, talking low.

Charlie was relieved to find out he was not entirely on his own, but would coordinate with Ben. While the LWD sensors provided data, Ben noted numerous properties visually, as well as from touch and smell that electronics didn't capture.

Drilling mud's chemical profile was inert and known precisely. The mud logger used what recirculated from the well to determine what was down-hole, based on returning rock fragments and composition of the tailings, which Charlie would determine in the lab.

Ben was quiet, but confident and intelligent with an easy manner. His full beard and hair were the same greyish brown as the mud he inspected, random waves embracing his hard hat's perimeter. The big guy's hefty build, round features, and brown eyes, reminded Charlie of a bear, yet friendly and nonthreatening. Given his size alone, he was a man you wanted on your side.

Charlie and the others exchanged nervous looks as they waited for Trey, expecting news on whether HQ sent up a second crew and the needed supplies. When Maguire returned his furrowed brow wasn't encouraging. He settled back in his seat and relit his cigar.

"Here's the good news," he said. "Everything's on the way. Should be here oh-dark-thirty tonight. Second shift comin', too. Bob's pickin' 'em up at the airport this afternoon. Gives 'em time to settle in and be ready to start diggin' tomorrow."

His scruffy white brows plunged downward.

"And here's the bad news." He prefaced the ominous statement by expelling a cloud of pungent smoke that hung above the table in the stagnant air. "They's sending up someone from management. They wants to know what's goin' on up here yonder. We's been diggin' too long with nada results. If we don't hit somethin' this time, they's shuttin' us down."

"So they's sendin' us some shit, and givin' us some shit," Big Dick quipped.

Trey grunted. "Y'all do have a way with words, Mr. Duncan. Here's the deal. After Dr. Phil flew outa here faster 'n shit through a screen door, he made some rude-ass comments 'bout this here operation when he done told HQ where to send his last check."

"HQ shoulda told him to stick it where the sun don't shine."

"I agree, Dick. But bottom line's the success of this dig. That'll decide whether we gets bonus checks or pink slips. Which would suck."

"Like a newborn calf.," Big Dick added.

Trey turned toward Charlie. "Y'all nailed it with the seep which, so far, has partly saved our asses. Without that, we'd be packin' right now. Shows there's somethin' there.

"But this next dig is deeper and costs a helluva lot more. They trust my experience enough to send what I asked for. *But* they's gonna be watchin' to make sure we knows what we's doin'."

Charlie held his gaze. There was something down there. The main reservoir fed the seep. All that aside, something heavy lurked in his chest.

Kind of like realizing a cougar was hunting the same elk you planned on eating yourself the coming winter.

What if he was wrong? What if there was nothing down there?

He'd look like an idiot, plus goodbye job.

No.

That wasn't it.

He had no doubts it was down there.

"So here's what we's gonna do," Trey said. "Ben, watch that flowback like you's lookin' for gold. Track depth and anything it's spitting out, 'specially return rate. Charlie, with Dr. Phil gone, you's gonna need to get Ben's samples tested ASAP. When y'all's done, radio the results."

He took another long drag, blew it out through his nose. "Now here's the worst part. Be warned that around halfway down, to prove the seismic ain't lying to us, they's gonna order us to pull core."

Charlie had seen enough, even as a neophyte, to know what that meant. All that pipe added to the drill stem, section by twenty-foot section, on the way down, needed to come off on the way back up. Then the bit needed to be switched out and put down again, section by section. After cutting core, more pipe pulling, change back to the tri-core, then add the pipe to get back where you were and resume drilling.

Trey turned to Big Dick. "Y'all's pipe monkeys and deck hands is gonna be pissed as hell. Y'all needs to have a come to Jesus meeting 'bout their attitude. Their back-ups, too. Process'll take eight hours, probably more. Any crap out of any of 'em and they's gone."

Big Dick agreed. "Gotcha. And you're right, they's gonna be pee-*issed*."

"Right. So do damage control, *now*," Trey ordered, then turned to Charlie. "Once we have the core, Littlewolf, ya'll's on again. Y'all's seen Dr. Phil do 'em before and y'all knows the tests. That area above the reservoir's a bit fuzzy. Could be a void, which ain't good. Might be a cavern, which'll eat us outa mud in no time flat. It could also be gas. If so, we gotta know before we gets there. Should be some sign in the core, 'cause it leaks out. Watch for it."

Charlie made a mental note. "Got it."

After that, Trey and Big Dick left to put together the shift rotation schedule for the second crew. Charlie and Ben went over their respective roles, the mud logger explaining exactly what he'd be looking for.

When everyone left, Charlie blew out a heavy breath and stared at the seismic survey. He knew he was right. But why did it still feel as if someone were holding a gun to his head?

BKSS LLC
ALBUQUERQUE
July 10, Tuesday
3:26 p.m.

Bernie ground his teeth as the anonymous client's rant dragged on and on. Furthermore, his deep voice ignited horrific memories of his Camp Pendleton drill instructor decades before.

"Explain to me why this woman's still alive. If you'd done the job right back in April, this problem wouldn't exist. What are you running, Keller? A bunch of amateurs?"

Bernie flinched.

How'd this guy know so much about the previous job? Some inside connection? Or did he deduce it from that woman's TV appearance?

Terminator sensed tension and sat up. The Rottie gave him a questioning look, then rested his muzzle on his good leg. His knuckles administered an affectionate noogie, signaling all was well.

At least as far as the canine was concerned.

"Listen, buddy," he replied. "I understand what you're saying. But you've got to understand. Not all jobs go as planned. Some things are beyond our control. Accidents happen. Our world is no more perfect than anyone else's."

"We're talking a lot of money here, Keller. You know damn well your so-called foiled plans could have been avoided. If you can't guarantee you'll get it done right this time, the deal's off. That woman needs to go. Permanently. She's a considerable threat to the people I represent. *Capiche?*"

"Yes, sir."

"If that bimbo went on TV once, it's a sure bet she will again. Do you hear me, Keller? Before long, she'll be on the cover of *People*, *USA Today*, maybe even *Time*. She'll be a celebrity.

Which means if anything happens it'll demand a full investigation."

"Such things tend to fade quickly."

"True statement. But her continued whining could result in irreparable harm."

What exactly constituted "harm" Bernie didn't know, neither needed to. "So what are you saying? It doesn't need to be subtle?"

"That's what we prefer. But timeliness is rapidly becoming paramount."

"What about the end of the month, like you mentioned before? Is that still on?"

"Preferably sooner. Depending on how vocal she is. Another TV appearance could be the tipping point."

Who this man was continued to pummel his curiosity. Government was largely impervious to attacks. Flaps came and went, but nothing changed.

Except the political players involved.

Maybe that was it. Some elected official, worried about reelection. Maybe Pearson himself, the guy who introduced the original bill.

Except he was some old fart. In office for decades. Even if he got voted out, he had a huge pension.

And could always switch to lobbying.

Aha! That was it!

While the facility was legal and the administration unimpressed with the flap, its completion was in phases. Only a small fraction of the lobbyist community was covered by the status quo.

Each year required a new funding round of Congressional approval.

Which could be influenced by irate constituents.

Congressmen already had such a facility and couldn't give a rat's ass whether their counterparts did. Zapping such a high dollar item now in the public eye could make some very happy while leaving others fighting for their lives in the event of an apocalypse.

Any number of PURF's hopefuls could have a serious problem with this woman, which explained the amount of money offered to neutralize her.

A figure high enough he had no doubts his contact wasn't the only one involved.

Maybe one of his cronies balked, knowing the details of the failed mission. Maybe that's what triggered this unpleasant conversation.

A seven-figure payment, the first number of which was not a *one*, was now in jeopardy. If this job cratered, BKSS was finished. In a business that depended on client referrals, a one-star review would take them down like TWA Flight 800.

On the other hand, if they pulled it off, that kind of payment would allow him to beef up their inventory. Get some of those mini-drones and fancy robotics. The right equipment could largely eliminate the human FUBAR factor. Then no one would ever call them amateurs again.

He tapped out two pills from the bottle in his top drawer and washed them down with a swig of Gatorade, its sweetness masking their bitter taste. Somehow he needed to reassure this guy they had this one in the bag.

"Okay, listen," Bernie said. "I get it. This is a far simpler job. Especially if that 'quiet' business if off the table. It shouldn't take that long."

"How long?"

"Right now my team's on R&R. As soon as they're back we're on it."

"By the end of the month?"

"I won't promise, but it's a good bet."

Cautions drummed his mind. Until he saw some cash he couldn't take the request seriously. In anticipation of the contract, they'd set out some surveillance devices to replace the ones that were removed, but hadn't started monitoring yet.

That wouldn't happen until the deal was consummated with cash. That last contract was a painful lesson in covering his ass with paperwork.

Or its equivalent in cash.

"We'll get on it as soon as we receive that retainer. Half up front, the rest when the job's done. We can't take action until we have that in hand. Meanwhile, she can go as rogue as she pleases. And you're right—in time it'll undoubtedly get worse."

He held his breath. What if BKSS lost so much credibility this guy wouldn't pay up until the job was done? Was it worth the gamble when he didn't even know who the hell he was?

"Fine. I understand," the man said. "I'm a business man myself. I'll get that wired by COB. Then I want to see your action plan. I want this taken care of by the end of the month. No later, understand?"

"Sounds like we've got a deal. The end of the month it is."

"What about that Indian?"

"The targets see each other from time to time. We'll see what we can do."

LSO LOGISTICS OUTPOST
July 10, Tuesday
5:20 p.m.

Charlie was loading up his plate with fried chicken and a heap of Cajun rice and beans when a white passenger van pulled into the compound. The dozen or so men who'd be second shift spilled out, falling over each other as they scrambled for the chow line.

Their interaction with the existing crew comprised various high fives and good-natured rough housing, making it clear the majority already knew each other. When the driver exited, Charlie did a double-take.

Bob Bentley.

The one who gave him the job.

An instant later, Trey and Big Dick were all over LSO's part-owner, pumping his hand, slapping his back, and providing a royal welcome. Bentley didn't recognize Charlie at first, actually asking where he was when he was standing right there.

"Where's my oil patch prodigy?" he asked, his unmistakable bass voice drawing everyone's attention as if a bomb had gone off. The roughnecks exchanged looks.

Big Dick and Trey knew exactly who he meant, and waved Charlie over.

"There you are," Bentley said as he pumped his hand. "I hear y'all's doing a bang-up job, son. Keep up the good work and we'll make it well-worth y'all's while."

"Thanks," he replied, uncomfortably aware of a multitude of dumbfounded looks. The sudden quiet broadcasted that praise from one of LSO's owners didn't set well with the workers. The hum of conversations resumed, but several men continued to stare, particularly the new arrivals.

After they'd eaten, Trey, Big Dick, Ben, Ben's shift counterpart, a guy named Larry, Bob Bentley, and Charlie headed for the office trailer to go over their plans for the following day.

As soon as they got settled, Trey turned to LSO's senior partner. "So, tell me, Bob. Who's coming up from HQ to check us out?"

Bob chuckled, a low and deep rumble deep in his chest. "None other than my illustrious brother, Gerald."

The misery-drenched chorus that followed indicated having Gerald Bentley around was not something to celebrate.

The Cheyennes still consider the badger very powerful. In ancient times it talked to people, if they met it on the prairie, it advised them what they ought to do and how they should live.
—*George Bird Grinnell in "The Cheyenne Indians: Their History and Lifeways"*

14. PLANS

SARA'S CONDO
July 11, Wednesday
9:03 a.m.

Sara sat at her kitchen table, impressed and oddly amused that Mike was wearing a suit, hoping to pass as an insurance salesman. The mics were off, their topic of discussion the dashcam videos. As always, her psyche imploded.

"They'd just killed Bryan and thought they'd killed me. Then acted like it was all in fun. What a bunch of horrible people."

Mike nodded solemn agreement. "They were some real goons, that's for sure." He reached up to twist his now-absent mustache, then countered by resting his chin on his fist. "That guy in the last frame is the one who told us to leave. It didn't take much to figure out what happened after that."

That memory had served her better trapped in her unconscious mind, but it was too late now. "He was the apparent ring-leader when they raided my cabin, too." She flexed her fingers, trying to forget.

"Bad people, alright. The entire bunch belongs in prison."

"I couldn't agree more." She closed her eyes, as if to erase the heavy feeling, then changed the subject. "Dad says everything's on

147

schedule for the deal on that condo to close within a week. After that, we can connect the two units."

She got up and led him into the living room where they scrutinized the shared wall.

"I'm surprised none of the fumes penetrated your place when that guy was cooking meth. That's quite a testimonial for the firewall. From what I've seen on my side, it's made of cinderblocks. Breaching it's possible, just noisy and messy. Plus a code violation."

Sara wrinkled her nose. "Let's call Dad."

She put Will on speaker as she and Mike continued to stare at the problem wall.

"One way we could get away with it legally would be to register the two units as one living space," Will speculated. "However, the down side is that would require various approvals, plus put it in the public record."

"Do you think they're watching such things?" Sara asked.

"No telling what their capabilities are. Do you want to take that chance?"

"No," she admitted.

"I hate to suggest this as former law enforcement, but we could just do it, then rebuild when the crisis passes."

Will agreed. "In my experience it's easier to get forgiveness than permission. Once you move out, I'll either sell or lease it to someone else. Unless you want to stay. Or you want all that extra space, Sara."

"Not really," she stated. "I think just doing it's our best bet."

"Unless some snoopy inspector shows up. I'll need a permit for the renovation and sometimes they just pop in to make sure the work matches what's stated."

"If this were Mexico, we'd just bribe the inspector," Mike quipped.

"If this were Mexico, there wouldn't be any code," Will added.

"Okay, how about this," Sara said, sitting on the couch. "We camouflage it as a closet in both units. Do you think an inspector would check inside?"

"You never know," Will replied. "And if he decided to show up, with our luck it would be the day we're tearing out the cinderblocks."

"Unless we do that after hours," Mike suggested. "Those guys work a strict nine to five. We'd just have to finish up before the next morning."

"It's also a matter of noise and if anyone complains." She mentally inventoried her neighbors and their propensity for griping.

"Thanks to firewalls, noise actually shouldn't be that bad," Mike said.

"True," Will agreed. "What dimensions would be most comfortable for you to get through?"

"I can step over, say, a foot, maybe two, and duck down a little. How about forty-eight inches high, twenty or so wide. Main thing is not to crawl."

"Got it," Will said. "Cement blocks are sixteen inches, so with alternate stacking, that's twenty-four or thirty-two. I have a ten-inch circular saw and can pick up a carbide blade this afternoon."

"Twenty-four would be fine. We can hide it with a utility panel. I know a guy with a metalworking shop who'll custom build," Mike said. "He can probably have it done by next week, no problem."

"Great. As long as the inspector isn't a deep thinker, that should pass," Will agreed.

"Unless he decided to inspect the wiring," Mike countered.

"Let's just hope that doesn't come up. I'll have the carpenter frame in the closet first thing, on Sara's side, too. Nothing illegal about that. Then all we have to do is cut through the wall. If we start right after quitting time, we should be done with the noisiest part before ten, when any neighbors would be more inclined to call the cops."

Satisfied they had a plan, they ended the call, then she and Mike discussed communications, potential passwords or coded messages if she was in danger, then what was on her calendar.

Which reminded her of the outstanding invitations for public appearances.

"I haven't called them back yet. But I'm pretty sure I'm going to accept most of them."

Mike looked at her as if she'd grown an extra nose. "You do realize that being recognized in public is *not* conducive to personal safety, right?"

She wrinkled her nose. "I wonder how I'd look as a blond behind a pair of Raybans?"

Mike chuckled. "Jamie Lee Curtis in *A Fish Called Wanda* comes to mind."

She burst out laughing. "I loved that movie," she said.

"Me, too."

LSO DRILLING SITE
July 11, Wednesday
9:50 a.m.

It took Charlie all of five seconds to understand why having Gerald Bentley around elicited a chorus of laments across the audible spectrum. The man was sarcastic, critical, and arrogant. A few years older, shorter, and stockier than his brother, his hair was lighter color, albeit greying, but more of it, compared to Bob's classic comb-over.

He chuckled to himself. *Generally, a much nicer scalp.*

While there was no question the man knew the oil business inside-out, his sardonic manner put everyone on edge. It was as if he were purposely trying to push someone into making a mistake so he could either rip him to shreds or fire him on the spot.

He even hollered at someone for failing to close the door on one of the porta-potties, claiming details were critical to any job, including taking a dump.

Bob introduced them, explaining how he found the seep and subsequent deposit. Charlie stood firm as Gerald looked him up and down.

Was it skepticism? Or racism? Doubts should resolve when he was proven right. Not much he could do if he just hated Indians, though Bob told him when they first met their great-grandmother was Cherokee.

"That seep ain't enough to cover all y'all's paychecks by a long shot," the man snorted. "This new dig better produce a dozen super tankers' worth. We get more crankcase oil leakin' from our truck fleet daily than we'll ever get from that there puddle."

While Charlie knew what was there, it was clear everyone else was painfully aware if the new dig failed they'd be heading for the unemployment line within forty-eight hours.

While mud logger, Ben, had Larry as a second shift replacement, there was no one to cover for Charlie. So far he hadn't worked with Larry, who was more animated than his counterpart and not particularly friendly.

Unlike Ben, he was clean shaven, blond hair unstyled in a classic oil patch mullet, while his grey eyes radiated confidence. He waved his hand indifferently at the situation, saying he'd do fine when Charlie was off-shift, tone implying he didn't need him at all.

Shifts ran 6:00 a.m. to 6:00 p.m., so Trey scheduled Charlie noon to midnight, thus covering half of each mud logger's shift. Otherwise, he'd be on-call. Shift changes were best described as organized confusion. As each replacement arrived, the men handed off officially with a fist bump or high five.

The track-mounted rig arrived from Fort Worth that morning. It was far more imposing than the deuce and a half's set-up, its bulldozer-style tracks designed to get just about anywhere.

The new dig started on-time at 19:00. Big Dick positioned the rig over Charlie's circle of stones, which Trey ceremoniously swept aside while the crew took up their positions around the new location.

Larry was on-shift, he and Charlie using radios for real-time communication to coordinate what showed up on LWD versus the mud log. The lab was a hundred feet to the west, where mud samples and the inevitable core would be hauled by the roustabout.

The jacks were down, tower elevated, rig flanked by a pipe truck and water tanker, all ready to go. A diesel symphony chattered in readiness as Charlie stood with Trey and Big Dick, awaiting the big moment. His nose wrinkled at the smell of exhaust carried by the afternoon breeze. The driller's eyes fixed on the toolpusher, awaiting his signal to begin.

"Well, Littlewolf," Trey yelled above the din. "We can't break ground without a name. What do y'all say we call it?"

Charlie balked. "Uh, I don't know," he yelled back. "I, uh, forgot about that." His gut contracted at the lie. Actually he hadn't, only hoped Trey had.

Call it?

A miasma of emotion churned in his chest. Bryan's words years before, *"When you name it, you claim it"* slammed his mind. Naming an animal, a car, or a canoe was one thing. Something about claiming this violation of the Earth Mother terrified him, making him accountable.

Yet, the situation truly was his doing.

His thoughts bounced like arrows missing their mark.

"*Nomen est omen,* Littlewolf," Trey prompted. "Good name, good results."

Badger popped into his head.

Badger lived underground. He could protect the Earth Mother.

"*Mahahkoe,*" he said.

"What's that? Some fancy-ass Indian name?" Trey asked.

"Cheyenne for badger. Who lives underground."

"Alrighty. I like it. Mean-ass little critters. *Mahahkoe* it is."

Charlie gritted his teeth as Big Dick gave the signal to the driller standing at the control panel to proceed.

As the bit penetrated the ground, Charlie high-tailed it to the lab, electrified with anticipation. Coordinating with Larry went well, dissipating his concerns.

By the time midnight rolled around, he signed off and headed for a cot in the supply room rather than going back to the bunkhouse. He'd slept on worse and it was more private, even if it was a little noisy from the generator.

If he got a call in the middle of the night it would be more convenient, plus save time in an emergency.

LSO DRILLING SITE
July 12, Thursday
2:09 p.m.

Early afternoon and just short of a thousand feet, Bentley ordered them to pull core. With the entire crew expecting it, no one was surprised and knew better than to grumble. As Big Dick had pointed out, the pay was the same.

Thus, the process began of extracting pipe to exchange the rotary bit for the core bit. While extracting the drill, the LWD generated more data, a process known as tripping. Charlie and Ben examined it together, comparing it with their drilling data. Everything continued to line up.

Just after the 18:00 shift change, the roustie and one of the roughnecks delivered the core, dropping it on the lab's outdoor sample table with a thud.

The food truck arrived about an hour before, drilling hands coming off-shift heading in that direction. Charlie was mid-shift, so ate at his post. As he sat down at the table, Trey joined him. He said hello as he gulped down his steak, then resumed staring at the core sample, wondering if Merry Gerry, as the men nicknamed Bentley, would join them as well.

Hopefully not.

When he finished eating, he glanced at Trey, then cut open the rubber sleeve end to end with an Exacto-knife, releasing the smell of chemically-tainted dirt. The sample revealed the stratification of the earth, though traces of drilling mud smeared its length. The inclination of the layers and their structure matched the seismic map. Determining its permeability, porosity, and fluid content would require closer scrutiny.

Trust your instincts, whispered to his mind, as he decided what to do first, hoping Trey wouldn't read anything negative into his hesitation.

He'd watched Dr. Phil enough times, yet suspected the guy went about it all wrong. He sniffed the lowest section of the sample. It smelled like dirt and drilling mud with the slightest hint of sulfur.

His hands wrapped around it. He noted its energy, then moved farther up, toward what represented the end closer to the surface.

Not as strong.

The trailer door opened—Larry, not Bentley.

"Hey," the mud logger muttered, joining them to scrutinize the sample.

Deferring to his experience, Charlie waited while Larry picked through some of the layers, rubbing it between his fingers, then sniffing it. "Let's take care of the basics, then see what else we've got. Like hydrocarbons and gas."

A hour or so later, the test results were complete. The electrical properties and clay chemistry were encouraging, indicating traces of hydrocarbons, though a bit gassy. They reported the results to the driller and Trey, who'd pass it on to Big Dick when he came back on-shift in the morning.

Drilling resumed around 11:30 p.m., Charlie heading for the rack as soon as he clocked-out at midnight. If all went according to plan, by the time he came back the next day they'd be getting close.

Oil is the excrement of the devil.
—Juan Pablo Perez Alfonzoas as quoted by Terry Karl

15. BLOWOUT

SARA'S CONDO
DENVER
July 13, Friday
1:05 p.m.

Sara stood in her closet, figuring out what to wear for her appointment with ambulance chaser, Kenneth Carlson. She lacked a "professional" wardrobe, her working days spent in scrubs. What she wore on TV was out, so she opted for black slacks and a lime green ruffled blouse. Wearing heels would dress up the slacks.

As she got ready two possibilities cruised through her mind. Either Carlson was truly interested in her case or didn't have enough to do.

Or maybe she didn't fully appreciate what her case represented. Somehow its scope was still very personal, her primary objective Bryan's final request.

It wasn't about money. The financial advice her father provided for the insurance proceeds proved sound. Her portfolio would bring in more than sufficient returns to live on, once quarterly dividends started rolling in.

Whether Will could make it to downtown Denver in time to join them remained questionable. She was comfortable either way. A final check in the mirror prompted her to put up her hair. Satisfied, she grabbed her purse and the accordion folder with the relevant information, then texted Mike she was leaving.

Carlson's office was downtown in the stoic brown brick Chancery building. No surprise he was in the Capitol District, a few blocks from the courthouse.

The building's adjacent garage had four levels, which was where she parked. Mike pulled into a space directly across from hers, to keep an eye on her SUV. An elevator connecting the parking terrace to the main building took her to the sixteenth floor.

Upon stepping out it was apparent Carlson's firm occupied the sprawling top floor. Whoever their clients were, they clearly didn't involve petty lawsuits.

The reception area to the right was luxuriously furnished in a rustic Wild West motif which included heavy, hand-crafted furniture and original paintings depicting the area's frontier history. Window walls offered a contrasting view of the roofs of various state and municipal buildings flanked by trees in the next block.

The receptionist was fiftyish, salt and pepper hair in a stylish bob, black business suit accented by a magenta silk scarf blossoming with a profusion of dahlias. Sara immediately felt underdressed as the woman escorted her down the long hall wafting the scent of *Black Opium*.

Apparently Carlson's employees were well-compensated as well.

When they reached another expansive waiting area she was handed off to a heavy, older woman introduced as Moira, who was friendly enough but whose makeup was a bit overdone. Sara sat as directed on a loveseat cleverly constructed from lodge pole pine.

"I expect my father will be joining us, but might be late," she said. "His name is William Montgomery."

"No problem, Mrs. Reynolds. When he arrives, I'll show him in. Mr. Carlson will be with you shortly. Would you like a cup of coffee or a soft drink?

"No, thank you. I'm good."

Actually, her mouth was a little dry, but the last thing she needed was the distraction of having to pee right in the middle of their discussion.

"Do you have a parking stub you'd like validated?"

"Yes, thank you, that would be great."

While waiting she did a mental inventory of what she'd brought along, hoping she didn't forget anything. The majority of information was on a thumb drive, which included the dashcam video of the wreck. Paper copies of the police report, Bryan's death certificate, and insurance claim on the truck were there, too. If all went as expected, she'd leave it all behind.

She couldn't quite imagine it wouldn't, based on her surroundings. Glancing around, she credited his decorator with showcasing the man's financial success in a warm and tasteful manner that made clients feel comfortable, yet conveyed the promise of wealth.

The fact an attorney with such a high degree of notoriety approached her settled on her mind like a movie trailer that promised plenty of action. How much would this change things? Would there be more publicity? Public outrage? What would Bryan think?

The past few months drama had swooped into her life, which, up until Bryan's death, had been nondescript. There was nothing outstanding about either of them. Just a normal young couple with day jobs who enjoyed the outdoors, once he was out of the military.

The events that brought her to this point were sudden and traumatic. In one afternoon her life transformed from an ordinary person to one she was only barely beginning to recognize—a young widow with a seven figure financial portfolio sitting in a high-powered attorney's office.

Tangled thoughts consumed her as the enormity settled, reverie ending abruptly with the sound of footsteps. She looked to her right, unexpectedly relieved—her father made it after all. She chuckled, wondering how fast he had to drive to get there on time.

"I can't believe you made it," she said, getting up to give him a hug.

"No problemo, my dear. Mercedes were built for the autobahn. It's like a thoroughbred stallion that needs to run at full throttle from time to time."

"Tsk, tsk, tsk," she teased. "That's not looked upon favorably by law enforcement, Dad."

He shrugged. "Amazingly, cops leave me alone. They probably figure I'm another attorney late for court who'll have my favorite judge take care of the ticket, anyway. They hate showing up at traffic court, especially on their day off."

She laughed at his rationale. "I hadn't thought of it that way. I suppose you're right. So, what do you think so far?"

"I think you've hit the big-time. By all appearances, this guy knows what he's doing. And if he's seeing you personally, all the more so. I'm sure he'll assign certain elements of your case to other attorneys, but so far this looks about as legit as it gets."

An imposing wooden door on the opposite side of the waiting area opened. A tall, athletic-looking man in his late forties beckoned them to enter. His clothes were more suitable for the golf course versus a court room, his faded blond hair in need of a trim. He didn't say a word, just motioned to sit down while he resumed his place behind a sprawling oak desk.

No greeting, no handshake.

Sara and her father exchanged a look, nonplussed as they sat stiffly in two high-back chairs.

"So," Carlson directed at Sara. "It's my understanding from your television appearance that you believe your husband was killed by the government or someone hired on their behalf."

"That's correct," she replied. "And I have substantial evidence to prove it."

"That's all well and good, Mrs. Reynolds. However, I don't believe that filing a wrongful death suit is in your best interest."

"But..."

He held up his hand. "Let me finish. You don't understand the gravity of the situation or whom you're dealing with. These people are no doubt livid over what's been exposed. And *people* is a misnomer. We're talking about the feds and multimillion dollar corporate interests.

"I realize that people who've been wronged as you have always believe they're in a David and Goliath situation where justice can be found in the courts. That is rarely the case."

Sara's cell phone rang. She apologized, taking it out of her purse to set it to silent. The 682 area code was unfamiliar. Whatever it was, it could go to voice mail.

"I'm so sorry. Please go on," she said, slightly rattled the conversation wasn't going as expected.

"It's my duty to warn you that to pursue this course of action is likely to put your life in jeopardy. These people do not tolerate intrusions into their business, especially when it's shady in nature."

Her thoughts continued to tangle, disconcerted by her misunderstanding of the meeting's purpose. "Oh. From your email, I thought you were interested in my case."

"You understood correctly. But my intent was to let you know you'd be making a serious mistake. I wanted to talk to you before you hired someone with less experience who may have pursued litigation to your detriment."

Her mind spun amid the unexpected development as Carlson continued.

"Such entities as you're dealing with don't fight fairly, Mrs. Reynolds. They already eliminated your husband, and probably intended to be rid of you as well. You're considering an action that will compound the trouble. I feel it my civic and moral duty to warn you, for your own good as well as anyone you care about, that you'd be better off leaving it alone."

She jumped when her phone vibrated the receipt of a text, but otherwise ignored it.

At this point Will spoke up. "Have you handled cases that prompted such a reaction?"

Carlson paused, mien thoughtful. "Yes, actually I have," he said, carefully enunciating each word. "More than once. I also became a target by getting involved. It would be bad enough if it involved a major corporation. They don't tolerate such things, believe me. But when the government is involved as well, the risk gets even higher. At best, it would drag on through the courts for years."

"It's not about the money but the punitive aspects," Sara said.

Carlson didn't agree. "Doesn't work that way. Your best bet is to move on, as quietly as possible. Now that you've spoken out in a very public way, you may already be a target. I would be very, very careful. And you, too," he added, looking at Will. "I assume you're her father."

"Yes. And I must say I see the wisdom in what you're saying. I, too, have some experience in such matters, which validates what you've shared. Thank you for your candor."

Sara's widened eyes fixed on the attorney. "You're right. I have no experience, except for the past few months. I've been stalked, both of my homes invaded, robbed, and infested with microphones and cameras. I've had enough and don't want that to continue. I guess I thought that going public would make me safer."

Carlson folded his hands on the desk. "That's no more than wishful thinking, Mrs. Reynolds. These people operate outside the law. They do as they please. Even when a preponderance of evidence is revealed, consequences are rare. The Karen Silkwood case many years ago is quite typical of how these situations end."

Sara exhaled sharply. "Okay. I guess that's that. Do you think there's any chance they'll press charges against me for revealing the information?"

"That's possible, but doubtful, unless you choose to pursue it further. They want this to go away, not drag on. The public tends to have a short attention span, which is what they're counting on."

"So true. Thank you for your time, Mr. Carlson. It's been extremely enlightening."

At this point the attorney stood, came around his desk, and extended his hand. He gave them each a firm handshake and came close to smiling. "You'll live much longer if you let it go," he reiterated. "But you still need to be careful. Retaliation is often a satisfying hobby to these people."

"Thank you again," Will said. "We appreciate your time and advice." Then he put his arm around Sara and steered her toward the door.

They took the elevator to the main floor, walked through the main lobby and out the revolving door in silence. Sara came to a stop, remembering her car was on the upper level.

"Don't worry, I'll take you up there," her father offered. "Mine's right over here."

"Actually, do you have time to talk a little about what he said?" she asked as they reached his car. "I never mentioned anything about creating a foundation or charity, either. But I suppose that can wait. For now."

"You won't need one if you do as he says and let it go."

Their eyes met, Sara wondering briefly if he'd paid Carlson off. Probably not, but was no doubt delighted by what transpired.

"Have you eaten?" he asked.

"Just a light breakfast."

"Why don't we grab a late lunch while we're here?"

"Sounds good. Though after what he said, I'm not sure I'm that hungry."

"How about *Lettuce Eats*? It's not that far. Let's just take my car and come back for yours."

"Okay."

Will started the car, backed out, and turned right on Lincoln. As she got settled in the passenger seat, the text came to mind. She took out her phone to check.

"Oh, my God!" she gasped. "No! No, never mind. Never mind! Take me to my car. I need to go to Belton. Right now. Something's happened to Charlie!"

"Just sit tight, Sara. I'll drive you to Belton. You're too upset to be driving anywhere."

Her free hand flew to her mouth, city blocks zipping by like the panic seizing her mind.

CHANCERY BUILDING, 16TH FLOOR
July 13, Friday
2:35 p.m.

Carlson tapped his fingers on his desk, staring out his window at the skyline as he waited for his golf buddy, a Colorado U.S. Federal District judge, to answer.

"Gray Watts here."

"It's Ken. Tell your friend it's taken care of. I doubt she'll make any more noise, much less file suit. She would have had a helluva case, you know. Worth millions. But I think she's sufficiently scared now she'll leave it alone. Especially if she listens to her father."

"Great news. I'll let him know he can stop worrying. Thanks so much."

"Anytime. Remember our deal. A round of golf and a case of Jameson. The good one aged eighteen-years, not the cheap stuff. I could've made a pretty penny from it, you know."

"Right," Watts agreed. "I'm sure we can make it up to you somehow."

"I'm sure you can."

"See you in court, Ken. Thanks again."

He set the phone back in the cradle, leaned back in his chair, and folded his arms. Now Gray owed him for a change.

Quid pro quo.

LSO DRILLING SITE
July 13, Friday
2:40 p.m.

The condition flag at the drill site's entrance flapped red instead of green. Local law enforcement evacuated everyone within a half-mile. Fortunately, that comprised mostly wildlife, the majority of which departed long before the bit cut ground. Big Dick and Ben took care of igniting the well so the hydrogen sulfide would flare off, though the sulfur dioxide produced in the process wasn't much better.

Trey stared out the trailer's small window at the pillar of flames as it roared skyward, a hundred feet or more into what had been clean mountain air. Noxious, black smoke belched even higher, caught prevailing winds, and departed for parts unknown. The conflagration's low frequency growl vibrated the floor and rattled windows, adding auditory ambiance to the unfortunate event.

He had a strange feeling about this dig from the start. The good news was that they definitely found something promising.

Very promising.

But at a steep price.

How he escaped, he'd never know. Perhaps experience rather than luck prompted him to stay back. The previous two mud cuts had indicated trouble was afoot, having high bottoms-up gas units. When the drill hit just over seventeen hundred feet, its hum changed pitch as RPM's spiked, putting him on full alert. Seconds later, mud puked out the return line like the earth had been on a cheap drunk the night before.

He instinctively yelled "Get down!" to the team, echoed by Ben, who was already on retreat, but it was too late, words lost in the blowout's initial blast as compressed gas exploded from the bore hole.

He hit the klaxon as everyone's high alarm went off simultaneously in an ear-splitting chorus. Before all the workers got their masks in place, two more were slammed by a snapped rig chain. Meanwhile, several dozen twenty-foot lengths of metal casing shot out of the ground like renegade NORAD missiles, some intact, others reduced to shrapnel.

Fortunately, he, Ben, and a few experienced roughnecks who felt it comin' got down, masks in place, just in time. Big Dick was taking the luckiest leak of his life behind the lab trailer. He joined him and the others to get masks on the downed men, then move them inside their makeshift infirmary. As such, it contained air packs, First Aid, and basic medical supplies, as required for hazardous operations.

The ones who got to safety on their own made it to their upwind muster point as indicated by the windsock, as if pursuing a textbook safety drill. The knockdowns, who'd come-to shortly after, were helped over there and given oxygen.

Two of the men nailed by the runaway chain had some serious fractures and lacerations, blood all over the place, but alive. All they could do was wrap them up with pressure bandages and give them a shot of morphine until they were transported to a hospital to be stitched up and checked for other injuries. Casing and shrapnel got a few, too, snapping bones like twigs.

The trailer resonated with whimpering, sneezing, wheezing, and coughing, a few gagging or vomiting. The pipe monkey and the two guys on the drill deck when it kicked were dead. Three others were dead, between the rig chain and casing debris. Another two were injured severely enough he had no idea whether or not they'd survive.

He called Life Flight for them specifically, knowing minutes counted. Those whose injuries required less urgent medical attention waited for an ambulance to the Belton hospital.

Trey's first aid skills were good. A certified EMT, which his position required, plus decades in the business, to say nothing of several years offshore. He'd seen plenty of ugly accidents, several involving limb amputations, even a decapitation.

But this one was pretty bad.

Especially on his watch.

Hydrogen sulfide, a.k.a. H2S or sour gas. A driller's worst enemy. Fifteen seconds, sometimes less, depending on the concentration.

Then you were dead.

Bad stuff.

The Brits used it as a chemical weapon during WWI. Back in 1975 it killed nine at a drilling operation in Denver City, Texas, eight of which were local residents, not oil workers, when the lethal cloud crept across their ranch.

He prayed this one wouldn't break that sordid record. Hopefully, those still alive would remain so. Not exactly something he wanted in his personnel file, much less his conscience.

He glared at his watch.

Where the hell was that chopper? What was taking so goddamn long?

He called again. The dispatcher explained. All local aircraft were in use. Theirs was coming from Boulder, ETA twenty-one minutes.

Damn it. That figures.

Another thought struck. What if the pilot was put off by that tower of raging hell on the other side of the compound? All he could do was pray the man was former military who'd flown in a warzone. He called back the dispatcher to check. Relief followed—the guy served in Kuwait, but he'd be given a heads-up.

All he could do now was wait. And think. Neither of which was pleasant.

It was impossible to tell whether it was H2S, the force of the blast, or flying debris that knocked the ones out who were still unconscious.

He guessed sour gas. Hard hats were more effective with direct blows than a concussive force. They probably saved the lives of some of the guys hit by that chain. Why the blowout preventer failed would be part of the OSHA investigation. Another nightmare to deal with when the current one passed.

The ones who were still out cold were administered amyl nitrite, the only thing they had on hand other than oxygen to treat H2S exposure.

So far they were breathing, but barely.

Everyone had been affected, some worse than others. He went over to check on his undocumented geologist, one of those still unconscious.

"Well, buddy," he said, regardless of whether he could hear him. "Y'all's done a mighty fine job finding something, alright.

Too bad it weren't exactly Texas friendly. I thought we'd lost you, too, there at first."

He patted Littlewolf's arm and hoped he'd recover. It wasn't the first time he'd had to administer CPR, but it was tricky with someone exposed to H2S. Good thing he knew to make sure all the toxic gas was out of his lungs first or he could have wound up in similar shape.

Why was Littlewolf away from his station, anyway? He would have been perfectly safe inside the lab trailer.

He'd probably never know. His thoughts wandered back to when Littlewolf named the borehole.

"Mean-ass little critters, alright. Somethin' sure pissed this one off."

*Our dead never forget the beautiful world that gave them being. They still love
its winding rivers, its great mountains and its sequestered vales, and they ever
yearn in tenderest affection over the lonely hearted living and often return to
visit and comfort them.*
—Seath'tl "Seattle", 1854

16. NIGHTMARES

DENVER TO BELTON
I-70 WEST
July 13, Friday
2:48 p.m.

Now it made sense. Will was so obsessed with accompanying Sara that he abandoned the telecon, leaving his boss speechless when he left in the middle of contract negotiations.

Grown up or not, she was still his little girl. She'd already been through so much. He shuddered to think if she'd been alone when she got more heart-wrenching news.

He knew his way around the area, but downtown traffic, as usual, was painfully slow. At least it wasn't rush hour. He continued down Lincoln as far as East Thirteenth where he turned left, heading for Speer Boulevard several blocks away.

"So tell me—what happened?" he asked.

Her eyes were wide with brewing panic. "I don't know. All it said was there was an accident. Victims taken to the Belton hospital. Sounded like a recording."

Her voice was strained with the hint of a whine, telling him from experience she was tripping past the door to unhinged.

"Working around a rig is damn dangerous. Any number of things could've gone wrong."

Her gaze remained fixed on some distant point beyond the windshield, worry defiling her features. "You know what's scary, Dad? Charlie and Bryan were born the same, exact day. How weird is that? Is Charlie meant to die in an accident this year, too?"

He reached over and squeezed her hand while they waited for another red light, parade of pedestrians filing past. "Until we know more, let's hope for the best. There's a wide range of how serious it might be."

"What a horrible day! First that lawyer and now this." Her voice ascended another octave. "Oh, Dad, is this ever going away? Will I ever have a normal life again?"

"I don't need to remind you that I agree with Carlson," he replied, hoping with every hair remaining on his head that she'd take the man's advice. "Your chances of a normal life are greatly improved if you quit pushing the issue. You're poking a hornets' nest."

She straightened in her seat, mouth agape. "Do you think whatever happened to Charlie wasn't an accident? LSO worked on PURF. Do you think they're after him, too?"

When the light turned green Will accelerated. "It's possible. But more a matter of what happened. Whether he was the only one hurt or others involved."

"Ha! What makes you think they care about collateral damage? They almost killed me, too, when they went after Bryan."

Once they reached Speer, traffic bogged down around the University. Sara kept staring straight ahead, grinding her teeth until they passed Confluence Park. Both sighed with relief when traffic opened up on North Federal.

"Don't catastrophize when you don't have the facts," he said. "Accidents in the oil and gas industry are not unusual. Have you texted back?"

"I'm going to call, see if I can find out anything."

"Good idea."

He mentally counted the number of signals left until they reached the Interstate, braced for a spontaneous meltdown.

"Hello? Yes, I'm calling about the accident at the drilling site. Yes, in Colorado. Someone called and sent a text. I was wondering how badly Charlie Littlewolf is hurt?"

Will held his breath.

"Oh. I see. Yes, on my way now. Thank you."

Fearful eyes stared down the road ahead, but her voice was closer to normal. "That was their headquarters in Texas. The injured men are on their way to the hospital. She didn't have anything on individual workers."

Will reached over and squeezed her hand again. "I'm not surprised. We'll know soon enough."

At the Interstate onramp at last, he gunned it, quickly merging to the inside lane where they zoomed past slower traffic. His nerves tightened, steeled for what awaited in Belton.

LIFE FLIGHT
2028 FEET AGL
EN ROUTE BELTON
July 13, Friday
3:20 p.m.

A blinding flash beckoned toward a place of peace and comfort. Silhouettes abloom with feathers blocked the way. Charlie sought for reason, awash in confusion.

Where was he? What happened?

He was looking for Ben when this horrid smell like the sulfur ponds on *Diné Bikéyah* engulfed him. Then that brilliant light, followed by his arrival in this soul-wrenching place. Every breath seared his lungs with liquid fire.

Eddies of blackness swirled as if leaking from another dimension. Voices, urgent but distant, infused the vapor with a dissonant hum.

A disturbance in the depths beyond twisted and turned, looming as death. A towering figure emerged, a colossal badger.

Fearsome eyes blazing with fury locked on his own. Words howled from the depths of the earth.

"At your call I come from the Sacred Mountain with our mother's warrior spirits. With my black medicine we protect the Earth Mother from your evil work. Go home, *Okohomoxhaahketa*. Return to your people where you belong."

Go home? *Was he dead?*

The badger vanished except for its eyes, which expanded, drawing closer, more probing, penetrating his soul. Circular pupils snapped like bow strings to vertical slits.

Eyes of a predator.

Cold mists twisted among the shadows, forming a hooded cloak around the glaring orbs.

A horned owl, the size of a man.

Whose death did it presage?

His own?

It faded amidst churning fog. Another creature appeared, six eyes in a rainbow of colors. A bulbous body the color of coal, eight spindly, hairy legs.

Vehoe, the Cheyenne word for spider, was a mythological trickster who lost his eyes. Was this monster here to claim his?

The giant arachnid bore its fangs, sextet of eyes boring into his soul. Though terrified, some rational part of him knew it was a nightmare.

A spirit animal, perhaps?

"What do you want? Why am I here?"

His words faded, engulfed by silence.

Walls materialized, trapping him with the spider. Ebony stone, smooth, shiny, and moist. A prison below ground. If he was dead, these were ominous signs. *Vehoe* was also their word for the white man, who spun his web over everything and kept it for himself.

That was it!

The white man tricked him into violating the earth and now he must pay.

This was not the long, peaceful path to *Yikáísdáhá.*

Every bad decision he ever made came upon him, forerunner to a tsunami of guilt. All his life he was more concerned with not making waves, not causing trouble, much less inviting it. If he could avoid a fight, he did.

How much had he caved instead of defending his beliefs? His people?

The distant tap of dripping water increased to a roar. The spider morphed into a huge heart, pulsing and straining to deliver blood to an unknown being. Cave walls crumbled. Infinity stretched in all directions. No moon, no stars, only the vacuum of space.

Was he floating? Flying? An eagle hunting at night? Or its prey, gripped by mighty talons?

No ground lay beneath, only emptiness. The sensation of falling stole all air from his lungs. Of course—no air amongst the stars.

A tiny glimmer of light. Then another and another. A constellation.

Átsé Ets' ózí.

The celestial warrior responsible for protecting his people.

A man's form emerged from within the points of light. He lifted his powerful arm, pointed an accusing finger.

Years wasted. Dishonoring his obligation to his people.

Unfit as a warrior.

His return to *Maheo* was as selfish as a spoiled child, motivated only by his need for help.

Such motions failed to purge the past.

If he was dead it was a bad death. He would go to some frightful place, forever. Or perhaps be stuck on earth, prisoner of the Earth Mother with others who violated her.

The star warrior dissolved, replaced by a familiar figure.

Eaglefeathers.

He likewise radiated disapproval.

All his efforts on Charlie's behalf in vain. His voice came as a blizzard's gale, words in Cheyenne.

"Fight. Confront your shadow. Prevail as the Sun at dawn."

171

The figure vanished.
All was dark and still.
No spirit animals.
No warriors.
No Eaglefeathers.
Nothing.

A suffocating terror closed around him, as if enclosed by a chrysalis—transform or die.

BELTON REGIONAL MEDICAL CENTER
BELTON
July 13, Friday
5:04 p.m.

A huge pillar of black smoke smeared the distant sky from cobalt blue to shades of grey. Visible from the hospital parking lot miles away, Sara estimated that raging portal to hell was no more than a casual jog's distance from her cabin. The hollow pit consuming her stomach deepened.

Will locked his car with the key fob. He came around to where she stood, took her arm, then gently guided her through the hospital entrance to its disinfectant-scented lobby. He passed the reception desk and went straight to the elevator where he pushed the button for the sixth floor ICU.

Sara followed, perplexed.

How did he know where to go?

Then she remembered.

The orange plastic chair was cold and unyielding as she took a seat in the crowded waiting room while Will inquired at the nurse's station. The woman to her right was reading, the old man to her left jerking periodically as he fought dozing off.

A cocktail of fearful emotions emigrated from her stomach throughout her body. Like her family went through three months before when she was in that very place.

Which was worse, not knowing?

Or horrible news?

Her father returned. He crouched down and relayed what he found out in a low voice.

"Charlie's in the ICU. He's in pretty bad shape, but alive. They paged his doctor to come fill us in."

"How'd you know he'd be in ICU?" she asked.

"Just a feeling, Sara. I figured we'd start here."

After a protracted wait, a doctor in green scrubs approached. The medium build, curly brown hair, and neat beard were familiar. The one who took care of her after the accident—Dr. Bishop.

Recognition claimed his features as well. "Mrs. Reynolds," he said, shaking her hand, then Will's. "It's good to see you. You're inquiring about your friend? Mr. Littlewolf?"

She cleared her throat. "Y-yes. Will he be all right? W-what's his condition?"

The physician's expression crumpled. "Not good. There's significant lung damage, a concussion, plus numerous bruises and contusions. Upon admission he was hypotensive, 67 over 42, and tachypneic, respiration 26. He's on oxygen and several meds. Chest x-rays show significant right pleural effusion. He wouldn't have survived except for his supervisor's first aid. That kept him alive long enough to get here."

Her hand covered her mouth as she absorbed the dismal news. "Will he be okay?" she asked, hand shifting to her heart, dreading the answer.

Bishop looked grim. "Unfortunately, besides the possibility of additional internal injuries, he shows signs of cerebral edema and laminar necrosis—cell death in the cerebral cortex. Like what happens with strokes. If there's damage to the basal ganglia, it could affect voluntary motor control and even cognition functions."

Charlie dealing with such serious disabilities was unimaginable. Knowing him, he'd prefer to die.

"When will you know for sure?" she asked, words crimped by her tightening throat.

"He's scheduled for a full body CAT scan early this evening. That should tell us more."

"Is he awake?"

"No. Not since the accident."

"What happened?" Will asked.

"From what I've been told, they hit a pressurized pocket of hydrogen sulfide. On top of that, shrapnel and flying debris. So far, six members of his team didn't make it. But at this point, his prognosis isn't the best. In addition to permanent lung scarring, there's the possibility of brain damage. The fact he hasn't regained consciousness isn't good."

Sara's hopes finished their fall into a hollow void. "Is there anything else you can do?"

The physician's tone shifted. "Possibly. If he stabilizes in the next twenty-four hours or so and we can extubate, we'll transfer him to a facility outside Aspen that does hyperbaric therapy. High pressure oxygen treatments. That's one possibility, in addition to what we can do here."

She grabbed the ray of hope like a lifeline. "That would improve his chances?"

"Possibly. It accelerates healing. Whether he'll be the same person after or not, well, that depends on how much permanent damage there might be. People sometimes recover from strokes, at least to some degree. Lung scarring, not so much."

"Yes, I've seen that myself when people have physical therapy. Does he need blood? I'm sure I could round up some donors."

"His coworkers already took care of that."

"Oh. Good. Can we. . .see him?"

"Only for a moment. The ICU's a busy place. We limit visitors for numerous reasons, as I'm sure you're aware."

Bishop motioned them to follow. Will placed his arm around her as they proceeded to an alcove where they donned gowns and masks. When properly suited up, the doctor led them through a pair of double doors with reinforced glass to a large, circular room filled with multiple beds separated by privacy curtains on metal tracks.

A chorus of beeps, some rhythmic, others urgent, accompanied the whoosh of ventilators and medley of moans.

Bishop paused by one of them, eyes solemn. Will's hands rested on her shoulders from behind. Hooks rattled as he pulled the nylon screen aside.

Besides being intubated, he was hooked up to a suite of monitoring equipment. Two separate bags, one with sodium nitrate, another with plasma, hung from a pole attached to the bedframe, tubes snaking down to IVs in both hands. The skin on his face was flaked and peeling, eyebrows and eyelashes mostly gone.

In spite of being unconscious, he looked tense. She placed her hand on his arm and gave a gentle squeeze.

"Fight, Charlie," she whispered. "You can do this."

The doctor cleared his throat. She and Will followed back to the alcove where they shed their sterile clothing. She glanced at the doctor as she deposited her gown in the bin.

"When do you think you'll have the CAT scan results?"

Bishop took a breath, let it out slowly. "Not before tomorrow morning. At the earliest. Possibly afternoon, with it Saturday."

"Do you have my number to let me know what you find out?"

"Let me check."

They returned to the nurse's station where he stepped behind the counter to bring up his file. "No. The only number we have is his employer's. Where can you be reached?"

She provided hers and her father's cell numbers. "So he might be transferred in a day or so?"

"Probably early next week. But only if he stabilizes and they have room." He pointed to the monitor. "His information here is incomplete. Do you think you could help fill it in?"

"I'll try."

"Do you know his address?"

"He lives in an old cabin outside Falcon Ridge. There's no street address. Rural Route, Falcon Ridge should do it."

"By any chance, do you know his date of birth?"

"Actually, I do. It's the same as my late husband's. September 9, 1981."

"Family members?"

"Not that I'm aware of. An ex-wife somewhere, I think."

"Religion?"

"Hmmm. I don't know." She thought back to his comments while they were out with the telescope. He had a spiritual side, but she had no idea how to pigeonhole it. "He's half Navajo, half Cheyenne. So whatever that would be."

"I'll just put Native American."

"Do you need anything else?"

"No, that should do it."

"So you'll let me know about the CAT scan and whether he'll be transferred?"

"Yes. I'll let you know when I have the results."

"Thank you," she said, unable to contain the sigh.

Will shook his hand, then guided her back to the elevator and out to the car.

BELTON REGIONAL MEDICAL CENTER
July 13, Friday
5:32 p.m.

Amid the familiar ambiance of hospital sounds, Kyle Bishop pondered his patient's condition while he scrutinized the information. His condition was grave. He'd never handled such a serious case before and so far hadn't gotten in touch with anyone who had. Protocol was instituted for situations where patients were unstable. If his patient were a member of one of the usual religions, he had specific pastors, priests, elders, or other representatives he contacted.

His brows drew together. What should he do for a Native American? Did they have a religion? Many converted to Christianity, but somehow contacting a priest didn't feel right.

He switched over to the internet, looking for the nearest reservation. The Navajo one was huge, sprawling across parts of New Mexico, Arizona, Utah and the southwest corner of Colorado. Cheyenne reservations were in Montana and Oklahoma.

All too far away to send someone.

He kept searching until a couple organizations showed up that supported the Native American population in Colorado—one in Denver, one in Boulder.

He noted the numbers, then returned to his office to give them a call, see what they recommended. Maybe they could send someone out who'd know what to do. Surely Native Americans had something for such situations.

Given the circumstances, it might be the best he could do.

It makes my heart feel sad as I do not know this land. We thought we should die,
and felt that I should cry, but I remembered that I was a man.
—White Eagle, 1881

17. INVITATIONS

EN ROUTE DENVER
I-70 EAST
July 13, Friday
5:45 p.m.

The drive back from Belton was quiet. Familiar miles walled by mountains slipped past while Sara's thoughts collided and rebounded like billiard balls.

The only worse days were when Bryan was killed or her mom passed away. Her eyes remained fixed ahead as they approached the square face of the Eisenhower tunnel.

"You're awful quiet, Sara," Will said as they traversed nearly two miles surrounded by reinforced concrete. "What's on your mind?"

She slumped deeper into the seat, as if every ounce of energy had drained. "Everything! Between Charlie and what that lawyer said, I have no idea what to do."

"Maybe the answer is nothing. For a while. Until you assess the situation."

"What do you think, Dad? What would you do?"

His profile shifted to a frown. "If I were you, I'd work on getting my life back on track first. It might be best to let the noise die down. Before launching an assault."

"Do you think going on TV was a mistake?"

"Possibly. Like Carlson said, it could push those people to retaliate. If they think you've given up, they might leave you alone. Then, after the smoke clears, if you still feel it's important, you could resume your fight. Gather your forces in the meantime. It's not like the core issue goes away."

"I'll tell you one thing, Dad. Right now I have no fight left. I didn't realize how much I cared about Charlie until I saw him lying there, not knowing whether he'll live or die. Or be the same. What a horrible prognosis! I'm sure he'd rather die than be disabled. Or some sort of vegetable."

She gazed out the passenger side window, face contorted with suppressed grief as mountains yielded to flatter ground.

Will reached over to pat her hand. "Hopefully that won't be the case. People wake up from comas from time to time and are just fine."

"God, I hope so. Or maybe he's supposed to join Bryan."

Her brain sizzled with another hostile data point as they passed the site of her second accident outside Lakewood.

Would going public put her in a similar position again?

It was Friday and the height of commuter hour, traffic at a crawl throughout the mile-high metroplex. By the time they reached Denver it was past dinner time.

She turned when she felt her father's gaze, deep concern in his eyes. "We never stopped for lunch. Have you had anything to eat today?"

It took a moment to remember. "A bagel and a cup of coffee."

"Call Connie. Have her meet us for Italian. You'll feel better after a good meal and a glass of wine. Help you see things more objectively."

"Maybe. But what about my car? I hate to leave it at the parking garage. What if those awful people mess with it again?"

Her brows lifted, mystified by his laugh.

"Right. About your car. While you were giving Dr. Bishop Charlie's information, Mike texted, wondering where you were. He was close to frantic. He was still at the Chancery building. I'm sure it's just fine. Maybe safer than your condo. That's the least of your worries."

"Oh, no! I forgot all about him. Was he mad?"

"No, not at all. He made a few jokes about you being too independent. It's okay. I explained what happened. Just stay with us tonight. We'll get your car tomorrow. For now let's get something good to eat and relax."

"Okay." She reached into her purse to dig out her phone.

"Well, well, well. It's about time I heard from you two," Connie answered, cheerful as always. "You two out goofing around again?"

Sara didn't know whether to laugh or cry. "We're so sorry, Connie. Charlie was in an horrible accident. He's in the ICU in Belton."

"Oh, honey! I'm so sorry! Is he okay?"

"No." Tears flooded her eyes. "He's unconscious and in really bad shape. They don't know if he'll make it or not. Or be disabled, if he does."

"That's awful! What happened?"

"Gas leak and blowout on the work site," she said, sniveling. "Six guys died. Really bad. Hold on a second." She dug a Kleenex out of her purse and blew her nose. "Sorry."

"Oh, Sara! That's horrible. Are you on your way back?"

"We're on Thirty-Six, almost to the Westminster exit. Want to meet us for Italian? We should be there in twenty minutes or so."

"I'd love to! I'll Uber so there's one less car."

"Great. See you there."

When she hung up she realized her phone was still on silent. There were multiple texts from Mike and her voice mail was full. One was Connie, the other numbers unfamiliar. She adjusted the audio, then checked the messages.

"Hello, Mrs. Reynolds. This is Davis Jenkins with NBC, host for the Today Show. I'd like to invite you to come to New York and be our guest. Call me back. Thanks."

That figures, she thought, and checked the next one.

"Greetings, Mrs. Reynolds. This is Caitlyn Butler with ABC. We hear your interview on Fox31 in Denver caused quite a stir. How'd you like to go to the network level? Give me a call. See you soon!"

The last one was George Noory with *Coast to Coast,* another invite.

"Oh, no. So much for laying low. Two networks and a radio show invited me to be a guest."

Will gave her the stink eye over the top of his glasses.

"Should I ignore them or tell them no? Calling back would be the polite thing to do. But I'm not sure what to tell them, other than being a big chicken."

He exhaled through his teeth. "I'd never call you a chicken, Sara. Listen. Now isn't the time to decide. Think about it for a few days."

"I suppose you're right." She couldn't help smiling. "It would be a real trip to be on *Oprah.*"

The cause of his pensive mien covered a multitude of possibilities.

"With midterm elections this year, I'm not surprised by their interest. Serious political implications related to your story could bring an abrupt halt to numerous Congressional careers. Regardless of that bogus State of the Union, any intelligent person can see it's a smoke screen."

Growing weary with the whole thing, she agreed. "I know, Dad. And Bryan didn't want them to get away with it. But I'm not sure I'm ready to join him in the hereafter trying to fix the system, either."

"Exactly. Just think about it for a day or so. Get Mike's take, too. He may know a few things about your case that we haven't discussed. Things that might make a difference."

"You're right. I don't have to decide today."

Her thoughts turned to what Patrice said—that there would be some trouble and she needed to be careful, but that public sentiment would be behind her. And, as always, the matter of whether she could live with herself if she let Bryan down.

Fortunately, they were almost to Boulder's *Italian Villa.* A headache incubated behind her eyes, telling her that, on top of everything else, she definitely needed to eat. Will parked in the back lot and they went inside. It was late enough there was no line, plus Connie was already there, waving from a booth on the other side of the dining room. They dodged the maze of mostly unoccupied tables to join her.

From that point on it felt like a normal day ending with a relaxing dinner in their favorite restaurant. The sweet taste of Sangria and creamy, garlic-kissed shrimp alfredo diminished her headache.

The worries tormenting her mind went undercover, but refused to be silenced.

BKSS LLC
ALBUQUERQUE, NM
July 13, Friday
7:17 p.m.

Bernie logged into his Swiss bank account, not sure what he'd do if the retainer wasn't there. Much to his relief, it was. Now to muster his men and put together a plan. His client would be screwed if that bitch kept showing up on TV, yappin' like his mother-in-law's obnoxious Pomeranian.

New Mexico desert extended beyond his window to the horizon—endless, unlike the job's parameters. Taking someone out quietly was a challenge. It was so much simpler when you just tracked the victim until you got off a head shot.

Obviously an execution.

But then you were done.

Less monitoring, less resources expended, less evidence.

Car wrecks were his team's specialty. He always loved demolition derbies, and they were even more exciting at seventy or eighty miles per hour. He taught the team everything he knew and they picked it up in nothing flat.

The precision they achieved should win an award, especially that one with the logging truck. *Perfecto!* Non-lethal damage required far more skill than the brute force required to flatten someone like a bug.

To keep up with emerging technologies, they needed to figure out how to hack self-driving cars. Same for the ones with safety features like automatic braking and collision avoidance. If done right, such interference would be impossible to trace and appear to be a computer glitch. Good news for him, bad news for the car maker.

Far more covert than severing a brake line.

With people tied more and more to consumer electronics, this kind of work would continue to demand more brains than brawn.

Definitely *not* his team's specialty.

So what was the best way to take this target out?

Poison came to mind first. Relatively easy, but if it didn't work fast enough and she got to the hospital, it not only wasted time but presented a detection risk.

They needed to review surveillance videos, identify her usual activities and personal habits, then find a vulnerability. If her schedule was going to include TV appearances, maybe they could get to her somehow there.

Studio security tended to be tight, but there were definitely ways to get around it. No doubt they'd send her a pass, probably via email. They hadn't been watching that, but should. Good job for his new IT guy. Use her pass as a template to create their own. Maybe slip something in her water and have her croak right there, on live feed.

He chuckled.

They'd deserve a bonus if they pulled that off.

The Reynolds chick was too young for a shell-fish toxin sponsored heart attack. She liked hiking up there around her cabin. Maybe they could borrow a bear somewhere.

Or something that would work in Denver.

Like cyanide-laced Girl Scout cookies.

He pulled up his encrypted email client and sent two key members of his team a link to a Skype tagup at oh-eight-hundred the following day. They knew damn well leave could be cancelled for an emergency.

Or lucrative job.

MONTGOMERY RESIDENCE
BOULDER
July 14, Saturday
8:16 a.m.

Sara awoke to her chirping cell, room filled with morning light. She swung her feet over the side of the bed, snatching it from the nightstand as she sat up. The area code was unfamiliar. The hospital, perhaps?

"Hello?"

"Mrs. Reynolds?" It was a woman.

"Yes."

"This is Caitlyn Butler with ABC. How are you this morning?"

"Oh! Ms. Butler! Hello. I'm doing pretty well, I guess. I got your message. Thanks for thinking of me."

"You're certainly welcome. So what do you think? Would you like to come to New York and be on our network news show?"

"I haven't decided, Ms. Butler. I'm in the middle of a, well, family health crisis right now. Until it's resolved, I don't dare leave town."

"I'm so sorry to hear that. We could patch you in from Denver, if you prefer."

"Oh. That would be much better. But I need to think about it for a day or so, if that's okay."

"I understand. Just let us know. I think there's a large audience interested in what you have to say."

"Thank you. Oh! I have another call coming in. I'll get back to you. Soon. I promise."

She switched to the other call.

"This is Dr. Bishop, calling about Mr. Littlewolf."

She held her breath. "How is he today?"

"Well, no worse than yesterday. No signs of respiratory paralysis, which is sometimes delayed after the initial exposure. He's extubated and so far stable, so we plan to transfer him to Aspen for HBOT—the hyperbaric oxygen therapy we talked about. However, they don't have any room right now, so we need to wait a day or two for an opening."

"I suppose that's good news. Better than bad, at least. What about the CAT? Did you find anything there?"

"The report hasn't come in yet. There appears to be some damage to the basal ganglia and a few signs of cerebral edema we're keeping a close eye on. It's too soon to tell if the effects will be permanent. We won't know until he wakes up."

"Any idea how long that might be?"

"I'm afraid not. The prognosis declines with each day he's unconscious."

"I was afraid of that. My contact information will be transferred with him, correct?"

"Yes. Once he's on his way, I'll text their number. If there's any change before then, I will as well."

"I appreciate it. Thanks so much for letting me know."

"Let's hope HBOT works. It's been known to help in these cases, sometimes rather quickly. He seems in fairly good health otherwise, so we'll see."

"I have my fingers crossed. Thanks again, Dr. Bishop."

After ending the call she took in a few deep, cleansing breaths. Being woken up by not one, but two calls, each with its own emotional kick, had definitely jump-started her day.

After a shower and getting dressed, she ambled downstairs, welcomed by the irresistible aroma of homemade waffles.

"Hey, honey." Connie greeted her with a hug. "Sleep okay?"

"Pretty well, all things considered."

Will joined them, the ensuing conversation centered on the pros and cons of more television appearances. Based on the latest invitation, Sara was once again determined to pursue it as planned.

"I can see how a lawsuit could get ugly," she mused. "But the main thing is how far they'll go to keep people quiet."

"It must be newsworthy," Connie noted, buttering her second waffle. "If it weren't, you wouldn't be getting so many invitations."

"What do you think, Dad?"

Their eyes met.

"Remember what Carlson said. It'll increase your chances of more trouble. You know I don't like it. But, since you won't give up this mission of yours, suicidal though it may be, that's why we hired Mike. If you feel up to it, that's your decision."

She rested her elbow on the table with her chin in her hand. "I'm afraid if I don't, I'll regret it. And if I wait, any interest will be gone, and opportunities won't be falling in my lap. There's also the people who donated to my cause. I owe them something as well."

His mixed feelings were apparent. "Windows of opportunity close as quickly as they open." He took a sip of his coffee, then leaned back in his chair. "We're behind you, Sara, one way or the other. I didn't raise you to be a shrinking violet. Even though I don't like it, I'm proud of you for not taking this lying down."

"Thanks, Dad." She wiped her mouth with her napkin, folded it carefully, and set it on the table.

"I'm going to do it. I can do the ABC interview from Denver. I'll call back the guy in New York about the *Today* show and see if we can schedule it for a week or two. Hopefully, by then we'll know how Charlie's doing. I don't feel comfortable leaving until he's out of the woods. With it talk radio, I should be able to phone in for the *Coast to Coast* interview."

"Sounds like a plan."

As soon as she finished her coffee, she called Davis Jenkins. He was delighted to set it up for Friday, July 27. Moments later his admin called to book her flight into New York.

Listen to the wind, it talks
Listen to the silence, it speaks
Listen to your heart, it knows.
—*Native American Proverb*

18. AMASANI

C harlie sensed movement. A figure stood beside him. A familiar warmth filled his heart. Only one person projected such pure, untarnished love.

"Where am I, *amasani*?" he asked in *Diné*. "Am I dead?"

"No, *Naalnish.*"

He smiled.

It had been many years since he'd been called by that name— *Diné* for "he works." Earned by helping with her weaving tasks when he was five years old.

"How is it possible that you are here?"

"It is I who is dead."

He gasped, breathing strained.

"You are dead? *Amasani*! No! When?"

"A few days past. I soon return to our sky father, *Ahsonnutli*, beyond the sacred stars of *Yikáísdáhí*."

"Are you here to help me cross over, too? Can I go with you?"

"No. I am here to help you as you helped me long ago."

"I helped you? With your weaving?"

"No. When you and your grandfather prayed for me. You asked that my spirit return and my body be healed. Do you remember?"

"Yes. I remember."

A quarter of a century scrolled back to when he was thirteen. He was living with his father, Little Bear, on the Northern Cheyenne reservation. It was mid-afternoon on a balmy spring day, his father and Uncle Joe out on the ranch branding calves. He was home with Eaglefeathers, helping prepare the evening meal, when the mail truck stopped out front. It rarely came, piquing his interest.

"Is it okay if I see what it is, grandfather?"

"Yes. Go, grandson. Maybe it is important."

He arrived at the mailbox as the truck disappeared amid a cloud of dust that irritated his eyes. He blinked it away and reached inside where he found a letter from his mother in New Mexico. A heavy feeling tightened his chest.

She rarely wrote.

Only when something was wrong.

He tore it open. Inside was a piece of three-ring binder paper with its holes torn through, the letter handwritten in pencil. It said:

Son, amasani *is ill. She is very weak and cannot get out of her bed. The reservation white doctors do not know what is wrong with her. I am afraid of losing her. I know your grandfather is a medicine man. I am asking you, son, to pray to the creator for* amasani *to get well.*

Mother

Every warm childhood memory of *Diné Bikéyah* involved his maternal grandmother. While his parents worked, he stayed with her until he was old enough to go to school. He thought of the special blanket she made him that kept him cozy on chilly nights.

Like her love warmed his heart.

What if he never saw her again?

He trudged back to the house, but couldn't go inside with tears dribbling from his eyes. If Eaglefeathers saw him cry, he'd think he was still a child. He sat on the wooden front steps, sniffling to hold them back.

Moments later, the door creaked opened. He bowed his head and wiped his nose on his sleeve as Eaglefeathers sat down beside him.

"What is wrong, grandson?"

He started to hand him the letter, then remembered—he couldn't read. Still battling renegade tears, he did his best to read the letter aloud between a litany of sobs.

A symphony of guttural sounds responded as the old man listened, finishing with a heavy breath.

"Do you want to help *amasani*?"

He wiped his eyes, then turned slowly to face him. "Yes. Of course. I will pray for her." He met his searching look. "You are a holy man, grandfather. *Maheo* listens to you. Will you help me pray for *amasani*?"

"*Maheo* likes it when children make a prayer, so he listens most carefully." Eaglefeathers's eyes drilled into his own. "Tell me, grandson. Are you ready to live as a young *Tsetsehestaestse* man? One who knows and understands our ceremonies and our ways?"

Charlie balked, conflicted. His parents fought defending their respective tribal ways. Loving both presented a dilemma.

While living in New Mexico with his mother he learned about *Diné* traditions from *amasani*. Living in Montana with his father and grandfather, he followed them.

So far they didn't seem that different, other than the language and various details. Years later Bryan told him their conflict reminded him of how Christians from different denominations argued about who was right, yet essentially held similar beliefs.

As he grew up he realized their arguments mostly centered around *Diné* being matriarchal while Cheyenne was patriarchal. Two strong-willed partners, each using their culture to justify their positions, which ultimately destroyed the marriage.

At the moment his main concern was helping his *Diné* grandmother. His gaze fused with his grandfather's.

"Yes. If it will help *amasani*, I want to learn more."

"Good. To help *amasani* our Creator needs to understand how badly you want him to help her heal."

"How do I do that?"

"You must sacrifice your heart for *Maheo*."

"My heart?" His hand flew to his chest. "How? What does that mean?"

"Admit that you cannot help her alone. Show that you will give up what you want in return for his help. To do that we can make a special sweat. Sweats are very powerful. They take effort to make ready, then you are very hot and uncomfortable. It is not easy. Your efforts tell *Maheo* how badly you want her to get well. It tells him you need his help. If it is not yet her time, he will listen."

"What must I do?"

"For me to help, you must ask in a special way. Tomorrow lay tobacco down and ask me with your words to help pray for your *amasani* to be healed."

When his father and Uncle Joe returned, he told them what happened and asked to borrow some tobacco to make the formal request.

The next day he laid down tobacco. Eaglefeathers accepted the offering and invited his friend, Two Moon, to join them the next day for a sweat. Charlie asked why, assuming his family members would be enough.

Eaglefeathers explained, "It is best when there are no empty spaces in the prayer circle when a sweat is for a special reason. Two Moon is also a medicine man. He is close to his Creator. Your father and uncle will be in the other two positions. You will sit in back, facing east, where you will pray."

That afternoon was spent preparing the sweat lodge a hundred and fifty yards north of the house near Rosebud Creek. His first task was to move the stones from their last use inside the structure back to the fire pit.

Uncle Joe showed him how to set the first five on the log base. One to the north, south, east, and west, then one in the middle. Each stone was the size of a grapefruit and heavy. His young muscles protested when he was only halfway done.

"Why are there so many?" he asked, grunting as he hefted another one to its new location.

"They represent each of the forty-four *Tsetsehestaestse* peace chiefs who lead our people," his grandfather explained. "Ten from each of our four societies, then four old man chiefs, who make the final decisions. The stones remind us to be like them. Wise, calm, kind, fair, and selfless as well as generous, hard-working, and brave."

As he stacked firewood around them, his grandfather continued to explain what would happen during the sweat.

"You asked for this sweat, so it is up to you to announce the purpose. Then you will pray for your *amasani* and the rest of us will pray along."

Pray in front of others? Especially with someone there from outside the family? His heart beat faster, but had little to do with exertion.

"How will I know what to say, grandfather?"

"You will pray from your heart. It will tell you what to say. The words come from your love and concern for *amasani*. Then *Maheo* knows how badly you want him to heal her."

The next day he and Eaglefeathers headed for the hunched-over structure covered with buffalo hides. Spring weather was fickle, temperatures erratic. The previous day's warmth had fled, replaced by a cloud cover that threatened another late snow.

He shivered, arms folded against the chill, his only clothing a deer skin breechclout.

His grandfather laughed. "Soon you will welcome a cold breeze, grandson."

As they walked, his grandfather gave him a few last minute instructions, distracting him from the cold.

Actually, most of his discomfort was trepidation.

What had he gotten himself into?

Echoes of his mother's disdain lurked in the shadows of his mind.

Was she right? Were the Cheyenne too serious about ritual, ceremony, and tradition? It wasn't like the *Diné* didn't embrace similar ones, like the sweat lodge. In her letter, his mother specifically mentioned his grandfather was a holy man.

Was she admitting defeat? Or recognizing both had merit?

"Are you listening, grandson?"

He blinked, jolted back from his troubling thoughts. "Yes, grandfather."

"Keep your mind on talking to *Maheo*. Keep praying out loud, not to yourself. Do not think about the heat. Do not watch the red-hot stones."

By then, they were there. The ember-laden fire felt good, though he couldn't imagine what it would be like inside the lodge.

Just before entering, Eaglefeathers looked deep into his eyes and added, "One more thing, grandson. Do not be afraid when the grandfather spirits come in."

Shivers crawled down his spine.

Why didn't he mention that before?

Did he purposely wait until it was too late to back out?

Except he wouldn't, because he really did want *amasani* to get well. He was doing this for her, not to please anyone. Except maybe *Maheo,* so he'd make her healthy again.

Charlie took a deep breath as he ducked inside. The scent of man sage welcomed him as he sat in back upon the branches that cushioned the ground. His uncle brought in the eleventh seething stone, pulled the buffalo hide door into place, and sat down.

The stones' red glow was the only light. Gradually everyone's seated form arose like shadows.

Eaglefeathers laid a piece of sweetgrass on each stone to bless it and the lodge. It's fragrant smoke mingled with sage, pleasant and calming. Charlie followed along the best he could when they sang the Badger Song, Grandmother Song, Buffalo Song, and Eagle Song.

When prompted to announce the purpose, he stammered, "*Maheo*, we are, uh, having this sweat to, uh, heal my. . ."

Silhouetted against the stone's soft glow Eaglefeathers shook his head.

Charlie's heartbeat pounded in his ears.

What was wrong?

Then he remembered.

"*Maheo*, the purpose of this sweat is to ask you to heal my *amasani*."

Water preheated beside the fire hissed as it touched the seething stones, delivering moisture to the warming air.

Pouring out his feelings came as easily as the life-giving liquid yielded to steam. He couldn't remember what he said, only that the words did indeed spring from his heart. His leaking eyes and nose joined the sweat coursing down his temples and chest as heat and humidity closed around him.

The others sang and prayed amidst the soothing whisper of the buffalo rattle, the din a distant accompaniment to Charlie's ongoing petition.

Every sweat had four rounds. During the pause between each one, the door was opened, allowing a blast of cool air to enter. Water was passed from Eaglefeathers to Two Moon, then Charlie, his father, and uncle.

Eleven more red-hot stones joined the others. . .Blessed with sweetgrass. . .More singing. . .

During the third round, enveloped by heat, moisture, sweetgrass vapors, sacred songs, and echoes of his heart-felt prayers, Charlie's concentration drifted away to a place where he had a vision.

One that troubled him for years.

It vanished as the round ended and a cool blast of air shocked him back to the present. Awakened from the nightmare, he didn't know how it would have ended.

Eaglefeathers's piercing gaze compounded the vision-induced fear. Did his failure offend *Maheo* and ruin the outcome? His grandfather tapped his forehead.

Stay focused.

When the water reached him he took a small sip, then poured the rest over his head. Grounded once more, he reminded himself why he was there. He made it this far, in spite of briefly slipping away.

Each round lasted about twenty minutes. A sliver of time that meant little under normal circumstances. Certainly he could make it through. He must, to make sure his prayers were heard. For his beloved *amasani* he could do this.

Shortly into the fourth round he sensed a presence. He prayed louder and more forcefully as another vision opened up. Rather than dread, this one brought love and hope. Especially when *amasani* appeared, smiling at him from in front of her little house.

More tears fell when she waved, his prayer punctuated with sniffling, but he didn't stop. His body and soul were ablaze from within. Without a single doubt he knew *Maheo* heard him.

She was going to be okay.

The singing stopped. He finished up his prayer with a final plea for *amasani's* health and a long life. Everyone turned toward him, faces animated with anticipation.

His reply, wordless like the answer he received, was a smile.

As the recollection faded back to the present, his grandmother reappeared. "Do you remember, *Naalnish*?"

"Yes. I remember. Very well. That was my first ceremonial sweat in the Cheyenne way. The heat burned the skin off my nose and ears. The first vision I had frightened me for a long time. I had nightmares about it for years. But it was worth it because then I saw that you would be okay and knew *Maheo* heard us."

"I felt your love and prayers. My body became light, as if part of me was lifting up, but it was the sickness leaving. I was filled with light and warmth and very soon after I was all better. You never told me about your bad vision, grandson. What was it about?"

He hung his head. "I have never told anyone."

"Why not?"

"I felt guilty. Like I did something wrong, because I drifted off and stopped praying."

"All visions have a message. Tell me. Maybe I can help you understand. When they frighten you, they are a warning."

He took in a deep breath.

"I was a tiny mouse chased by a hungry fox. He was right behind me. I was running as fast as I could through a field of tall grass. There were lots of rocks and boulders in the way as I fled to my den. I was exhausted and kept falling. I couldn't breathe. It nearly caught me. Then the cool air woke me up."

He shivered. "Between my parents arguing and the white man telling us we were savages, I didn't know who I was or where I belonged. I was running away. Now I know."

"That is good. You understand messages from the spirit when you are ready to listen. Until then you are reminded, not always in a kind way. Do you ever wonder how the vision would have ended?"

Renewed fear gripped him in an icy wave. "I was afraid I would not make it to my den and the fox would eat me."

"Why don't we find out?"

In an instant, the vision was back, trailing all its terror. With no other choice, he focused on running faster until he reached his den. At last he scrambled to safety, where he turned around.

The fox was gone.

Wild snarls mingled with the piercing cry of an eagle drew his attention skyward. Tightly gripped by the raptor's unrelenting talons, the unfortunate fox writhed vainly to free itself.

His predator's efforts to secure a meal had resulted in becoming one himself.

Charlie didn't know whether to laugh or cry.

Saved the last possible instant by the grandfather spirits.

All those years he suffered through recurrent nightmares, all he had to do was focus on his intent instead of forcing himself awake.

Maintain his concentration, like Eaglefeathers said.

"See, *Naalnish*? Refusing a vision offends the Great Spirit. It forces you to learn the same lesson in a more difficult way."

"You are so wise, *amasani*. I miss you so much."

"I miss you, too, *Naalnish*. Because of your work and honest heart, *Ahsonnutlim*, our creator, heard your prayers and those of your family. He helped me heal so we were together for many more years."

"Will I be healed as well, *amasani*?"

"If it is the will of our Sky Father. Do you remember what I taught you when you were a little boy?"

"I remember, *amasani*. To seek joy, happiness, confidence and peace. To honor the Earth Mother by using her gifts wisely. To do my best. To never be wasteful, but honest and generous. To use my hands for good and to help others." He smiled. "Those are like what the forty-four peace chiefs teach us, too."

"Yes. Your goodness lifts us all because we are all connected in spirit. When you use the Earth Mother's gifts, show you are grateful. Make an offering and create something you are proud to give back to her."

She placed her hand on his head and closed her eyes as her blessing continued.

"Honor her and you will receive good health, guidance, and protection in your everyday life. You will have power, strength, and courage to live long and do great things for your people. As my dearest *hatsóí ashkiígíí*, you bring me much joy."

Her hand lifted, its feathery touch gone. "Because I love you, *Naalnish*, I leave you with another special gift. It will comfort you with my love when you are sad, discouraged, in pain, or confused."

"Thank you. I love you, *amasani*. You are a great blessing in my life."

She kissed him on the forehead, waved as she had during the sweat vision, then evaporated into the mist, departing to her eternal home beyond the Milky Way.

Her admonition echoed through him, similar to much of what Eaglefeathers said. Certain words stood out, guilt staging an encore.

"When you use the Earth Mother's gifts, show you are grateful. Make an offering and create something you are proud to give back to her."

No wonder the Earth Mother was offended.

He didn't make an offering.

Teach us love, compassion and honor...that we may heal the Earth, and heal each other.
— Ojibwa prayer

19. INTUITION

COSMIC PORTALS
DENVER
July 14, Saturday
3:12 p.m.

Patrice scrutinized the current positions of the luminaries and planets on her computer screen. Someone was in trouble.

But who?

The feeling started the day before. Was it only because it was Friday the Thirteenth?

No. Of course not.

That superstition only played out if the transits cooperated.

Too few realized the Gregorian calendar was a bad joke. A hopelessly inaccurate jumble of numbers, courtesy of sundry egomaniacal Roman emperors. It no longer related to the cosmos in the slightest. The Sun, Moon, planets and stars marked time. Even the Bible said they were for "times and for seasons."

Not the whim of self-serving humans.

Sometimes, however, the date's numerology had meaning. The previous day was a four. In general, that related to building a foundation. She could always remember that because the cusp of the fourth house represented home, new beginnings, as well as midnight, the start of a new day.

Actually, the four derived from the date's actual total of twenty-two. A very significant number. The Master Builder. It governed things of the earth. Laying a foundation upon which great humanitarian efforts were built. Paving the road for others to walk and follow.

Which implied something of great import occurred.

She huffed out a breath. The cosmos could be so vague. Its energies never lied, but could be elusive and interpreted in a multitude of ways. Possibilities were not only endless, but mind-boggling as they affected everyone on the planet in a unique way.

After-the-fact they were crystal clear. But precise predictions were difficult at best. The Universe offered guidance, not step by step instructions.

The day before there was a New Moon at twenty degrees Cancer. A partial solar eclipse that opposed Pluto.

Uh, oh.

Not good at all.

That not only fit Friday the Thirteenth, but could be bad for anyone with planets or chart energy points at that degree, especially their sun or moon.

Pluto, god of the Underworld, was ominous. He ruled death and transformations, which included intense, life-changing experiences. Eclipses exacerbated the effects, which lingered for months. Heaven help anyone with a birthday that day who'd have that unfriendly energy in their solar return, making that day and perhaps the entire coming year a rough ride.

Curious which of her clients might be affected, she pulled up her database for all the natal charts she had on file, looking for anything at twenty degrees. When the names came up, the first one that jumped out was Sara's friend, Charlie.

The one with whom she'd shared a psychic link. Whose ascendant was 20:34 Libra.

That had to be it.

She brought up his natal chart and checked to see how the eclipse affected it.

The air fled her lungs.

It hit him, alright, like one of Zeus's lightning bolts. Squaring his ascendant while the eclipse and Pluto rode his Midheaven/Imum Coeli axis, suggesting major life changes.

Neptune opposing his Sun from the 5th house was likewise worrisome. Sneaky Neptune made things disappear, in this case possibly his essence and self-identity. Saturn and Mars in an uncomfortable stand-off indicated a change of direction and restructuring for his thoughts and status generally.

There wasn't a friendly aspect to be seen.

All were critical, stressful, and life-changing.

Or worse.

Her hopes sagged. She'd seen friendlier death charts.

After debating whether to call Sara, she decided to tune-in directly on Charlie first. A possibility, given they connected that way before.

She closed her eyes, seeking his essence.

Nothing but static.

No sentient response at all.

Without a doubt he was in serious trouble, either physically, mentally, or emotionally.

As she reached for her phone, it rang. She jumped, then laughed when she saw who it was.

There are no coincidences, absolutely none.

"Hello, Sara. What happened to Charlie?"

Stunned silence responded.

"Sara? Are you there, sweetie?"

"Y-yes," she stammered. "H-how did you know?"

"Bad vibes. Been troubling me since yesterday. I looked at the transits to his chart, especially that solar eclipse, and figured it was probably him. Upon having that telepathic conversation a few months back, our hearts connected. So I sensed he was in distress. Is he going to be okay?"

"I have no idea, Patrice. He's in bad shape. I was going to ask you that very thing."

"Hold on. Maybe the Universe will cooperate with a specific question."

She generated a horary chart, identified the planetary significators and their house placements. The eighth house of death was empty—

—except for the vertex, the mark of fate.

"This definitely shows an intense situation, Sara. He's headed for a long, transformational journey. It doesn't mean he'll die. He might, but if he does, it's his time. Like most significant events, it was fated. Meant to be. If he recovers, he'll be a different person. Transformed. Either way, he's headed where the Universe wants him to be. What happened?"

"Big accident at the drilling site where he works."

"Drilling site? For what? Oil?"

"Yes. They hit a gas pocket and the rig blew up. It damaged his lungs, plus he has a head injury. He's lucky to be alive. Six guys weren't as lucky."

"Wow. That doesn't seem like an appropriate job for a Native American."

"I know. He had doubts, too. But he said he felt that was where the Great Spirit wanted him to be. Makes me wonder how benevolent this Great Spirit might be."

"There's always a reason, Sara. Something significant will come from this. Let's send lots of prayers and positive energy his way to help him along the path." She paused, then added, "Whichever direction that might be."

"I will. Thanks, Patrice. I feel a little better now. You can't argue with fate, I suppose. Oh, by the way, he actually wanted me to ask, but I think you already told me. Did you actually have a telepathic conversation with him a while back? He wasn't sure if he imagined it or not."

She laughed. "Yes, we did. Loud and clear. We had quite the discussion, actually."

"Great. If, uh, I mean *when* he wakes up, he'll be happy to know that."

"I saw you on TV the other night," Patrice said, gently steering the conversation to another subject. "You did great!"

"Thanks. I have a bunch more invitations, some at the network level. I'm a little worried, but feel as if it's something I need to do." She giggled. "Fate, I suppose."

A well-worn crease asserted itself between Patrice's eyebrows. From what she'd already seen, Sara was in for a soul-stretching year. Difficult as it may be, that was how people evolved and became who they were meant to be.

"Good luck, sweetie," she said. "Follow your heart. It won't lead you astray."

As much as Patrice believed that, hers nonetheless grieved when any of her extended family of clients and friends were faced with difficult times, usually courtesy of Saturn or Pluto.

LSO LOGISTICS OUTPOST
July 14, Saturday
4:18 p.m.

Trey sat at his desk staring into space, physically, mentally, and emotionally drained. The stub of a burnt-out cigar reposed in a metal ashtray, its acrid odor reflecting his mood. For the entire day he'd been debriefing his men, one by one, gathering their personal accounts while everything was fresh in their minds.

When he was done interviewing the ones onsite, he'd visit those in the hospital or call those recovering at home. In many cases, they wouldn't remember, but he was required to ask.

Investigation aside, he sincerely wanted to know how they were doing. He cared and was rooting for them to make a full recovery. His heart grieved for those who died. Young men, good workers, some with families.

At times like this the oil business became the fiery pits of hell.

He needed as much information as possible before OSHA showed up Monday morning. It was his job to know exactly what happened and why, long before they released their official report.

The pounding in his skull crescendoed to an intolerable level. He opened a drawer to fetch an aspirin.

The bottle was gone.

In its place a Styrofoam cup.

His throat burned. It seemed only yesterday he gave the bottle to Littlewolf. He shook out three tablets, forced them down with the tepid dregs in his LSO mug.

He rubbed his face with both hands, determined not to cry.

Gradually, the story was coming together.

No surprises, really.

Something that could never be entirely avoided.

Where there was oil, it was common to find gas. Just the way it was. There appeared to be plenty of oil down there, too. Once the gas vented, they could get to it. Meanwhile, he needed to get through the investigation, then replace the annihilated equipment.

Over a million dollars' worth.

His head defied the aspirin by pounding some more.

The next interview was the last, at least there at the site.

Which was good.

Except it was Gerald Bentley.

Maybe he should take another aspirin. Better yet, all of 'em. With a shot or two of Old Crow.

Why was Littlewolf away from his station? He had no business out by the rig. None, whatsoever. Gerald was in the trailer, too, so maybe he knew.

Maybe that ornery bastard sent him out for something.

At any rate, he'd know soon enough.

Assuming the man would tell the truth.

Littlewolf was still in the hospital, unconscious. He'd probably never see him again, whether or not he survived. Not only did he genuinely like the guy, it was a huge loss to the business.

The trailer door opened and Gerald stepped inside. Trey took a deep breath and stood up as LSO's obnoxious part-owner and CEO entered his office.

They shook hands.

He sat back down, turned to a fresh page in his notebook, and set up the recorder on his cell phone. He braced for the worst and looked him square in the eye.

"Good afternoon, Gerald. I'm sorry y'all had to be here for this shit storm." He held his breath, expecting a lambasting from the depths of oil patch hell.

Strangely, the man's usual acerbic manner was missing, replaced by a humble solemnity he'd never seen before.

"Don't apologize, Trey. You run a clean ship. One of our best. Shit happens. And unfortunately, it just did."

"Yeah. Sure did." When Bentley chuckled softly, he was taken aback, mystified.

"Pretty lousy birthday present, eh, Maguire?"

"What? It's y'all's birthday?"

"Yeah. Yesterday. My sixtieth."

"Y'all's shittin' me, right? What the hell is y'all doin' up here?"

"Doris was gonna throw me some big, goddamn party. Kids and grandkids all comin' in, big-ass barbecue, fireworks, the whole nine yards. I don't like being this old, Trey. Don't need to be reminded, much less pretend it's somethin' to celebrate. Total horse hockey. So I left. Ran away. Came out here. Watch a new dig, visit my brother. Be somewhere I don't feel like such an old man."

Trey's jaw went slack. "Holy Christmas, Gerald. I don't know what to say."

"I guess it serves me right. I sure as hell won't forget this one. Talk about fireworks! Plus now, I really feel old as hell."

"No shit. That sucks."

"Sure does."

"So tell me, Gerald. What exactly went on in the lab trailer? Y'all was monitoring LWD with Littlewolf, right?"

"Yeah. It showed somethin' was up. RPM spiked, torque and resistivity dropped, looked like we hit a void. Depth matched that shadow on the seismic. We radioed the mud logger to find out what was going on when the return rate jumped, too. Classic gas signature. When the guy didn't answer, I decided to go out and take a look."

The man stopped as his features crumpled.

"As soon as I got up to go check, Littlewolf told me to stay put. Said it was his job. That he'd do it."

His voice broke and big, bad, Gerald Bentley began to cry.

"It took Bob more 'n forty years to get over me running over his dog with that old Ford pickup, clear back when we was kids." He paused, sobbing, and wiped his nose on his shirt tail. "He's never gonna forgive me, Trey, if I done killed his Indian."

Trey's eyes defied his earlier edict and teared up. He wiped the moisture away, fitting the pieces together, while he waited for Gerald to get a grip on himself.

When LSO's CEO stopped blubbering, he cleared his throat, hoping to squelch his own emotion.

"Here's how the cow ate the cabbage, Gerald. Our first shift mud logger, Dan, told me he knew things was going south when the flowback came shootin' out like explosive diarrhea. When the ground began to shake, he got up and ran like hell to the muster point. Exactly what they're told, over and over, in safety training. He took off his headset to get his mask on, so didn't hear y'all. Littlewolf got there just as it blew."

BELTON MEDICAL CENTER
July 15, Sunday
1:50 p.m.

Charlie sensed a presence. Opening his eyes failed. The soul-crushing weight remained, confirming he was alive, like *amasani* told him. Surely it didn't hurt this much to be dead. Every breath filled his lungs with pain soaked in suffocating fire.

The realization someone was speaking in a grandfather voice stirred within his soul. The reverent, beseeching tone indicated prayer, but he couldn't understand the words. Not *Diné* or *Tsetsehestaestse*, and certainly not English or Spanish.

Who was it?

Why was he there?

Mysteries and ceremonies came to men like Sweet Medicine from within the earth. Was that where he was?

Why else were some sounds muffled, others not? Though distinct, the man's speech came as if from a great distance.

Perhaps he *was* within the earth. Swallowed by an angry Earth Mother.

The prayer ended and the man began to sing, accompanied by the rhythmic swish of a rattle. Even without understanding the language he recognized it as an honor song. Its healing effects settled upon him with an unexpected sense of peace.

The singing faded.

Again all was deathly still.

Wisdom comes only when you stop looking for it and start living the life the Creator intended for you.
—Hopi Proverb

20. BUGS

Sara's hand trembled as she hung up. Caitlyn Butler had a cancellation for Wednesday. As promised, she arranged conducting the interview from Denver. While she knew it was the right thing to do, airing the most traumatic event of her life on network TV evoked a sick, heavy feeling.

The raucous cry of some obnoxious bird lured her from the sofa to the living room window. There on the neighbor's fence, its black and white tuxedo-like feathers iridescent green in the morning sun, perched a magpie. It flew off to her left, showcasing its long, wedge-like tail.

In spite of its majestic appearance, many considered them no more than a formally-attired crow worthy of eradication.

Was that how she'd be viewed? A nicely dressed nuisance making unwelcome noise on national TV? An annoyance that likewise should be eliminated?

Some undoubtedly saw her that way. But that was the price of exposing the government's outrageous behavior.

Her thoughts ambled down various paths, coming to rest on Charlie.

How was he doing? Would he be transferred today?

She found the Belton hospital in her contacts and pressed connect. Rather than bother the doctor, she asked for the ICU nurses' station.

"ICU." The woman's voice sounded far too cheerful.

"Good morning. This is Sara Reynolds. I was wondering if Charlie Littlewolf was transferred? Dr. Bishop mentioned that was the plan if the HBOT place in Aspen had room."

"Let me check, Mrs. Reynolds."

Several minutes elapsed before the woman returned. Long enough she began to worry. Had something horrible happened? Were they hunting down the doctor to convey the bad news?

"Hello, Mrs. Reynolds?"

She relaxed, relieved it was the same person. "Yes."

"I apologize for the wait. Mr. Littlewolf was transferred early this morning to the hyperbaric treatment center in Aspen. Would you like their number?"

"Yes, please."

She entered it in her phone. If that course of treatment didn't work, no telling what the prognosis would be. What would constitute the worst case scenario, other than death?

No.

Think positive.

He was young, in good health otherwise, and getting the best possible care. The odds were in his favor. If he was meant to die, he would have by now. When he woke up, she should be there. If she was at the cabin, she'd be that much closer.

The more she thought about it, the better it sounded. Mike could check out the cabin. With that suspicious truck in the area, more than likely it was infested again with bugs. She snickered, wondering how the guy reacted when he saw the mics they'd taken out of her car. Maybe they could talk to Rhonda about that man she saw. Ida, too, if he stayed at her RV park.

"Call Mike," she said, summoning her phone's voice commands as she resumed gazing out the window.

To her relief, he picked up on the first ring.

Hopefully, that would always be the case.

"Hey, Sara. What's up?"

"Hi, Mike. There's been some action out by my cabin, plus Charlie's been transferred to a hospital in Aspen. I'd like to drive out there for a few days so I'm closer if he wakes up. I need to be back by early Wednesday afternoon for a TV interview."

"Okay, I'm in. But back up a little. What kind of action?"

"Liz Hudson saw a black pickup heading for my cabin. Someone else told her some creepy guy was staying at the RV park about the same time. His truck was black, also."

"When?"

"Before the holiday." She braced for his response, knowing he wouldn't like the long delay, much less the fact she'd known for over a week but forgot to tell him.

"That's almost two weeks ago! But worth a visit, I suppose. I'll stay at that RV place, see what else I can find out, especially if they have security cameras. They should remember me. I threw out an unruly guest of theirs one time, back when I was a cop. When do you want to leave?"

"Can you meet me at Dad's place at noon?"

"Sure. Are you okay taking both vehicles? If they're in the area, no sense advertising my involvement, same as here."

She squirmed, uncomfortable. "I don't know. If they're still there, I'm not sure I want you that far away."

"I'll never be farther than a few car lengths. When we get to Falcon Ridge, hang out at the store until after I check in. Then I'll text you to meet me at your cabin."

"I guess that'll work."

She texted the plan to Will. He replied with news as well.

Condo deal closed. Framing closets this week.

RURAL FALCON RIDGE
BARBIE'S RV PARK & MARINA
July 16, Monday
2:37 p.m.

Gravel crunched beneath the Tacoma's tires as Mike pulled into Barbie's RV Park and Marina's parking area. He didn't have a reservation, but didn't figure he needed one. It was tourist season and the place had boating access to Lake Wilson, but with luck one of their trailers would be available. Not seeing any cars, it looked like a good bet.

It was off the beaten path with few of their RV hookup spaces ever occupied, other than their own half-dozen rentals. It was almost as if the place were a well-guarded secret. He'd heard rumors that it was a money laundering front for the Mexican mafia.

Such was not the problem of the local police, unless they otherwise broke the law. That one belonged to the feds, one group he was no longer inclined to assist.

The place had questionable guests from time to time, like the one he bodily evicted a few years before. Mrs. Schwartz, who probably out-weighed him by a good forty pounds, could have easily done the job herself.

All things considered, he didn't trust them. The fact that one of their recent guests gave another local "the creeps" testified to their cliental. However, in this case that could work in his favor.

He climbed out of his truck, casually scanning the property for video surveillance. Light reflected off metal in a tree near the lake. He made a mental note to check closer when he used their dock later to go fishing. If they had cameras in the rental units, possibly he could hack the source.

Upon leaving Falcon Ridge PD he spent his down time sharpening and upgrading his electronics expertise. Such devices represented powerful weapons, which cut both ways. Keeping up with technological advances was essential for protecting his clients to say nothing of himself.

Especially in Sara's case, considering the evidence indicated she was being tracked by professionals.

Yeah, right. Maybe semi-professionals.

He headed for the office, the repurposed garage of their small frame house. Inside, the woman he remembered waited behind the counter. Her appearance was far removed from the usual image conjured by the place's name. Her frizzy hair and weight were exactly as before, about as far from a slender, good-lookin' blond as a person could get.

As he recalled, her name wasn't Barbie. Rather, the place was named after their daughter or something. For all he knew, perhaps their dog.

What's that woman's name? His usual tactic to remember names employed mnemonics, a trick learned in the Academy.

A potato came to mind.

Ida hoe that owns this hole.

"I know you," she stated. Her scratchy voice suggested a long-term relationship with cigarettes. "You threw that jerk out two years back who refused to pay 'cause of a dead roach. You still a cop? Or find a better way to make a livin'?"

He smiled, wondering what 'bugs' he might find. "For now, I'm retired. Do you have any vacancies? I'd like to do some fishing for a couple days."

"Sure. It's been slow after the big holiday rush. Some OSHA guys checked in today, investigating that oil well blow-up, but that's it."

He signed the register, listing his address as Denver with his regular cell number. She handed him a receipt. The rate for such a sub-par place—a tin can, actually—was an outrageous $295/night. He'd stayed in five-star hotels for less.

"Is cash okay?" he asked, lip twitching as he stifled a grin.

"Much appreciated."

He handed over seven hundreds to cover the room plus taxes. While she retrieved his change and the key he glanced around. Two cameras. One in the corner behind the counter, another behind him, over the door. Old technology, probably hard-wired to a monitor somewhere.

"Good luck fishin'," she said, handing over some worn-looking bills and grungy coins. "Breakfast's in the party room at nine, sharp."

"Thanks."

Should he ask about the guy in the black pickup?

Nah. Not yet.

Back at his truck, he collected his gear, then found his assigned RV among the others.

It rocked slightly as he stepped inside. Old, but clean enough, even if the Clorox odor was a strategic move to mask the mold. He tossed his bag on the bed, then swept for bugs.

If there were any cameras, they were well-hidden. As far as he could tell, no microphones, either. Definitely nothing wireless.

Perhaps a requirement for their usual cliental.

That worked for him, but he'd still only talk to Sara or Will from a fair distance away, just to be sure.

He knew the man who owned the grocery store fairly well, where he'd pick up some bait tomorrow. He used to patrol the area regularly in return for some of the best free coffee ever.

At some point everyone wound up in there for something. A fishing license, six-pack of beer, or a bag of chips. It was a good bet the black pickup guy showed up for something. The screen shot from the dashcam video could confirm if it was the same person who harassed Sara before.

But first things first. He texted Sara he was heading her way. She replied she'd do likewise.

Before starting the truck, he set the stopwatch on his phone.

Such things were good to know.

**SARA'S CABIN
RURAL FALCON RIDGE
July 16, Monday
3:09 p.m.**

Sara arrived first. The mics and tracking devices on the ground were gone. Everything outside looked normal, so she gathered up her overnight bag and computer, then went inside. She glanced out the window as Mike's truck pulled up, surprised when he just sat there.

Her satellite phone chirped.

Come get my RF detector. Check for cameras and mics before I come in.

When she got to the car he showed her how to use it, then she went back inside. Just like the condo, there were more bugs than before.

So much for the effectiveness of deadbolts.

These were smaller and higher tech but, as far as she could tell, audio only. She scrutinized the ceiling fan in the living area, where she and Charlie had found several. The detector didn't pick up anything and nothing was visible, but it was up there a good fifteen feet or so. To examine it more closely, she needed the extension ladder under the deck.

She fetched binoculars from the desk to check visually. Wanting to be sure, she texted Mike, who responded the instrument's range was sufficient to pick anything up—unless it was a stand-alone with an SD card.

The rest of the cabin was clear, but the wrap-around deck and back patio had cameras watching both doors.

She shuffled down the steep, rock-strewn driveway to his truck with her report.

"What do you think? I'd like to zap them all. They'll probably come and plant them again after I leave, but I'd have some privacy in the mean time."

"That's fine with me. Can you get the cameras? Then I can help with the others."

Her nose wrinkled. "*If* I get the ladder out from under the deck."

"I'll get it."

His mischievous smirk prompted her to lift her brows.

"I'm sure we can put them to good use," he explained.

She sniggered, remembering when she and Charlie relocated one after the raid to monitor the contents of the downstairs commode.

Mike brought the ladder around back as far as he could while staying out of camera range. Screwdrivers and pliers in hand she went to work. The tools were useless, devices either glued or installed with double-sided tape.

Unable to pry them loose, she considered a hammer, reminiscent of the dashcam's fate, which prompted her to remove the memory cards instead. Finished outside, she retrieved the ones indoors, including another tiny camera on the ceiling fan.

Ladder back where it belonged, they sat at the kitchen table strategizing.

"It's a sure bet they used your ladder to set those things up," he said. "You should get one of those steel cables to secure it to the two-by-fours under the deck with a heavy lock. Why make it easy for them? Meanwhile, before we leave I'll dust them for prints."

"Good idea," she replied. "I can't believe I never thought of that."

"That's why you pay me the big bucks. Let's see if there's anything on those SD cards."

She set up her laptop with the appropriate cable. The one from the fan showed someone leaving, but no face. The back door, nothing, but the front door showed a familiar face as he relocked the door.

"How'd he get a key?" Sara gasped.

Mike shrugged. "As a rule, commercial locks have a limited number of keys. It's not that hard to get a hold of all of them. A locksmith could probably design a unique one for you."

She blew out an exasperated sigh. "Great. Wish I'd known that before. Better late than never, I suppose. Another thing for my to-do list."

"I can take care of that for you if you like."

"That would be great." She closed her eyes and inhaled slowly, trying to dismiss the stress that had already provoked a muscle spasm in her neck.

"So what's the plan while we're here?" he asked.

"I want to drive down to Aspen tomorrow to check on Charlie, even if he's not awake," she said, fingers massaging the twinge. "What else should we do while we're up here?"

She stifled a smile when he reached up to stroke his long-absent mustache. "Why don't you let it grow back, Mike?"

He chuckled. "I just might do that. For now I see it as a ridiculous habit I need to break."

"But a harmless one."

"I suppose. But I recently saw some guy in an old black and white movie doing it. When I realized how stupid it looked, I shaved it off that night. Okay. Back to the plan. I'll see what I can find out about that black pickup. I also want to find out if there's any connection between him and the RV park. Something about that place doesn't feel right."

Sara's mouth fell open. Ida Schwartz definitely had a rough side, but she never suspected anything criminal.

"I played *Mah Jongg* with that woman!" she exclaimed. "I wonder if she had anything to do with either wreck? My memory started to come back at one of our games. I wonder if she mentioned that to them?"

"No telling. They might be just fine, but I don't trust them. Who saw the guy that said he gave her the creeps? I'd like to talk to her. Show her the screenshot and see if it's the same guy."

"That would be Rhonda Wheeler. She lives in the green cottage, just north of the RV park."

"Hmmm, that name's familiar. So her house is lakefront?"

"Yes, I believe so."

"Okay, great. I'll skip the dock and just stroll along the shoreline fishing. It'll support my cover, if nothing else. So we're set. You go see your friend and I'll chat with Mrs. Wheeler. We'll just chill out, like we're up here for a break. By the way, driving the speed limit it takes four minutes and seventeen seconds to get here."

Sara didn't know whether she liked that or not. Far better than the usual police response time. But in a real crisis, like that last raid, probably not fast enough.

A lot could happen in four minutes.

ASPEN
MOUNTAINVIEW THERAPY CENTER
Hyperbaric Unit #3
July 16, Monday
4:38 p.m.

Charlie was familiar with cold. Whether Colorado or Montana, winters imposed months of sub-freezing weather. This cold, however, was different. Not as bitter, but penetrating. His ears popped, as if descending from *Novavose*.

The sensations beckoned forth a vision from the encroaching fog.

Eagles Peak, the first night of his failed ceremonial fast. A month shy of eighteen, just out of high school, and heading for college in a matter of weeks.

It was mid-August, but mountain nights were cold, frost common and snow possible at elevations above the treeline, where connection with the grandfather spirits came more easily.

The soft folds of his grandfather's buffalo robe and *amasani's* blanket got him through the night, but by afternoon the next day the sun was scorching hot. Angry rays seared the surrounding rocks and talus, resulting in a piercing glare. For some reason, flies were profuse, their buzzing irritating.

His stomach growled, protesting its emptiness, and the paint on his body itched. Afflictions overwhelming, he glowered across the desolation to the pines below.

Sensing Eaglefeathers's stare, he fixed his eyes in the direction of their cabin, wishing he were there taking a nap. He squirmed beneath the scrutiny, scratching his arms and chest.

"Grandson, when you are uncomfortable you must pray harder. *Maheo* will help you."

The pleading in his grandfather's eyes was no match for his rebellious teenage soul.

"I am sorry, Grandfather. I am hungry and thirsty. My head and stomach hurt. I don't want to do this. I want to go home."

"You must try, grandson. It is important. You told me you were ready to be a man. Finishing all four days will make you stronger. It will help you the rest of your life. If you are thirsty, I have something that can help you."

The old man's knees creaked as he got up from the ground to fetch his medicine bundle in the shade of a nearby boulder. He removed a root that was shaped like a human hand, cut off a piece, then peeled it with his knife.

"Here. Try this, grandson."

"What is it?"

"It is called Big Medicine. It will help your dry mouth and see you through."

Charlie frowned as he took it, sniffed it, then put it in his mouth. Much to his surprise, saliva returned.

But thirst was but a tiny fraction of his discomfort.

He lacked the resolve required to complete such a difficult task, much less the maturity to understand how such a sacrifice could help him in any possible way. Would it bring back his dead father, whom he missed horribly? Reduce his fears about what awaited at college? Explain why life was so unfair, not only to him, but all his people?

This was Eaglefeathers's idea, not his. Four days and nights sitting on the side of a mountain enduring extremes of heat and cold while his body screamed for nourishment was the last thing he wanted to do. When he said he was ready to be a man, he had no idea what he was getting into.

How could enduring this misery possibly make him a man?

He spit the Big Medicine into his hand and tossed it on the rocky ground.

"I want to go home, grandfather. I am sorry, but I do not want to do this."

"You are sure that you do not want to continue?"

"I am sure. What's the point of sitting here four days with no food or water? I am tired and hungry. I want to go home."

Eaglefeathers studied him a long moment.

"I am disappointed, grandson. The suffering you cannot bear now is nothing compared to what will come later. This will make you stronger. *Maheo* will bless you with patience and confidence in what you can bear and achieve."

"How can my suffering now make any difference later? It doesn't matter in the real world, grandfather. It is different now than when you were young."

The old man's voice was firm. "Life's challenges do not change. I promise you they do not get easier. You will need *Maheo* even more as you grow older. Connecting with him now will give you faith that he is always near when you need him."

"I will connect with *Maheo* when I need him. Right now all I need is food."

His grandfather's eyes glazed with disappointment.

"I named you for a mighty Cheyenne chief and warrior. One of the greatest chiefs who ever lived. Without his bravery and vision, we would not have returned to our homeland. I can see I made a grave mistake. You are not a warrior. That makes me sad. Only warriors survive in this world."

"My father was a warrior and he didn't survive."

Eaglefeathers's voice acquired an edge. "Agent Orange in Vietnam gave Little Bear cancer, which killed him. He lived an honorable life. Without proving yourself a man, no honorable *mésèhée* will have you. A respectable Northern Cheyenne wife is important. She assures your success and happiness. Instead you will marry a *kòhóméháe*, a coyote woman, you cannot trust. She will trample your heart and turn on you like a rabid dog."

"Like my mother did to my father?"

Eaglefeathers held his gaze. "Yes."

"I'm sure I can do better."

His grandfather's perusal was that given a foolish dog at its fourth odiferous encounter with a skunk. He patted Charlie on the back, got up, picked up his buffalo robe and medicine bundle, then plodded down Eagles Peak without looking back.

Charlie knew instantly he'd made a tremendous mistake, but didn't have the courage to admit it. He gathered up his blanket, and trudged toward home, deliberately staying several yards behind.

Step by heavy step, his grandfather's words at the sweat the day before came back loud and clear.

"You have reached the age to become a man. Northern Cheyenne men your age earn their first medicine bundle, a *vonàhé'xá'e,* fasting for a purpose at the sacred mountain. Do you see yourself as a man, grandson?"

He caved with self-recrimination. He claimed he was, but only in years, not in spirit. Even his white brother, Bryan, refused to sympathize or validate his rationale for quitting, accusing him of having a recto-cranial inversion. He never quite knew exactly what that was, but it didn't sound good.

Neither he nor Eaglefeathers spoke of it again until four years later when the old man lay dying in his arms and advised him once more to return to *Maheo.*

The memory faded, wounded spirit aching with regret.

He hurt him in a way that he could only understand now that he was a father himself.

Worst of all, his grandfather's prophecy came true.

That description of a *kòhóméháe* fit his ex-wife better than his hunting knife fit its beaded buckskin sheath.

If he'd understood the power of prophecy possessed by a medicine man, that alone would have convinced him to tough it out.

It is better to have less thunder in the mouth and more lightning in the hand.
—Apache Proverb

21. DOGS & CATS

BKSS LLC
ALBUQUERQUE, NM
July 17, Tuesday
8:01 a.m.

Bernie realized this job didn't require the entire crew. Thus, there was no reason to call everyone back from R&R. He'd do it himself—make sure it got done right—but it was too risky to leave the state. That left two candidates: Johannsen and his latest recruit, Paul "Mac" McCullough.

Mac was former CIA, a spook with IT skills of the same caliber as Reynolds. LaGrange referred him, which vouched for his abilities, but was suspicious in itself. Covert audit or capability assessment, perhaps?

Either way, he was grateful to have someone onboard with real-life experience for a change. The man's intelligent hazel eyes were packaged in a nondescript scruffiness that could pass for anything from homeless vagrant to Fortune 500 CEO.

Yeah, considerable potential. If anything happened to Johannsen or he continued to screw up, this guy was plug and play.

Was he a plant?

Could be. But not worth worrying about.

He logged into the call, the two men already present.

"Hey, boss. Wazzup?" Johannsen asked, wearing a disheveled white T-shirt and yawning as if he'd just woken up.

Bernie stifled a grin when his team lead sat up straight and glared, apparently noticing an unfamiliar person on the call.

"Johannsen, this is Mac. Mac, Eddie Johannsen, team lead."

Johannsen grunted; Mac smirked.

Maybe serious competition would motivate Johannsen to sharpen up.

"Here's the deal," Bernie said. "The client took his sweet-ass time, but finally paid up, so we're good to go. He insists upon a quiet job. Nothing flashy that brings the target additional publicity. He wants it done by the end of the month."

"We've had a great turn of luck at her condo, which might help," Johannsen said.

"Go on."

"The unit behind hers is being remodeled, top to bottom. Everything's torn out, clear to the studs. Perfect to wire the place. She won't be able to get rid of them without tearing out the walls."

Bernie's eyebrows shot up. "Good work, Johannsen. But when a transmitter's involved, they're detectable. I wouldn't put it past that woman to rip out the walls. So far she's killed more bugs than Black Flag."

"Good one, boss," Johannsen chuckled, no doubt ass-kissing. "So don't bother?"

"I didn't say that. That's an older condo. See if you can hardwire the mics into an old landline. All we'd have to do is activate it with Ma Bell. Go ahead and get a job on the construction crew."

"Roger, that."

"What about suicide? They're quick and popular for nuisance witnesses," Mac suggested.

"A little too popular. Might make the news. Harnesses take care of the kill, but suicide notes are harder to fake," Bernie responded. "Knowing her family, they wouldn't buy it. They'd make all sorts of noise."

"We have recordings of her voice, right?" Mac noted. "How 'bout we synthesize it, make a suicide phone call or video. Just need VGI software."

"Not a bad idea, but let's see if we can come up with something simpler."

"So what are you thinking, boss? Poison?" Johannsen again, looking smug that Mac's idea was shot down.

"Actually, yes. Something that works slow, but not too slow, no known antidotes, and untraceable in an autopsy."

"I bet she don't go through the place with a Geiger counter," Johannsen said. "An old army buddy owes me one. He works for a company that makes industrial x-ray units for non-destructive testing. I'll bet he can line us up for cheap with a used or returned unit."

Impressed with the creativity, he hated to shoot it down as well. "Good in theory, but not as simple as it sounds. Besides logistics tracing and security, which is tight for radioactive sources, shielding is next to impossible to breach. If you do, you're dead, too. Nice try. Keep thinkin'."

"How 'bout another wreck? Third's a charm, eh?"

"That bitch has squawked on TV how she's nearly been killed twice. A third one would get publicity, which the client insists we avoid. Needs to be subtle."

His thoughts drifted back to his original idea, cyanide laced cookies. He chuckled to himself, picturing Johannsen decked out in a Girl Scout uniform hawking them door to door.

But cyanide worked too fast and was probably traceable. Others, however, might have potential. Sarin, perhaps.

"A former colleague might be able to help," Mac said. "We were knocking back a few beers in Virginia a month or so ago. He told me some former KGB-type looking for fast cash sold him a cache of designer poisons. Stuff left over from when the USSR folded, back in the 80s. Former spies from Slavic states were desperate for money. I could see if he still has any."

"Now you're talking!" Bernie thumped his desk with his fist and bellowed, "That's *exactly* what we're lookin' for."

Terminator shot to his feet from beneath his desk. He rubbed the dog's head in reassurance, but the canine's glare clearly stated, "Apology not accepted." He emitted a whine-saturated yawn, turned his back on his master and stretched, butt in the air, then cast him a side-long glance as he laid back down.

"Payment's authorized up to $5K," Bernie went on, choking back a laugh. "The usual deal: Half up front, remainder on delivery. Johannsen, you're familiar with the chick's condo, so you're on deck. Mac, good job. Get Johannsen's contact information for the hand-off."

LAKE WILSON SHORELINE
July 17, Tuesday
8:30 a.m.

Always alert to some obnoxious little ankle biter, Mike turned around at the high-pitched yipping of a small dog. An older woman was strolling his way from the cottage behind him. Early sixties, grey-streaked hair pulled back in a bun, a few untamed wisps blowing in the morning breeze. While a little on the chunky side, she wore a friendly smile.

An old Beach Boys song popped into his head. He grinned. *Help me, Rhonda* was exactly what he was hoping for.

He tipped his lure-embellished fishing hat, then pulled it down far enough to shade his eyes as the dog sniffed his feet.

"Don't worry, she won't hurt you," she said. "How's fishin' today?"

"Good morning, ma'am." He stooped down and let what looked like a Jack Russell - Yorkshire mix sniff his hand. Satisfied, the dog ran off, chasing a dragonfly. Back to his full height of five-feet six, he asked, "Is it okay if I fish here?"

"Certainly, but thanks for asking. Lake itself and the shoreline aren't mine. You'd think it was, the taxes I pay."

"The government always gets their share, don't they? Hi. I'm Mike." He held out his hand and she returned his firm shake.

Nice to meet you, Mike. I'm Rhonda. Rhonda Wheeler."

Mnemonic name reminder notwithstanding, why's she seem so familiar?

He looked down when something rubbed against his leg. He leaned over to pet an orange tabby, another pudgy grey and white feline strolling along behind—quite the entourage.

"You look familiar," she stated, echoing his thoughts.

"You do, too. I used to be a cop with Falcon Ridge PD. You probably saw me on patrol from time to time. Had to break up a disturbance next door a while back."

The woman's countenance switched from friendly to one that was unmistakably uncomfortable. "Oh. Uh, I think I may have been a bit of a disturbance myself, a few months ago. I had some health problems that made me a little, well, crazy. Got arrested one time. Was that you?"

He barely caught his mouth before it fell open. "The mailbox incident?"

Her sheepish wince presaged her answer.

"Yes. That was me. I can't believe some of the things I did. All thanks to those old mines, polluting our water. Was in the hospital a couple weeks getting cleaned out. I have a good filter system now. Too bad those miners aren't still around so I could send them the bill. From the hospital, too."

"No kidding. Pretty irresponsible. Too many, even today, just take the money and run."

"That's for sure," she agreed. "Like that oil company not far from here. Guess they had big problems last week. I could see the smoke for a couple days, over toward Eagles Peak. Too bad it didn't scare 'em away."

"Not if they found what they're looking for, it won't. So you've lived here for some time?"

"All my life. Grew up in this very house. Never had a reason to leave."

He jerked his thumb toward the RV Park. "What kind of neighbors are they? Do they get a lot of people partying?"

"No, not as a rule. They're pretty selective. Had a bunch of bikers come in one time. RVs, bikes on trailers, an entire caravan.

These were older folks, not kids. Some even retirement age and fairly well-behaved. The racket those Harleys made, though, was horrible. People complained. They didn't let them come back. I'm sure that hurt. Filling that place up would mean a nice bunch of cash."

"So their guests are normal folks? Just here fishing or getting away from the city?"

"Mostly. There was some guy here a week or so ago, though, who was pretty creepy. Cold eyes, mean look. Could tell by how he walked. Gave me the willies, all along my arms. He's stayed there before."

Bingo.

"Oh? Was he fishing?"

"Not that I know of. Never saw him by the water. No, wait. I saw him on the dock a couple times, but he was either having a smoke or on his phone. I asked Ida about him. She said he was her husband's nephew. Sam's sister's son. She doesn't like him, either. Didn't say much, but her sour face said it all. He lives around Denver somewhere. She said he was here on a job."

More than ever he appreciated the practice he got as a cop not reacting to anything someone might say. "A job? What kind of job?"

"Who knows? Couldn't have been much of one. He was only here a day or so."

He set down his fishing pole and pulled the screenshot from his inside pocket. "Is this him, by any chance?"

She gasped, hand flying to her mouth. "Yes, that's him, alright. Is he in some sort of trouble?"

"Maybe. I've been asked to keep an eye out. Would you be willing to call if he shows up again? Without telling the neighbors, of course."

"Of course." She accepted his card and read it over. "So you're not with the police department any longer?"

"Nope. Decided it was time to do something else."

"Good for you. Life's too short to do otherwise. I'd rather live in this little house my grandparents built and have my life to myself than do anything else. I taught school long enough to get a small pension, which does me just fine."

"True enough."

"Well, I've kept you from fishing long enough. Good luck. I hope you find that guy and keep him away from here. I usually feel pretty safe, but not with the likes of him around."

"I'll do my best. Have a great day, Mrs. Wheeler."

"You, too."

He tipped his hat again, then turned back toward the water. He squinted against the sun's reflections from its green depths, wearing a satisfied grin.

His dubious host's relative. Not much of a surprise there. With local ties, finding out his identity should be a cinch.

MOUNTAINVIEW THERAPY CENTER
ASPEN
July 17, Tuesday
10:14 a.m.

When Sara walked into Charlie's room, the last thing she expected to find was a big redneck with a shaved head sitting there in jeans and a red plaid work shirt. The fact he was reading *The Geophysical Journal* and smelled like Dove soap seemed even more out of place. The bed, however, was empty.

He turned his head, startled, then immediately set aside the periodical and stood up, wearing a huge grin.

"Howdy, ma'am. I'm B-b-b-, uh, Dick Duncan. I, uh, work with Charlie." He held out his hand.

So this was Big Dick.

She shook his rough, beefy hand. "Sara Reynolds."

"Nice to meet y'all, ma'am. We's pretty much shut down right now. Trey's dealin' with OSHA, we needs to replace the blown equipment, and clean up the rest of the blowout sh—, uh, 'scuse me, stuff, on the drill site."

She stepped past him to sit on the chair on the other side of a small table, prompting him to park his bulk back in his own.

"The boss wants me to keep an eye on our guy, here. If it weren't for him, we'd all've been headin' back to Fort Worth a long time ago. We wanna make sure he gets the best possible care. Plus, when he wakes up, we gotta little somethin' for 'im. So are y'all a friend o' his?"

"Yes, I am. Charlie and my husband were close friends for over twenty years."

"Oh. Y'all's got a husband?"

She fought back a smile at his crestfallen look. "Well, yes. I did. He died a few months ago, in an accident." Any trace of humor fled. "Or so they said."

"It wasn't that one on that county road outsida Falcon Ridge, was it?"

"Actually, it was. You heard about that?"

"Yeah, sho' did. Boss got his ass chewed out royal-like 'bout it, too, by the local sheriff."

"Why?" she asked, taken aback.

"Oh, uh, somethin' 'bout our 'quipment bein' a potential hazard. In the way, or somethin'. Big stuff, on that narrow road, I s'pose. Wanted us to be extra careful, when we pulled out."

"Did your equipment cause it?" *Or did his boss drive a black SUV?*

"No, no, not at all." He avoided her eyes. "I reckon he just wanted us to be careful."

She watched him squirm, recalling the pictures Bryan took that day. So they were the ones drilling on the secret site. "So what exactly were you doing up here? Fracking?"

"No, ma'am. LSO was puttin' in a geothermal system. Same general process, though. Drillin', casin', and such. Just lookin' for a heat source down there insteada oil."

"Isn't LSO Bob Bentley's company?"

"Yes, ma'am. Do you know him?"

"Not really. Just his wife. It's real nice of you to be looking after Charlie," she stated, changing the subject. "Is he having one of the treatments now?"

"Yes, ma'am. They took him down just over an hour ago."

"Is he still unconscious?"

"'Fraid so, ma'am. Out like a chipmunk crossin' the Interstate." When she shuddered, his expression fell. "Not out perm'nent-like. More like a light. Out like a light. Which could always come back on, eh?"

"Hopefully."

"Yeah. Hopefully, fo' sure. Trey wants him to be comin' back, real bad."

Fat chance, she thought. While she sincerely hoped Charlie would fully recover, it was doubtful he'd have any inclination to return.

About then, an orderly pushed a gurney through the door, a male nurse following. They got their patient settled in the bed, acknowledged them with a nod, then left.

She flew out of her chair.

"Wait!"

The nurse stopped and turned around, a lanky guy in his late twenties.

"I was wondering if I could talk to his doctor and find out how he's doing?"

"Are you Mrs. Reynolds?"

"Yes."

"Great. I'll tell his doctor you're here."

"Thanks."

She sat back down, hoping the doctor would have good news. Charlie's color looked better. But until he woke up they wouldn't know if he had brain damage, permanent or otherwise. At least he was down to only one IV besides the feeding tube.

His doctor arrived moments later, a bosomy middle-aged black woman with a kind demeanor and complex network of braids. "Good morning," she said, extending her hand. "Denise Johnson, Mr. Littlewolf's physician."

After getting past introductions, Dr. Johnson explained that so far they were optimistic. "He just got here yesterday and after only two treatments, his vital signs have stabilized quite nicely. Blood pressure and respiration are approaching normal range. There's evidence of unilateral COP—cryptogenic organizing pneumonia—in his right lung, so we have him on steroids.

"We'll do a CAT scan tomorrow and see how things are progressing neurologically. We've had excellent success in the past with similar cases. We'll know more when he regains consciousness."

Sara asked a few specifics about his condition based on what Dr. Bishop told her, earning a surprised expression until she explained her medical background. They chatted at a professional level for a while, Sara encouraged by the time the conversation ended.

When the doctor left, she got up and walked to Charlie's side. Eyes coated with hopeful tears, she ran her hand down his arm.

"You need to come back, Charlie," she whispered, not caring whether Big Dick heard or not. "A bunch of us here are rooting for you."

"Amen."

She turned toward Duncan, eyes spilling their contents in a heart-felt duet with the big Texan keeping watch.

We the people of the Morning Star, as long as Maheo *is in the blue sky we will walk on earth.*
—*Chief Morningstar a.k.a. Dull Knife (Northern Cheyenne)*

22. MISERY

When Sara walked into Charlie's room the next morning she stopped dead in her tracks. Big Dick was nowhere to be seen, but Charlie was sitting up in bed eating a bowl of oatmeal.

"You're awake!"

"I guess...you could say...that." His halting voice sounded like tires on a gravel road.

She set her purse on the chair she occupied the day before and stepped to his side, relieved almost to tears. "You seem pretty awake to me. How do you feel?"

"A roadkill...comes to mind. Run over...by LSO's...deuce and a half."

His left hand slipped over his right side as he emitted a small cough. She shrunk with a sympathetic cringe.

"But you're alive and awake. I've been so worried about you. Are you in a lot of pain?"

"It hurts to...breathe. It's...unpleasant."

Seeing him suffering nearly unleashed the tears, but she held them back, suspecting that would send the wrong message. Her hand rested on his shoulder.

"I'm so sorry, Charlie."

"Me, too."

His laugh attempt failed miserably, causing him to close his eyes and grit his teeth.

"I should go and let you rest."

"No! Please. Stay."

"Are you sure?" His pleading eyes conveyed a definite *yes*. "Okay. So, is your friend, Dick, still around?"

His laugh failed, hand still gripping his ribs. "You met...Big Dick?"

"I did, yesterday. Interesting guy."

"He left...a while ago...to report back...to Trey. He gave me ...this." He picked up a business-size envelope from the bed tray. "What...is it? My eyes...aren't working...right. Everything's blurry. It's probably...my last...paycheck."

Sara took it from his hand to take a look. "Charlie! It's a check, alright. But it's for $75,000!"

His gasp triggered a coughing fit. She debated between handing him the oxygen mask or his water container. He grabbed the former, breathing slowly with his eyes closed for several seconds.

"Are you...serious?" His voice was barely a whisper.

"Yes! A seven and a five followed by three zeros. Seventy-five thousand dollars. Wow!"

"Huh. That must be...the bonus...Trey told me...about. I kinda doubted...it, actually." Gradually his mouth formed a smile. "I don't know...if it's worth *this*, but...it's pretty cool."

"I'll say! It's fantastic!"

His eyes grew distant. "I've never...had that much...in my life."

"What are you going to do with it?"

"Don't...know. Maybe...new truck. Maybe...save it."

"Do you plan to go back to work when you're up to it?"

"Not going...anywhere. Until my eyes...work right. And that's... only part...of it."

"What do you mean?"

His lids closed slowly, then opened again. "I can't tell...if I'm asleep...or awake. I see...and hear things. Noise...all the time...constant hum. People's voices are...muffled. Except the ones...in my head. There's this...blur. Like a rainbow...around everything. I'm like...in a fog." He closed his eyes. "I don't know...if you're real...or not."

She laughed. "I am, as far as I know. That's probably normal, considering what you've been through. I was dizzy for weeks after my concussion. Worst case, maybe you'll need glasses."

"I...don't know. This feels...strange. I'm not...on...pain meds. Steroids for...pneumonia. And oxygen...treatments. That's all."

Her mind wandered, processing what he said. "I'm sure it'll eventually go away. So when can you leave?"

He hesitated, eyes searching hers. "They said...a few days...maybe the weekend. Once I'm...steadier...on my feet. I'm supposed to...take it easy...for a couple...weeks. What day...is it?"

"Today's Wednesday. July 18. You've been out of it for five days. So that sounds like you'll probably be out by this weekend. What do you plan to do? Do you want to stay at my place? Either the cabin or Denver? Until you feel like yourself again?"

His eyes met hers again, lingering for what seemed a long moment. "Thank you...but no. I need to go...somewhere else."

"Really? Where?"

"I need to go...home."

"Charlie, you shouldn't be alone."

"I won't...be. *Home*...to the...reservation."

"The reservation? Why?"

"I don't know. That's...what I was...told."

"By whom?"

He paused. "Not...sure. But...it was very...clear."

"I told Dr. Bishop back in Belton you were Native American." She couldn't help giggling. "Intuitively obvious, actually. Did he have someone come out to see you?"

"I don't know. I recall...someone. Couldn't understand ...language. I have...strange dreams. Visions....Not sure. But that...is where...I need to go." His fist covered his heart. "I feel it...here."

"Which reservation? How are you going to get there if you can't see to drive?"

He appeared caught somewhere between embarrassed and apologetic. "I was hoping...you'd help...put me...on a bus."

"Forget a bus. Are you kidding? I'd be glad to drive you, Charlie. Where do you want to go?"

"Montana."

She blinked. "Montana. On the other side of Wyoming."

"Yes. That is where...it usually is." He smiled.

She wrinkled her nose at the sarcasm, but couldn't help smiling back as she retrieved her phone from her purse. "What's the nearest town?"

"Busby."

"Okay. Here we go. If we leave from here, it's around 600 miles. If we leave from Denver, it's 488. I'm thinking I could drive you in your truck and have Connie follow, so she can take me back home. That way you'll have it when you're able to drive again."

"You'd do...that for...me? I'd never...ask for that."

"Charlie. You know I would. A road trip will do me good."

"Thank you. You are...a true...friend."

She laughed as she patted his hand. "I hope so. That's a long drive, but we can do it in a day. Connie and I will spend the night somewhere and drive back the next day. So you have no idea why you should go there?"

His eyes held hers, though they appeared unfocused.

"Yes...and no. I need to...reconnect...with my people. I've been away...too long. Whatever is wrong...with me...our medicine man...can fix. I need...a sweat."

"A sweat? What's that?"

He gripped his side again. "One of...our rituals. Purification...of mind, body...and spirit. Maybe...all I need."

"Kind of like the sauna at the gym?"

He grew thoughtful. "No. More. Much more. We pray and...sing to *Maheo*, our creator. When I was thirteen...my *Diné* grandmother, my *amasani*, was...very ill...on her...deathbed. My grandfather was a medicine man...We had a special sweat for her...*Maheo* healed her and...she lived a long life."

"I think that will be very good for you."

"Yes. So tell me. How...are you? Any trouble...or anything?"

She told him about the visit to the lawyer, then her decision to continue her quest, starting that evening on network television. "I plan to show a clip I put together from the dashcam video. I think if people see what they did it'll have more impact."

His face clouded. "Aren't you worried...you'll piss them...off?"

"A little. Dad hired a bodyguard for me. Mike Fernandez." She laughed. "Actually, my case is why he quit being a cop. He's up here with me now, seeing what else he can find out. You know that guy at the end of the video?"

"The one...leading...the raid?"

"Yes," she said with a sneer. "*That* one. He's been seen around this area again. Plus, there were new bugs in the cabin. And it turns out he's a relative of that Schwartz couple, who own the RV park down on the lake."

"Do you think...you're in...danger?"

"I wouldn't doubt it. But that's what Mike is for."

"Where is he...now? Here? At the...hospital?"

"No. At the RV park, pretending to fish. There was no sign of anyone around so I told him I'd be fine. When I get back we'll head for Denver. Do you have your phone so you can let me know when you'll be released?"

He gestured toward his phone on the bedside table. Sara picked it up and gave him a look. "I'm surprised this still works. Maybe getting a new phone should be first on your list."

"Will you help...pick one out?"

"I'd be happy to. Let's do that first thing when we get to Denver."

His eyes blinked closed as he agreed, facial muscles tense. Talking was wearing him out, something she remembered too well, to say nothing of his breathing difficulties. Her brain still balked when too much data flooded it at once.

Before she left she couldn't resist planting a kiss on his forehead. "I'm so glad you're better. I couldn't bear the thought of losing you, too. Let me know when you'll be released."

His eyes eased open and met hers. "Thank you. This is...the second time...you've helped...me. *Ná-améhahtomēvo.* I owe you. I'll let you know...when...I find out."

She held his gaze amid a torrent of unexpected emotion. "Okay. See you then."

Before she got to her car, the tears broke loose. To see someone who was usually the picture of health so debilitated tore any control over her tear ducts to shreds.

At least he was awake. But the possibility he'd never fully recover blared a troubling refrain.

SKYVIEW APARTMENTS
LAKEWOOD, COLORADO
July 18, Wednesday
6:40 p.m.

Eddie Johannsen hadn't felt so violated since the last time his father beat the crap out of him when he was sixteen. Lying to his friends about the black eye, claiming he got it fighting one of the school's football jocks.

He sucked in a long drag of his cigarette, awash in humiliation, then exhaled forcefully, as if to dismiss the volatile mix of emotions churning in his gut.

That stupid bitch went on TV *again*.

At the network level.

It was bad enough she aired the dashcam video that recorded him talking. Someone sounding like him could be explained away.

But the final frame, which stayed on screen for a horrifying four and a half seconds, was a clear and recognizable shot of his face.

Holy shit.

He slumped into the couch as he took another sustained drag, held it a moment, then blew it out through clenched teeth.

What a fuckin' idiot.

Why the hell didn't he just take out the SD card? Now it was a good bet his stupidity would go viral across the entire civilized world.

Lurking out there on the web forever, waiting to be found by his mother, sister, two ex-wives, son, and everyone else, most of whom didn't know what he did for a living.

They would now.

Unlike his mother's brother, Uncle Sam, they would *not* be proud, much less amused, by his chosen profession.

Hole-ee shee-it.

His phone lit up next to his can of Bud Lite, visual preamble to its audible ring. *Hmmph.* With so many candidates, who'd be first in line to rip him a new asshole? Upon seeing who it was, any remaining pride imploded.

"Hello, Ma."

"Edel Wolfgang Johannsen. Bist du ein mördreisch beruflich? Spinnst-du! Bist du verückt? Scheisse! Wie gehts?"

He slumped into the cushions, ten years old again as she reamed him out for being a crazy idiot in her native tongue. Sadly, the only German he knew was acquired under similar circumstances.

"Ma, I know. You're upset. But if you want to talk, it needs to be in English. *English*, Ma. No *Deutsch*."

"Wie bitte? Nein Deutsch? Warum nicht? Bestimmt mein Sohn ist ein Dummkopf. Bist du blöd? Hmmmph."

He braced himself while her brain switched to English, shaking his head at the familiar dig that he was too stupid to learn German.

Maybe he would have if she hadn't slapped him upside the head whenever he made a mistake.

"Edel. *Mensch!* Vat's de madda vit you? *Dein Großvater*, he do zuch things in de camps *aus Deutschland* vit *der Krieg.* It is zometimes vhat one must do. *Die Arbeit*, to work *ist güt.* But you should not be *sehr glücklich* about it. *Pfui! Du bist* disgrace *die Familie. Dein Opa* turns in *das* grave."

"Yeah, yeah, I know, Ma." He reached for his beer while conducting a mental inventory of his liquor cabinet. The phone vibrated with another call.

Could it possibly be any worse than this one?

"I'm sorry, Ma. I've got another call coming in. It's my boss. I need to take it."

"*Ja*, you do dat. *Sprechst du der meister.* Tell him *es tut mir leid,* that you is sorry you be *ein Dummkopf. Du bist gar nicht schön,* Edel. *Alles klar? Einverstanden? Mein Sohn ist ein* disgrace. *Gute nacht.*"

"Goodnight, Ma."

He took a deep breath and switched calls. "Hey, boss."

"Nice job, Johannsen. Not exactly the kind of publicity I'm looking for."

The fact Keller wasn't yelling generated hackles up and down his arms. When the man yelled he got over it far quicker. Instead, his voice was an octave lower, intonations cutting to the bone.

"How many times have I told you cock-wads to shut your holes during a job? You may as well call the FBI and give them a DNA sample, too. You need to keep your sorry ass in your apartment until you make some serious changes to your appearance. Then consider going to South America for something more long-term, like plastic surgery. Got it?"

"Yes, sir." He stifled a grin, relieved. *Did this actually mean he wasn't getting fired?*

"So listen up, numbnuts. Dye your hair. Get brown contacts. Online, not the corner drug store. While you're at it, get some indoor tanning shit and do something about that pasty lookin' skin, too. I know you hate hats, but get one. Shoot for an Hispanic look.

Middle-Eastern, or something. Looking like a terrorist is better than that asshole on TV. Then, and only then, should you set foot outside your front door. Not one second before. Understand?"

"Roger that. Do you think the police'll be lookin' for me?"

"I doubt it, but it's possible. The local cops saw you before, also thanks to one of your screw-ups, but didn't actually catch you in the act. Now they have concrete evidence that you caused the wreck. It's every bit as incriminating as being caught on surveillance video, government sanctioned or not."

"So I'm likely to get arrested. For doin' my freakin' job."

"Based on the public reaction I expect to that broadcast, Johannsen, that's the least of your worries. You're more likely to get lynched at Dairy Queen by a gun-toting' soccer mom. Do you hear me? Lay low. Don't go within ten miles of the chick's condo. Even when you've cleaned yourself up. I'll get someone else on that construction crew."

"Roger that." He ground his teeth, not sure whether to ask or not, but he needed to know. "Uh, what about that pickup? Is that still on?"

He held his breath during the silence that followed, wincing when Keller's reply was the man's pet expletive. If that meant no, he was probably all but fired.

"It depends, Johannsen. What have you learned? Anything?"

He paused, not sure if it was a hypothetical question or he expected an answer.

"Well?" his boss prompted. "I want to hear it. Make sure you've actually learned something." He cleared his throat. "Again."

He hung his head, feeling as if he were back in high school, getting chewed out for flunking algebra.

"Uh, well, yeah. I guess no unnecessary talking during a job."

"Very good. What else?"

"Hmmm. Let's see. If I ever have to deal with another dashcam, remove the memory card instead of bashing the crap out of it."

"Excellent. What else?"

"Um, uh, I can't think of anything else, boss."

"Okay, let me help you out. I'm glad you enjoy your work. But try not to have quite so much fun on the job. It's unprofessional. Save your celebratin' and jokes for after, understand? Killing as a business is one thing. People might understand that. Doing it for sport or fun is another. We've already been accused of being amateurs. There's a good chance we'll get fired for this. *Very* good chance. And any potential clients out there who saw tonight's newscast sure as hell won't be calling any time soon."

"Roger that."

If that happened, the rest of the team would finish him off for sure. He cringed at the thought as he ground out his smoke. He stared at the ashtray's logo, swiped from his Stardust hotel room in Vegas after getting paid for the last job.

Maybe *literally* his last job.

"So, uh, what about that pickup?" he asked, bracing for the worst.

Another long silence.

"Mac hasn't gotten a hold of the guy yet. Apparently, he's hard to catch. If all goes as planned, yeah. Don't fuck it up. Understand? I mean it, Johannsen."

"Roger that."

As usual, Keller hung up without saying goodbye.

His phone went off again before he could set it down. Ex-wife number one. Had their twelve year old son also seen the broadcast?

He sunk back into the cushions and slammed the rest of his beer. A spectacular, operatic quality belch doubled as a scream of frustration.

Forget it.

That's what phone mail was for.

His ass-chewing quota for one night had already been exceeded.

Whoever is out of patience is out of possession of his soul. Men must not turn into bees who kill themselves in stinging others.
—*Jonathan Swift*

23. BUSTED

SARA'S CONDO
DENVER
July 18, Wednesday
8:52 p.m.

Sara leaned back on her livingroom couch, shaken but smiling, as her father popped the cork on a bottle of Brut Champagne, then poured its contents into chilled glasses. She sipped the bubbly after a series of toasts, hoping the clip had the desired effect on the show's audience.

No matter how many times she viewed it, that video never failed to whisk her back to the most heart-wrenching moment of her life.

"Well, what do you think?" she asked. "Was it a mistake or will it get people stirred up?"

"It made me cry," Connie stated, tearing up again. "And it would have, even if you weren't our daughter. It's horrible what they did. Inexcusable."

"I've got to admit, it affected me, too," Will agreed. "But I'm more inclined toward vengeance. I'd love to see them all hang."

Mike's derisive snort reflected agreement. "The fact they were so flippant about it is what got me, even when we were there with the ambulance. They deserve to go down. Hard."

"Your hostess was speechless," Connie added. "It was clear she had no idea what you'd been through. Sharing that video put people right there. That had far more impact than the last interview. The only way to connect with people is when there's emotion involved. You definitely did that."

"What do you think the general reaction will be? As far as my ultimate goal."

Mike's eyes locked on hers. "What exactly *is* your ultimate goal? Revenge?"

"Somewhat. Bryan didn't want them to get away with it. And neither do I."

"What do you think he meant? Individually? Or more?" Will added.

"I think he wanted people to know how their tax dollars are being wasted by a corrupt government at the beck and call of corporate interests. Expose how Congress and the elite take financial advantage of everyday citizens. Bribing lawmakers and agencies to favor profits over people's health."

Anger smoldered as she went on. "Elected officials are supposed to represent the people. What intelligent person of either party would approve of PURF? Much less the blatant murder of anyone who threatens to expose it."

Will's eyebrows lifted. "That's a pretty big order, Sara. That would require taking down the entire system. And a corrupt one, at that."

She paused to take a sustained sip, bubbles tickling her nose. "I don't know what I'll accomplish. But there's no telling who might take up the sword with me. The more people who speak up, the more momentum it gains."

"Every flood starts with a single drop," Connie said.

"Not taking it lying down is the most important point," Will said. "PURF is bad enough, but what they did to Bryan to hide it is flat-out wrong. People who don't believe such things happen are only fooling themselves."

Sara set her glass on the coffee table and picked up her phone to check her GoFundMe account. "Wow! Donations are rolling in. There's now over seventeen thousand dollars in there. I need to set up something officially, maybe a nonprofit."

"Either that or donate it to Judicial Guardian, who's already exposing corruption and taking them to court," Will suggested. "They're swamped in this environment and every dollar helps."

"Good point. I'll have to think about it and how much I want to do personally." She frowned as possibilities paraded through her mind. "Do you think they're still going to come after me? If something happens to me now, won't it confirm how messed up things are?"

"You never know. Intimidating the government isn't possible. If you anger them, they're not above simple revenge. If you're no more than a buzzing mosquito, you're okay. However, that guy whose face just got a rather dubious debut on the airwaves might be out for some payback. At least we know what he looks like."

Mike literally growled. "I can't wait to get my hands on that bastard."

"Me, too," Will agreed. "Right, wrong, or indifferent, I hold him personally responsible for that wreck."

"At this point I have enough information to find out exactly who he is," Mike stated. "Once I find out where he lives, I think a visit's in order."

Multiple red flags waved in Sara's mind. "Shouldn't we let the police handle it?"

"We can't," Mike replied, words bearing a bitter edge. "Falcon Ridge PD was directed to close the case and quit asking questions. We knew this guy's team orchestrated the wreck, but with them operating under government auspices, our hands were tied. We can't go back and get him or anyone else for that wreck. It's a done deal."

"But. . ." Sara protested.

Mike cut her off. "Just listen. With PURF no longer secret, there's a good chance that contract ended. Once they're working for a non-government client, that protection's gone. Then they're just common criminals. What we need to do is get him on an additional charge. Catch him messing with either of your homes, your car, or some other criminal act that presents a threat to your life or well-being."

"So we need to get him on new charges?" she asked.

"Exactly. We need to post this place as well as your cabin and various points around your property with *No Trespassing* signs. That puts anyone on notice and makes being there a crime. We have our own surveillance devices to catch him or anyone else red-handed. As far as I can tell, this is something we'll take care of on our own."

Will topped off everyone's glass, finishing the bottle. "You're right. This is an entirely new situation."

"What about a restraining order?" Connie suggested.

"They're a joke as far as protection is concerned, but it would add to the charges. Make it easier to arrest him."

"So, when do we get this place ready, in case he shows up?" Sara asked.

"It's too late to start tonight," Will replied. "We'll break out that wall sometime after five o'clock tomorrow."

SKYVIEW APARTMENTS
LAKEWOOD, COLORADO
July 19, Thursday
8:18 a.m.

Eddie picked up his phone, not surprised by who was calling. An ominous feeling like a bad case of the flu hit the moment he woke up, instincts screaming trouble was afoot.

"Hey, boss. What's up?"

"Nothing good," Keller replied.

"Did we, uh, lose the contract?"

"Not exactly, but close. Real close."

"Yeah? How's that?"

"The client insisted that I do some housecleaning before proceeding. Sorry, Johannsen. You're fired."

Eddie's heartrate followed the crest of an adrenaline blast. He shot up from the couch and paced between his galley kitchen and living room.

"*What?* I'm fired?"

"Our client is not a forgiving man. You're off this job."

"What about future ones?" The response was a long pause. Too long.

"Boss? Did you hear me?"

"Yeah, I heard you. Your public appearance last night is bad for business."

Fiery indignation raged. He clenched his teeth. Losing his temper would add to the strikes already against him. Begging or acting like a wuss would only piss him off. If he played it cool, he'd probably eventually let him come back.

He forced a deep breath, let it out slowly. "Okay. You know how to reach me. This wasn't my fault, you know."

"Actually, it was. Then you topped it off by stepping in your own shit. Goodbye, Johannsen."

The connection went dead.

Months before he'd asked why he always hung up without saying goodbye. Keller told him it was simple: He only said it when he really meant it.

Shock morphed to blind rage.

"*Shit!*"

He pitched the phone at the couch. Instead of landing on a cushion it bounced off the arm and fell on the carpet. He kicked it toward the kitchen, where it disappeared under the refrigerator. He bellowed an F-bomb that would flatten Milwaukee, retrieved the damn phone with a fly swatter, then dropped into his TV chair, staring into space.

His hand trembled as he lit up a much-needed smoke.

Now what?

This work was all he knew. His mother signed the papers for him to enlist in the army when he was seventeen. He had a talent for special ops and loved his work. He stayed in for over ten years, getting out only because wife number one insisted, saying their son needed his father to be accessible. She left shortly after, anyway.

Having him around 24/7 while he looked for work must not have been like she expected.

After that, he spent five years working a variety of meaningless jobs from construction to selling cell phones at Verizon. Which was where he met wife number two. They married after two months, which was how long that one lasted.

Then he met Bernie.

The past two and a half years had been great. He was back in his element, once again thriving on the challenge and excitement. He was good at his job. Sure, he made mistakes. Who didn't? Screw-ups or not, he got the job done.

How could this happen?

What now?

He needed income. Unemployment benefits weren't an option, not without proving he left legitimate, verifiable work. Mercenaries didn't get a W-2 or 1099. He still had money in the bank from the last job, but not much. Most of it went toward paying cash for his new truck.

At least he had that. Never again would his vehicle be repossessed.

Talk about humiliating.

This way, whatever else happened, he could live in his prize Ram.

For now he had enough cash to last a few months.

But then what?

Like Keller said, since his illustrious TV appearance, he'd be *persona non grata*.

Everywhere.

Legitimate jobs or otherwise.

This was all that stupid bitch's fault. They should have finished her off at the wreck site. And would have, if he'd realized she was still alive.

What the hell was she trying to prove? Not only releasing all that information, but then going on TV to whine about it. How much was she being paid for those appearances? Probably a boatload.

Well, one thing for sure. Now that he was off the job, he could do as he damn well pleased. The disguise was a good idea, anyway, so he'd still do that. The things he ordered to do so should be there the next day. Once that was done, he was a free man.

Knowing the frequency of the devices in her condo, he could still monitor them.

Why not?

He had nothing better to do.

No doubt that new guy, Mac, would take care of the hit. The second he saw him on that telecon he smelled trouble. Maybe why he got fired, the newscast a handy excuse.

Another thought struck.

Unless he got to her first.

It wasn't about money anymore.

Now it was personal.

Eddie was numerous things, but he wasn't a quitter.

This was definitely not over.

SARA'S CONDO
DENVER
July 19, Thursday
5:09 p.m.

Earlier that day Sara went shopping for *No Trespassing* signs. She didn't have any trouble finding some for the cabin, but it wasn't as simple for the condo. She finally found a stylized one in brown that blended with the front door without looking too glaring. She stuck it in place with double-sided tape, wondering if it violated the condo owners association's outdoor aesthetics deed restrictions. If so, she'd know soon enough.

After dinner Will and Mike started cutting away the sheetrock in the new closet. Will used his circular saw to score the firewall where the opening would be. Sara cringed with every blow as they chipped it away with sledge hammers.

Billows of pulverized cement filled the air, covering everything with thick, grey dust. A series of sneezes drove her to the downstairs bathroom to wet a wash cloth to hold over her nose and mouth. She opened a nearby window. The breeze that swept inside wasn't what she had in mind, so she set up a small fan.

Hacking and sneezing, the two men swept manageable weights of the dusty mess into black plastic contractor bags. When they were done, they hauled them out to Mike's truck to take to the Dumpster on the far side of the parking lot while Sara got busy with the vacuum cleaner.

That accomplished, she made a pitcher of iced tea, less than thrilled by how much dust migrated to the kitchen. They'd barely settled down to relax when Sara's phone chirped an incoming text.

"Great! Charlie's getting released from the hospital tomorrow morning."

Will glowered. "So you and Connie are driving him to Montana?"

"Yes. We'll pick him up, then stop at the drilling site, or what's left of it, to get his truck. He wanted to stop by, anyway, to thank them for that huge bonus. We'll come back here for the night, then head for Montana Saturday morning. We'll drive back Sunday."

Mike looked puzzled. "Sounds like a plan. Should I assume I'm riding shotgun?"

Will looked relieved as Sara confirmed it, then shifted the subject back to the present.

"I've been thinking—"

The men exchanged that *heaven help us* look she knew too well.

She narrowed her eyes, then put it out there. "You froze the surveillance devices and disabled the audio, making it appear no one was home," she said. "None of the cameras are facing the back wall, so they won't see the work in progress or that a closet had suddenly appeared. *However*, someone has been in here before to plant their devices."

"Correct," Mike agreed. "So unless the guy's a total idiot—which is possible, based on his tricks so far—if he's ever in here again he'll probably notice. It's only a small closet, so maybe not. But if so, our advantage could be blown."

Sara bit her lip. "That's what I was thinking. Hopefully, he'll be behind bars before that."

"It's a gamble," Will added. "But we'll know if he gets in again, courtesy of our own equipment. Then we'll just have to deal with it. Its benefits outweigh the risks." He took a drink, then stared through the open closet door to the roughed-out opening. "You know, maybe we should aim one of our own cameras toward the closet."

Mike chuckled, drawing questioning looks. "Good idea. I'll get the one from the cabin's ceiling fan out of my truck."

A few minutes later, it was secured to the picture frame over the couch, pointing in that direction.

After that, they secured the opening with a shoring box from half-inch plywood. At least the sawdust didn't fill the entire condo and was easily swept up with a broom.

Mike had picked up the custom-made faux utility panel at the metal working shop earlier that day. The magnetic latch opened from either side, allowing her to escape, if necessary. They screwed it in the wooden frame, then stood back admiring their work while Sara rested her hands and chin on the broom handle.

"I'm hungry. Want to go out? Or call for pizza?"

No one had a better idea, so she opted for the latter.

"Okay, time for a sound test," Mike proposed as he set a decibel meter on the other side of the room. "Let's see how quietly I can get in."

They all cringed at the metallic screech when he pushed it open. WD-40 did the trick, but the closet door squeaked as well. Fortunately, that was easily remedied the same way.

While they waited for the pizza, Sara painted the closet walls, grateful Home Depot was able to match the pale grey on the adjoining walls.

She was just finishing up the baseboards when the pizza arrived. Before adjourning to the kitchen, Will surveyed their work wearing a satisfied look.

"Okay. Now all we have to do is wire the com system between the units. Then I can go ahead and hire some workers to get the other side finished up." He grinned at Mike. "That way you won't have to feel like you're living in a bombed out building anymore."

Mike met the comment with a wry grin. "Do I get to choose the wallpaper?"

Will laughed. "Sure, why not? No telling how long you'll be there."

"True. I might just sign a lease when this job is over. I hate moving."

"Who doesn't?" Sara agreed. "But who uses wallpaper anymore?"

The rest of the evening was spent installing the intercom system, including silent alarm buttons, in case an intruder eluded the motion detectors. Placements included the master suite next to her bed, the adjoining bath, her office, which doubled as a spare bedroom, then the kitchen. All were silent, but would send an alert to their phones.

Flashing LEDs, which Will claimed could wake the dead, would activate throughout Mike's condo, which they'd install as soon as they returned from Montana.

It was after midnight by the time they finished. She gave them both a tired but appreciative smile.

"Thank you, both of you. I feel safer already."

Some of you think an Indian is like a wild animal. This is a great mistake. I will tell you all about our people, and then you can judge whether an Indian is a man or not.
—Young Joseph, "Chief Joseph", January 1879

24. RELEASED

MOUNTAINVIEW THERAPY CENTER
ASPEN
July 20, Friday
10:05 a.m.

The familiar drive went quickly, as trips always did with someone to talk to. Sara and Mike chatted about the progress at the condo, then brainstormed code words for emergencies and scenarios where she might be in danger. It helped to know what to watch for.

"Situational awareness," he called it.

Until a few months ago she never thought, much less worried, about such things. Even before her father hired Mike, when she was wearing her Glock on a regular basis, she never tuned in like she should to every surrounding detail.

Bryan always joked, "Just because I'm paranoid doesn't mean no one is following me."

But who wanted to live on constant alert?

Nonetheless, realizing how vulnerable she'd been did not generate a good feeling. Actually, she knew better, but was too distracted during the time she and Charlie were trying to find Bryan's data stash.

When they arrived at the hospital, Mike waited in the car while she went inside to see if Charlie was ready. She stopped dead when she saw him just inside the lobby. He was not only ready, but waiting in a wheelchair. He looked uncomfortable, perhaps embarrassed, but such facilities didn't allow patients to walk out on their own, no matter how good they thought they felt.

Furthermore, he was wearing an over-sized white T-shirt and what looked like pajama bottoms, hospital-issue paper slippers on his feet. It took a moment to realize why he wasn't wearing regular clothes.

His features were slack, eyes droopy, looking more exhausted than when she'd seen him days before. She could practically hear Bryan telling him he looked like "pounded shit."

He'd actually been released?

Wow.

Maybe they needed the space. Apparently they had a waiting list. Good thing he was going somewhere to finish recovering.

He sat up straighter when he saw her.

"Okay, great, you're all set," she said with overdone cheerfulness. "Wait right here while I get the car."

"No," he objected firmly. "Get me...out of here. Now."

Her eyebrows shot up at his impatience. His voice sounded a little better, but still raspy.

Nonetheless, she'd never seen him so edgy. She pushed him out to the car where Mike got out, holding the door open for him to get in.

He just sat there, glaring at Mike in a deep shade of unfriendly. The reason took a moment to register, having forgotten their shared past—Mike being the one who arrested him for trespassing at the wreck site. The ex-cop seemed to understand and took the lead, extending his hand and introducing himself.

"Mike Fernandez."

Charlie glowered.

"He was only doing his job," she reminded him quietly. "He wasn't happy about it, either."

"That's right," he stated, still holding out his hand. "If I agreed with how that case was handled, I wouldn't be here today."

Charlie's scowl remained, but he relented and took his hand. Then he gripped the wheelchair's arms and pushed himself to his feet. He stood there a moment, swaying, then dropped back down.

"Between not...being able...to see...or breathe...and this vertigo crap, I feel like...I've been taken apart then...put back together by...a one-eyed possum," he grumbled.

Sara rested a reassuring hand on his shoulder, much as she had with her physical therapy patients what seemed a lifetime ago. "It's okay, Charlie. I'm sure it won't last."

Mike stepped over and helped him into the passenger seat.

Sara remembered too well how she felt after her accident. That, combined with the convoluted mountain roads back to Falcon Ridge presented a perfect storm for him to regurgitate. Taking Highway 82 was straighter, but its westward heading added several extra miles versus going through Meredith.

"Do you think you might get car sick, Charlie?"

"I hope not. But it's...possible. I'm sorry, Sara. I'd hate to...puke in your...new car."

Mike was quick with a solution. "I'll get some barf bags from inside."

While they waited, he adjusted the seat to semi-reclined and closed his eyes, muttering, "This is...bullshit."

She snickered as she went around and settled into the driver's seat. She'd never heard him cuss before. *Ever.* No doubt he picked up a bad habit or two around all those roughnecks.

Mike returned with a handful of barf bags, a bottle of water, and a Dramamine, courtesy of the hospital. He handed them over, then climbed in back. Charlie gulped down the pill, then leaned back and closed his eyes.

"Get me...out of here. Please."

"Do you still want to stop at LSO?" She couldn't help wondering if he'd want his coworkers to see him in such a state.

"No. They're not...expecting me. I'll go by some other...time. When I feel like a man...instead of a...road kill."

She reached over and patted his arm that rested on the console. "It's only been a week, Charlie. You nearly died. Give yourself a chance. We do need to pick up your truck, though. I'll park a ways back and send Mike in. How's that sound?"

"Good. Thank you...for understanding."

"Do you have your keys?"

"They're in...the truck. Above the...sun visor."

They were no sooner on the road than he was asleep. Not wanting to disturb him, she and Mike didn't converse, only exchanged concerned looks in the rearview mirror. When they reached the state highway outside Falcon Ridge, Sara dreaded waking him up, but needed directions.

"Charlie," she said softly. No response. She reached over and tapped his arm. He bolted awake, eyes wide, then gasped a few times to catch his breath.

"I'm so sorry," she apologized. "We're almost there. I need directions to LSO."

He gave instructions, then dozed off again.

His doctor actually released him in this condition? Had he hidden how he felt? Or checked himself out? LSO's workman's comp insurance would undoubtedly cover any expenses, so it wasn't likely they threw him out because of that.

One thing was certain: He wasn't in any condition to be on his own.

His directions were clear, so she found the turnoff without any trouble. The SUV jostled down the rutted dirt road, huddled beneath pines mixed with deciduous trees and bushes.

Charlie's eyes cracked opened. Another hundred yards and the road split. The left fork widened into a parking area while the right led up a hill to the worksite, where a few trailers were visible.

"Here. Right here," he said.

She hit the brakes.

"My truck should be...toward the far end." He shot Mike another icy look. "I'm sure you know what it looks like. And yeah, it still has New Mexico plates."

She wanted to smack him for another veiled reference to his arrest. His usual behavior was reserved and polite. Then again, Bryan was always cranky when he didn't feel well, too.

As Mike got out, Charlie squinted out the windshield toward the other vehicles. No cars, only trucks of various makes and sizes. "How many do you...see over there?" he asked.

"Oh, ten or twelve."

"Good. I thought...I was seeing double. Most the workers...don't have a vehicle. I wonder what's...going on?"

"Want me to find out?"

"No! They'd be all...over you. Like Trey says, 'like a duck on a...June bug.' Oh. I know. OSHA. Last people I...want to talk to."

He leaned back again and closed his eyes. Mike paced down the row of vehicles to the end, then turned around with his arms akimbo. He shrugged, then headed up the hill. The next thing she knew, he was coming back down.

On foot and not alone.

"Uh, oh," she mumbled.

Charlie's eyes popped open. "What's wrong?"

"Your truck wasn't there so he went to check. You're not seeing double this time, either. He's on the way back and someone's with him."

He looked as if he wanted to melt into the seat. "Oh, no. Big Dick?"

"No. This guy has white hair. And a mustache."

"Oh. Terrific." His pained look implied he might need one of those barf bags after all.

When the two got to the car, he pressed the button to roll down his window. The man stooped over to peer inside, wearing a huge grin.

"Is it ever good to see y'all, Littlewolf! How's y'all doing?"

He cleared his throat and forced a weak smile. "Thanks, Trey. I feel like...crap."

"Better 'n dead. Don't take this wrong, Littlewolf, but y'all looks like you's been rode hard and put up wet. Y'all doin' okay?"

He held his gaze a moment. "I'll live."

"This must be y'all's friend, Sara." He favored her with a smile saturated with Texas charm as he reached in front of Charlie to shake her hand. "Big Dick told us all about seein' y'all at the hospital."

I'll bet he did, she thought, taking his hand. "Nice to meet you, Trey."

"So'd y'all get that check okay? Or did Big Dick run off with it? He said he was thinkin' of goin' to Vegas while we's shut down and all."

Charlie's smile was weak but sincere. "Yes. Thank you...very much. It was a surprise. Nearly made me...pass out again."

The Texan laughed, loud and hearty. "Good. Y'all deserves every penny. Where's all y'all headed for now?"

"I'm going to stay...with family. Until I...get back...on my feet."

"You know we'd love to have y'all come back whenever y'all's up to it, right?"

"Thanks. We'll...see."

"Here's y'all's keys."

Charlie pointed at Mike standing beside him, who took them, then wasted no time heading back up the way they'd come.

"Sorry to hold y'all's truck hostage like that."

"No problem. Thanks for...looking out for it."

"I wasn't 'bout to let one of them roughnecks drive off with it, get drunk, and smash it to pieces. Wouldn't put it past some of them partying with us down and all. But I's holdin' y'all up. It's good to see y'all. Keep in touch, okay, Littlewolf?"

"I'm not sure...I'll have...a signal. Or email...Thanks again, Trey. Say hello...to the guys. Especially...Big Dick."

"Sure thing. Take care," he said, then stood back as she pulled forward to the split to turn around and wait.

When Mike appeared in Charlie's Ranger he waved her ahead. She stepped on the gas, wincing at every bump and jolt until they got back to the main road.

"Would you mind...stopping by my place? I need to...pick up ...some clothes. And a few...other things."

"I'd be happy to. No reason to hurry."

Fortunately, Charlie's breakfast continued to stay where it belonged. As soon as they were on their way again he emitted a gigantic yawn, closed his eyes, and went back to sleep. She knew the way, so didn't wake him until she pulled up in front of his cabin, Mike right behind.

"Charlie, we're there," she said softly.

He opened the door, swung his feet around, then hesitated.

"Do you need some help?"

Both hands covered his face. "No. I'm fine."

"Why don't you let me help you?"

"No. I told you...I'm fine."

He slid out slowly and shuffled along, one hand on the fender for support. He paused several seconds when he reached the end of the hood, then staggered forward like a blind person until he disappeared inside.

Several minutes passed. She was just about to check on him when he came out. The baggy T-shirt was replaced with an unbuttoned denim work shirt, the PJ bottoms with a pair of jeans, sockless feet in a pair of unlaced hiking boots. A multi-colored Navajo blanket was draped over his arm, a duffel bag slung over his shoulder as he shuffled toward the car.

She got out to help, whether or not it would injure his pride. He didn't argue when she took his bag, then placed it in the cargo area while he slowly resumed his place in the passenger seat, blanket on his lap while he fumbled with buttoning the shirt.

Once they reached I-70 he leaned the seat back all the way, closed his eyes, and went to sleep.

Sara's mind buckled with concern.

How could any responsible facility release him in such horrible condition?

Charlie's eyes were closed, not so much to sleep as to block the unfocused images. Not being able to see clearly was bad enough.

Compounded by the noises in his head, the combination was unbearable.

They were more horrific in the hospital. Not only the everyday sounds of medical personnel and equipment doing their jobs, but the other patients.

As if his own misery weren't enough, he was painfully aware of the suffering of every soul in the facility. He perceived their thoughts. Their pain. Their depression. Their hopelessness.

Whatever the Christian concept of hell might be, surely that was it.

It was quieter now, but far from silent.

What was that humming sound? More than that—a roar. Was it the car? If so, it had some serious mechanical problems.

No. The car was new, Sara seemingly unaware.

The earth, perhaps? Was that what it was? He could always feel her energy. That was how he found the oil. But someone turned up the volume to full blast.

Oh. . .

Right.

He violated her, knowing it was wrong. No telling how she'd unleash her wrath.

Perhaps already had.

The realization evoked a shiver that penetrated to the bone. He unfolded his blanket, released the seatbelt, and wrapped its soft, colorful folds around him.

"Are you okay, Charlie?" Sara asked. "You can turn off the a/c vent on your side if you're cold."

He reached forward and did so, got the blanket tucked in all around him, then reconnected the seatbelt.

Ahhh. Much better.

Visions resumed, but pleasant ones. *Amasani* made him that blanket when he was a young child in New Mexico. He helped card the wool and collect dye materials, not knowing the blanket was for him.

He thought back to her visit in the hospital. Seeing her and feeling her love softened the sting that she was gone. Her hugs always warmed his heart.

Now he understood the "special gift" she promised to leave. Like never before, the blanket's every fiber radiated that same love, not only to his body, but his heart and soul.

One has to face fear, or forever run from it.
—Crow Proverb

25. ROAD TRIP

SKYVIEW APARTMENTS
LAKEWOOD, COLORADO
July 21, Saturday
8:20 a.m.

Eddie scrutinized his reflection in the bathroom mirror. The alcohol-soaked wad of toilet paper used to get rid of the dye stains along his hairline left a glaring white line where it likewise removed the fake tan.

Damn it.

He combed his hair forward to cover it up, but after years of wearing it straight back, it rebelled by sticking out straight.

"Fine," he grumbled, and pulled on an NRA baseball cap.

He *did* look different. So much so, every time he passed a mirror, he did a double-take. Which was good. His hair had gone from dirty blond to black, his ice-blue eyes now seeing the world through brown contact lenses.

Cool—built-in sunglasses.

He grinned. He should ditch *Johannsen* along with his father's Scandinavian appearance and just go with Eddie Schwartz, his mother's maiden name, or one of his aliases. For a lousy hundred bucks he could change it legally.

Great idea.

A whole new identity.

He'd always been clean-shaven, something he acquired a taste for in the military, but maybe a bit of scruff would work, too.

Fortunately, his beard was dark enough, it didn't give away his dirty little secret.

Confident he was no longer recognizable as that infamous dude on TV, he was ready to venture out. First, the grocery store to pick up a twelve-pack, then that Reynolds bitch's place to see what was going on. With luck, maybe he could still get a job with the construction crew.

He chuckled—for which looking Hispanic couldn't hurt, though contradicted by his six-foot-three frame.

The bugs inside her place had been extremely quiet lately. Maybe she was out at the cabin again. Or did another search and destroy bug sweep.

He ditched the hat for his headset, turned on his laptop, and logged into BKSS's surveillance website, grinning that Keller hadn't blocked him. He'd check the condo's audio first, then try the cabin.

Aha! Voices!

That was her, all right, but who was that other person? Definitely a guy. Her old man? Maybe.

Wait—there were two different guys, maybe more. WTF? A quick channel switch to video showed nothing—out of camera range.

Damn!

He switched back to audio. Everything was silent. They must have left.

Oh, well.

No problem.

This was definitely worth a drive-by to see what the hell was going on.

With one final glance in the mirror, he put on the hat, grabbed his keys and wallet, then headed out to his truck. As he backed out he promptly remembered why he never wore a hat—he may as well have blinders on. He snarled with frustration as he flipped it around, replicating an appearance he despised on others,.

Checking the result in the visor's vanity mirror busted him up.

His own mother wouldn't recognize him now.

SARA'S CONDO PARKING LOT
DENVER
July 21, Saturday
9:15 a.m.

Sara sat in the driver's seat, pairing her Bluetooth with the car's media system, then inserting the ear bud while Mike waited by her open window. Even with communications along the way, they reviewed their plan once more before heading out to pick up Connie.

He adjusted his holster to a more comfortable driving position, looked satisfied, then rested his arms on the window frame.

Sara's mind cycled. Should she get her Glock? She'd been less diligent carrying with Mike around. And he was now, so she could leave well-enough alone.

Or maybe not.

He'd be in a different vehicle for hundreds of miles.

"Hold on," she said, fumbling in her purse for the keys. "I need to get my gun. If nothing else, I shouldn't leave it here when I'll be gone a day or so."

"Good idea," he agreed.

She narrowed her eyes at the glaring *No Trespassing* sign as she went inside, then climbed the stairs to the office where she kept it in the bookcase. As she lifted it from the hollowed out tome, she realized that was pretty stupid. The spooks found her other one in that very spot. Her father would flip out if he knew.

Oh, well. Dealing with that could wait.

Not wanting to wear it while driving, she nonetheless retrieved her holster, just in case. Getting it out from the dresser's bottom drawer, her shoulder-length curls flopped into her face. When she tucked them behind her ear, something hit the floor.

The ear bud.

Charlie was in such a hurry she didn't bother doing anything with her hair other than brush it out. The quickest remedy was a French braid. She started at the crown, tucked in a few strands from each side until it was all included, then braided it to the end where she secured it with a hair tie.

She reinserted the ear bud.

There. Much better.

When she got back, Mike still stood between their vehicles. "Okay, I think we're good to go," he said. "I'll follow you to Boulder, then wait in that shopping center on Lookout, just down from the turnoff to Will's."

"Sounds good."

As she eased back in the driver's seat she glanced at Charlie. His eyes were closed, seat reclined, and looked no better than the previous day. Worse, in fact. Probably too much activity. He sounded a little better, but still hoarse, breathing raspy and labored.

It was apparent he slept in his clothes. His shirt was still buttoned wrong like the day before, but she didn't want to embarrass him by pointing it out. She lambasted herself for not insisting that he sleep on the futon instead of the couch, even if she had to help him up the stairs. He hadn't eaten much, either, just a few bites from a can of vegetable soup the night before and a piece of dry toast and coffee that morning.

Not good.

She tossed the holster in back, then put the handgun in her purse on the console.

"Gearing up...for a game of...cowboys and...Indians...when we get to...the reservation?"

She muttered, "Uh huh," as she pulled on her seatbelt, not sure whether or not he was joking.

Mike climbed into Charlie's pickup, then signaled her to go ahead. Again, she eyed her passenger with concern. "You doing okay? There's no hurry. You can rest up a few days here, if you want."

His eyes remained closed. "No. That is where...I need to be. Thank you for...taking me. I'm sorry for...being so much...trouble."

"Oh, shut-up, Charlie. You know you'd do this for me if things were reversed. Just let me know if you need to stop. To rest, eat, stretch, pee, whatever. Our plan is to grab something in Casper, but we can stop sooner if you need to."

"Whatever you do...is fine. I'm really...not hungry."

"Okay. How's your stomach otherwise?"

"Fine."

"Okay, great." She forced a smile. "Let's roll."

They drove in silence, until she got on Highway 36, heading north. Seeing his eyes were open, she decided to bring something up that had been troubling her since the night before.

"I'm sorry you're so uncomfortable around Mike."

"*Hmmmph.* He put me...in handcuffs...threw me in a...squad car, then shoved me into...a jail cell and locked...the door. I can't...forget that."

"I'm sorry, Charlie. He was—"

"—just doing his job," he snarled, a bitter mocking tone riding his scratchy voice. "Yeah, yeah, I know. Like Johannsen...at the wreck. Or your cabin. Just doing...his job."

She flinched, remarks hitting the bullseye.

He exhaled through his nose. "I'm sorry, Sara. Every time...I see him, it brings...all that back. If I felt better...I could probably...tolerate it. I'm sorry it...bothers you."

"No, no, it's okay," she replied, eyes fixed on the road. "I get that. I'm just sorry it upsets you. He's actually a pretty good guy. When we get to Dad's, I can tell him we've decided we're okay and send him back to help with the condo."

"Sara, no—"

"Listen. I can drive your truck and Connie can take her car. Dad can take Mike back to Denver. Connie going was my original plan, anyway."

"No. I'm fine. I think it's...a good idea...to have someone ...looking out for you."

"Are you sure? I'm okay with just Connie. And I do have my trusty handgun."

"No. I mean it...Forget I said...anything. Please. I appreciate what...you're doing."

"Okay."

Her eyebrows pinched together. Bryan was inclined to hold grudges, too. She stifled a sigh.

At least the two men weren't riding in the same vehicle, a sure recipe for spontaneous combustion of the testosterone kind.

HIGHWAY 36 NORTH
July 21, Saturday
9:24 a.m.

Eddie's grin was so wide his cheeks hurt. Had he hit the motherlode or what? He had no idea where they were going or why, but it looked as if he had the whole crew in his sights. As he drove along a hundred yards behind the cop, driving what he was sure was the Indian's truck, he tried to fit the pieces together.

So the Indian was alive, but looked like an extra from *The Walking Dead*.

What the hell happened?

Did Keller manage a hit, albeit a failed one?

And why was that small town cop there? Was he undercover? Or no longer on the force? He suspected he was a troublemaker, clear back at the accident scene. Asked too many questions, didn't like his attitude.

Clearly they were up to something. It was just a matter of what.

They exited in Boulder.

He followed.

The chick's old man lived up there. Was he going along, too? When they reached Lookout Drive, the cop pulled into a shopping center while the chick's SUV made the turn into her father's residential area.

WTF?

Eddie turned into a Valero station a half block away, hoping he had time to top off his tank. He secured the nozzle, then leaned against the truck with his arms folded.

What was going on?

Was the cop some kind of secret?

He threw back his head and laughed.

Busted!

He paid cash for the gas, then pulled over to the air station to check his tires, keeping an eye out for any movement by the Ranger or the chick's return. If he hadn't seen them leave together, he'd think she wasn't supposed to know he was following.

He lit a cigarette and sucked in a long, thoughtful drag. This was way more fun than taking orders from Keller. Maybe getting fired was a good thing. Maybe he was meant to work alone. He'd done most the work, anyway, then taken all the flack. This was much better.

When he saw her SUV returning he stomped out the cigarette and jumped in the cab. There was another person, a woman, in the car now, the Indian in back. As expected, the cop followed. He waited until a few cars passed, then did likewise.

They kept going north, then got on Highway 119, obviously not returning to Denver. They continued past Longmont, eventually returning to Interstate 25, still heading north.

Where the hell were they going?

INTERSTATE 25 NORTH
July 21, Saturday
10:38 a.m.

Just past Wellington, the road was straight, converging to a dot on the horizon. Sara's side view mirror showed Charlie's truck a hundred yards or so back. Nothing but grass-strewn, rolling prairie stretched in all directions. Traffic was sparse, an occasional eighteen-wheeler or pickup towing a travel trailer.

"Sure is desolate country," Connie commented, switching the sun visor to the side window.

"Definitely. I'm sure glad Mike is back there. This isolation is creepy. If anything happened, like rolling your car in a ditch, it could take weeks before anyone found you."

She glanced at Charlie in the mirror. He'd said nothing since leaving Boulder. Wrapped in his blanket, more often than not he looked as if he were sleeping. Now his eyes were open but unfocused. Why the frown? Was he not feeling well? Did he need a barf bag?

"Charlie? You doing okay?"

"Someone is...following us."

Besides being hoarse and short of breath, his voice lacked emotion.

"Yes, I know. That's Mike. In your truck."

"I know that, Sara. There's someone...else. Farther back."

"There is? How do you know that?"

"Because I...see him."

Sara checked her rear and side view mirrors. All she could see was his truck, perhaps another vehicle some distance behind it, no more than a dot. As touchy as he'd been lately contradicting him seemed ill-advised.

She did her best to remain calm even though a spark of anxiety sizzled in her chest.

"What else can you tell me?"

"It's black...a Dodge pickup. The guy...from the raid."

Her heartrate bolted into hyperdrive.

How could that be?

She voice commanded the car's media system to call Mike.

He picked right up. "Is everything okay?"

His reply blared into her ear via the Bluetooth. She blinked hard and turned down the volume. "Maybe not. Is there someone behind you?"

"Yes, but quite a ways back. I can't tell what kind of vehicle it is, except it's not a semi. Why?"

"Charlie says we're being followed. By a black pickup."

"A Dodge...Ram," Charlie prompted.

Sara passed on the information, fear's heavy cloak folding around her.

"I'll slow down and see if he moves in closer so I can get a better look."

"Okay. I'll slow down, too."

Trying not to hyperventilate, she disengaged the cruise control, slowing from just over seventy to sixty-five.

Or maybe she should speed up.

If only there were an exit somewhere, the only option jamming it into four-wheel drive and going cross-country.

Which a pickup could easily do as well.

She stayed on the call, nerves on full fight-or-flight alert.

How could Charlie know such a thing?

There was no denying the certainty in his halting voice. Whether crazy or spot-on, either justified the knot in her stomach.

Those people caused two wrecks in the past few months, one of which killed her husband.

Vehicular homicide was their specialty.

Panic smoldered just below the flash point, her only comfort that Mike was right there.

Could he stop them? *How?* Shoot out their tires?

What if she and Connie had gone alone?

She reached over to her purse with an unsteady hand, fingering the gun.

Which wasn't loaded.

Not unusual, considering it was stashed away, but in all the rush she forgot to grab a box of bullets.

"The guy's closing in," Mike reported in her ear. "He's about fifty yards back. I can't see the driver, but it *is* a black pickup. Hard to tell on the make. It has a huge after-market bumper with a full grille guard. When we left Boulder I noticed one like that parked at a gas station. Shiny black with tinted windows. Other than being fairly tall, the driver looked Hispanic."

"Eaglefeathers will...stop him."

Based on his tone, Charlie may as well have said the sky was blue or the sun rose in the east.

Sara studied him in the rearview mirror. His eyes were closed, brow suggesting intense concentration.

"WHOA!"

The volume of Mike's exclamation crackled through the ear bud, loaded with unmitigated shock. "Whoever it is, the guy just swerved across the inside lane to the median, then back to the shoulder and stopped in a cloud of dust. Looks like he had a blowout."

Mouth agape, Sara checked Charlie via the mirror. His eyes were open amid a strange, satisfied simper.

"Did you do that, Charlie?"

"No. My grandfather...did."

Her neurons fired, searching vainly for an explanation, rational or otherwise. "How?"

"Doesn't...matter. No one will...follow us now. We are...safe. He will...protect us."

Tension sculpted Connie's face. "What's going on?"

Sara wasn't sure herself. "We were being followed, but the guy had a blowout or something."

Shock radiated from her startled features. "And Charlie had something to do with that?"

"No, it was...Eaglefeathers," he confirmed from in back. "We are fine...now. It's...okay. Just keep...driving."

"Did Charlie just say he had something to do with that?" Unvoiced questions inflected Mike's voice.

"Indirectly, Mike, but yes."

"Wow. It's a good thing he's on our side. I'll call your father and put him on alert. If it's the guy from the video, he may be headed back to your place, figuring we'll be gone. Also, that he's modified his appearance."

"Good idea."

She ended the call, then glanced back at Charlie. His eyes were fixed somewhere far away, his enigmatic expression one she'd never seen before—on anyone.

Dr. Bishop's words mingled with Patrice's regarding Charlie's post-accident fate.

This was not the same man she sat with under a blanket gazing at the stars.

INTERSTATE 25 NORTH
July 21, Saturday
10:50 a.m.

Eddie crouched down to examine the front driver-side tire. The tread was split from the steel belt, almost as if it melted. A brand new Michelin with less than two thousand miles. The truck hadn't even been off-road yet.

It had to be defective.

Shaking his head, he realized he had no idea where the jack assembly was, much less how to get to the spare. YouTube worked great for such things, but his cell signal was so weak the video wouldn't load.

He spit out an expletive, then dug the owner's manual out of the glovebox. The jack assembly was under the passenger seat.

He got it out.

Okay. . .Why the hell was the shaft so goddamn long?

Oh. . . A crank to lower the spare from beneath the rear undercarriage.

The process alone, particularly the learning curve, took far longer than expected. The first thing he'd do when he got back was buy an after-market bed-mounted spare kit so he'd never have to go through this crap again.

By the time he finished up, close to an hour had elapsed. He tossed the damaged tire in back, not bothering to secure it underneath. It was going back, anyway, so why bother?

He lit a cigarette, then stared down the highway to where his quarry had long since disappeared. Catching up might be possible, but at this point why bother?

Screw it.

Their being gone was valuable information in and of itself.

He swung a U-turn across the weed-infested median and headed back. His lucky little excursion had revealed a significant amount of intelligence, even if he didn't know where the hell they were going. He was willing to bet their destination was far enough away they wouldn't be back that day, maybe longer.

With them out of the picture, there was plenty he could accomplish back in Denver.

From the moment the British set foot in North America, they began driving off native residents. By 1830, the continent's original inhabitants retained only one hundred thousand of the approximately million square miles in the United States east of the Mississippi River.
—Unworthy Republic, p. xv

26. WYOMING

CHILI'S GRILL AND BAR
CHEYENNE, WYOMING
July 21, Saturday
11:22 a.m.

It was a solemn bunch who sat in Chili's ordering lunch. They chose a place a few blocks from the Interstate across from the airport, in case the man in the black pickup fixed his blown tire fast enough to catch up.

Their original plan was to stop halfway in Casper, but after the unsettling incident, they all agreed to stop earlier. Sara, on the booth's inside seat, wasn't hungry, but needed to eat. Still shaken, her entire body tingled. No wonder they called it *shock*, the sensation like being zapped by an electrical charge.

She braced her arms against her ribs, trying to still her hands gripping the menu. Familiar with is contents, she scanned it with unseeing eyes for several moments before her mind settled down. Seeing they had lettuce wraps, an all-time favorite, she decided on them.

Charlie, directly across the table, was quiet, almost sullen, ignoring Mike beside him. It was as if he had a force-field around him, pushing the man away. He looked somewhere between disgruntled and offended, perhaps thinking they didn't believe

271

him, either about what caused the blowout or the man returning to Denver.

Sara did, but wasn't sure why. He, too, stared at the menu, but didn't appear as if he were reading it. Remembering he couldn't see very well, maybe he couldn't.

"Do you need some help, Charlie? she asked.

"I'm fine... I know...what I want."

Mike gave him repeated sideward glances, as if he were within stinging range of a man-sized scorpion. Connie, next to Sara, usually chipper and optimistic, suddenly looked her age and entirely overwhelmed. Even her auburn hair drooped.

So much for a simple road trip.

To think she'd actually considered leaving Mike behind. Then again, it was apparently Charlie who saved the day.

But how?

She was dying to ask him what was going on, but knew it wasn't something he'd explain in front of everyone else.

Maybe he wasn't sure himself.

The waiter, a young Native American with a ponytail trailing down his back, came by with water and took their drink orders. Everyone requested iced tea except Charlie, who wanted a cup of hot water with lemon. The waiter gave him a friendly nod, which softened the persistent furrow in his brow.

Her neck was tightening up, vestiges of anxiety coupled with dual whiplashes the past few months. She dug an ibuprofen out of her purse as discreetly as possible and chugged it down.

She looked up.

Charlie was watching with knowing, steady eyes.

She smiled.

He scowled.

She'd never seen him so stressed.

A tremendous roar thundered overhead, rattling the windows.

Charlie straightened, eyes wide, as if ready to dive beneath the table.

Goosebumps slithered up her arms when, in a flash, his expression mirrored Bryan's when they left the PURF site—one of sheer panic.

A glance outside revealed the source, an incoming Southwest Airlines 737. His eyes closed as his shoulders relaxed, hand clutching his right side.

Her thoughts wandered back to what the doctor told her. No doubt his recovery would take much longer and be far more difficult than expected.

If at all.

Going to the reservation, for whatever reason, was a good thing. He'd been traumatized, physically and emotionally. Chilling out with his own people and reconnecting with his roots was what he needed.

Part of it was potentially PTSD—not surprising, considering—which also might not ever go away.

Connie ordered a Cobb salad; Mike, a hamburger with onion rings; and Charlie, scrambled eggs, bacon, and toast. They ate in silence, the only exception a few favorable comments about the food.

At one point, her eyes met Charlie's across the table. His response to her unvoiced concern chilled her to the bone—that of a cornered animal. One that was lost and very frightened.

When the check came, Charlie held out his hand.

"I will pay," he said. He squinted at the tab, then pulled enough bills out of his wallet to cover it, plus a generous tip. He tucked them in the folder and set it on the table. "Can we...go now?"

Everyone scrambled to get up, uncomfortable with the unexpected directive, but hesitant to argue.

Connie wrung her hands. "Uh, if you don't mind, I'd like to use the little girl's room."

"And I need to wash my hands after those lettuce wraps," Sara added.

"We may as well all make a pit stop while we can," Mike agreed. "We have a long drive ahead."

When Sara came out of the bathroom, Charlie was standing out front, alone. She high-tailed it out the door, hoping to speak with him, even for an instant. She stepped up beside him and touched his arm.

He jumped like a spooked rabbit.

Her hand jerked back.

"I'm so sorry. I didn't mean to startle you. Are you okay?"

He stared straight ahead. "The only thing...I know right now is...I'm going where...I belong. How about...you? I saw you...take that...pill."

"I'm fine, Charlie. Just a little stiff. Don't worry about me."

"Why didn't you...say something...about my shirt?"

"Your shirt? Oh." She glanced over, seeing he'd buttoned it correctly. "Didn't seem important."

"It looked...stupid."

"I'm sure no one noticed. By the way..."

Before she could ask what happened with the black truck, the others came out. Connie put a snug arm around her, the side hug saturated with unspoken understanding.

"Would you like me to drive, Sara?"

"Thanks, but it's okay. I'm fine." While tempting, keeping an eye on Charlie in the rearview mirror scored higher than fatigue.

Everyone piled back into their respective vehicles, topped off their tanks at a nearby filling station and picked up a few bottles of water, then filed back to the Interstate. Sara took the lead as they headed out across the most sparsely populated state in the contiguous United States.

Certainly the last place to run out of gas.

Or be alone, more grateful than ever that Mike was right behind.

Once beyond the city limits, desolate prairie soared past again, southbound traffic often miles apart. Charlie, swaddled again in his blanket, quickly dozed off. Connie took her tablet out of her tote bag.

"Any word from Dad?" Sara whispered.

Her step-mother sniffed before whispering back, "Every twenty minutes. He's going to spend the night at your place. Make sure everything's okay."

"Good idea."

"I love these crossword puzzles. I haven't had time to do any for a while."

"I know the feeling. They'd probably be good exercise for my brain."

"How's the concussion?"

"Better. But there are still times it feels like I hit a mental wall and my head might explode."

Connie's concerned gaze pierced her peripheral vision. "If you change your mind about driving, honey, just let me know."

"Thanks. I will."

Smalltalk ceased, any topic of interest nixed by the back seat passenger's imposing presence.

The terrain changed. Towering rock formations littered the vast steppe with a variety of crags and buttes as if Zeus or some other Mount Olympus deity had slung them asunder. Connie put away her tablet, commented on the unusual terrain a few times, then dozed off.

Sara's mind wandered with the advancing odometer, concern for Charlie's wellbeing dominating her thoughts.

If only Bryan were here, to help him through this.

Her, too, for that matter. Things had been so hectic following his death she'd barely had time to mourn other than at night, when crying herself to sleep over the cold space beside her had become the norm.

Charlie helped her through it as much—actually more—than her parents. He missed Bryan, too, their shared grief creating a bond. He took considerable risks helping solve the mystery of Bryan's death. Even to the point of being arrested.

No wonder he hated Mike.

She thought back to bailing him out and taking him to the impound to pick up his truck. Due to the fact the incident was directly related to helping her, she never expected him to pay her back. Yet he did, protests notwithstanding.

They'd gone through so much together the past three months.

That raid on her cabin remained a regular on her nightmare playlist. The man dozing in back was far different from the one who'd defied a band of armed commandos, standing fearlessly before them as her protector.

Where she found the courage to step around him and order them out of her house she'd never know. Strange how she felt less fear then with a cadre of automatic rifles pointed at her than she did now.

She chuckled to herself, remembering when he called her Wonder Woman.

A glance in the mirror indicated he was sound asleep, breathing regular but wheezy.

Could he recover from this?

Hopefully.

But once they got to the reservation, Charlie would be gone from her life, too.

Her throat closed and eyes teared up. She dug a tissue from her purse to wipe her eyes and nose. The last time she'd gotten emotional while driving, triggered by Sarah McLachlan's *Angel* on the radio, she'd been run off the road by a semi loaded with freshly cut logs.

She hadn't listened to music while driving since.

Alright.

Enough.

Get a grip, Reynolds.

If either of her passengers saw her crying it would make it worse. She didn't want anyone worrying about her. The looming meltdown needed to end, *now*.

She bit her lip, took a few deep breaths, then focused all her attention on the road ahead. Trees clung to rugged bluffs, landscape greener. The GPS on the dash explained: Chugwater Creek.

After passing Wheatland an hour later, the Laramie Mountains came into view, their profile chopping the western horizon. The Bluetooth dinged. Her attention shifted from endless pavement to the dash; Mike's usual text.

Everyone doing okay up there?

She dictated her response via voice command, low enough it missed a few syllables.

Yes. They... bo... sleep.

How are you doing?

OK.

Another hour and the road veered in the same direction as the glaring sun plodding across a cloudless sky. Rolling hills rumpled flatland, an occasional pond, exits to multiple small towns, most invisible from the highway.

The trip meter declared three hours eighteen minutes and a hundred and eighty-four monotonous cruise-control miles had transpired since leaving Cheyenne.

At last green highway signs promised approaching civilization. More ranches, fence lines, and stylized ranch gates, living time capsules of the untamed wild west. Billboards sported cowboy motifs promoting Casper's restaurants and real estate.

Sara ached, muscle spasms searing her neck in concert with twinges from her pinned hip. Tension from the incident with the black truck had never entirely dissipated, either.

Green exit signs beckoned.

Her Bluetooth dinged. Another text from Mike.

Should we stop to top off our tanks?

She stretched the best she could behind the wheel, debating. The fuel gauge read a hair above half. The Lexus was getting great mileage on the open road. No doubt that was enough to reach Sheridan, another hundred-fifty miles away. A couple more hours, give or take.

Keep going? Or stop?

A glance at her slumbering passengers provided the answer.

I'd like to keep going. Do you need to stop?

No.

See you in Sheridan.
She smiled. The perfect title for a chick flick.

LAKEWOOD, COLORADO
July 21, Saturday
12:33 p.m.

The route to his apartment took Eddie past the dealer where he bought his truck, so he stopped to ask about the tire. They referred him to a Michelin dealer a few blocks away, so he headed there.

The technician, a skinny black kid about nineteen, was as mystified as he was about the damage, having never seen anything like it before. The manager showed no qualms about replacing it.

He stood outside the open service area having a smoke while the kid removed the damaged tire from the rim and set the new one.

"Do you want it back in the spare compartment, mister?" the kid asked.

"Yes, I'd appreciate it. Sure is a bitch to get to, ain't it?"

The kid laughed, but had undoubtedly done it enough times it only took a minute. He tipped the kid ten bucks, picked up a Whopper at the Burger King around the corner, then returned to the freeway. By then, he'd killed enough time that lunch time traffic had lightened up.

He no sooner stepped into his apartment when his cell rang.

His hopes soared.

Keller telling him to come back, perhaps? He pulled it from his pocket expectantly. The 240 area code and number were unfamiliar. He debated. Probably another one of those damn calls about a car warranty when his truck was brand freakin' new.

"Yeah," he snarled, ready to tell the guy, or most likely recording, to piss off.

The voice was deep, harsh, and abrupt. "This is your contact. I'm at the airport. I need you here now or the price goes up."

It took a moment to register.

WTF? Was Keller on something when he fired him? Did he forget to tell Mac?

Eddie grinned. Didn't matter. Either way, he could still do the job. Hell, after what that dumb bitch did, he'd do it for free.

"Which airport?" he asked. "Denver?"

"Centennial."

"In Englewood?"

"Yeah. What's your ETA?"

"Uh, as soon as I can."

"Not good enough, dipshit. I'm on the tarmac. Need an ETA."

"Uh, it's around ten miles. Depending on traffic, half-hour or less. Where?"

"General aviation, north end. Stay on South Peoria where it splits to Bronco. First exit. Hard right into parking lot. I'll meet you on the building's north side."

"On my way."

He pounded down the stairs to his truck and zoomed off. Highway 6 took him to I-25, mind on fire with anticipation. This was too perfect. If he hadn't had that cursed flat he would have missed the call or been hopelessly far away to make it in time.

Was he on a roll or what?

He damn near missed the Arapahoe exit, cutting someone off, bad, barely making it amid squealing tires and the angry blast of a horn. Traffic lights plagued the way to Peoria, but the guy's directions from there were perfect. He parked at the far end of the lot and checked his watch.

Twenty-two minutes.

He got out and headed toward the designated place.

After a few minutes, the person he assumed was his contact came around from behind the building. The man strolled down the sidewalk with a slight limp, then sat on a bench under a tree. Older guy. Mustache, somewhat stooped over. Khaki cargo shorts and a Hawaiian shirt.

No one else in sight.

Eddie stood there a moment, thinking. Was it a trap? Past wrong assumptions slammed him like a wrecking ball. This seemed too good to be true.

Was it?

The guy spotted him and stood up.

Would he be shot point blank? Or the opportunity of his life?

He set his jaw and walked the rest of the way.

"You working for Mac?" the guy asked, voice like crushed ice.

"Uh, yeah."

He removed a Crown Royal bag from his thigh pocket. Eddie held his breath, on full alert. He opened it, then extracted a test tube with a smiley face sticker. It contained three long cotton-tipped swabs.

"Did Mac tell you how to use this stuff?"

"No, sir." His hopes crashed, dipping toward the horizon.

"Alright, listen up. Don't touch it or you're dead, understand? Works best injected or ingested. That or sustained physical contact. Long enough to reconstitute. Is your mark male or female?"

"Female."

"Wine glasses are good, better yet a toilet seat. It's a sure bet she'll use that. It dries clear with no residue."

"Perfect," Eddie chuckled.

"Any questions?"

"Yeah. What is it?"

"Hell if I know. Some Russian shit left over from when Reagan ended the Cold War. It works. Gotta go. Good luck."

He slipped the test tube back in the bag, pulled the golden strings tight, and handed it over. Without further ado, the man turned and walked toward the back of the building where he signaled a twin-engine Cessna Corsair in the holding area. The engines chattered as the props started to turn, then ramped up to a steady roar.

Eddie grinned.

He was still alive and the chick as good as dead.

> *They were the best cavalry soldiers on earth. In charging up toward us they*
> *exposed little of their person, hanging on with one arm around the neck and one*
> *leg over the horse, firing and lancing from underneath the horses' necks, so that*
> *there was no part of the Indian at which we could aim.*
> —*Captain Anson Mills, June 1876*

27. MEMORIES

ENROUTE SHERIDAN, WY.
July 21, Saturday
3:18 p.m.

Rolling prairie graduated to steeper hills, then the Big Horn Mountains, road no longer straight. Sara's Bluetooth dinged. Another *RU-OK* text from Mike. Two hours later a town called Buffalo promised gas and snacks, Sheridan another thirty-five miles.

Road weary and achier than ever, Sara checked the fuel gauge. The warning light was on, but she kept going. If she stopped now, she might not ever get back in the car.

At least Mike was right there if she ran out. Hopefully he wouldn't, either.

Before long, an increase in billboards confirmed their arrival in Sheridan was imminent.

The rearview mirror reflected movement in back.

Charlie coughed and cleared his throat. "Where are...we?" he asked, squinting at a passing sign.

"Almost to Sheridan."

"Already? Have you...stopped...for gas?"

"Not yet."

"How much...do you have?"

She glanced at the fuel gauge. "Not much. I'm running on fumes. I'll take the first off-ramp and find the nearest gas station."

"No. Take the...third exit. There's one...not far from there where...my grandfather always went. It has...a convenience store, deli...and tobacco shop. Eaglefeathers always bought...the best pipe tobacco...there. I need some...for my uncle."

"Your uncle?"

"Yes. I will stay...with him...on the reservation. He is a... medicine man. I need him...to help me."

Multiple turns later, his directions brought them to the Common Cents Travel Plaza, a modern-looking shopping center with a vast parking lot designed for big rigs. Gas pumps were around back. She pulled into one, Mike claiming the one beside it.

"I will pay...for the gas for...both of you," Charlie said. "They have...good food. We can all go...inside to get...something to eat."

"Sounds good. How much farther to the reservation?"

"Busby is about...eighty miles." He opened the door and started to get out.

"Hey! Where are you going?"

"I will pump...the gas for you."

"Nonsense. I can do it. You just relax." He paused, but didn't close the door. "Charlie. I mean it. I can do it."

He hung his head, hesitated another moment, but obeyed.

She got out, craned her neck to work out the kinks, then walked over to the neighboring pump to update Mike.

Back at her own, she designated a cash sale and set the dispenser in place. While gasoline gushed into the tank she placed both hands against the rear hatch door and leaned forward to stretch her lower back. The nozzle clunked. She secured it back on the pump, tore off the receipt to take inside, and glanced at the meter: *22.9 gallons.*

The tank held twenty-three.

She glanced upward with a silent prayer of heartfelt gratitude. Muffling a groan as she got back in the driver's seat, she followed Mike around front and parked.

COMMON CENTS TRAVEL PLAZA
SHERIDAN, WYOMING
5:59 p.m.

While the others strolled over to the deli, Charlie fumbled a hundred dollar bill and a twenty from his wallet and laid it on the counter for the gas. As the young indigenous clerk rang up the sale, Charlie eyed the tobacco hanging on hooks behind the counter, trying to remember which one Eaglefeathers bought.

The labels blurred. Unknown fears swamped his mind, interrupting the task at hand.

What was wrong with his eyes? Were they going to be like this the rest of his life? What if Uncle Joe couldn't help?

"Can I assist you, sir?"

He blinked and turned toward the voice. Confusion burst upon him in a suffocating wave. His eyes were at counter level. The original clerk had either vanished or morphed into an imposing elder with long braids dappled with grey.

Before he could respond a voice from the past replied, "Yes, thank you. I would like four bags of Bull Durham."

His eyes widened and mouth fell agape.

Eaglefeathers towered beside him. The elder handed him the requested number of pocket-sized, muslin bags secured with red pull strings.

Like the ones in his grandfather's medicine bundle.

Years rolled back. The excursion from New Mexico with his father and grandfather. When Eaglefeathers named him *Okohomoxhaahketa*; Littlewolf in English.

His *Diné* mother nixed the official naming ceremony. The main reason Eaglefeathers came to visit. His father, Littlebear, was angry. *Very* angry. Rather than send him home to Montana on a Greyhound bus, his father insisted on driving, apologizing the entire way. When they arrived at the reservation, his grandfather named Charlie in a private ceremony with him and his father.

"Sir? Can I help you? Are you alright?"

The elder vanished. Charlie gripped the counter, journey back to the present as unsettling as the departure. He cleared his throat.

"Yes. I would like...three small bags, please."

The young man looked confused, regarding him as if he'd sprouted horns. "I'm sorry, sir. Which brand would you like? We do not have bags. Do you mean the small packages?"

His eyes closed, then blinked open as he drew in a deep breath through his nose. "Uh, right. Sorry. Bull Durham. I'd like some ...Bull Durham." He squinted toward where the bags had been, seeing only a rack with various packaged brands on hooks.

"I've never heard of that brand, sir. I'm afraid we don't carry it."

"Oh. Uh, okay. Then three...packages. Of your best one. Whatever...that is."

The young man held one out. "This is our most popular."

"That will...be fine."

He pulled another twenty from his billfold, collected his change and the plastic bag with his purchase, then made his way over to join the others.

Sara's eyes met his. "Are you okay?"

"I honestly...don't know."

Connie ordered a pizza, the cop a pulled pork sandwich, and Sara braised beef. Charlie got a burrito, but his appetite had disappeared at the tobacco counter. They ate in silence, then waited while the cop grabbed an espresso shot, prompting Sara and Connie to get cappuccinos.

Sara snuck another pill from her purse when she thought no one was looking. Her posture and tension around her eyes showed she was hurting.

Guilt roared through him.

Some day he'd make it up to her. He should be looking out for her, not the other way around.

The cop held the door as they filed out to their vehicles, Charlie instinctively heading for his truck. His hand searched his pocket for the keys, startled when they weren't there.

He sensed everyone's stare.

"Over here, Charlie," Sara called, her smile stiff. "I need your help finding my way back to the highway."

He ground his teeth at his foolish mistake, avoiding everyone's eyes as he climbed into her SUV.

Once everyone was settled in and buckled up she asked, "So now where, Charlie? Should I get back on the interstate?"

"No. There's a...shorter way."

Familiar with the alternative route, he directed her to Highway 314.

They crossed the Tongue River. A few miles later, a blue Montana-shaped sign emblazoned with a rising sun and jagged snow-covered peaks announced they'd crossed the state line.

ENROUTE MONTANA HIGHWAY 314
July 21, Saturday
6:46 p.m.

The two-lane highway growled beneath the tires, unlike the purr of the interstate, the road's rhythmic undulations like moguls on a ski run. Prairie grass sprawled upward to striated buttes. Whatever glacier carved them out eons before hadn't been sufficient to wipe them off the map, only claw vainly at their craggy sides.

Like the white man tried to wipe out Native Americans, Sara thought. *Yet, still they remain.*

No wonder Charlie's people were so connected to the land. It was everywhere to be seen. Upon it their lives depended, even though its harsh environment likewise threatened their survival. The two were well-matched.

Rugged.

Stoic.

Unconquerable.

So this was Charlie's home. It fit. The spirit of the land revealed more about him than she'd ever been able to discern. It explained that feral aspect she witnessed when he confronted the commandoes. Something her Western European blood could never entirely comprehend, despite being drawn to it in an inexplicable way.

You are beginning to understand who I am.

The words came directly into her mind. Their eyes connected in the rearview mirror. Goosebumps tickled her arms. Her own thoughts or imagination? Or merely the hypnotic effect of driving nine hours?

Shifting her attention back to the landscape, the vegetation looked greener, more soothing to the eye. Ironically, *God Bless America* sang through her mind.

From the mountains, to the prairies, to the oceans, white with foam. God Bless America, my home sweet home. . .

Before long a large creek appeared to the left, sustaining a rich, green valley filled with trees and vegetation. The roadway yielded to its path, no longer straight.

"That's...Rosebud Creek," Charlie volunteered from back. "Not too far ahead...off the road a ways, is an...open valley and small lake...where a great battle...took place. The white man...calls it the...*Battle of the Rosebud.* My people call it...*Where the girl ...saved her brother.*"

"That's an interesting name for a battle," Connie commented, then leaned over to extract her tablet from her bag.

"In our culture...women can be...warriors, even though...not all men qualify. Some men...were always needed...to maintain the...camp."

"I love it!" Sara said, laughing. "Gender equality at its best. So what's the story behind the battle?"

"Oh, no!" Connie interjected. "I was trying to find it online, but there's no service out here."

Sara glanced in the mirror, relieved Mike was right there. Would it be this way the rest of the trip?

"There's only service...along major...highways or cities," Charlie explained, as if reading her mind. "But that's...okay. I can tell you...about the...battle. What you'll find...online is...usually wrong. My grandfather told me...the story many times."

"Do tell us," Connie prompted. "It makes the area so much more memorable with a story attached."

"The battle took place...June 17, 1876."

"Seriously? That's my birthday!" Sara remarked, adding, "Okay, like a hundred-plus years later."

"Next year we can celebrate both," Connie added. "Sorry, Charlie. Go ahead."

"During the battle...a Cheyenne warrior...Comes in Sight...had his horse shot. While running away...from the soldiers, his sister...Buffalo Calf Road Woman...rode to his...rescue. Comes in Sight jumped...onto her horse and the two...got away."

"That's a great story," Sara said. "Did you win the battle?"

His laugh triggered a string of coughs. "Yes. General Crook had...a thousand soldiers...and two hundred scouts from...our enemies, the Crow and Shoshone. Chief Little Wolf...and Crazy Horse had...about three-hundred-sixty...warriors. We fought so well...they thought there were more. Crook got...his ass kicked...and returned to Goose Creek...outside Sheridan. This was about a week...before the Battle of...the Little Big Horn. Which we call...Battle of Long Hair. Crook's retreat...left Custer's troops short...a thousand men. That contributed...to their loss."

"Ha!" Sara said. "Perfect. Bryan always said 'Custer had it coming.'"

Charlie grunted derisively. "Yes, he did. Little Wolf...was a great general. He led and trained...warriors. The white men were impressed...how we hung over the side...of our horses while running...and fired at them...quite accurately. When we went to battle...we wore our best clothes...in case we were to meet...our Creator. We also...wore paint. Only Cheyenne...used paint in battle. It was inspired...by a vision Crazy Horse had. Paint is earned...through pledging...solemn ceremonies...and provides protection."

Ho'néoxháahketa   Vóohéhéve
Little Wolf   Morning Star
(1820 - 1904)   (1810 - 1883)

* * *

A rare photo taken in Washington, D.C. (1873) of the two strongest and bravest Northern Cheyenne Chiefs of the Western Plains Indian Wars of the late 1800s. They led the Morning Star people 1,500 miles north to Elk River (Yellowstone) from the barren land at Darlington Agency in Indian Territory, Oklahoma. The Northern Cheyenne claimed victory over many battles with the U. S. Government Army, never surrendering in their fight for their right to live in the land where they were born.

"Like what you wore when those commandoes raided the cabin? It certainly protected us then."

"Yes. The lightning bolts...on my cheeks show...the power of *Maheo*. The white dots represent...the hail in his dream. History books claim...Crazy Horse was Oglala Sioux. His mother was... but she died when he was...very young and he was raised...by his father...Chief American Horse. And he...was Northern Cheyenne."

"Are you related to Chief Little Wolf?" Connie asked.

"Yes. He's my uncle...several generations...back. He is one of the two...most important chiefs...at that time. The other was...Morning Star. In history books...he's usually called...Dull Knife."

"That's not a very complimentary name," Sara said.

"It isn't. His brother...gave it to him...because he didn't...want to fight. He was a...holy man and peace chief...A ceremonial man...who carried the...sacred red pipe."

"A peace chief? There's more than one kind?" Sara asked.

"Yes. The other is...warrior chief. Like Little Wolf...The people chose him...to be one of the four...Old Man Chiefs of the council...of forty-four chiefs...when he was only forty...years old. He carried the...sweet medicine bundle...a huge responsibility...day and night. On the reservation...we celebrate his homecoming...every April 1st."

"That's pretty impressive," Sara said. She pointed out the windshield. "What's that building, up there on the left?"

"That's the...Kirby Saloon. It's a bar, grill...and casino."

"Out in the middle of nowhere like this?"

"There are lots...of ranches we can't see. And we're getting close...to the reservation."

"This is a beautiful valley," Sara commented. "How does it stay so green? Do you get a lot of rain?"

"No. But lots of snow. There are many...open running spring waters...that flow into...Rosebud Creek. That creek flows...all the way to...the Yellowstone River."

"Look, Charlie!" Connie pointed to a green sign. "*Entering Northern Cheyenne Indian Reservation.* You're almost home!"

Sara glanced at the mirror to see his reaction. His eyes were glazed with tears.

"My ancestors paid...with their blood for...our homeland," he said. "They had to fight...the soldiers many...times. They basically walked back...from Oklahoma with a...few horses and rifles...and only sixty warriors."

Sensing how much the reservation meant to him, her eyes burned as well, every mile worth it to bring him home.

A short distance later, the road ended at a T-intersection with a stop sign and blinking red light. Arrows on a sign dead ahead indicated Billings to the left and Busby to the right.

Connie's tablet chirped multiple times. "Oh! I have a signal again."

"Which way, Charlie?"

"Right. Keep going 'til you see...the forty-foot tipi. Then turn right...at the road...just before that."

She turned as instructed onto Highway 212. "Forty foot tipi? Seriously? What's it made out of?"

"Wood."

A short time later, Connie pointed out the windshield. "That must be it, up ahead."

Sara squinted at the massive grey conical structure still a few hundred yards away.

"Years ago...it was a community center," Charlie went on. "Now it's abandoned...and falling apart. But still standing...and no one wants...to tear it down. Eaglefeathers told me...there used to be a small mercantile store there...but it's gone now, too."

The road crossed a creek, the towering tipi just ahead when Sara turned right on a dirt road to their final destination.

When there is true hospitality, few words are needed.
—Arapaho Saying

20. UNCLE JOE

NORTHERN CHEYENNE RESERVATION
MONTANA
July 21, Saturday
8:04 p.m.

Vice-like tension crushing every muscle released its grip, confirming he was where he belonged. For the first time since waking up three days before, Charlie's vision was crystal clear. Everything was identical to how he remembered it.

Identical.

The smell of sun-parched grass amid dry, dust-ridden air. Timelessness made his head spin. He closed his eyes and drew in a breath until the effort was arrested by pain.

When his lids eased open, panic struck like a flaming arrow. The auras were back. Now, mere heartbeats later, things were no longer the same. There were more houses, albeit small, humble ones, most with tin roofs, but fewer tar-paper shacks and trailers. The trees were taller, but not as many.

What was going on?

"Where should I go now, Charlie?"

Sara's question jolted him back to the present. Or at least what he thought was the present.

"Stay on this road...for about a mile and we'll be...at my uncle's ranch. There's a gate."

Weathered power poles lined the heavily rutted dirt road, clouds of dirt spewing behind them.

He grinned. The ex-cop was eating their dust.

The SUV crept forward, dodging dogs or a host of children of various ages. All stopped whatever they were doing, wide eyes fixed upon the unexpected paleface visitors in the big, fancy car.

When a wooden gate loomed before them, the ex-cop got out to open it, then closed it after both vehicles passed through.

A ranch style house painted sky blue appeared on his right. Poised above ground level, its porch of several steps indicated the presence of a full basement. The car eased to a stop.

"Is this it, Charlie?"

"Yes. This is...it."

Sara pulled off the road and stopped. Fernandez drove up beside her and rolled down the passenger-side window. "Should I leave the truck here? Or somewhere else?"

Charlie directed the answer to Sara.

"Here is fine."

She passed it on to the ex-cop, who pulled forward and parked. He got out, walked their way, and climbed in back across from him. The door banged closed with a hollow echo. He flinched when Fernandez reached toward him, then held out his hand to accept the keys.

Charlie forced his eyes to meet his. "Thank you for...bringing me home. I will go...now."

"Do you want us to wait and make sure everything is okay?" Sara asked, releasing the rear hatch.

"It's fine. My uncle has...a good heart. He will help me...or get someone who can."

He got out, gripping the sack with the bags of tobacco and his blanket, then collected his duffel bag from the back, strap slung over his shoulder.

He stood there a moment and blinked, wondering if his eyes were playing tricks again. The last time he'd been there was for his grandfather's burial. The house's siding changed abruptly from blue to tan and the bur oak beside it stretched toward the sky. A garage materialized as well as a small barn in back, the surrounding property strung with barbed wire.

Two horses stood beneath a box elder beside the barn, tails swishing.

He shifted his weight to keep his balance when his knees weakened to rubber. He blinked again.

It remained the same.

Which was real?

The front door opened and Eaglefeathers stepped out. His heartrate doubled.

Everything smeared with prismatic light.

The man morphed into Uncle Joe, his father's younger brother. Relief washed over him. The man's approach was slow and leisurely, as if Charlie being there was nothing unusual. He came over and stood before him.

"*Okohomoxhaahketa?*" he asked in Cheyenne.

Charlie stared into the man's questioning eyes.

"Yes."

He set down the blanket on the duffle bag, got out a package of tobacco from the plastic sack, then bent over slowly and placed it on the ground in front of him.

"I, uh, I need you to...to help me."

His uncle looked at it for a long moment, then back at him without picking it up.

Panic consumed him.

Is he refusing to help me?

He stooped down to retrieve it and placed it back in the sack, grateful Sara was still waiting.

Should I leave? Now what?

He hung his head, avoiding the man's eyes.

"Keep it until tomorrow," Joe said, patting his back. "Then we will talk."

His anxiety dissipated when the man wrapped his arms around him in a firm hug. "Welcome home. You are family. But first, won't you bring your friends inside? If you've come from Colorado, you've had a long drive."

The passenger side window of the SUV hummed open. "Is everything okay?" Sara called over.

"Won't you come inside?" Joe replied. "I'm sure you could use some food and a cold drink."

"Thank you," she said, "That's very kind of you." She pulled farther onto the property and turned off the engine, then everyone piled out.

"Joe Whitewolf," he said, holding out his hand, first to Sara and Connie, then Fernandez. "We haven't seen Littlewolf for a very long time. Thank you for bringing him home."

He placed an affectionate hand on Charlie's shoulder as he led them toward the porch where his wife and two teenage boys, both with long braids, stood watching.

"This is my wife, Star, and our two sons. Winter Hawk was named for her grandfather, and Risingsun is my youngest child. He is named after Star's great-grandfather."

Once inside, they were greeted by yet another family member, a large black dog named *Náhkòhe* for his resemblance to a bear cub.

The canine made a beeline for Fernandez, tail snapping back and forth as if greeting an old friend. He crouched down, grinning, as he greeted the mutt by name, then scratched him behind the ears.

Joe invited them to sit down and relax on a sprawling sectional couch which bore the scars of long-term family activity. As they all got settled, the dog remained by the ex-cop's side, ignoring everyone else.

Charlie didn't know whether to be jealous or accept the fact the ex-cop might be a good guy after all, based on such a blatant canine recommendation.

"We've been waiting for you since last week, Littlewolf," Joe said. "We knew you were coming home to the sweat lodge, that you needed to be with family."

Charlie's throat ached with emotion. No wonder he felt so compelled to come home.

"We have an elk roast and vegetables from the garden heating up," Star said. "How does some fresh baked pan bread sound?"

Star looked the same as he remembered, other than a few grey streaks accenting her waist-length hair. She motioned to her sons, who went into the kitchen to gather what was needed to set four places at the huge dining room table, the family having eaten hours before.

"Our sons got a young bull elk last fall up the head of Eaglefeathers Creek," Joe explained.

"Come, sit at our table," Star invited. "There's elk, roasted potatoes, radishes, onions, and corn on the cob." She turned to her younger son. "Prepare the food offering and take it outside to the grandfather spirits while our guests get settled."

Risingsun prepared a plate with small portions of meat, corn, potatoes, and a radish and went out the front door.

"I'll put on a fresh pot of coffee," Star went on. "Sara, before you leave you must teach me how you made that fancy braid in your hair. I've been around braids all my life and never saw anything like that."

Sara laughed and agreed.

As soon as Risingsun returned, they loaded up their plates and dug in. The buzz of dinner conversation faded in and out to a distant time when a different group gathered around that same table. Memories blended seamlessly with the present, except with different faces.

Back then, Uncle Joe had two young daughters and a son, plus Star was pregnant.

Where were the other cousins he remembered?

Of course—like himself, they were grown, these two born sometime after his last visit.

Following dinner, Connie helped the boys clear the table. Sara demonstrated how to make her "fancy braid" on Winter Hawk while Star and Risingsun watched. Then Star tried it, the young man's bearing one of fixed forbearance. Joe and Fernandez lounged on the couch swapping hunting tales like old friends.

Charlie remained quiet as past and present tangled together. Eventually, conversations wound down. His entourage exchanged glances, then got up to leave.

"We really appreciate your hospitality, but it's time for us to get going," Sara said. "Is there a motel in Busby where we can stay? If not, we can probably make it back to Sheridan before dark."

"The nearest motel is in Hardin, about an hour away on the way to Billings, so it's out of your way. You're welcome to stay here, if you like," Joe offered. "We raised a large family and have plenty of room."

"Thank you, but we've already imposed enough. We can just go back to Sheridan. Besides, you and Charlie have some catching up to do."

Joe's laugh came from deep in his chest. "I'll say we do. But it's not a problem for you to stay. It's the least we can do."

"Thank you, that's very kind, but you've already done so much, feeding us that wonderful meal. It's a good thing you made that pot of coffee, though, or I'm afraid I'd fall asleep."

"Then let us do one more thing for you," Joe said. "Pray for your safe return."

No one argued as Joe took the lead and petitioned *Maheo* that they return home safely.

When he finished, Connie said, "I haven't done any driving so far today. I can do the honors back to Sheridan."

"Stay on Highway 212 until you get to the Interstate," Joe said. "After sunset 314 has a lot of wildlife. Everything from skunks to elk."

Sara nodded agreement. "Thank you. I understand. We have lots of wildlife in Colorado, too."

She stepped forward and gave Charlie a firm hug. "Stay in touch, okay? I'm sure you'll get better in no time now that you're home."

His eyes burned as he thanked them again, the transition from caring friends to family more difficult than expected. As Sara followed Fernandez and Connie out the door, she gave him one final, lingering gaze that constricted his throat.

Would he ever see her again? Why did it feel as if the circumstances might not be favorable?

Consumed by ominous impressions, he failed to appreciate the laughter when *Náhkòhe* clearly wanted to go with his new friend, Risingsun holding him back as the dog barked farewell.

When Connie started the car, everyone went back inside except Charlie, who remained on the porch until the SUV disappeared in a cloud of dust.

Once he was back inside, Joe said, "You are very tired. I will take you downstairs where you will stay until you are ready to leave, one way or another."

Charlie grabbed his things, then lagged behind as he struggled to follow down bare wooden stairs to the basement. His uncle led him to a small room with a twin-size bed and dresser. A worn, grey rug covered most of the linoleum floor, a blue and white Cheyenne flag on the wall. He set his bag, tobacco, and *amasani's* blanket on the bed, then tried to keep up as he was shown around.

His cousins occupied another downstairs bedroom, plus a bathroom they'd all share. The rest of the basement was unfinished, but well-utilized. A washing machine and dryer were in one corner, a weight bench in another. On the far side, a block and tackle hung from the rafters for dressing out game, beside it a door that led outside at ground level,.

Being a medicine man and rancher, his uncle was well-provided for by the community. He was expected to be home and accessible when needed, which kept him from holding a regular job. Furthermore, he'd inherited eighty acres from Eaglefeathers, who received it by similar means, passed down through the family after acquiring it from the Indian Allotment Act of 1934.

Another part of him snarled at a world that imposed a far different scenario on too many of his people who'd view his primitive cabin back in Colorado as luxury accommodations.

Do you look upon the midnight robber and assassin as being a Christian, and trusty man? These Indians had not done one single wrong act to the whites, but were as innocent of any crime, as any beings in the world. And do you believe that Indians cannot feel and see, as well as white people? If you think so, you are mistaken. Their power of feeling and knowing is as quick as yours.
—*William Apes, 1836*

29. SURPRISES

MIKE'S CONDO
DENVER
July 22, Sunday
1:54 a.m.

Eddie parked his truck about a hundred feet from the vacant condo. The need for a speedy getaway wasn't likely, so no big deal. No one would notice at this hour, but no sense taking unnecessary chances, either.

He wore jeans, a brown t-shirt, and lightweight jacket to carry the test tube in the inside pocket. Nothing dramatic enough to arouse suspicion. Mercury vapor security lighting cast the area in pinkish orange, walkways marked by solar-powered path lights.

If anyone saw him he'd easily pass as a shift worker, either coming or going. Most windows were dark, a few flickering with a television broadcast viewed by some unfortunate insomniac.

He decided earlier not to bother wiring up the adjoining condo. Wasn't his job anymore. Besides, if she was dead in a few days, what did it matter? Nonetheless, while he was there, he wanted to check it out, see exactly what was going on. Something about it smelled fishy. Steps, quick and silent, took him to the empty unit's patio door where he donned a pair of neoprene gloves.

As expected, the sliding glass panels were locked, but unobstructed, allowing skillful entry in a matter of seconds.

He grinned at how lucky he'd been to discover the chick was out of town. The ultimate break-in convenience, like when she was at her cabin. In such situations he left his weapon in the truck. Being unarmed lessened the charges if, perchance, he did get caught.

His flashlight confirmed the place was being remodeled. Stripped down to the two-by-fours, all sheetrock gone, except a closet on the far side, walls intact.

Weird.

Rolls of pink fiberglass insulation were heaped up toward the back, some already nestled between uprights on the walls and rafters above.

Why such a complete renovation? A fire, perhaps? The only furnishings were a heavy-duty gun cabinet and an old metal desk. Strange, in what was supposed to be an unoccupied unit.

Or was it?

He held his breath, listening.

Silence.

He crept up the stairs. He checked each room to confirm no one was there. Thus assured, he slipped the flashlight in his back pocket and turned on the light. It revealed a double bed and dresser.

Was someone actually living there? He opened a drawer. Socks; another, T-shirts; yet another, men's underwear.

Interesting.

He took out one of the T-shirts, held it up. Men's XL. He folded it the way he found it and put it back. The bottom drawer contained jeans and a few pairs of khakis. He took one out. The waist was around thirty-eight, in-seam thirtyish. Like the shirt, he replaced it exactly how it was.

No doubt the ex-cop in that entourage was staying there. As he'd already figured out, he was protecting the Reynolds bitch.

He chuckled.

Good to know.

He turned off the light, hit the switch for the one on the stairwell, and treaded back down to the main floor. He glanced around one more time now that he could see better, then sat on the stairs, planning his next move.

Her place was bugged, so his entry would be monitored by his former employer.

Damn! He had the frequencies and could have turned them off.

Did it matter?

Did he care?

Would they?

If he was still on the job—for free, no less—why the hell would they?

With luck, which so far had been off the charts, he could get in the same way as here. If there was one thing Keller taught him, it was to always have Plan B. The first time he'd been there he was lucky enough to have her key. Since then, the lock had been changed, probably compatible with one of his masters.

Except he forgot his ring of skeleton keys at his apartment.

Damn!

He was good at picking locks, not so much a deadbolt.

The windows were too high off the ground without a ladder. Furthermore, if he broke one, they'd know someone had been there. The less they suspected, the better.

Another thought struck. Knowing the cop was staying there, maybe he should put one of those swabs to good use there as well.

Sure, why not?

But where? Guys only sat on the can to take a crap while the broad would make multiple contacts. Would one be enough? What other options were there? Certainly there wouldn't be any wine glasses.

Coffee mug, maybe.

He got up and turned on the kitchen light. Sure enough, one sat on a makeshift plywood countertop next to the roughed-in sink. He picked up the black cup, its interior sullied with a puddle of dregs.

Would the cop wash it before using it again?

If he simply rinsed it out without disturbing the rim, it might not be a problem. If he washed it, which was possible, given the bottle of detergent on the window sill, it wouldn't work.

He chuckled. Maybe he should wash it for him.

Except if he was a really, really good cop, he'd notice and suspect something.

If the guy only washed the inside and maybe the rim, the handle still might retain enough.

What did he have to lose?

Yeah.

Do the toilet *and* the mug.

He went back upstairs to the master bath, sat on the edge of the tub across from the toilet, and removed the vial from his jacket. Now that he was about to open it, a wave of foreboding hit. Something about that happy face gave him the willies.

He held his breath as he removed the stopper, set it on the tub beside him. Reached in and plucked out one of the swabs. Balanced it on the edge of the tub as he replaced the stopper and returned the vial to his inside pocket.

He lowered the toilet seat, picked up the swab, then carefully traced a path around it. Waited a moment for it to dry. As promised, not a trace. He grinned as he put it back like he found it.

He returned downstairs, no longer concerned with being quiet. He picked up the mug by the handle, then wrapped his thumb and forefinger around the bottom as he rubbed the swab all around the handle, especially the inside, then the rim. He laughed at the FBI seal with "10 Year Service Award" below. It got a few extra swipes.

There.

He balked. Where exactly was the damn thing, anyway? Oh, well, a few inches shouldn't matter. He set it on the plywood, hoping the guy wouldn't notice if it was a little off.

What now with the used swab?

He looked around. A black contractor bag leaned against the far wall. He dropped the swab inside, shaking it by the edges until it disappeared within the debris.

His eyes shifted to the closet.

Something was off.

Why was it finished when nothing else was? Curious, he opened the door. A huge utility panel covered most of the back wall, which was made of cinder blocks.

He frowned.

What the hell could be behind it, given there was a freakin' firewall?

Ha! Wiring the place wouldn't have worked, anyway.

He tugged it open a crack.

Light shot through the opening to another closet beyond the concrete blocks.

Holy shit!

His hand clamped over his mouth, too late to stifle the spontaneous snigger that snuck out.

He went back to turn off the lights, got his flashlight back out, and stepped through the opening, grinning.

This day just kept getting better and better.

Maybe he should take what money he had left and go to Vegas before this lucky streak ran out. Make up for last time, when the only thing he came home with was an ashtray.

He turned off the flashlight and slowly turned the knob on the other side. Pushed the door open ever-so-slowly, grinning when it didn't squeak.

Parking lot security lights filtered through the blinds, barely enough to see. Fortunately, he knew the layout, having been there multiple times. He crossed the living room with slow, stealthy steps, heading for the stairs.

He crept up, one at a time, slow and careful, just in case anyone was there.

Halfway up, he noticed a light beneath the door of the spare room.

He stopped dead.

Shit.

Now what?

Retreat?

Or press on?

He'd gotten this far, so why not?

What he needed to do wouldn't take that long. He held his breath and crept the rest of the way upstairs, then toward the master suite, hoping the floor wouldn't creak in betrayal. Defused lighting from the security lamp outside the bedroom window was just enough to see.

He tiptoed into the adjoining bath. Lifted the toilet lid and knelt on the floor. Careful fingers extracted swab number two. He swiped it around the seat, chuckling to himself.

Here's a little bathroom humor back-at-cha, bitch, he thought, recalling when the feed from her cabin displayed a turd circling the bowl instead of its intended view from the ceiling fan.

He swept the light around, looking for anything else.

The glass next to the sink.

Perfect.

He got up to retrieve it—

—froze when he heard a soft thud.

He stashed the swab back in the tube, inserted the stopper, and dropped it in his jacket pocket. Holding his breath, he snuck back to the hall. The light was still on in the other bedroom, but no further noise or sign of movement.

Was someone there? Or only intended to give that illusion?

Should he go back and do the glass?

No.

Not worth the risk.

He tiptoed down the hall toward the staircase.

The closed door flew open, flooding the hall with light.

A red dot danced on his chest.

Shit.

SARA'S CONDO
DENVER
July 22, Sunday
2:44 a.m.

Will glared at the intruder, Glock leveled for a body shot. Before he could utter a word, the man bolted toward him, kicked the gun out of his hand, then pounded down the stairs. He cussed as he picked it up and followed, flipping lights on along the way.

"Hold it right there!" he yelled.

As expected, the guy kept going. But even more to his astonishment, didn't head for the front door.

What the—?

When he got to the living room he saw the open closet door. Which explained why the motion detectors picked him up, not the door alarm. He dashed inside the closet, reaching the opening just as the man exited through the other condo's front door.

Pursuit was pointless.

Starting a fire fight in a condo complex was definitely a bad idea. With a growl of frustration, he stepped the rest of the way into the other unit, closed and locked the front door, then returned to Sara's place.

He sniffed.

The guy was a smoker. Not that it would help find the SOB.

He went into the kitchen to glare out the window just as a pickup roared by, lights off, heading for the front gate. He cussed. Too fast to get the license number, even if he could have seen it, assuming it was him.

Who else at that hour?

Another thought struck. The place was gated. How'd the bastard get in? It took a moment before he answered his own question. The remote, courtesy of Sara's purse, lost in the wreck.

He jumped when his cell phone vibrated inside his sweat pants pocket. A text from Mike to both him and Sara.

Turn off the devices, it said.

Before Will could ask how, Sara texted, *Done.*

Seconds later, it rang. Mike followed by Sara. He connected them in a conference call, then collapsed in a kitchen chair to explain what happened.

No one was happy, yet not surprised, and relieved everything on his end seemed okay.

"Did you call the cops?" Sara asked.

"Not yet. It barely happened," Will replied.

"I certainly don't feel very safe knowing he's been there again," she said, voice saturated with stress.

"Yes, definitely report it," Mike agreed. "That gets it on record in the Colorado Crime Information Center system. Perps don't risk breaking and entering without a reason. If it wasn't robbery, then why? Sara's life is in danger. No telling what he was up to. I'd specifically check for poison."

Will stomach lurched. "Agreed. I'll call as soon as I hang up. They can help look for evidence."

"Definitely," Mike said. "Don't wait, do it now. Let us know what they say."

He hung up and punched in 9-1-1.

"9-1-1. What's your emergency?"

"Someone just broke into my daughter's house." He provided his name and Sara's address.

"Has the suspect left the premises?"

"Yes."

"Any injuries?"

"No."

"I'll send someone out."

He paced the floor for forty-five minutes until two officers arrived. The gaunt features of the tall one, whom he estimated to be at least six foot five, implied he was the one in charge. His baby-faced partner barely looked old enough to be a rookie.

Will explained the complex situation as succinctly as he could along with what they knew about Johannsen, including what he drove.

"The CCIC shows a break-in and theft reported at this address back on June 11," the younger cop stated. "Are you familiar with that?"

"Yes. Two handguns and a computer were stolen. Most likely the same person."

Preliminaries taken care of, he took them over to Mike's condo to figure out how the intruder got in. It didn't take long to surmise the break-in probably occurred via the patio door.

He shuddered, struck by a bolt of *déjà-vu*—the same MO as when they stole Sara's gun, laptop, and Bryan's server.

No distinguishable prints were found on either door.

By the time they were back on Sara's side, he realized the one he thought was a rookie was actually the senior officer.

"So you believe your daughter's life is in danger?" he asked.

"She's being stalked, electronically and physically. He's tried to kill her twice using car wrecks. That's why I hired the bodyguard."

"Maybe the suspect came to kill her, then left when she wasn't home."

Will disagreed. "No. He pursued them when they left for Montana, so he knew she was out of town. Which is why I'm here, watching the place."

The cop's scrutiny switched to unveiled skepticism. "If his intent is to harm your daughter, why would he break in when she's not home?"

Will exhaled hard. "I don't know. Plant more bugs? Poison her teabags or toothpaste?"

"You think the perp is that sophisticated?"

"Absolutely," Will insisted. "Common criminals don't set up surveillance devices in their victim's house. Speaking of which, we have a few of our own."

He removed the memory card from the camera directed at the closet. Using Sara's laptop they viewed its contents. All it showed was a glimpse of his silhouette as he came through, then his subsequent escape. Total elapsed time, two minutes fifty-two seconds.

He cussed silently that the camera wasn't infrared.

They dusted the kitchen cupboards for prints. Too many, none discernible.

Nothing inside appeared disturbed. Dinner plates were sparkling clean, no sign of powder or residue. Glasses and silverware likewise looked untouched. Same situation with the fridge, which appeared exactly as he remembered.

"Probably not enough time to do anything in here," Will speculated. "Besides, I probably would have heard him. In my experience, it's pretty hard to sneak around in a kitchen. I have the feeling he was here to do something very specific."

"Such as?"

"I don't know. Plant or collects bugs? Leave something harmful?"

They filed upstairs where they dusted for more prints. As expected, again everything appeared undisturbed.

"If this isn't your place, how do you know whether or not anything is disturbed or missing?" the lead cop asked.

Will saw where they were coming from.

"You're right. My daughter will be back some time tomorrow. If she discovers anything amiss, we'll call back and you can update your report."

The three returned downstairs where the lead cop sat at the kitchen table to fill out what looked like an index card. While he was doing that, the tall one asked, "How qualified is this bodyguard?"

Will straightened, trying to read the guy's intent. "Former FBI, sheriff's deputy in California, officer in a small town in Belton County. I worked for the Bureau, too, as an analyst."

The one at the table exchanged a look with his partner. "*Hmmph,*" he responded. "Then what do you need us for?"

Will was taken aback. "Because you're the local police. With a report on file you can get a warrant and arrest him."

"Your video shows someone broke in, but with no evidence for anything missing. Technically, no crime was committed. We'll file a General Occurrence report, but it's unlikely anyone will be assigned to the case without substantiation. If you or your daughter find anything suspicious let us know and we'll update the GO."

"What's the best way to do that?" Will asked.

He stood up and handed Will the card. "It's all right here."

It had his name and the name of the officer, the offense reported, and where to call to obtain the case number to report new or additional information. The other side listed services provided by the Denver Police Department.

Will thanked them, shook hands, then watched their Crown Vic squad car until it disappeared around the corner on its way to the gate.

He knew the guy was up to something. Something sinister. What else but poison? A timebomb, perhaps, loaded with lethal gas?

If such was the case, it was more important to protect Sara than worry about finding evidence. If she wound up sick or worse he'd never forgive himself.

As a precaution, all the dishes and glasses went in the dishwasher. He started a cycle, then dumped all open liquids down the drain: A carton of milk, cranapple juice, the remains of a two-liter bottle of ginger ale.

Back upstairs, he checked her bathroom again. He tossed out the old tube of toothpaste, plus a new one still sealed in the box, just in case. Grabbed a bottle of mouthwash, dumped it down the toilet, with a bottle of ibuprofen. Didn't see anything else.

The glass.

He used a tissue to pick it up, just in case, and took it downstairs, where he somehow managed to squeeze it in the dishwasher, then restarted the cycle.

As the water swished once again, he wondered if that was the very evidence he needed.

Oh, well. Too late now.

He collapsed on the couch, staring at the closet, mind bombarded with defeat. Now they knew the units were connected. When Mike was there, it would be a different story. They wouldn't come in that way, but if whoever it was came back, no doubt someone would be watching or obstructing that closet door.

Their entire project was a total waste.

He went back upstairs, turned off the light, and laid down, but too wound up to sleep.

The guy's intent bombarded his mind with vain, random flashes. Was it no more than a common burglar? Not the person they thought? Or someone besides that Johannsen guy? Someone else pissed off by her public appearance?

But most important of all, why?

His belly twisted into a Gordian knot.

Something was wrong.

But nothing specific came to mind.

Sometimes I go about pitying myself. All the while I am being carried across the sky by beautiful clouds.
—Ojibway saying

30. PONDERINGS

NORTHERN CHEYENNE RESERVATION
July 22, Sunday
5:50 a.m.

Charlie slept like a rock. So deeply, in fact, that when he awoke it took a moment to remember where he was. The pale light of a new day whispering through the narrow basement window established his location—Uncle Joe's.

The situation far exceeded his expectations. The mattress was comfortable, plus the added bonus that the basement was cooler than the rest of the house. Best of all, it was quiet. He sat up and set his feet on the rug, worn velvety-soft by years of traffic. Much nicer than his cabin's bare wooden floors.

For the moment, at least, his eyes behaved.

The smell of freshly brewed coffee wafted around him from upstairs. The homey aroma further lightened his mood. It was a new day. His gaze fell upon the Cheyenne flag, the tribal symbol's white spiked square design on a field of sky blue. The warm feeling increased. Even though he'd only lived there relatively short periods of time, it always felt like home.

As soon as he stood up, dizziness made a strong comeback. Hand on the dresser, he steadied himself until the vertigo ended. Folded his blanket and laid it carefully on the bed.

His vision tunneled.

He sat back down, head between his knees, like the nurses showed him. When it passed, he picked up his jeans from the floor. Stepping into them would no doubt end with his head impaled on the wall beneath the tribal flag. He sat on the bed until he got his legs inside, then stood long enough to zip up.

Pausing to catch his breath, he recalled how he resented the nurses helping him. At Sara's he just slept in his clothes. Somehow, the night before he managed to get out of them and sleep in his underwear.

He eased upright and hefted his duffle bag onto the bed. He unzipped it slowly, staring at its contents as he tried to remember what he'd hastily stuffed inside.

A T-shirt seemed easier than what he'd worn the day before with all those buttons. He dug one out and tried to put it on. He thrashed around, unable to get it past his shoulders, breathing impossible with both arms over his head.

He sat down, bent over, yanked it back over his head, then tossed it aside, gasping. If it weren't for Star he'd just wear his undershirt, but that would be horribly disrespectful. Sufficiently defeated, he grabbed the denim shirt off the dresser and put it on, careful to line up the buttons with the correct holes.

Buttons. Another nuisance vehoe *invention.*

The waiter in that Wyoming restaurant probably thought he was drunk or high on something.

He eyed his boots, remembering what it was like getting them on the day before.

The energy such a small task required was incomprehensible. Forget it.

Barefoot was good enough.

While his mind lingered on simple things now difficult, he wondered how he'd deal with those stairs. Coming down was one thing, going up quite another.

What should he take upstairs now to avoid additional trips later?

After breakfast he'd formally ask White Wolf for his help as a medicine man. That meant offering the tobacco again, so he needed that. He dropped it in his pocket, recognizing an unexpected advantage to the shirt.

It also meant going outside.

For that, especially on a ranch, he needed something on his feet.

Maybe there was something in the closet. He got up carefully, stepped over, and opened the door. Sundry clothes hung inside, a pair of well-worn moccasins on the floor.

He smiled as he slipped them on, then sat back down.

What about the other things he brought?

No.

Those weren't needed until there was a sweat.

He used the bathroom, then made his way up the stairs one at a time, gripping the handrail and stopping several times to catch his breath.

When he got to the top he paused long enough for his breathing to settle, then shuffled toward the kitchen. Everyone was already at the dining room table eating breakfast.

Náhkòhe's nails clicked across the floor as he came over to sniff his feet, then lick his hand.

"Sit down, Littlewolf," Star said as she got up. "How do you take your coffee?"

"Black...is fine," he answered, then lowered himself into a chair.

She was back moments later with a steaming mug of brew. "Help yourself to some breakfast burritos," she said.

"Thank you. I really...appreciate it."

Moments later the boys helped their mother clear the table, then went outside. Joe came over and sat beside him.

"I believe we have some business to conduct," he said. "When you're finished, meet me outside, beneath the bur oak."

"Yes, uncle."

He finished eating, took his plate and mug to the kitchen in slow motion, and thanked Star. Careful steps took him out the front door. The early morning freshness was awash with memories.

The visions he had while unconscious were growing dim, but the mailbox out by the road brought back the one of *amasani*. His vision blurred, but this time with tears.

Now she really was gone.

At least she came to tell him goodbye. Her gift was beyond priceless. He would die before he'd ever give up that very special blanket.

He sighed with resignation at the sad reality, then wrapped his fingers around the railing and made his way down the steps, one by one.

As stated, his uncle stood beneath the tree to his right. He'd changed from his usual rancher garb to traditional Cheyenne beaded and fringed regalia, including a black silk scarf headband, presenting the unmistakable persona of a medicine man.

He looked so much like Eaglefeathers Charlie blinked a few times to make sure he was seeing correctly. The only difference to how he remembered his grandfather was the amount of grey in his long braids.

Convinced it was his uncle, he removed the tobacco from his pocket and walked slowly and deliberately in his direction, step by step.

Their eyes met.

He squatted down to set the tobacco on the ground, swaying slightly as he arose.

"White Wolf. I lay this...offering...at your feet to...respectfully ask...for your...help."

His uncle's countenance was one of solemn scrutiny. "Explain what you want from me, Littlewolf."

"I need your help...to get well. I also want...to return to...the *Tsetsehestaestse* way and...the teachings of...my grandfather."

His knees buckled.

Strong arms reached out just in time to keep him from falling. Once he was steady again, White Wolf leaned over and picked up the tobacco.

Charlie's eyes teared up with relief.

"We will go inside and you will tell me more. I can see it is difficult for you to be walking around."

He led Charlie back to the house, then down the hall to another room where they sat on wooden chairs facing one another. The faint scent of cedar and sweetgrass hung in the air, walls lined with shelves filled with herbs and other medicine man paraphernalia.

His uncle followed Eaglefeathers's footsteps and became a medicine man, Charlie's father, Little Bear, unable to do so due to failing health.

"Eaglefeathers came to me in a dream a week past," White Wolf stated in Cheyenne. "He said you come, so I expect you. You are not well. What happen that you come home?"

It took Charlie several moments to digest what he said. Besides his brain not functioning to full capacity, it had been years since he'd spoken the language conversationally. The last time had been with Eaglefeathers, fifteen years before. When praying the native words flowed from his heart, but everyday speech was far different.

If he made a mistake, *Maheo* knew his heart and what he was trying to say.

Now he would look stupid.

He glanced down, hoping his shirt was buttoned correctly.

His uncle's eyes narrowed, then he explained in English.

"There will be two sides to our relationship. One will be as it has always been, as family, where I am Uncle Joe. The other will be as a healer as I show you how to get well, then finish what my father, Eaglefeathers, began. When we are working, you will address me by my *Tsetsehestaestse* name, *Ho'néohvó'komaestse*, and we will speak our language."

A surge of anxiety surged through him. "I, uh, it has been...many years since I've spoken... *Tsetsehestaestse*. What if I don't...understand?"

"You will in time. Our language is rich and powerful. It is the only way that much of what you must learn can be expressed. I have wondered when you would come back home where you belong and complete your life's path as intended by *Maheo*."

White Wolf folded his arms and switched back to Cheyenne, speaking more slowly. "Speak our language as you are able. Mistakes okay. You learn when use it. Now answer question. Why come you home?"

His head pounded, still disconcerted by the dramatic change in his uncle's persona. He didn't know what he expected, but this wasn't it. Eaglefeathers was strict, but never so stern.

Between needing to catch his breath every few syllables and trying to remember the Cheyenne words with his dysfunctional brain, he faltered through explaining about his job and the accident.

When finished, he braced for a lambasting for working in an industry so harmful and disrespectful to the Earth Mother.

Much to his surprise, none came.

"If *Maheo* sent you there, was reason. Experience force you confront death. Prepare spirit for destiny. You remain very ill. Is this best *vehoe's* medicine do for you?"

"No. They not...want me leave. My doctor...she cry. She beg me...stay. I did not intend...my decision hurt her."

"I thought your doctor was man."

"That was...first medicine house. This was...second one, where I...woke up."

"Why did you leave? No money?"

"No. LSO's chief...pay everything. I leave...because I could not...endure noise. I not...sleep or rest."

White Wolf looked puzzled. "The noise of sick persons and medicine people working in *vehoe* medicine house?"

"No. Noise...in my head. I hear all sick people's...thoughts, felt their...misery and despair. It was worse...than pain. This was where...I should be. So I leave."

His uncle unfolded his arms and leaned back in his chair. "Do you believe I can heal you?"

"Yes. Or I not...be told...come here."

"Who told you come home?

Charlie's gut wrenched. "Badger. He very...angry at me."

"Why? What you do?"

"I violated...Earth Mother. My work chief...told me name...borehole. I name it...*Mahahkoe*...to protect her."

White Wolf looked surprised, but said nothing, so Charlie continued.

"After blowout...badger tell me...go home."

"One does not play games with *Mahahkoe*. He did as instructed. Why think you something wrong with eyes?"

It was as if he were a little boy again, helpless and confused.

"I am stranger...trapped inside...damaged body. Everything ...blurry. Wrapped in...strange fog. Sometimes what I see...is not there. It is memory. It change...when I blink and concentrate. I see...strange dreams. I know things...but don't know...how or why. Sometimes I hear...people's thoughts."

He paused to take a breath and remember the Cheyenne words. "On journey here...dangerous *vehoe*...follow. Eaglefeathers tell me...he follow us. Then he make *vehoe*...truck get...broken tire. I see it...like flying bird...in my mind."

Renewed vulnerability and fear constricted his throat. He looked away while he regained control.

"I am afraid...I become...*ononovàhéhe*...crazy person. Medicine keeper say...injuries cause...brain not work right. What I see...not dream. Is...true. When...in medicine house....I hear someone...pray and sing...honor song. I smell sage...I have...good feeling. Did not understand...what he say. It was...strange talk....Not ours. I not know...who it was...or if real."

His uncle's stern demeanor dissipated. "That I know. Your medicine keeper much concerned. He call National Congress of American Indians in Denver. Not know your tribe, they send Leaping Elk, an Oglala Sioux, to see you. Your name tell him you Northern Cheyenne and he call me. That was day after Eaglefeathers say you come."

White Wolf smiled as he continued. "*Maheo* tell him call. It confirm dream. Leaping Elk tell me of your illness and we pray and fast for you. Plan ceremonial sweat for you tomorrow. It is held, whether or not you arrive. Is good you here. Will bring more answers. About sweat—did you bring anything with you?"

The gravity of his words carried implications he understood too well. The sacred items Eaglefeathers gifted him should have rightfully gone to White Wolf.

He cleared his throat. "Yes, *Ho'néohvó'komaestse.* I bring ...Eaglefeathers medicine bundle...sacred red pipe...eagle bone whistle...and buffalo horn cap."

"That is good. We use them tomorrow."

Charlie's mind drifted to whether he'd be allowed to keep them.

"The pipe carry many prayers," White Wolf said. "It see all ceremonies of our people. Grandfather spirits come help."

"Yes. I know...its power. It carry...my prayers to *Maheo*...and he answer."

A crease appeared between his uncle's brows. "How is it you know its power? You use it?"

"Yes. My white brother...was murdered. It help me...find killer."

"The same *vehoe* Eaglefeathers stop on journey here? *Ok kliwŭs?*"

"Yes. *Ok kliwŭs.* One who kill another. He murder my white brother. "

Their eyes locked for several moments before White Wolf cleared his throat and continued. "You tell me more over time. This afternoon prayer cloth ceremony begin healing journey. Now rest your body and prepare your spirit."

SHERIDAN, WYOMING
COMFORT INN
July 22, Sunday
7:40 a.m.

The group consuming the complimentary breakfast at the Sheridan Comfort Inn was far from comfortable. It was no fault of the establishment, to be sure. The coffee was rich and fresh, the culinary selections warm and plentiful, the buffet expansive.

But considering what happened on the home front during their absence, no one was in a cheerful frame of mind. Sara hadn't slept since her phone wailed that raucous intrusion alarm the night before.

She was still worried about Charlie, but he was in good hands. Now her anxiety-ridden thoughts turned to her own family entrenched in *her* problems and ongoing threats because of *her* decision.

One her father explicitly opposed from day one.

The fact the passageway had not only been discovered, but actually *used* by the intruder annihilated her sense of control like an explosive demolition. All that planning, expense, and effort, only to have its primary purpose not only defeated, but used against them.

An unsavory blend of failure, worry, lack of sleep, guilt, and anxiety conspired inside her mind, inviting her stomach to join her throbbing head.

It would be hours before they stopped for lunch, so eating was required, whether she felt like it or not. Her racing thoughts and frayed nerves, however, robbed the blueberry muffin she selected of any appeal She cut it in half and buttered it, then took a dutiful bite. Its sweetness beckoned as her mind tripped through a variety of less appetizing scenarios.

Maybe she needed to move. Denver was a large city. There was a good chance she could find another place she'd like. Preferably, one that was not only gated, but with onsite security. Even if they didn't have her lost remote, tail-gating was easily accomplished, unless a guard was on-duty 24/7. Who could often be fooled with a good story or suitable bribe.

Perhaps she should leave the city entirely. Move closer to her father and Connie. She no longer had a day job, so it didn't matter.

But how long would that work, anyway? If they wanted to find her badly enough, they would.

Especially when the government was involved.

No one was invisible anymore.

Except maybe those under a witness protection program.

She finished the muffin and got up to replenish her coffee. She needed the caffeine, even if her hands were already shaky. She smiled at Connie as she sat back down, even as her mind switched to her upcoming television appearance, scheduled for the coming week.

Should she cancel or not?

Proceeding as planned with it already booked made sense. Without good reason, it would be rude and appear flaky to decline so late. Like Will said, windows of opportunity eventually closed.

Publicity was doing some good. More calls and emails for interviews kept streaming in, many from national magazines. Not so much those blatantly controlled by the government, but those focused on personal freedom and an individual's Constitutional rights.

The muffin restored her appetite, driving her back to the buffet to help herself to some fruit salad and a piece of French toast. As she sat back down, she hoped it would clear her head, which tended to fog when her blood sugar was low. Not that it would do much for lack of sleep.

Maybe she just needed to write her own book, then go on a promotional tour. Or do a podcast, focusing on the various bits of evidence Bryan uncovered. There was so much that hadn't been mentioned with the limited news coverage. She had enough incriminating material related to collusion for a full-length documentary series.

So much more corruption existed than what was acknowledged, even considering the fact the government's antics were well-known and accepted by so many.

Then there were the ones with their heads in the sand entirely.

Both were at fault.

She finished the last strawberry and piece of cantaloupe, then got out her tablet to check her email. Her flight information to fly into La Guardia the following Thursday was there. A picture of the person who'd pick her up at the airport was attached as well.

Her hotel reservation had her checking out Saturday, but if she wanted to extend it to do some sightseeing, she could. A document with guidelines for live guest interviews and the schedule for make-up and so forth were also included.

Hopefully, she could get Mike on the same flight and a room in that hotel. With all the excitement she hadn't thought about him going along, too.

She opened the folder where she kept interview requests. One of the magazines was headquartered in New York City, another in St. Louis. With luck, she could work them into the same trip.

She responded to the emails, mentioning her travel schedule, expecting it to depend on whether the *Time* reporter was available. She assumed *The Liberty Digest,* which had a relatively small circulation, would jump on it, saving airfare. All she'd have to do was work in a layover on the way back, unlikely to be an issue with first class tickets.

Feeling eyes upon her, she looked up. Mike and Connie were both smiling, patiently waiting.

"Sorry," she muttered, and got up.

They took the elevator to the third floor, gathered their bags, then checked out, using Mike's credit card. When they got to the car, he offered to drive. She didn't argue.

The long, but gratefully boring, drive was nonetheless underscored by palpable tension.

Indians never whip their children, nor punish them in any way.
—George Bird Grinnell in "The Cheyenne Indians: Their History and
Lifeways"

31. COLORS

SKYVIEW APARTMENTS
LAKEWOOD, COLORADO
July 22, Sunday
10:45 a.m.

Eddie sat at his kitchen table with his third cup of black coffee, debating. Should he call Keller or not?

His cell rang.

Ha.

Should've known.

"Hey, boss."

He held his breath, unsure whether he'd get kudos or an ass-chewing.

"First, I'm no longer your boss. Second, what were you doing at the target's condo last night? If you mess up this job any further, Johannsen, you'll be blackballed so deep you'll never work again. Including flipping burgers at McDonald's. I mean it, numbnuts."

Eddie laughed. "Everything's cool, boss! Everything's cool! I keep my promises. I accepted the delivery. Trust me when I say that guy would not have been happy if I didn't. There was a window of opportunity with the bitch out of town, so I made the plant. Everything's good to go. No need for further action. A few days, give or take, and the problem should go away."

Keller was dead silent.

"You still there, boss?"

"I am *not* your boss. Tell me exactly how this went down. Where'd you make the pickup?"

Eddie explained everything that resulted from his run of incredibly good luck: the condo parking lot; the flat tire; the pickup; then the passageway from the unit next-door, though he left out the fact someone saw him.

"I must say, Johannsen, I'm impressed. I'll be watching to see if all goes according to plan. You damn-well better hope so."

Eddie grinned as he ended the call. While the man never said so out loud, he suspected he'd get his share of the job's payment when the bitch was confirmed neutralized.

In fact, he wouldn't be surprised if he got a bonus *and* his job back. Keller was tough, but fair.

Best of all, revenge truly *was* sweet. *Schadenfreude,* one of the few German words worth remembering, summed it up nicely: relishing your enemy's ill fortune.

Paybacks are a bitch, eh, bitch?

He chuckled as he lit a cigarette and took a long drag.

Life was good.

WHITE WOLF'S RANCH
NORTHERN CHEYENNE RESERVATION
July 22, Sunday
1:08 p.m.

The towering oak beside the house offered relief from the midday sun. Within its shade, all facing east, Winter Hawk stood with his brother on his left, mother on his right, father next to her, then his mysterious cousin.

As always for such occasions, White Wolf looked magnificent. Traditional ceremonial clothing transformed him from an exceptional father into an imposing and powerful medicine man. Fringed deer hide shirt beaded across the chest, back, and sleeves. Fully beaded blue moccasins with the white

Cheyenne flag. Buckskin pants, long braids criss-crossed with half-inch strips of red trade cloth, and a black silk scarf folded into a headband, ties fluttering in the summer breeze.

The sight never failed to swell Winter Hawk's psyche with awe and pride that part of him issued from that great man's loins.

He, too, was dressed in traditional clothing, though with far less ornamentation. Furthermore, his recent growth spurt had created a huge gap between his buckskin pants and moccasins, which were cramping his toes. In the fall after the deer hunt, he'd help tan a hide from which his mother would make new ones, his current garb then packed away until his brother grew into them.

As the son of a medicine man he was privileged to attend and assist at numerous ceremonies, this being one of them. The prayer cloth's purpose was to cleanse Littlewolf by wiping away evil spirits that had gotten a hold of him, inside and out.

Which, judging by the looks of him, was apparently a lot.

Several feet in front of White Wolf an earth-filled abalone shell held glowing coals from the woodstove that Winter Hawk placed there earlier. A stack of five neatly folded cloths of as many colors rested beside it, their unfurled dimensions a yard-square.

His father opened the ceremony with a prayer. Then Winter Hawk along with the others went through the graceful motions of blessing their mind, body, and spirit with the Earth Mother, from which they'd been created.

His father turned to Littlewolf and said in *Tsetsehestaestse*, "Now we all pray to *Maheo*. We call upon him, his spirit helpers, and badger from the Sacred Mountain, to remove the evil spirits that have befallen you. We pray that you will heal and live a long life serving *Maheo* as well as your *Tsetsehestaestse* brothers and sisters."

Following the prayer, they sang five sacred songs, their lyrics functioning as prayers that invited the Creator and his spirit helpers to attend.

While the words of the Badger song issued effortlessly from Winter Hawk, his cousin faltered. Every few moments he stopped, gasping for air, sometimes coughing.

He looked sicker than anyone he'd ever seen. Except perhaps someone very old.

Really old, and ready to die.

He continued to sing, now into the Grandfather song, hoping Littlewolf would be alright. His father hadn't said much about him. In fact, he couldn't remember his cousin being mentioned by name until about a week ago, when he learned he was coming. All Winter Hawk's other relatives—various aunts, uncles, and a multitude of cousins—lived nearby, most on the reservation, no one farther than Billings.

His father told him Littlewolf's father died when he was fifteen.

The same age he turned six months before.

At the thought of losing his father—or mother or any of his siblings—his throat closed, choking off part of the Grandmother song. He resumed singing, earning a concerned glance from his mother beside him.

But even if such a tragedy were to befall him, one of his many relatives would take him in. As his parents had with some of his other cousins, or anyone else on the reservation, when the need arose. Even those who suffered in poverty had family. They helped one another, however they could.

As he sang the Buffalo song he recalled Littlewolf's mother didn't want him, either. She was *Diné* and lived in New Mexico. For some reason, she threw both Littlewolf and his father out. Then he lived with their grandfather, Eaglefeathers, who died seven years after that, a few months before Winter Hawk was born.

Littlewolf was in college by the time his grandfather crossed over, but regardless of age, how could he survive, all by himself like that?

Buffalo song complete, they sang the Spirit Calling song. No doubt Littlewolf's spirit was lost and wandering around out there and needed to be called back.

When its last verse ended, he stepped forward and picked up the sweet grass braid lying beside the abalone shell. He broke off a section and placed it on the glowing coals.

Aromatic smoke lilted skyward, its vanilla-like fragrance blessing the air while his father prepared the cloths. He unfolded each one, let it fall open, then held them by one corner, until all were free. Winter Hawk added more sweet grass to the coals as needed until each was blessed.

Yellow.

The color of the sun. Kind to all creation, providing light and warmth to all living things.

Red.

The "blood we wear." Reminder to honor his ancestors with every action, every day, and be proud of his heritage as a red man.

White.

Wisdom, as shown in the white hair of the elders, earned through many winters.

Blue.

We the people of the Morning Star, as long as Maheo *is in the blue sky we will walk on earth.*

Black.

Victory. Defeating the enemy, in whatever form it presents itself. Why his father wore a black cloth wrapped around his head for protection from evil spirits released from those who came for help.

White Wolf knotted the cloths together, then shook them as one. Primary colors sailed the summer breeze as the layers rippled together. Next, he blessed them through the sacred smoke in the four cardinal directions, plus one to honor *Maheo*, each motion accented by the deerskin fringe on his sleeves.

Then he turned to Littlewolf and methodically engulfed him in a kaleidoscope of color, each sweep starting at his feet and moving upward. First, his left side, leg, arm, and shoulder in front; then in back.

Next, his back; then his right side, leg, arm, and shoulder in back followed by in front. Upward across his chest, over the heart, face, and head. The knot swiped the sides, back and front of his head, resting briefly on top, until the rainbow of colors fluttered back down in front.

The cloths snapped with one final shake, then Star held open a bag where he deposited them by holding the knot. Fabric contained, Winter Hawk and Risingsun followed him to their aging Ford Explorer.

The vehicle bumped across three miles of an ancient dirt road, originally a footpath worn by his ancestor's feet, to Eaglefeathers Butte. They rode in reverent silence so as not to disturb the spirits, ceremony not yet complete.

The road ended.

Winter Hawk got out and removed two five-gallon plastic buckets from the backseat. He kept one and handed the other to his brother, then the trio walked the last hundred yards to where the headwaters of Eaglefeathers Spring gushed from beneath the looming rock formation.

White Wolf left a tobacco offering at the base of a young tree, removed the prayer cloths from the bag, untied the knot, then retied them over one of the branches.

Freed colors caught the breeze, captured bad spirits seeking freedom, only to be escorted into the earth by good spirits that resided by the spring.

Sobered by the dark spirits left behind, his father offered a short prayer of gratitude. After that, Winter Hawk and Risingsun picked up their respective buckets and collected fresh water for the next day's sweat.

He and his brother returned to the car, both short of breath from their heavy loads, their father waiting in the driver's seat. Water placed in back with the hatch closed, White Wolf turned the key and drove back to finalize the ceremony.

Back at the house, Littlewolf was sitting in a lawn chair beneath the tree, Star coaxing him to drink a big glass of water. At their approach, his cousin got up and everyone resumed their places in line.

White Wolf offered a lengthy prayer of gratitude and petitioned *Maheo* to bless and heal Littlewolf, that his afflictions depart with the evil spirits, and his health and vigor return.

Once again they blessed themselves with the Earth Mother and the ceremony was complete.

Littlewolf turned to White Wolf, bowed his head, and shook his hand.

"*Néá eše,*" he said, then did the same with Star.

Winter Hawk was next. Their eyes connected with an unexpected sense of familiarity, his handshake electric, teasing his natural curiosity.

Who is this prodigal cousin about whom I know so little? There's something different about him, something I can't figure out, yet I feel I know him.

Littlewolf moved on to shake Risingsun's hand, then Star collected Littlewolf's drained glass and headed back to the house, White Wolf and his brother right behind.

His cousin's eyes shifted his way, connecting again with his own. Winter Hawk stepped over to see if he needed anything, motioning for him to go ahead and sit back in the lawn chair.

"Thank you again—*Néá eše*—for...helping today," Littlewolf said. "It is a great honor...for you to work with...a medicine man like...your father. I will always...remember...the time I spent with...our grandfather, Eaglefeathers."

"I've heard much about Eaglefeathers. I'm sorry I did not know him. I was born a few months after he crossed over."

Littlewolf smiled. "I remember...that your mother...was expecting a child...back then. So that...was you."

He smiled back. "Yes. I guess it was."

"Eaglefeathers is always...with us in spirit. He was here...today. Watching. He is very...proud of you."

The hair on Winter Hawk's arms stood up.

How could he speak such a thing with unwavering conviction?

Humbled as well as startled by the compliment, he didn't know how to respond, so switched to more practical matters.

"Do you need anything, brother? More water or something to eat?"

"No, thank you. I'll just rest here...a little longer."

"Okay. If you're still here, I'll check back when I water the horses."

Winter Hawk waved, then returned to the house where his mother was fixing the evening meal. He gazed upon her a moment, unable to imagine her not being there someday, then hurried downstairs to his room, wiping his eyes.

He'd always been a serious, obedient son who took his responsibilities seriously. For that reason he was likely to be the one from among his siblings to follow in his father's footsteps.

Somehow his cousin's comment confirmed that.

Parental discipline came in the form of cautionary tales. Stories of how someone once resisted their destiny, then paid heavily for his disobedience. It made perfect sense to learn from others' mistakes. That was what listening to the elders was all about.

They talked about Eaglefeathers from time to time, saying he died of a broken heart, but never mentioned who broke it.

He couldn't imagine hurting any of his loved ones like that. How could anyone who'd done such a thing ever hold up his head before *Maheo*?

The Earth is the mother of all people, and all people should have equal rights upon it.
—Chief Joseph, Nez Perce (1840-1904)

32. AFTERMATH

MONTGOMERY RESIDENCE
BOULDER
July 22, Sunday
6:05 p.m.

While Will and Mike wasted no time heading to Sara's condo to search for any missed evidence, she took advantage of the quiet by taking a nap. When Will got back, they'd go out for dinner, then she'd spend the night.

She closed the blinds, stripped down to her underwear, and got under the covers. Usually she napped on top, but she was determined to get some sleep after getting so little the night before.

Her head and body ached, muscle spasms in her neck and back from the long, tedious drive. Whether on her side, back, or stomach, something hurt. She got up to dig through her purse on the dresser for an ibuprofen. Popped it in her mouth and gulped it down.

Deep breathing combined with conscious relaxation gradually nudged the discomforts to an unwilling retreat. As the pain ebbed, the visage of that loathsome person in the video popped into her mind.

The person trying to kill her was in her home.

Again!

And just like that, her neurons exploded.

Even with Mike nextdoor, her sense of security was decimated. Their secret entrance not only discovered but *used!*

Just what she needed in the wake of everything else. With her appearance on the *Today Show* less than a week away, she needed to start compiling talking points.

Should she air the dashcam video again or not?

While she wanted the audience to know what they'd done to her, she didn't want to come off as a whiner. Maybe still use it, but edit it down a bit more.

Her primary objective in going public was to expose the corruption operating beneath the guise of government. Show how far they'd go to hide it.

Corruption that robbed the people of benefits they should enjoy, not corporations.

The financial data Bryan gathered indicated the facility cost $6.8 billion. All to benefit lobbyists promoting their corporate sponsors' requests to lawmakers. Congressmen who were elected to represent legal voters, not campaign financiers.

Including those suffering in poverty, like those she'd seen on the reservation, to say nothing of homeless veterans.

Until now, she never understood why other races hated whites. She was white and never did anything horrible to anyone, much less because of their ethnicity.

As far as she was concerned, it didn't matter if someone was yellow, black, red, green, or orange. If they were honest, caring, law-abiding, hard-working, and didn't impose radical views on anyone else, it made no difference.

Live and let live.

She *did* have a problem with those who exploited such people or wanted something for nothing, no matter what color or economic class they belonged to.

Thanks to Bryan's data as well as her own research, she was horrified as well as ashamed of what her ancestors had done. Early immigrants came to America to escape religious and economic oppression imposed by European royalty.

But sadly, it didn't take long before they carried on the same tradition, shoving Native Americans aside as they systematically stole their land, then attempted to annihilate them when they refused to cooperate.

Why was the conquering spirit glorified? Accepted as okay? How could people who claimed to be Christians justify genocide against indigenous people? Not only those occupying the American continents, but parts of Asia and Indonesia as well?

After tossing and turning for the better part of a hour it was apparent sleep wasn't going to happen. Her mind was hopelessly abuzz, prompting her to finally get up and put her clothes back on.

She tiptoed from her room, down the hall, past Connie snoring in the master suite, to her father's den where she turned on his desktop computer. She searched on "colonization," needing more information on America, especially settlement of the west.

While Christopher Columbus was the fall guy, her research indicated he had been respectful toward indigenous people and expected the same of his crew. However, those that came later with evil intent quickly changed that.

Her mouth hung open in shock when she discovered inhumane treatment of indigenous people was approved by the Pope himself. The first papal bull issued for King Ferdinand in Spain after Columbus returned from the Caribbean stated: *"All people of North America are no better than feral animals and may be slaughtered at will."*

And that bull was followed by another that accompanied the North American land grants: *"All land grants will be governed by the same rules as the land grants in Spain, to which you have been accustomed. Thus, as usual, any people populating your land defined by the land grant here issued are your slaves."*

So, in truth, the blame traced all the way back to the Vatican. *Wow.*

That was definitely *not* in history books.

Numerous church-sponsored schools existed on several reservations. However, it was impossible to forget that their original view of native peoples was to anglicize them to justify their existence. Thus, they were forced to cut their hair, abandon their culture and language, and adopt European style names, supposedly for census purposes.

She'd heard that following World War II the Vatican assisted numerous Nazis by issuing new names and birth certificates that enabled them to acquire passports via the Red Cross and escape.

Surely there was no love lost between the papacy and the Jews, but helping Nazis escape?

Another *wow*.

No wonder people were losing respect for organized religion. She was no Bible scholar, but was nonetheless certain Jesus never taught any such thing.

Victors wrote history from their own point of view, justifying, down-playing, or downright denying such atrocities. In many ways, black slaves were treated better. They were considered property that had value. Enslavement was wrong, but an unfortunate fact for millennia. All races and ethnicities were victimized at one time or another, often by their own kind.

Conversely, Native Americans were an obstacle to supposed progress. They refused to give up their land or become slaves, for which they were driven from their homes and exterminated. If not directly, by forced removal from ancestral lands to parts of the country no one else wanted, coupled with other hostile policies and directives.

American history books described Indians as savages and brutal aggressors, neglecting to mention they were only defending what was rightfully theirs.

What would Americans do if they were invaded? She knew what those she knew would do—exercise their Second Amendment rights and fight back.

Exactly what America's original residents had done. No wonder they declared Custer got what he deserved.

She fumed at what she'd been taught in elementary school that early explorers *discovered* America.

Stolen was more like it, for their royal European sponsors.

Bryan's passion made more sense than ever. His friendship with Charlie opened his eyes. Now she understood why they took his life and her own was in danger.

They were threats, exposing the corruption.

A government of, by, and for the people had devolved into a sham. Now the ruling class included corporations. Such entities protected their turf and their assumed right to exploit others by whatever means necessary.

She needed to write a book. Conveying the scope and depth of such deeply rooted corruption was not something conveyed in a ten minute interview.

Furthermore, the "Powers that Be" would not approve of her narrative. The instructions she received from the television station made it clear that she was not in charge of the interview.

Her host would ask and direct the topics, not her.

All things considered, why was her story suddenly news worthy?

Her eyebrows drew together.

Was she being set up?

Let her air her grievances, then make her a martyr, like Bryan?

An example to others?

Or appear as a fool?

Would she accomplish anything? Or do no more than paint a gigantic target on herself?

EN ROUTE BOULDER TO DENVER
July 22, Sunday
6:15 p.m.

Mike's thoughts rolled through peaks and valleys not unlike the distant Flagstaff Mountains as Will gunned his E350 from the Diagonal onto Highway 36's express lane. Compared to the six and a half-hour drive from Sheridan, the familiarity of the twenty-five mile trip to Denver was almost relaxing. He was tired but hyped by the prospect of examining the crime scene.

By the time they'd arrived in Boulder, Sara was clearly worn out. Connie suggested she stay the night. Much to his relief, she didn't argue, confessing that rather than rest while Mike drove, she spent the entire time obsessing on the fact her home had been violated yet again, wondering *Who? Why? More bugs? Or worse?*

He had the same questions.

Compromised sleep the night before left him fueled solely by adrenaline, discipline, and determination while his stomach writhed with self-recrimination and frustration. All their work linking the two condos was an utter waste.

He remembered setting the dead bolt, but knew he hadn't secured the patio door. Inexcusable for an ex-cop. What kind of a body guard neglected something so simple?

"Are you feeling as bad as I am about this mess?" Will asked, interrupting his dismal thoughts.

"Worse," he lamented. "It's my fault he got in. That was so stupid."

"Hmmph," Will said. "We both blew it. I let him get away. I should've shot the bastard."

"Not necessarily. He's not working alone. Besides, the paperwork's a bitch."

Will chuckled. "Yeah, I know."

"We need to check for more bugs. Sara may have accidentally frozen the cameras when she was in view."

"Could be. Worst part is now they know the units are connected. They also know that we know they know." Will's laugh sounded more like a snort. "I sound like Abbott and Costello: 'Who's on first?'"

"Right."

Will followed the express lane as it merged with the I-25 HOV toll road. The spaghetti bowl tangle of highway interchanges swarmed with vehicles traveling in all possible directions. Megatons of concrete and towering pillars whizzed past, one of many as they made their way across Denver to the southeast side.

"The real question is why? What the hell did he want?"

"Good point," Mike agreed. "Whoever it might be, if their prime objective is to take her out, there've been plenty of opportunities. But they haven't. When there's a contract on someone, it usually doesn't take long before it's a done deal."

"True. But they've been subtle from the start, resorting to car wrecks. So what do you think they're up to? Just harassment?"

"I doubt that, but it's possible. I don't think we should assume her life's not in danger. Me being here would be pretty pointless if that's the case."

His shoulders sagged. Not that he'd done any good so far, plus he'd irritated her Indian friend.

"I think we should be on the lookout for other threats," Will stated. "Poison, other types of accidents, biologicals. I already got rid of some stuff while I was there. Now that I've thought about it some more, I want to dump all the food and every toiletry item she's got, just in case. For all we know, he came back again after I left."

"Makes sense. I need to find out exactly who this guy is. The trip threw me off track. The perp has relatives who run that RV park by Sara's cabin. The truck following us met the same description as the one seen snooping around her place. My cop's intuition screams that's no coincidence."

Will agreed. "Too much circumstantial evidence."

"Precisely. We have a pretty good mug shot from the dashcam video, even if the one we got from the surveillance camera isn't any good. I've worked with far fewer leads in the past. Way fewer! When we get back from New York, I'll pull whatever strings necessary to find out exactly who this asshole is, where he lives, and pay him a visit."

"Sounds like a plan, Mike. But he's probably just a pawn. What we need to know is who he's working for. Then we'll be on our way toward some real answers. If need be, I can call in some favors, too."

The green sign for Exit 201 to Hampden loomed ahead. Will eased over to the outside lane to leave the freeway behind, then wound through mixed use properties to the condo complex.

Mike went right to his unit where, as far as he could tell, everything was how he left it. He got his kit to dust for prints out of his truck, but had no better luck than Denver PD. No surprise, considering all the workers that were in and out of there before he moved in, plus if the perp had the intelligence of an avocado, he wore gloves.

"I'm still getting bids for the remodel. Sorry things are moving so slowly," Will stated when he joined him back in Sara's unit. "I'll tell them to get the kitchen together first."

"I've gotten pretty spoiled going out to eat, but home cooking is starting to sound mighty good." He chuckled. "Even mine."

"Are there any big black garbage bags at your place? All I can find here are the white kitchen variety."

"I'll go check."

He returned with a partially filled black contractor bag that Will filled up with everything from Sara's refrigerator, plus any open containers in the cupboards. After that, Will sprayed down the counters sink, table, and fridge, inside and out, with Clorox Clean-up until the place smelled like an indoor swimming pool.

"Let's see what we've got upstairs," Will stated.

Mike checked her bedroom for anything that looked suspicious while Will went to work in her bathroom, tossing all remaining cosmetics and toiletries that escaped his first cleaning frenzy.

"She's going to kill me for this," he commented, "but I can't take any chances."

Mike continued to assess her bedroom, floor to ceiling, while Will sprayed down the sinks and counters in the master bath, then went down the hall and did the same in the guest bathroom. On a hunch, he stripped the bed, stuffed everything in the washing machine in the laundry room, started a cycle, then used her Dyson to vacuum everything.

"Well, what do you think?" Mike asked.

Will was at a loss. "I don't know what else we can do. All I know is she's not going to be happy about replacing all that stuff and putting the place back together. Fortunately, I'm sure my wife will help."

"It bothers me we didn't find anything definitive," Mike said.

"Yeah. Me, too. He was up to something and we still don't know what."

"If you think of anything else we should do, holler. I'm going to that Ace Hardware just up the road to get a dowel for my patio door. Then, since Sara's staying with you tonight, I'll go back to my old apartment and finish cleaning it out. My couch is still there plus a few other things. Dishes, pots and pans, that kind of stuff. I need to be out by the end of the month. With the New York trip coming up, I need to get this out of the way now."

"Did you get reservations okay?"

Mike nodded. "I lucked out and got the seat right next to hers for the flight and a hotel room on the same floor."

"She's definitely independent. But the fact she forgot about you shows you're doing a good job of being unintrusive."

"Or not intrusive enough."

"Maybe. You can be sure she'll tell you to back off if you cross that line. Do you want some help with that couch?"

"Nah. It's after eight. I'll find someone tomorrow. I've had enough for today."

"Yeah. Me, too."

What is man without the beasts? If all the beasts were gone, men would die from great loneliness of spirit, for whatever happens to the beasts also happens to man. All things are connected. Whatever befalls the earth befalls the children of the earth.
—*Chief Seattle, Suqwamish & Duwamish*

33. SWEAT

WHITE WOLF'S RANCH
NORTHERN CHEYENNE RESERVATION
July 23, Monday
9:20 a.m.

Prairie grass rippled in the breeze for as far as Charlie could see, spilling over gentle hills and around random trees. As with every summer it was turning brown, but its feathery waves remained soothing to behold.

As it had for thousands of years.

Gazing upon it his eyes behaved, what he remembered identical to the present. He was still weak and achy following the prayer cloth ceremony, but his anxiety had dissipated, mind more alert.

Without a doubt this was where he belonged.

He sat behind the house in a lawn chair, sipping a mug of bear root tea, White Wolf's prescription for his damaged lungs. It tasted exceptionally good, his body embracing its medicine. Even its aroma was enticing, prompting him to inhale its healing vapors as deeply as he could.

The wind shifted and he detected a hint of smoke. An hour ago his cousins lit the fire to heat the stones for the sweat lodge ceremony. He smiled, aware of how much effort was involved.

When he was their age he helped do so as well. That was when he learned how it was done, like White Wolf's sons were now.

His last sweat back in Colorado had been a solitary event. It facilitated an appreciation for the more usual family or communal sweat lodge. Doing all the work himself was nothing compared to missing the support and companionship of tribal and blood relations.

The past several years had been far lonelier than he realized at the time. Now more than ever he knew nothing could replace being near family.

Absolutely nothing.

If any good resulted from the accident, this was it—bringing him home.

While Bryan was the closest friend he ever had and truly like a brother, nothing could match the bonds of shared blood. Cultural ties and beliefs, the rituals and ceremonies that bound them together and to *Maheo* were stronger than life itself.

The back door from the basement opened, followed by White Wolf heading his way. Charlie downed the last swallow of his drink and stood up.

His uncle scrutinized him from head to toe, his eyes as troubled water.

"Nephew, I must ask. Are you ready? Do you feel strong enough to endure four rounds of the sweat ceremony?"

His uncle's concern was well-placed. He, too, wondered, yet craved the renewal, cleansing, and hopefully healing effects. He took a slow, measured breath.

"I am weak, but the prayers...of the grandfather spirits will give me strength...for all four rounds. I know it will help me. I need this, uncle. I remember...my first special sweat for my *Diné* grandmother...when *Maheo* heard our prayers and healed her. I am ready to sacrifice...my mind, body and spirit...for our Creator's help."

His uncle looked pleased. "I remember that sweat. I was doorkeeper. Okay. That is good. Remember you must drink lots of water and bear root tea. I will show you how to make it. Yes, our grandfather spirits will be there."

"I do have one concern, uncle." He looked away for a moment, embarrassed.

A crease appeared between White Wolf's eyebrows. "What is that?"

"I do not know if I am...strong enough to walk...to the sweat lodge." Its location was one hundred and fifty yards north of the house with a slight upward grade.

The man smiled, looking more like Eaglefeathers than ever before. "We will provide transportation for you, Littlewolf. One of our ponies will be honored to take you there. Tell me, when was your last sweat?"

"About a month past."

White Wolf's surprise was evident. "A month? You surprise me, Littlewolf. Where did you attend a sweat lodge?"

"Eaglefeathers...built one beside our cabin...years ago. It returned to the...Earth Mother. So I built...a new one."

"By yourself?"

"Yes."

His uncle didn't respond for several moments, his ebony eyes saturated with surprise. "That is good news. You are farther along the Red Road than expected. The stones will be ready in a half-hour. We leave soon. We will need those items you brought with you."

"Of course. Come. I will get them."

Gratefully, the back door led directly into the basement and his room, eliminating the stairs. With his uncle's help he hefted his duffle bag onto the bed, then guided its zipper open. Earlier that day he'd taken out his clothes and placed them in the dresser.

What remained were the sacred items, plus his badger hide; ceramic jar from his *amasani*; the black hat that belonged to Eaglefeathers; and the old man's medicine bundle.

While he'd earned the hide and the jar was a gift, the others were given him on the assumption he'd follow in Eaglefeathers's footsteps.

What Eaglefeathers wanted, not him.

His acceptance was based on false pretense. When the old man died, Charlie stashed them away, as if to hide his own shame. Until a few short months ago they'd languished in the cedar chest he and Bryan built.

Until Bryan's death, when he needed answers. Only then had he given them any thought.

During all those years previous to his awakening, how many grandfather spirits were not hailed, prayers not heard in *Maheo's* sacred realm?

He handed each item to his uncle, one by one, too ashamed to make eye contact.

The eagle bone whistle in its leather pouch.

Buffalo rattle.

Buffalo horn cap.

The sacred red pipe in its deerskin bag.

Would his uncle want the hat, too? Charlie used to wear it in remembrance of his grandfather until he realized its "eye of the medicine man" hatband possessed significance he'd failed to earn.

He left the hat in place, and braced himself.

Would he be chastened?

Thanked?

Ever see them again?

He turned his head cautiously to see his uncle's reaction.

White Wolf's huge, rancher hands cradled them as he would a newborn child as he clutched them to his breast. Tears dribbled down his weathered features like spring runoff in a rocky creek bed.

Charlie's eyes spilled their contents as well, conscience laden with guilt.

"Forgive me, uncle," he whispered. "These...should be yours."

White Wolf set them down on the bed and rested his hands on Charlie's shoulders. "No, Littlewolf. They were given to you for a reason. They watched over you and led you home where you belong so they can bless us all. The sacred red pipe has made many prayers of healing for our Northern Cheyenne people."

Just then Star called inside from the back door. "Husband? I am heading up there now. Are you ready?"

White Wolf stepped to the bedroom door and motioned her inside. Moments later she stood beside him, wearing a floor-length navy blue sleeveless dress, her white-streaked hair unbraided and flowing down her back.

"We must make a prayer of thanks, wife," he explained, gesturing toward the objects. "Come see what has returned home."

Pure joy captured her features as a reverent hand reached out to caress each one. White Wolf cleared his throat and bowed his head, Charlie and Star doing likewise, as he prayed in *Tsetsehestaestse.*

"*Maheo,* our Creator. We thank you for the safe return of my nephew, Littlewolf, and each of these sacred items. We are grateful for your many gifts that allow us to connect with you in prayer that we may have your blessings and wisdom in our lives."

Then, beaming with heartfelt gratitude, he turned to Star. "Please take these with you. We'll meet you there after I get Littlewolf settled on Risingsun's pony."

"Please take this up there, too," Charlie requested, handing her his blanket from the foot of the bed.

Star rolled everything up in the blanket and left, White Wolf right behind her to fetch Risingsun's chestnut mare from the barn. Moments later he met Charlie outside the back door.

"This is Spring Thunder. I am sure you two will become close friends."

Following the introduction, Charlie stepped toward her slowly and made eye contact for a long moment. Then he slowly stepped to the side, still within her sight, and stroked her neck from her ears down.

When she responded with a friendly snort, his uncle boosted him up on her bare back, then picked up the dangling reins and with Charlie's help, guided them over the horse's head.

For a few euphoric moments Charlie forgot how much he still hurt as he followed White Wolf along the well-worn path to the sweat lodge. Like so many other things left dormant and neglected in his indigenous soul, it had been years since he'd engaged in any equestrian activities.

At one point he leaned over and wrapped his arms around the mare's neck, relishing the earthy smell of horseflesh and leather. She bobbed her head gently and snorted in reply, acknowledging the embrace.

Yes, they would be great friends.

His thoughts drifted to the horse he had in New Mexico. A beautiful appaloosa mare. His wife complained repeatedly about taking care of her when he was away for any length of time with his forest ranger job. One time he came home to discover Rosina had given the horse to her brother. The man promised Charlie he could ride her whenever he liked, then turned around two weeks later and sold her at auction.

What on earth ever possessed me to marry that woman?

That decision had definitely not issued from his brain. Why couldn't she have been more like *amasani*, the kindest, most loving person he'd ever known?

How his daughters, Carla and Charlene, were doing likewise crossed his mind. He needed to call them.

No, maybe write, with his voice still scratchy.

They didn't need to know how close he came to getting killed. Being back on the rez in Montana was easy enough to explain.

Calling would be better, though. Maybe he'd sound more like himself after the sweat.

When they arrived, Charlie dismounted and handed the reins to Risingsun, who tied his horse to a nearby tree. His cousin patted Spring Thunder on the flank, then picked up one of the water buckets from its place warming beside the fire and toted it inside the sweat lodge. *Náhkòhe* sat nearby, having followed the boys as soon as they set out to start the fire.

Charlie sat on the handcrafted wooden bench on the north side and watched while White Wolf made sure everything was in order. One wooden chair held a pile of several towels, another the things Star delivered. He reached over to fetch his blanket, carefully placing the other items on the seat.

A buffalo skull rested on a small mound of soil a few feet from the fire pit—an invitation to the buffalo spirits. In years past, the buffalo meant life. It fed, clothed, and housed them, its bones providing tools.

Then their generous numbers were annihilated by the invasion of *veheo*. The skull invited those same blessings to return, the ever-present hope that vast numbers of the animals would once again roam the prairie.

White Wolf praised his boys for a job well done, then the men and boys stepped behind the domed structure to remove their shirts and replace their jeans with cutoffs.

His uncle gathered up the sacred items, lifted the buffalo hide door, and ducked inside where he sat cross-legged on the south side of the fire pit.

One by one, Winter Hawk picked up five seething stones, carefully rolled each one in the dirt to remove the ashes and soot, then took them inside. Moments later the scent of sweet grass drifted outside as White Wolf blessed the stones, himself, the lodge interior, water, then each of the sacred items.

He connected the stem and bowl of the sacred red pipe, loaded it with tobacco, then handed it to Winter Hawk, who brought it back out and placed it on a badger hide on the roof, bowl facing east.

With everything ready to go, he went back inside where he passed behind his father and circled around to the other side so he was by the door. Star followed, then Charlie, and Risingsun, who went past his mother to sit beside his brother.

Along with the others, Charlie got settled on the man sage branches cushioning the ground, blanket folded beside him. He took a moment to catch his breath, then felt around for a suitable switch to help coax the toxins from his body.

Situated at last, he realized that was where he'd been for the special sweat for his *amasani* when he was Risingsun's age. He gave his cousin a smile, deciding to share that experience with him later.

He felt a warm bond of affection with both young men, being raised much the same as he had been by a medicine man showing them the way. Their strong spirits were apparent, radiating respect, obedience, and all the qualities expected of an honorable *Tsetsehestaestse* man.

Already Winter Hawk was far wiser than himself, accepting the teachings versus wasting time with skepticism and confusion. With the perspective of years, plus being a parent himself, he cowered with shame at his former behavior. Eaglefeathers had been so patient with him, as had everyone else, for that matter.

Except his mother, whom he tried his best to think of in a positive light. Often it was easier not to think about her at all.

Winter Hawk brought in six more stones, then reached over and pulled the door closed, eliminating all light save that from the seething stones. White Wolf placed more sweet grass on all eleven, then instructed everyone to bless themselves.

Right hand on his blanket, Charlie cleared his throat as he prepared to announce the sweat's purpose. As with his last one, he found that his initial thoughts were not correct as the spirits prompted him to declare something different.

While healing from his physical injuries was part of it, first he had to be cleansed at the spiritual level.

"The purpose of this sweat is...for me to cleanse my soul of the...foolish, selfish person I have been. I ask *Maheo's* forgiveness...as well as all of you...and my grandfather, Eaglefeathers."

He paused, partly to catch his breath, but mostly to get a grip on his emotions.

"May I leave that part of me...behind...Be purged of the mistakes I made...that hurt so many...good people." His lungs begged for air, breathless from the soliloquy.

Appearing as no more than a red-cast shadow, White Wolf picked up the buffalo horn cap, dipped it in the bucket, and sprinkled water on the stones. A subtle hiss, then the smell of steam permeated the lodge. The high-pitched call of the eagle bone whistle invited the grandfather spirits to join them. The others began to sing while Charlie prayed aloud, petitioning the grandfather spirits and *Maheo* to make him whole again.

Breathing grew more difficult with the increasing heat and humidity. Would he make it, as promised, through all four rounds?

His fingers gripped the blanket's soft folds on the ground beside him, drawing from the love it contained.

While their culture differs from ours in some respects, fundamentally they are like ourselves, except in so far as their environment has obliged them to adopt a mode of life and of reasoning that is not quite our own, and which, without experience, we do not readily understand.
—George Bird Grinnell in "The Cheyenne Indians: Their History and Lifeways"

34. QUESTIONS

SARA'S CONDO
DENVER
July 23, Monday
2:08 p.m.

The stench of chlorine hit Sara like an invisible wall. Her father warned her she wouldn't be happy. A huge understatement, further exacerbated when her cupboards were all but stripped bare.

She dropped down in a kitchen chair in disgust. The last thing she felt like doing was going to the grocery store. Her focus had to be on preparing for her upcoming interview, not getting her home back in order.

Maybe things upstairs were better.

To her disgust, it smelled even worse. Her bed was stripped to the mattress and everything on her bathroom counter gone.

Gone!

She opened a drawer in the vanity.

Empty.

As were all the others.

Damn it!

She ground her teeth and growled with disgust. Her home was a total disaster. Who did more damage, the jerk who broke in or her father and bodyguard?

If there was anything she didn't need right now, it was this.

Fueled by anger and frustration, a headache and nausea from the stench provided another nice, "Welcome Home."

OMG, what were you thinking, Dad?

She folded her arms, trying to remind herself he meant well. Only trying to protect her. Mike, too.

But still...

Having a tantrum, however, wouldn't help.

She inhaled deeply with the intent of calming herself down, but instead the chemical-laden air caught in her throat, causing a coughing fit that left her gagging and eyes watering.

Fine.

Forget it.

Anything she needed to do here could wait. Go back to Boulder until after the New York trip.

She grabbed her laptop from the office, then returned downstairs where she picked up her purse and overnight bag from the road trip, which contained some toiletries, at least. Deadbolt secured, she returned to her car, which was nearly out of gas.

How typical.

She swung by her mailbox, finding the usual stack of unsolicited requests for money, as if every charity, nonprofit, and political organization on the planet knew about her sudden influx of wealth. One nondescript envelope without a return address evoked a mystified look. She started to open it, curious, then stopped.

What if it contained something toxic? Some deadly white powder that would drop her in her tracks?

Ewwww.

She deposited the entire stack in the trash can located beside the battery of mail boxes for that very purpose, then wound her way out through the complex's gate to the nearest gas station to fill the tank, glancing at her watch.

Nearly three o'clock.

So far the day was a total waste.

Considering her luck so far, it was no surprise when every traffic light was red until she got to I-25. She was sailing along at last on what she hoped to be the home stretch of Highway 36 when her navigation system alerted her to a wreck at the Northwest Parkway interchange.

No exits offered a reprieve for an alternate route. She compressed the brake as she caught up to the bogged down traffic, then proceeded at a crawl. Over a half-hour later she reached the Highway 287 exit, which took her to Highway 52, which meant more lights, but at least she was moving.

It was after five by the time she pulled into the driveway, set the brake, grabbed her things, and blew back inside, nearly colliding with Connie.

"What's wrong, honey?" the woman asked, features etched with concern.

She growled with exasperation. "My place is a total wreck. It stinks so bad I got a headache the moment I walked inside, then nearly choked to death when I went upstairs. Is it okay if I stay here a few more days? I absolutely *have* to get my act together for Friday. One more distraction and I swear, I'll go bat-shit crazy."

Connie laughed and wrapped her arms around her in a sympathetic hug. "Of course. And don't worry. I'll drag your father down there tonight or tomorrow to get it cleaned up. I can't believe he and Mike left it that way."

"I know. They meant well, I'm sure. But I just can't deal with it right now."

"That's fine. Go get settled. I'll call when dinner's ready."

NORTHERN CHEYENNE RESERVATION
July 24, Tuesday
8:42 a.m.

Judging by how light it was, it was later than his usual wake-up time. Charlie checked his phone, amazed he'd slept over twelve hours. No wonder he felt rested, the best night's sleep in a long time. Even better than after the sweat at his cabin over a month before.

He sat on the side of his bed, awash in the lingering euphoria of the day before. With the help of the grandfather spirits he had, indeed, made it through.

Between the heat and humidity, breathing had been no simple matter. A sharp pain in his side kept him from inhaling as deeply as required, fears looming like a prairie thunderstorm that he'd suffocate.

Determined to do so, he'd taken short, shallow breaths sufficient to pour out his heartfelt desires to the grandfather spirits while the others sang the third verse of the Badger Song.

A vision opened up in startling detail. *Amasani* and Eaglefeathers stood on *Novavose*, the sacred mountain, aglow in the light of Father Sun. Peace and love poured into his heart, then throughout his body.

The tightness in his chest relaxed. Healing, moisture-laden air poured into his lungs. It hurt, but so far was bearable. A few breaths later, a gut-twisting spasm erupted within his ribcage. He coughed, again and again, so deeply his breast-bone burned.

His lungs convulsed and heaved, eventually expelling a huge glob of phlegm. He hocked it on the ground in front of him, gasping with surprise when it no longer hurt to breathe.

The break arrived moments later. As doorkeeper, Winter Hawk scooped up the loogie with a spade shovel and took it outside. After that, the usual break procedures of water and a breath of fresh, cool air went on as usual while Winter Hawk brought in the next eleven stones.

By the third round, breathing was no longer a problem. Tears of gratitude mingled with sweat as he thanked the grandfather spirits and *Maheo* from the depths of his heart. Their gift of sweet grass scented steam coupled with stimulating his body with the man sage switch had cleared his lungs, process initiated by the bear root tea.

During that round more visions appeared, of how Bryan and Sara blessed his life. He relived the good times—hiking, fishing, hanging out in their cabin as friends do.

His white brother was always there for him.

Laughing, encouraging, even admonishing at times when Charlie did something stupid. Adventures together, a bond that even death couldn't destroy. Their shared connection linked to the heavens and Coyote star.

His favorite story as a youth in New Mexico, the *Diné* legend of the Hero Twins, appeared before him in fully animated splendor. Being born the same day, he and Bryan considered themselves cosmic twins, endearing the story to him even more.

In truth, now they actually *were* fighting monsters together, but from different realms.

Without warning, the vision faded to black.

Something about it felt wrong. Sara came to mind. Was she in danger? Or simply a reminder Bryan was gone?

His eyes burned at the vivid reminders of loved ones lost. He missed them horribly—his father, Eaglefeathers, and most recently, Bryan.

Again the grandfather spirits spoke peace to his heart. While their respective life journeys overlapped for a time, each was an individual with his or her own journey.

Let go of the past and seek your own destiny.

The fourth round he saw himself healthy again. Wholeheartedly living the *Tsetsehestaestse* way. Completing a fast on the sacred mountain and participating in a sun dance. Achieving what Eaglefeathers saw all along.

His grandfather appeared amid echoes from the past.

"You have reached the age to become a man. Northern Cheyenne men your age earn their first *vonáhé'xá'e* fasting for a purpose at the sacred mountain. Do you see yourself as a man, grandson?"

This time his reply sprang from the depths of his heart and soul.

"Yes. It is time for me to be a true Tsetsehestaestse man."

By the time the fourth round ended, he felt cleansed and renewed, physically and spiritually. His purpose for the sweat had been fulfilled.

Star returned to the house while the men gathered outside with the sacred red pipe. Seeing White Wolf engage with its powers and send their prayers to *Maheo* brought another twinge of guilt for keeping it from him for so long.

Yet, his uncle's joy at receiving it was a special gift to them both.

When anything was taken for granted, whether life's comforts or loved ones, their worth was seldom recognized.

Until they were no longer there.

Lessons in appreciation were seldom easy.

After sending their petitions to *Maheo* via the sacred red pipe, the boys dismantled the sweat lodge. They hung the buffalo hides on drying racks, uncovering the white sheets placed beneath, which they gathered for Star to put through the wash.

While his cousins were so occupied, he and White Wolf returned to the house where they were met by the aroma of baking bread. Star was freshly showered, her long hair in a ponytail, midday meal simmering on the stove. He and White Wolf each headed for a shower, returning with their long hair likewise in ponytails. By then the boys returned and took their turns doing the same.

When they were all seated at the table, White Wolf turned to Charlie. "Pray for us."

He balked, having never made such a prayer before. "I don't know much of how to pray like that."

"Pray in the best way you know how."

He took a deep breath, glanced around the table at the expectant looks, and decided against the mock blessing Bryan taught him as a teen: *Good food, good meat, good God, let's eat.*

Neither Uncle Joe's nor White Wolf's persona would be amused.

He closed his eyes.

"*Maheo*, we thank you for the sweat lodge ceremony and the grandfather spirits. *Maheo*, thank you for my uncle and his family and their home. *Maheo*, I am happy to come home for their help. *Maheo*, you give us this food and you help us today. *Maheo*, I want my life to be good again. *Néá eše*."

"Risingsun, you can make the food offering," his uncle said. "We will wait for you."

As soon as he got back, Charlie dug in. It was the best elk stew he'd had since, well, possibly *ever*. It was normal to be hungry after a sweat, but that was no ordinary sweat. His sense of taste had returned as well as his appetite, after being compromised by nausea ever since the accident.

Eyes fixed on his bowl, he gobbled it down as if it might be his last meal. He paused a short time later, fork midway to his mouth, when he heard Star say, "Where's Charlie?"

He looked up. Multiple eyes were upon him, everyone wearing a smile.

"Oh, *there* he is!" Star declared.

Everyone laughed, including him.

"Forgive my poor manners," he apologized. "This is just so good and I am so hungry."

"No one is complaining," his uncle replied. "We are all very happy to see you doing so much better."

After enjoying the hearty meal, White Wolf motioned for him to follow to his medicine room. Charlie sat in a wooden chair, his uncle in the chair across from him, while he lit a sweet grass braid and blessed the room, then left it to smolder in an abalone shell.

"How do you feel, Littlewolf?"

"Good, uncle. I can breathe. It only hurts a little now when I take a deep breath."

"Where does it hurt?"

Charlie pointed to slightly above his waist on the right side.

"To finish healing, burn this cedar or light this sweet grass, call your spirit back. Use it to bless yourself, brush away the rest of the evil spirit. Pray the best way you know how. Pray. Pray for your family and your children to have a good life. The more you pray for others, the more *Maheo* will take care of you."

His uncle got up and placed a small circular piece of buckskin on a table. He gathered a few different jars from the shelves lining the room and proceeded to place some of their contents upon the leather patch.

"This medicine bundle will help finish the healing of your lungs. It has red earth paint, bear root, and Big Medicine. Do not take it off, even when you sleep. You must continue drinking bear root tea until it no longer hurts to breathe."

He tied it closed with a piece of leather lacing, blessed it with the sweet grass, then placed it around Charlie's neck.

Gratitude coursed through him as a stream swollen with melting snow. The sweat and grandfather spirits helped his lungs so he could breathe again. At last he was on the mend, both physically and spiritually.

To his disappointment, however, his eyes were still not working properly.

"What about my eyes, White Wolf? When will they be healed as well?"

His uncle looked puzzled. "What makes you think they are not?"

"Because things are not the same as they were before."

He'd given him a strange look, then said, "It will take time, Littlewolf. Eventually you will adjust."

Charlie came back to the present, eyes fixed on the Cheyenne flag. Like everything else, it had an aura around it, causing it to appear translucent.

The knowing look behind his uncle's eyes the day before made him nervous—the one adults wore when they humored or teased a young child with stories about Coyote or monsters so they'd behave.

Was that his uncle's way of telling him things weren't going to get any better? Was he doomed to see the world in this blurry, headache-provoking way the rest of his life?

The blowout occurred only eleven days before, though it felt far longer. Like another lifetime. Big Dick yelling at complainers to, *"Man up, y'all! Quit actin' like a bunch of damn pussies!"*

He smiled at the similarity to what Eaglefeathers tried to get him to do years before.

Man up.

Exactly what he needed to do.

The grandfather spirits heard his prayers.

He was alive, his body no longer ached, and he could breathe again.

The enticing whiff of coffee brewing upstairs was impossible to resist. Apparently he wasn't the only one who'd slept in.

When he got to the top of the stairs, he smiled, realizing for the first time since his arrival he wasn't out of breath. He greeted Star and White Wolf in the kitchen, then headed for the coffee pot.

His uncle stepped in front of him, arms folded.

"Not yet, Littlewolf. First you must drink your bear root tea."

SARA'S DENVER CONDO
July 24, Tuesday
1:50 p.m.

Sara sat at the same desk where she'd prepared various reports and presentations during her high school and college years. It felt comfortable, providing a timeless sense of déjà-vu. This time the task at hand was to enlighten the *Today Show's* audience on the sordid side of Western World history.

As if that were going to happen from one short interview.

She was a logical, intelligent person who valued information, but knew all too well not everyone thought like she did.

She smirked.

Too many didn't think at all.

Tomb Raider above the bed caught her eye, confirming her heroine agreed.

That said, presenting factual data tended to impress anyone with half a brain. Facts didn't lie or distort like opinions. Furthermore, having them on hand provided credibility.

Her experiences were facts that she could back up with tangible evidence, like the dashcam video and everything they released to WikiLeaks.

Another fact was how outrageous it was for the government to spend billions of dollars on a facility like PURF when there were so many genuinely needy people in the country, especially veterans and Native Americans.

Congress knew it was wrong, legal or not, or they wouldn't have hidden it in the Black Budget.

And what about the country's aging roads, bridges, dams, and power grids?.

One way or another, for this upcoming gig, she needed to be prepared. One thing was clear—those with satisfactory lives were rarely concerned for those less fortunate.

She knew because she'd been one of them.

Thus, she started googling the information she needed, determined to find appropriate factoids, quotes, or statistics to back up the injustices, particularly against those citizens who'd been lost and forgotten.

She easily discovered there were over forty thousand homeless veterans—enough to populate a medium-sized town.

What she'd seen on the reservation opened her eyes like never before. Had she awoken there, not knowing where she was, she would have thought it was a Third World country, not the United States of America.

When she googled the per capita median income for Native Americans on reservations, it was a mere $29,097, compared to $41,994 for Americans nationally. On the Pine Ridge Reservation in South Dakota, the per capita income was the lowest in the country at $1,539 per year.

How could any reasonable person not see something wrong with that?

Her thoughts shifted to Charlie. How was he doing? Hopefully better. He was in such a debilitated state when they dropped him off. At least his family appeared reasonably comfortable besides being some of the nicest people she'd ever met.

She leaned back in the chair, ready for a nap. Her energy level still wasn't what it was before the accident. But her life had never been so upended before, either.

After this interview, she vowed to take a break and rest. Plan out exactly what she hoped to accomplish and how. A podcast or YouTube channel sounded better each day. Then she could say whatever she wanted, however she wanted, whenever she wanted.

Provided the site didn't censor her, which was known to happen. Another one of Bryan's favorite gripes.

In what was supposed to be a free country why should the truth be outlawed? What was happening? No wonder Bryan, who'd served his country in the military, was incensed.

Loneliness filled her heart, reminding her again that he was gone forever. She got up and stared out the window at the unending cars along the Diagonal.

He was lucky.

He didn't have to deal with it anymore.

Among the Cheyennes, the men were energetic, brave, and hardy; the women virtuous, devoted, and masterful. Their code of sexual morality was that held by the most civilized peoples.
—George Bird Grinnell in "The Cheyenne Indians: Their History and Lifeways"

35. ANSWERS

NORTHERN CHEYENNE RESERVATION
July 25, Wednesday
7:08 a.m.

Charlie sat on the ground beneath the sprawling oak, *Náhkóhe* lying beside him. White Wolf mirrored his pose, both immersed in the crisp morning air. In spite of the sense of hope from the sweat and being able to breathe again, his eyes still refused to function as they should.

What good was a warrior who couldn't see?

Was this an affliction he'd have the rest of his life?

At least his voice was back to normal and he didn't have to stop every few words to draw in a painful breath. In another day or so he'd call his daughters. They usually spoke every week and it was now close to two.

Most likely his ex was telling them what an undependable loser he was, even though his child support was now caught up. No telling how she spent it. Probably not on his girls.

White Wolf's countenance contained that same enigmatic bearing, which was becoming more and more suspicious. Yet, the man's high cheekbones, long braids, and eyes dark as night projected a peace he'd not known himself for many seasons.

The fact his uncle looked and sounded so much like Eaglefeathers, however, made it difficult to remain grounded in the present reality.

So far, as he'd been informed upon his arrival, all their formal discussions had been in *Tsetsehestaestse*. At first it was difficult, but after the sweat it was not a problem. Thoughts as well as speech easily slid back to another time, another life.

Perhaps another lifetime. Or genetic memory, encoded by his ancestors DNA.

"Tell me what you see," White Wolf asked. "How do I look?"

Charlie flexed his fingers through the dog's silky coat as he stared into his uncle's eyes. "I can see you are a man, but there is a glow around you. It has many colors, like a rainbow."

"How deep is it?"

"As deep as a stream to gather water or where a fish can swim, but not a man."

"Look past me, *Okohomoxhaahketa*, past that tree and over to the barn."

Charlie squinted as he tried to focus. He could tell that was what he was looking at, but it was awash in the usual fog. Illusive, as if he could see what lay beyond.

"It is as dirty glass. It is there, but not real. It looks like I could walk through it."

He sensed White Wolf's piercing stare. "Do you know why?"

Charlie met his gaze, frustration rising. "I do not."

"When you first arrived, your eyes seemed to be working correctly, yes?"

"Yes."

"Then it became troubled again, as raging water."

"Yes."

"Do you know why?"

Charlie's patience was evaporating with the morning dew. He wanted to know what was wrong with his eyes, not taunted by endless questions. A scream of frustration lurked within his chest. White Wolf was his uncle, one of the tribe's elders, and a highly esteemed medicine man. He owed him the highest level of respect.

Thus, he took a deep breath, swallowed his pride-laced confusion, and again responded.

"I do not."

"Do you want me to tell you?"

The tension burst free in a sarcastic laugh. *Náhkòhe* jumped to his feet, then licked his face. He hugged the dog, then patted the ground and his canine friend laid back down.

"Yes!" he exclaimed. "Why? Why can I not see as before?"

White Wolf responded with that same suspicious smile. "You are seeing more."

The words swiveled through his mind and landed in his heart, where they burned as embers. Yet, he questioned them.

More?

More of what?

Surely, one of them was crazy. It made no sense. Yet the statement's truth rolled through him as thunder.

"I do not understand," he responded, impatience falling under humility's sharp arrow. More than ever he felt lost, damaged, and horribly stupid.

"You are seeing many things you did not perceive before your journey began."

"But my eyes are worse. I am seeing less, not more."

What was White Wolf saying? Could his eyes not be healed? His eyes burned with unshed tears. Awash in futility, he seized his lower lip in his teeth to squelch the unmanly reaction.

"No, *Okohomoxhaahketa*. You are seeing more. Much more. You must learn to choose and focus on what you want to see. Like when you arrived and saw things as they were."

"Why was that the case then, but not now?"

"You were seeing the past."

White Wolf laughed at Charlie's wide-eyed gasp. *Náhkòhe* wagged his tail, as if thumping his back in congratulations.

"You are surprised, Littlewolf?"

He thought back to that moment when they drove onto the reservation. It reminded him of when he and his father had come for his naming ceremony. Like the old man buying tobacco in

Sheridan. He'd seen it as it was years before. The same with his uncle's house, which back then had been Eaglefeathers's.

He wasn't recalling an event, he was looking back in time.

"Yes! It was the past. But how could that be?"

"You are crawling from a cocoon, *Okohomoxhaahketa*. Like the caterpillar abandons his old life to develop wings and fly."

"Then what is that I see glowing around you? The past?"

"It is my life-force. It is my past, present, and future. It is everything I am. It is what you must learn to perceive and interpret in others. But that is enough for today. You must practice controlling what you see. Then we talk more."

MONTGOMERY RESIDENCE
BOULDER
July 25, Wednesday
10:52 a.m.

Sara dreaded going back home, but had no choice. She'd left in such a huff after seeing, much less smelling, the mess she hadn't thought to gather the clothes she needed for her interview. After that, Connie and her father cleaned it up, as promised, *i.e.* aired it out, restocked her fridge with staples, ran her linens through the wash, and made up her bed.

It should be fine now.

Probably the best since clean-freak Bryan departed.

Nonetheless, something about it still gave her the creeps. Having her home violated by someone trying to kill her didn't exactly resonate with Home Sweet Home. Visions of that evil face visited her far too often, day and night.

She shuddered, then straightened with determination. Staying any longer was ridiculous. Besides packing, she still had the finishing touches to do on her notes.

The past few days it was too easy to go chat with Connie over a cup of coffee or gaze out her window at the Diagonal every time her mind wandered. Its steady flow of traffic, day and night, was hypnotic and thus, in some inexplicable way, soothing.

All those people with their own destinations, their own victories, heartaches, and problems.

She turned from the window, determined. Disciplined albeit unenthusiastic, she packed up her laptop, placed her laundered road trip clothes in her bag, grabbed her purse, and ambled downstairs to the kitchen.

"Going home already?" Connie asked, tone etched with disappointment.

"I have to. I still need to pack, plus finish up a few things," she said, forcing a smile. "Oh! I need to text Mike. Tell him I'm heading home. He's been staying at his old apartment, packing up what's left and cleaning the place." She took out her phone and did so before she forgot.

"Won't you at least stay for one more cup of coffee?" she pleaded. "*Please.* I just made a fresh pot. I'll miss having you around. Besides, I need your help finishing off these cinnamon rolls."

Sara cleared her throat. "If I'm not mistaken, those bear a very strong resemblance to Patrice's spiral galaxies."

Connie giggled. "Now that your father knows about Patrice it really doesn't need to be a secret. But if I tell him now, he'll know I lied when I said they were from a new French bakery out by Niwot. C'mon. Have one. Or two. And another cup of coffee." She picked up the plate and waved it beneath Sara's nose.

Their euphoric aroma was too much to resist. "Okay. Why not?"

By the time she forced herself to leave over an hour later they'd drained the pot and finished the pastries. When she got to where Highway 36 merged with I-25 she had to pee so bad she considered exiting to find the nearest restroom. Noon time traffic, however, convinced her to stay the course.

By the time she got home, she flew inside, leaving everything in the car as she raced for the downstairs half-bath, which she reached just in time.

Feeling much better, she retrieved her things from the car and headed upstairs.

What should she do first? Pack? Or finish organizing her presentation?

"Research notes" was more accurate, given the interview would be directed by host, Davis Jenkins. Nonetheless, high school and college debate experience taught her how to sneak in what she wanted to say by bending her response.

She snickered.

Either that, or like politicians, flagrantly ignore the question and say whatever she wanted, even if it was entirely out of context.

Getting her notes in order won out, so she headed directly into her office to get to work.

WHITE WOLF'S RANCH
NORTHERN CHEYENNE RESERVATION
July 25, Wednesday
12:20 p.m.

The family gathered around the dining room table for their midday meal discussed their respective plans. It was White Wolf's turn to say the prayer at a Tribal Council meeting. Star had her shift at the food bank, and the boys had ranch and garden chores.

"What would you like me to do?" Charlie asked. "Now that I feel stronger, I can help."

White Wolf didn't agree. "*Néá eše*, Littlewolf, but your task is to get well. I want you to walk. If you feel strong enough, run. It doesn't matter where. Just move. Study what you see. Meditate. Focus on what and *when* you want to see."

Charlie couldn't quite hold back his conspiratorial smile. "I could take Spring Thunder instead of walking."

His uncle's look was sympathetic, but he shook his head. "No, Littlewolf. You must rebuild your strength first. A few days ago you couldn't even walk to the sweat lodge. Your feet need to be on the ground. You are still healing from a serious injury. I do not want you falling off a horse." He chuckled. "First you must learn to control what you see. You might chase a buffalo that was there centuries ago."

Charlie could see his point, but was let down, nonetheless. He'd been longing for a ride since that enticing whiff of horseflesh two days before.

"Here is what I want you to do," White Wolf went on. "Now you know there is nothing wrong with your eyes. You must learn to use this new gift from *Maheo*. When you see something that changes with time, like a house or tree, study it. Concentrate on looking to the past. A month, a week, a year, many years. Then return to the present. Practice controlling how far back you see."

"What about people? Or animals?"

Could he see them as a child or several years younger? What about older? Was that what their aura would reveal?

"Not yet, Littlewolf. They are too complex. For now. Their life force will confuse you. Thoughts and feelings take time and experience to read and understand. Only trees and buildings. Maybe cars and trucks. You must learn to control time. Concentrate on what you see with your eyes. *Sight only.* For now, ignore any feelings or thoughts, which will relate to the items' experiences or owners."

When they finished eating, everyone set out for their respective destinations.

Náhkòhe beside him as usual, Charlie walked for several yards, then ran along the dirt road. It felt good until his strength gave out, sooner than expected. He bent over, hands on his knees, to catch his breath, but it didn't hurt and was vastly improved.

It was hot, sun a blazing furnace, the air dry. He resumed walking, wishing he'd remembered to bring a water bottle.

Which reminded him, he hadn't consumed his quota of bear root tea.

A majestic box elder maple to his right drew his attention, as if beckoning him closer. Its branches spread wide, offering welcome shade.

He focused on its branches, then the girth of its trunk. As he concentrated on going back in time, slowly at first, he watched its leaves change to the brighter green of spring, then shrink back to buds. Time rewound some more, leaving it naked and covered with snow. A large branch appeared, which had fallen the previous winter from its burden of snow and ice.

Yet, in the tree as it now stood, it had not been missed. He backed up through fiery autumn colors, back to green, though its general size was only slightly reduced. He accelerated his time view to years instead of months. The trunk grew narrower, its height and width shrinking as well.

Once it became little more than a stick no taller than himself, he stopped and reversed time to watch it resume its current size. While it did, he pondered its lessons. Surely there was a reason he'd been drawn to this particular tree.

Or perhaps, as a plant totem, it had chosen him.

Such trees brought joy and wonder to children every autumn when its winged seeds fluttered groundward like little helicopters, where many would later germinate. Yet, its wood was weak and brittle, subject to breakage from snow, ice, and wind. In spite of such setbacks, it recovered, new growth disguising past damage.

He shifted his gaze to the dirt road ahead, pondering the message. After absorbing what these traits said about himself, he started to continue his trek, but *Náhkòhe* was no longer beside him. He glanced around, spotting him sniffing the ground a few yards beyond the tree.

"Let's go, *Náhkòhe*," he called, whistling, but the dog ignored him for more interesting pursuits. He almost left, knowing he'd catch up eventually, then decided maybe he was trying to tell him something, too.

When he approached, the dog's tail went crazy. He pranced about, excited, then went to a spot where the vegetation was greener and started to dig. Charlie hunkered down beside him and helped push aside the soil, which was increasingly cool and moist.

A bit farther down, wetter still.

Encouraged, he kept going until the hole was about a foot and a half deep and a small, albeit muddy, puddle lay below. That was good enough for the dog, whose big head ducked down and lapped up a long, noisy drink. When he stepped back, Charlie scooped some into his hands, then splashed it on his face and arms, relishing its cool touch.

He thanked the dog and his Earth Mother as he gathered more, scrutinizing the particles of suspended soil until they settled, liquid mostly clear. He sipped, its taste sweet and cool. He drank his fill, then removed his shoes and plunged his feet in its depths.

Eyes closed, he thanked the box elder for its message. He, too, would greet spring with its promise of new growth. Likewise, he made a prayer of gratitude to the water for its gift of renewal.

Later he would bring tobacco to leave an offering. In the future he'd be better prepared.

When rested, he replaced the dirt while *Náhkòhe* waited by the road, ready to move on. As their trek resumed, he observed how a few other trees had increased in size, then eventually shifted to houses, either as they were built or, conversely, deteriorated.

Each object retained a suggestion of a blur, which he suspected was the future. In time he was sure such an exercise would address that as well. As White Wolf mentioned, other impressions lingered at the threshold of awareness.

By the time a few hours passed he was tired, yet pleased with his progress. He called to his canine friend a few yards down the road to return home.

As they walked back at a leisurely pace, his thoughts returned to the box elder's encouragement. But it was still unclear what was happening to him and why.

**SARA'S CONDO
DENVER
July 25, Wednesday
4:52 p.m.**

Getting her notes in order and filling in a few more research blanks took Sara most the afternoon. This was one of those projects that would be abandoned as opposed to finished. Thus, at a certain point she called it good and printed out what she had, mainly because she was hungry. It was almost five o'clock, the last thing she'd eaten those sinful cinnamon rolls, as tempted by her evil step-mom.

Which had turned out to be a stellar idea, the caffeine blast exactly what she needed to break the inertia. Her energy was still running low and stomach a little wonky, probably from all that sugar.

She took the bundled-up laptop down the hall to her bedroom, laughing that her bed was not only all made up, but the covers turned back with a mint on her pillow.

What would she find in the fridge?

She chuckled again when she found a gourmet take-out meal from Central Market. Grilled salmon, spinach and feta salad, even a bottle of wine along with the expected eggs, butter, milk, and condiments. She set the wine aside for another day, remembering the last time she drank alone.

Satiated, she headed back upstairs to tackle the next chore: packing.

Deciding what to wear for the interview wasn't easy. Again, it wasn't because she had a huge wardrobe, but the opposite. Business attire simply hadn't been necessary, much less her style.

If she were going to continue along this path, that had to change. It wasn't like she couldn't afford it—rather it was something she found boring. Making a fashion statement had never been a priority, but now it could make a difference in her credibility. The public always judged women based on their wardrobe.

Dress for success and all that.

When she got back she'd go shopping, like it or not. Shop-a-holic Connie would be delighted to go along. She pawed through the choices in her closet, wishing she still had that slinky, royal blue dress that was Bryan's favorite. She had another one that was similar, but a rich shade of magenta.

Sure, why not? Throw a little glamour out there. Finding it toward the back, she looked it over and decided it would work. It complemented her hair, which she'd wear down in its cascade of natural curls.

That decided, she packed casual attire for any sightseeing they might do. Maybe the Statue of Liberty, Empire State Building, or Times Square. She never heard back from *Time* or *Liberty Digest,* so there was no need to change their flight reservations.

When she entered the adjoining bath to grab her toiletries, she remembered. All her shampoo, conditioner and makeup were gone.

Panic exploded in her chest.

Could that be why she felt so drained? Was there something in her house making her sick? Had she already ingested something poisonous?

No.

That was impossible.

Wasn't it?

They knew that jerk was there Saturday night. But what about other times? Her place was deserted—a lot—and it could have been done long before they hired Mike or modified the surveillance equipment to their advantage.

Maybe it *was* possible.

On the other hand, the road trip drained her reserves. Then, upon arriving home, she had no choice but to shove it all aside to focus on the trip, which was now imminent.

That was probably all it was—stress.

Carry-on luggage zipped up with its fluorescent orange tag secured, she set it by the door. That complete, the reality of being a guest on a popular TV show ripped through her in a breathless wave of trepidation.

She flopped down on the bed, suddenly exhausted.

Unless she felt better, forget any tourist attractions.

She gasped, hands flying to her mouth.

Was she pregnant?

A barrage of mixed feelings swarmed her like fireflies. What a miracle that would be! That last time with Bryan, they failed to use protection.

Could it be?

After two car wrecks and all that surgery? When was her last period? Had she had one since the first wreck? She couldn't remember.

Could stress cause them to stop?

Probably.

It was easy enough to check, but she didn't feel like going to the drug store. It could wait until she got back from New York. For now, she just needed to get through this interview and worry about that later.

She'd be gone for a few days. Maybe getting away was all she needed. She could replace her makeup in New York. Hotels always had shampoo and conditioner. Shopping on Fifth Avenue for clothes and toiletries could be fun, even though retail therapy wasn't her thing. She could actually afford to go to the more exclusive stores.

Even if she felt up to it, whether or not Mike would agree was another story. Especially after being on national TV. She giggled, imagining his bored response at being dragged along.

She forced herself to get up to go to the bathroom. As she did, a random memory popped into her head. Her mom, counseling her as a young child to squat, never sit, on a public toilet.

She smiled as she sat there a moment, wondering whatever brought *that* to the surface?

She got up, deciding to go ahead and take a shower now so her hair had a chance to dry before she went to bed. With no reason to get dressed when she finished, she donned her Grumpy Cat nightgown, then laid down again, mentally reviewing her itinerary for the coming day.

Share cab with Mike to the airport, check-in, find gate...

Her eyelids drooped, then closed.

What seemed moments later her phone chirped. The clock read almost nine. Fatigue weighted her body with dozens of additional pounds, a dull headache behind her eyes.

A heavy arm reached over to pick up the phone. A text from Mike.

Everything OK over there?

Yes. Just dozed off.

Getting your beauty rest for Friday?

:-D Right.

Her eyes closed again.

If only!

Getting up early to get to the airport, plus a long flight across two timezones had as much appeal as a root canal.

Why'd she feel so awful? More tired than when she got home. The past week catching up with her? Or something else?

Her medical training jumped in with a series of prompts.

Anemic? Maybe.

Thyroid? Another maybe.

Cancer? Probably not.

Even if she was pregnant, that couldn't possibly make her feel this badly—could it?

Another possibility electrified her with sheer panic.

Her mother died in her forties of ALS, commonly known as Lou Gehrig's disease.

Could that be her fate, too?

Sara was in college when she died, but she'd watched her waste away for years before she finally succumbed.

Would life be so cruel to do that to her, much less her father, who'd watched his wife fail day by day with an insidious disease with no known cure?

She started to text Connie to see if she remembered her mother's early symptoms, then stopped. No need to scare her as well when she didn't know for sure.

Googling "ALS" on her phone brought up several references. Per Mayo Clinic:

"Amyotrophic lateral sclerosis (a-my-o-TROE-fik LAT-ur-ul skluh-ROE-sis), or ALS, is a progressive nervous system disease that affects nerve cells in the brain and spinal cord, causing loss of muscle control. ALS is often called Lou Gehrig's disease, after the baseball player who was diagnosed with it. Doctors usually don't know why ALS occurs. Some cases are inherited. ALS often begins with muscle twitching and weakness in a limb, or slurred speech."

Two unnerving statements jumped out: *"Some cases are inherited."* Not good. And *"Nerve cells in the brain and spinal cord?"*

She'd suffered two concussions in as many months.

Two!

Could that trigger it?

Oh, my God!

Maybe she should get in to see a doctor right away. There was an emergency clinic a few blocks away.

Then again, a few more days weren't going to make that much difference, no matter what it was. At least she hadn't had any muscle twitches or slurred speech, other than that time she got sloshed sucking down that bottle of Shiraz.

There were no easy fixes or magic pills for any of the possibilities. They'd want to run tests, possibly lots of them, and she was scheduled to fly out tomorrow.

No, it would have to wait until she got back.

Suck it up, Buttercup, as Bryan always told her.

Mind over matter.

Maybe it was all in her head.

Nothing but stress.

Tears filled her eyes.

That was exactly what they told her mother before lab tests confirmed the dreaded diagnosis.

A white man has a mind that sleeps without peace. A red man has a mind that sleeps with peace. —Pete Risingsun

36. TRAVELS

DENVER INTERNATIONAL AIRPORT (DEN)
July 26, Thursday
8:11 a.m.

Sara sat on her suitcase amid the human throng in Denver International's massive concourse. Its poor logistics were enough to make anyone dizzy and disoriented. Passengers were herded like animals through a zig-zagged rope maze toward security, a path that was claustrophobic in spite of the facility's size. Based on her position, she was about halfway there.

As if the place's outlandish outward appearance weren't enough, its completion had been over-schedule and over-budget. Huge underground tunnels were inaccessible and dismissed with superficial explanations. The creepy murals that once covered the walls caused such a stir they were removed. Conspiracy theorists had a ball with the place.

All she wanted was to get to her flight, settle into her seat, and go back to sleep. It felt like the worst hangover ever. She must have picked up something during that road trip. Certainly better than some dread disease, but something bad, nonetheless. A few places they ate on the way home were pretty iffy.

Digestive issues were rare for her, but she had a full suite of them now. The dull headache didn't help, either.

Salmonella, perhaps?

People died from botulism!

Yuck! No telling what it was.

Good thing first class had its own bathroom.

She glanced over at Mike, who said he felt crappy, too. His posture sagged and eyelids drooped. What a pair they made. If someone were to kill her, they'd be doing her a favor.

The fact they were both not feeling well seemed to confirm they picked up something in Wyoming. Connie was okay, but may not have eaten the offending food.

Yet, it seemed a long delay for food poisoning. Maybe it wasn't that at all. Maybe the flu.

Great.

She couldn't bring herself to cancel the interview at the last minute, and therefore hadn't.

Maybe that was a bad idea.

Now it was too late to back out. United 303 left at 9:54 and was scheduled to arrive in New York at 3:36. She rarely got motion sickness, but at this point it was a possibility. When they got into the airport's main concourse, hopefully there'd be somewhere to buy some Dramamine.

The line shuffled forward. She got off her suitcase, swaying as the place swirled around her. Mike reached over, supporting her arm.

"Are you okay?"

She closed her eyes and swallowed. "I guess."

Taking a deep breath, she shoved her bag forward with her foot. Upon closing the space between her and the next person, she sat down again, stomach churning.

As they got closer to the security portal, she took off her shoes and dug through her purse for the documentation pertaining to her array of surgical hardware.

The walk-through screamed.

A woman security officer took her to the side where she showed her the information. The woman pointed the hand-held device at the designated areas, which confirmed the existence of metal. Sara looked her straight in the eye, relieved when she waved her on.

She found a place to sit and replace her shoes, head spinning when she stood to retrieve her bag.

Maybe skipping breakfast was a mistake.

But even her usual cup of coffee had no appeal.

NORTHERN CHEYENNE RESERVATION
July 26, Thursday
11:20 a.m.

Charlie and *Náhkòhe* sat in their favorite spot beneath the oak. Sunlight danced through its leaves, sparkling like the insights tickling his mind. Once he understood what his blurred sight represented, it didn't take long to figure out how to control it.

He hadn't dabbled with the future, however. Intuitively it felt as if that were sacred ground on which he should only tread for a very specific, noble purpose, not idle curiosity.

The dog got up and wandered off, returning moments later with a stick, which he dropped at Charlie's feet. He smiled as he obediently gave it a hearty toss, watching his four-legged friend bound after it. As the game continued, his thoughts wandered to whether he could see places beyond his line of sight.

When *Náhkòhe* returned the next time, he instructed him to sit and stay, scratching his big, bear-like head to dispel his disappointed look. Arm draped around the animal's muscular body, he closed his eyes and tuned his mind to his home back in Colorado.

It resolved before him, like when he and Trey used the drone to view the drilling site. He zoomed in, only mildly surprised when entering through the door wasn't necessary. Everything appeared the way he left it. A soft pang of homesickness struck as he looked around.

His favorite chair, his coffee mug in the sink, fetishes on the mantle, and all that hung above it. Things that represented some of the most important times, people, and events of his life. He was glad he brought his grandfather's sacred red pipe, medicine bundle, and various other items with him, at least.

But something wasn't right.

His cabin was bugged, similar to Sara's. He growled. *Náhkòhe* echoed his response, bringing him back to the present. He gave the dog a reassuring hug, thoughts shifting to LSO, then Trey and Big Dick.

Dirty industry or not, they treated him well. Which reminded him of the check in his wallet. He'd open a bank account and deposit it the next time they went to Lame Deer. He grinned at the prospect of handing it to the teller and cashing it. What he'd do with all that money, cash or otherwise, he had no idea.

Any recollection of the accident remained hidden, perhaps lost forever. The last thing he remembered was monitoring the LWD data stream, then leaving the trailer, but couldn't recall the reason.

If he could see the past *and* remote locations, could he access an instant replay of the accident?

He'd never know unless he tried.

More than ever he could relate to how Sara must have felt watching the dashcam videos. Reassuring himself that it was in the past and he was still alive, he took a few deep breaths to dispel the anxiety.

The fear twisting his gut gradually settled. He took another breath, then blessed himself with the earth. Its gritty feel between his hands brought an unexpected sense of peace. He made a prayer that he might learn the truth according to *Maheo's* will, then eased his thoughts back to the last thing he remembered.

It took several moments before the scene resolved in his mind, startling him when it did. It felt strange to see himself sitting in the lab trailer next to Gerald Bentley, monitoring drill data. They agreed something wasn't right, so he tried to reach Ben on the radio.

When the mud logger didn't respond, Bentley got up to go check. He stopped him, saying he'd go, because it was part of his job.

Besides, Bentley was getting on his nerves and he needed a break.

His view shifted to outside, watching himself from above, as if from the trailer's roof. A huge commotion with lots of yelling. The ground pulsated. Klaxon alarms screeched. Mayhem reigned as mud gushed from the borehole like a geyser. Casing burst from the well, slamming some of the men along with a broken chain. Then an ear-splitting explosion that mocked the loudest thunder.

Several workers dropped to the ground, himself included. Trey, Big Dick, and anyone else who was mobile wore gas masks and started putting them on those who were down. Then they dragged them as far from the well as possible.

Amid the chaos he noticed several men's spirits hovered above the site, looking startled. Big Dick carried his lifeless body to the trailer where Trey gave him CPR, then started an IV. A short time later, he and someone else were loaded on a helicopter.

The medevac chopper landed and EMTs ported him inside the Belton Hospital. ER personnel swarmed around him administering treatment, then sent him to the ICU. A psychic form of fast-forward settled in when the action assumed a daily routine.

Various people came by. Sara and her father, even Big Dick and Trey. An elder showed up. Speaking what he now recognized as Oglala Sioux, he performed a healing ceremony. He remembered bits of that, but wasn't sure if it was real until White Wolf explained.

Some day he must find and thank him.

A few days later an ambulance took him to the Aspen facility, where he observed his hyperbaric treatments, a few each day, to the point he finally woke up.

That much he remembered. Feeling cold, sensing movement, then opening his eyes. Prone within the confines of a clear cylinder, it was as if he'd been blasted into the future by some portal or science fiction scenario.

Fortunately, a nurse nearby noticed he was awake. The woman's smile dispelled his panic even before she'd explained where he was and why.

His eyes flew opened. His ribs rose and fell with rapid breaths, his skin crawling with goose flesh. Between witnessing the accident that almost killed him and discovering he now had the ability to observe it, it was as if he were caught between one dimension and another.

To his relief, the bur oak loomed beside him. He flattened his palms against the ground, seeking tangible assurance he was back in the present.

His lids fluttered closed, mind spinning and twisting as wool on *amasani's* spindle, plying threads of coherent thoughts together for understanding.

Upon feeling grounded, he reopened his eyes. He jumped, startled, heart pounding like a ceremonial drum.

He wasn't alone.

Náhkòhe and White Wolf stood before him, wearing concerned expressions.

"You are learning to use your abilities," his uncle stated.

"Yes," he said, breathless. "But I am confused. Men died in that accident, yet I survived. Now I am different. What happened to me?"

In most cases his questions earned nothing more than a penetrating look. To his relief, his uncle sat down across from him, projecting compassion.

"Death-like experiences awaken you. They open the door to your destiny. You always had these abilities, but they were asleep. Even among our people your gifts are rare. We have been waiting for you for a long time, Littlewolf."

The statement's truth roared as an echo through a vast canyon. His unbelief wasted decades. How much longer might it have taken without Bryan's death?

"But I returned to the red road months ago. I planned to come home by summer's end. Did my injuries cause me to see these things I couldn't before?"

"No. Your spirit coming back did. Had your intent to come home been undecided, you would have died and another take your place."

The unexpected response served up more questions than answers. "Another? I do not understand."

White Wolf's eyes became as timeless orbs within which all truth resided. His voice lowered, as if revealing something that shouldn't be spoken aloud.

"You are a healer, Littlewolf. You need these sacred abilities to help your people. You must only use them how and when *Maheo* allows you to. They are used to achieve what the Creator wants, not you as a man."

Charlie drew a sharp breath. Though barely audible, the words electrified every cell in his body. Never again would he be the same as before the accident.

Nor want to be.

Yet the concept of being a healer conflicted with what he'd done. A heavy blanket of guilt settled around him. "That accident was my fault. Without reading the Earth Mother and telling them where to dig, it would not have happened. I used my abilities for myself and *vehoe*. Is that why I had to suffer?"

"No. It was the will of *Maheo*. You took your ability to read the Earth for granted. As is often the case, you created the path to your own destiny without understanding."

"What about those who died? Am I a murderer?"

"No. It was their time."

"Then why did I have to suffer as I did?"

"It was a portal through which you had to pass. Until you know suffering, you cannot relieve another's pain. Until you know healing, you cannot work with *Maheo* to heal another. Until you know a life force stronger than muscle, you cannot mend muscle. Until you have seen death, you cannot comprehend life. Experience provides the path to understanding which leads to wisdom."

"Is that why I now have these abilities? To heal people?"

White Wolf folded his arms, eyes fixed upon him as if debating whether or not to continue. Charlie held his gaze, pleading with his eyes. While what he was learning was unsettling, it was likewise reassuring.

To his relief, his uncle's stern presence relaxed.

"Healing others is but a small part," he went on. "I will try to explain. *Maheo* gave you five senses to learn about this world. You see, you hear, you smell, you taste, you touch. There are spiritual senses as well that perceive the spiritual world. The Grandfather Spirits give them only to a privileged few. They are sacred and very powerful.

"Your spiritual eyes have opened. Other gifts will come with time and your worthiness. Continue to ponder what you have learned today. You must understand who you are and what you will become. Then I will teach you more. In time, you will teach me."

They were a typical Plains tribe of buffalo hunters, possessing energy and courage, and taking rank as one of the most hardy and forceful tribes of the great central plains.
—George Bird Grinnell in "The Cheyenne Indians: Their History and Lifeways"

37. REVELATION

NBC STUDIO 1A
NEW YORK, NEW YORK
July 27, Friday
7:15 a.m. EDT

Fueled by adrenaline, Sara felt better, even after getting up several hours earlier than usual. She enjoyed being fussed over by the makeup people who also complimented her dress, helping her feel confident and optimistic.

Stress could definitely affect a person's health, and she'd had plenty. The thought it might be anything more serious had been shoved to the back of her mind.

The day before she'd no sooner gotten settled in her hotel when the producer called to go over last minute details regarding the script. The interview itself would be spontaneous, but they'd start with the dashcam clip to introduce her experience and motivation for going public.

That morning she forced down a light breakfast, nausea still clawing at her throat, but it seemed controllable enough to ignore. Mike would be in the studio audience, keeping watch, making sure there were no threats. By the time the show's live cameras started to roll, excitement surged.

She was about to be a guest on a popular show viewed by millions.

What better way to get her story out than that?

See, Bryan, she thought. *I'm doing what I can.*

As the dashcam video ran on the monitors, she watched the studio audience's reaction. Most were open-mouthed, some covered their eyes, others wiped away tears. Their sympathy brought a lump to her throat, which she commanded to retreat. The last thing she wanted to do was break down as she had previously, whether it generated additional compassion or not.

Nonetheless, people could relate to someone with vulnerabilities. Even superheroes had weaknesses.

Except perhaps Lara Croft.

Davis Jenkins was fortyish with black hair and blue eyes that looked color-enhanced by contacts. All that aside, his friendly manner seemed sincere and felt comfortable.

"You've been through a horrific experience," he began. "Fill us in on the context of what we've just viewed."

She fixed her eyes on him, slightly distracted by the blinking red lights on the camera behind him as it zoomed in.

"My husband and I were cross-country skiing in an area not far from our cabin in the Colorado Rockies. We saw something suspicious in a remote area, so Bryan took pictures. After we left, this black SUV broadsided our truck on a blind curve, like you just saw."

Murmurs from the audience implied additional shock and concern.

"So was this discovery entirely accidental? You just happened to be in the wrong place at the wrong time?"

"Not exactly," she admitted. "My husband had reason to believe something was going on and wanted to confirm it visually."

"So what exactly did he suspect?"

"That there was a multi-billion dollar underground facility being built, funded by taxpayer dollars, but intended to benefit corporate personnel."

"In other words, the PURF facility."

"Correct."

"The one the president assured us is perfectly legal in a State of the Union address."

"Yes."

More muttering issued from the studio audience.

"So how exactly did your husband know about this?"

Her breath caught in her throat. The answer was a double-edged sword. "Bryan found the information online."

"It was readily available?"

She winced at the direction this was going. "Not exactly. He, uh, did quite a bit of research to piece it all together."

"Did this research involve hacking classified government computers?"

She paused, uncomfortable. "Yes, I'm afraid so."

"Unless I'm mistaken, such activities are illegal." Jenkins's eyes bored into hers. "How did he, and now you, justify that?"

She balked, nausea returning with a vengeance. Gritting her teeth against it, she replied, "He felt that spending that much to benefit lobbyists was wrong. So many people are suffering. Thousands of veterans who served their country are homeless. Native Americans, the original residents of this country, from whom we virtually stole it, are living in poverty."

"So tell me, Sara. Are you and your late husband socialists?"

She sat up straight, mouth agape, head starting to pound. "No, no, not at all. But we believe it's wrong for corporations to be running the country. Ours is supposed to be a government of, for, and by the people. How can the government spend so much money—$6.8 billion, if I'm not mistaken—to benefit those who are already rich, yet say there isn't enough in the budget for those in need, right here in the United States?"

"That project provided jobs for thousands of people," Jenkins noted. "Didn't they benefit, albeit indirectly?"

The direction of his comments was entirely unexpected, nothing she'd prepared for. What was he doing? Attacking her or giving her a chance to justify her actions?

She swayed as the room swept around her, mind searching vainly for the statistics she found.

Why couldn't she remember?

She'd never been one to have stage fright or be intimidated by crowds. She wasn't afraid, just confused.

What was wrong with her?

If she couldn't get the numbers right, she was better off not giving any at all.

"I'm sorry, Davis, but I'm afraid those numbers have escaped me for the moment. I'm sorry, but I really don't feel very good. . ."

The glare of studio lights impaled her vision. Daggers of geometric color danced before her eyes. The sides closed in as a tsunami of disorientation washed over her. Her digestive system, conspiring with the erratic visual input, decided that adrenaline alone was insufficient reason to behave.

Fortunately, Jenkins apparently noticed she did indeed appear ill and cut to commercial. Seconds later, she vomited all over his Armani suit, then went limp as studio lights faded to black.

NORTHERN CHEYENNE RESERVATION
July 27, Friday
5:39 a.m. MDT

Charlie bolted awake, consumed by a heavy, overwhelming sense of dread.

Something was wrong.

Very wrong.

While he avoided peeking into the future, he knew what he'd just seen hadn't happened yet. White Wolf told him such glimpses were a warning to be acted upon.

It didn't make sense.

He sat on the edge of the bed, curling his toes through *Náhkòhe's* sleeping form.

He closed his eyes and prayed.

Maheo, help me. What was that? What does it mean? What am I supposed to do?

Sara was in danger.

Physical, life-threatening danger.

How and why was unclear. But seeing her father, his wife, and himself scattering ashes along the same trail where they'd released Bryan's months before had ominous implications.

Was he simply remembering the previous spring?

No. This was autumn. Mountainsides ablaze with color, peaks newly capped with snow.

Were those commandos about to catch up with her at last?

He had no idea what time it was, but it was early. The window set high in the basement room faced the eastern horizon, *háyílkááh* in *Diné*. The sky above was black, still alive with stars. Time still remained until the coming of dawn.

Perfect.

As he embraced *Tsetsehestaestse* spiritual traditions, *amasani's Diné* teachings awakened as well. Whenever he stayed with her she made him arise before daybreak. Together they welcomed Father Sun with an offering of corn pollen and the day's first prayer.

Not having any, he retrieved tobacco from the dresser instead, then quietly left the house through the basement door. His favorite spot beneath the oak provided a perfect view. While he awaited the heliacal rise, he made an offering and blessed himself with the earth, then continued to pray, asking *Maheo* and his spirit helpers for guidance.

Gradually, the constellation known to his mother's people as *Tłish Tsoh* came into view. Seen as a big snake, it was part of the constellation familiar to the west as Canus Major. Unsurprisingly, it was associated with winter healing ceremonies on *Diné Bikéyah*.

However, being a snake, venom came to mind.

Without a doubt, something out there threatened Sara's life, but he needed more information—and knew how to obtain it.

Fortunately, White Wolf told him to use it as needed and left it in his care. He went back inside to retrieve what he needed to communicate directly with the grandfather spirits.

Back outside, he spread the badger hide on the ground, then placed the sacred red pipe and its stem upon it. He made another offering, then held the stem aloft and offered it to the circle of life and its Creator at the center.

He connected it to the bowl, cradled it in the crook of his left arm, filled it with tobacco, then touched it to the earth. The match burst to life, blinding him a moment, before he could proceed.

Once lighted, he released the first puff over the stem to bless it, then four more as he sent his prayer heavenward with the smoke.

A short while later, a vision of Sara's condo entered his mind, more specifically her bedroom suite with its adjoining bath. For whatever reason, her toilet bowl was overflowing with writhing, black, red-eyed snakes.

By the time the sun bleached the horizon, banishing the stars, no further information had come, so he closed the ceremony. He cleaned the pipe with an ash tree twig, then returned it to its bag.

He had to talk to her. Maybe she'd make more sense of it.

Which wasn't simple.

There was no cell service for miles.

He hadn't driven since his arrival. There'd been no reason to. His vision had stabilized as he gained the ability to control it, however. It's not like he had to go to Ashland, much less Billings. Only far enough for line-of-sight to a tower.

But first, he needed to talk to White Wolf, have him confirm his interpretations. Back at the house the kitchen light was on.

Good.

He came back inside through the front door. White Wolf stepped into view wearing a startled expression.

"You are up early, Littlewolf," he stated. "You look troubled."

Charlie followed him back into the kitchen where his uncle resumed making coffee.

He filled the tea pot with water to make his morning dose of bear root tea, then proceeded to tell him about his dream, the message discerned from the stars, then his impression from the sacred red pipe.

White Wolf leaned back against the counter, arms folded across his chest. "The snakes are *mo'óhtáeheséeo'ótse*. Black medicine. Very bad. We will fast for her."

"The dream was of the future?"

"Yes. A warning. Such visions invite action. Sometimes preparation, such as an enemy coming. Sometimes prevention. Which can be dangerous, unless *Maheo* approves."

"But if I don't, she will die."

"Yes. But you must be careful. You must never offend *Maheo* by using such knowledge in a selfish way."

"Would saving her life be wrong?"

"If it is her time, it would be of no effect. But as long as there is free-will, there is a chance it can be changed."

Which was exactly what he was counting on.

NBC STUDIO 1A
NEW YORK, NEW YORK
July 27, Friday
7:45 a.m. EDT

Mike sprang from his seat in the front row of the studio audience and onto the set, barely catching Sara's limp body as it slid from the chair. As he eased her to the floor, her body started to convulse. He knelt beside her, turned her to one side, then waited while she jerked and writhed.

An eternity later, she grew still.

He eased her over to her back.

"Sara? Can you hear me?"

Unseeing brown eyes stared back from a lifeless mask of starkest white. Disheveled dark hair occulted her shoulders, a contemporary *Sleeping Beauty* in a blaring pink dress.

He scooped her up and carried her backstage, where the studio's female EMT awaited with a gurney.

He placed her upon it, stepping aside as the woman started CPR. To his left, one of the producers called 911.

After a few minutes, Mike took over.

Still nothing.

When the woman took his place, he spotted an automated external defibrillator, or AED, on the wall beside the First Aid Kit. By the time he retrieved it, two uniformed first responders joined them.

Mike handed over the device, deferring to them to assume control as he explained their failed attempts at conventional CPR.

An EMT of oriental descent tore open the front of her dress and placed the paddles on her chest.

"Clear!"

After a few attempts, it elicited a weak, unsteady heartbeat.

It didn't hold.

He set the AED to fire at regular intervals, mimicking a pacemaker, while his black cohort started a drip of Ringer's.

"Does she have a history of seizures?" he asked Mike.

"No."

"Diabetes? Any other chronic conditions?"

"No. I have no idea what's wrong. There've been threats against her life. It's possible she was poisoned, but I don't know where or how."

"Okay. That helps. We'll take her to Perleman. They have a good poison unit."

Mike and the attendants transferred her to the EMT's gurney. It hummed along the floor toward the emergency exit, accented by the AED's rhythmic beeping. Fortunately, the studio was on the first floor, ambulance waiting at the curb on tree-lined West 49th.

While the oriental attendant loaded her inside, the other turned to him and asked, "Are you her husband?"

A jumble of thoughts ripped through Mike's mind. Some bodyguard he was, given the circumstances. Furthermore, not being a family member, he wouldn't be allowed to stay with her or given any information on her condition.

"Y-yes," he stammered.

The attendant waved him aboard.

"Stop!" someone yelled.

The studio's medic dashed up to him, waving Sara's purse. "You'll probably need this," she said. "Good luck!"

"Thank you," he said, then climbed inside.

In spite of a Code Three replete with screeching siren and flashing light show, they crept down West 48th past Rockefeller Center with the rest of the city's bumper to bumper morning traffic.

One-way streets necessitated a convoluted path that included Times Square, as well as parts of Fifth and Lexington Avenues. A trip that took over twenty minutes to travel two miles. No one, especially the cadre of yellow taxis, yielded so much as an inch.

The siren fell silent as it pulled into the tunnel-like ER loading area of Perleman Emergency Center, a few blocks from the East River.

Once inside, Mike took care of the admittance process, beyond grateful to find the information he needed in her purse. That complete, he collapsed into a seat in the waiting area and buried his face in his hands.

He'd been on high alert since Sara threw-up, then convulsed into a tonic-clonic seizure on the sound stage. Training and law enforcement experience brought his instantaneous reaction.

Now that the crisis was past, or at least out of his hands, the enormity of what just occurred fell upon him like an F-5 tornado.

In his work as a cop he dealt with strangers, where the emotional component was missing. He cared, but in a detached, professional way.

This was different.

Besides growing to like Sara as a person, he was directly responsible for her wellbeing. It was more than a good-paying job.

Their relationship had developed to the point it felt as if she were his adopted daughter.

An unfamiliar feeling of helplessness collapsed his heart.

He shoved it aside, forcing his thoughts to more practical concerns.

Poison was the only logical explanation.

But how?

Where?

He and Will cleaned her condo.

Some toxins worked instantaneously. Had someone there, perhaps on the *Today Show's* staff, compromised her in some way?

He'd scanned every member of the audience for anyone suspicious. None of the staff backstage set off that instinctive alarm known to anyone who'd worked around those with criminal intent.

Did he miss someone?

If so, any evidence back at the studio would be gone by now. His thoughts whipped back and forth. Frantic for her life on one hand, wondering at the *modis operandi* on the other, his failed efforts pummeled by both.

Sara's cell rang inside her purse. He fumbled around inside, finally finding it in an exterior pocket.

"H-hello?" he answered.

"Uh, who's this?" The voice was male and vaguely familiar.

"This is Mike. Who's this?"

"Oh. This is Charlie. Is Sara there? Is she okay?"

His shoulders slumped. "No. She's not. We're in the ER, here in New York."

"I was afraid of that. Was she on TV?"

"Yeah. But part way through she got sick and passed out. So far she hasn't woken up."

"She's been poisoned."

"I agree. But how? Where?"

"Her father should go to her home and check her toilet."

"Her *toilet*?"

"Yes. There is poison. He must be careful. Whatever it is, it's very dangerous."

Relief he hadn't missed something at the studio was spontaneously trampled by the realization he and Will blew it at her condo.

But how could Charlie know such a thing?

"Do you have any idea what it might be?" he asked, thoughts drifting back to the black truck incident during their roadtrip.

"No. Only that it's deadly. I will pray and fast with my uncle for her doctor to know what to do."

"I told them it was probably poison. This is supposed to be the best hospital for that. But if Will can find out more, it'll improve her chances. Thanks, Charlie. Take care."

As soon as he hung up and retrieved his own phone, it struck him.

Call Will.

Making unfortunate next-of-kin notifications during his law enforcement career was business as usual.

This would be the hardest call he ever had to make.

> *"You have to look deeper, way below the anger, the hurt, the hate, the jealousy, the self-pity, way down deeper where the dreams lie, son. Find your dream. It's the pursuit of the dream that heals you."*
> —Father of Olympic Gold Medal Winner, Billy Mills (Oglala Lakota)

38. TRANSITS

MONTGOMERY RESIDENCE
July 27, Friday
7:05 a.m. MDT

Will had barely turned on the TV to watch the *Today Show's* delayed broadcast when his cell went off. He and Connie exchanged puzzled glances as he picked up.

"Hey, Mike. Is everything okay?"

"No. Far from it. You haven't seen the broadcast yet, have you?"

"Not yet. It's just coming on now."

"Well, don't be surprised if Sara's segment is edited out. It didn't go well. She got sick right in the middle of it and is now in the hospital."

Panic fired in his chest. "Oh, no. What happened? How is she?"

"Not good. So far she's still unconscious. But get this. She got an interesting call from Charlie that I picked up moments ago. He said she's been poisoned. He said check out her toilet at the condo."

"Holy hell! So we were right about the break-in. That son of a bitch!"

"I can't believe we missed that," Mike lamented. "I was thinking of things that could be ingested, not contact."

"Me, too."

"If it's organic it'll show up in UV. Do you have one of those flashlights?"

"No, but I can get one easily enough. Actually, I'll call in a favor from someone who knows his way around this stuff. Hopefully he can get here soon enough. If not, I'll call Denver PD. I don't want to chance compromising evidence or do something that could get it thrown out of court."

"Excellent point. That should definitely provide enough evidence to get an attempted murder indictment."

"Hey, it looks like they didn't edit it out. I'll call you back."

Connie's eyes were wide, silently begging to know what was going on. He grabbed the remote, hit *Record,* and gave her a quick rundown, then proceeded to watch the debacle unfold on network TV.

COSMIC PORTALS
BOULDER
July 27, Friday
7:30 a.m. MDT

Patrice was seldom up that early, but didn't want to miss Sara on TV. Thus, she got out of bed in her apartment above the shop, brewed up some coffee in the Pyrex pot that had belonged to her mother, and turned on the television.

The day before she looked at Sara's transits for that day and didn't like them. The Sun was transiting her 8th house and up to no good squaring Pluto and trining Saturn. Uranus, the biggest troublemaker of all, was stirring up a few things as well. Over all, a very volatile situation was unfolding.

Furthermore, Mercury was retrograde, a time when communications were best described as one gigantic, cosmic FUBAR. Mercury was also retrograde for the accident that killed her husband earlier that year. As a Gemini, it was Sara's sign ruler and thus had a strong, often negative, effect. As a Virgo, Mercury had a heavy influence on her husband as well.

Thus, she wasn't surprised, but still horrified, when Sara was put on the defensive by a host who was usually Prince Charming. The fact she was no longer on the set following the commercial break, at which time the program switched to another segment, did not bode well.

Sara's solar return suggested it was going to be a difficult year, whether or not she pursued her plans.

This was a classic example of how things could go wrong.

She also wondered about her health.

Something told her she was physically ill, on top of everything else. She knew from her own experience that stress was a major contributor to serious disease.

That poor woman had certainly had her share of that.

Upon the sudden loss of a spouse, the survivor had a thirty-six percent chance of developing PTSD.

Patrice's two bouts with cancer had both come in the wake of difficult life situations. Her sixth sense, however, told her it was something else.

Something sinister.

Still in her nightgown, silver hair in a single braid that trailed down her back, she crept downstairs and into her office. The coffee shop opened at 7:00 a.m., but the woman she hired as manager took care of that, so most days she didn't make an appearance until around 10:00.

The murmur of early patrons and aroma of freshly brewed java and baking spiral galaxies drifted through the beaded curtain as she turned on her computer. Her astrological software program came up, allowing her to see what was going on in the cosmic neighborhood.

Saturn, the king of karma, was in cahoots with Neptune, who was sneaky and not to be trusted as the ruler of poison, drugs, alcohol, and illusions. Someone was definitely messing with her.

Her second house, which included a person's physical body, was loaded with transiting malefics—a stellium of the little devils, *i.e.* Saturn, Pluto, and Mars.

Not good. Every one of them a threat to her health and well-being.

There were so many other hostile aspects she kicked herself for not checking early enough to warn her. Yet she hated to set someone up with a self-fulfilling prophecy by warning them in advance.

Astrological predications were tricky. What appeared ominous could turn out not to be a big deal. Just another challenge, perhaps no more than a bump along the road of life, enabling the person to learn and grow.

But this was no pothole.

More like a sink hole, that could consume her entirely.

It was two hours later in New York, so the unfortunate event was already in Sara's past. No telling where she was, what she was doing, or what she might be going through.

Wanting her to know she was thinking of her, yet not be too intrusive, she decided to text her. Invite her to call if she needed someone to talk to.

She snuck back upstairs, where she grabbed her phone and messaged: *I'm here if you need me, sweetie. Looks like the planets are kicking your butt.*

NORTHERN CHEYENNE RESERVATION
July 27, Friday
7:50 a.m. MDT

Sun-parched prairie rolled past on all sides as Charlie drove along Highway 212 back to White Wolf's. The drive back from outside Lame Deer where he found cell service gave him time to absorb the events of the past few hours. He didn't question what he'd discerned, knowing its source was *Maheo*. However, it was taking time to adjust to the abrupt acquisition of such startling abilities.

White Wolf's statement the day before that the accident provided a jolt to wake up senses he already had made sense.

Like thunder in the dark of night.

Amasani taught him that thunder's return hailed the onset of spring, vibrating the Earth and waking up hibernating creatures of all kinds, from bears to insects. Thus, during the winter, ceremonies were not held where drums were beaten or rattles shaken, so as not to disturb the natural cycle.

Had the vibroseis trucks awakened the Earth Mother, instigating her rage?

Between that and the subsequent drilling, no wonder she exploded.

Now he understood why *Maheo* didn't reply to his prayers about working for LSO. The blowout's intent was to jolt his soul awake to these other senses.

They woke up, alright.

Previous whispers were now a roar.

Awareness of how important his abilities could be humbled him, but prompted impatience to hone his skills. The Creator expected him to use these gifts to help others. He'd wasted enough time foundering in unbelief.

His mouth formed a rueful smile as he recalled his reaction when the ex-cop answered. The instant he heard that man's voice instead of hers, he'd been annoyed.

Then, upon learning she was unable to answer, he was consumed by a blanket of light, admonishing him for his hostility.

Fernandez, like himself, was trying to help.

In that instant, his anger evaporated, replaced by a warm sense of gratitude. Shedding that huge lump of resentment had been a revelation in itself. To complete the process, he needed to ask the man to forgive him for his previous behavior.

Each day brought important lessons and new understanding. Now he was hungry for more, to discover all the things of which he was now or would be capable. As he neared the house, he hoped they could get down to the business of learning. If White Wolf had any healing calls today, that was okay—they would be important experiences for him as well.

It felt good to be back in his old truck driving again, now that his eyes were beholden to his will. The sense of freedom he'd lost following the accident had been restored. It felt as if the recent past were a different lifetime, the present a promising new one.

The vision of Sara's condo awakened him to the responsibility he carried. The poison used was extremely dangerous. Some didn't have an antidote. It was good she was in a hospital where they could start some sort of treatment to purge it from her system. There were limitations to western medicine, but it was a good start to get her stabilized, at least.

An urgent need fell upon him to assure her recovery. He'd seen White Wolf heal people in astounding ways. So far, he hadn't been told anything about the process, only that it involved correcting life energy flows with the help of *Maheo*.

The auras around all living things, even rocks and minerals, were also beginning to make sense. How to interpret and work with them, however, had not been explored. How much would be intuitive, experience, or learned through White Wolf's tutoring?

So far, he'd looked to the past and remote locations. As soon as he got back, he hoped White Wolf would help him see what Sara's aura reflected about her current condition.

The thought of those red-eyed snakes took his breath away. Permanent damage was almost assured.

Whether or not he could help hammered his mind. He'd always cared about her as a friend. Now he couldn't bear the thought of losing her.

COSMIC PORTALS
BOULDER
July 27, Friday
1:22 p.m.

Patrice sat with her usual mid-afternoon latté, staring into its caramel enhanced depths. Sara's fate stuck in her mind like a stationing planet. The fact she hadn't responded to her text was a bad sign, especially considering all that ominous eighth house activity. Unable to stand it any longer, she retired through the beaded curtain to her reading room to give her a call.

Fear flooded through her when a man answered.

"This is Patrice, a friend of Sara's. Can she talk?"

"Who's this?" he asked, abruptly enough she was taken aback.

"This is Patrice Renard. A personal friend. To whom am I speaking?"

"Mike Fernandez."

"Oh! You're her bodyguard, correct?"

"Yes. Did she tell you that?"

"No, her step-mom, Connie, did." Her stomach fell with the realization things were as bad as she feared.

"Will's wife, right?"

"Yes. Is she okay?" She didn't like the long pause that followed.

"Here's the deal," he said at last. "I can't give out that information without Sara's permission. She's in the hospital and they're doing everything they can. I suggest you call Will's wife for the details."

"Okay. Thank you. I'll do that."

An ominous, empty feeling crept up from her stomach and lodged in her throat. Should she call Connie or not?

They'd known each other for a long time, been through a lot together. Maybe she needed someone to talk to. It never hurt to know that someone cared enough to call.

She found her number and pressed *Connect*. Connie picked up moments later.

"Hi, girlfriend. It's Patrice. I just tried to call Sara and talked to Mike. Is everything okay?"

"Oh, Patrice! It's not okay at all." She sounded as if she'd been crying. "Sara's been poisoned by something bad. She's been unconscious ever since she passed out at the TV studio. She's in the hospital, there in New York. Can you tell if she's going to die?"

Patrice drew a sharp breath. She'd seen death charts far less threatening than what Sara was dealing with, so it was a distinct possibility. However, it was unethical to answer such questions.

"I can't tell you that, girlfriend. Like Yoda says, 'Always in motion, the future is.' Much of it depends on what she wants."

Free will could have a huge influence, one way or the other. However, how much free will was in effect if she was unconscious? Besides, planetary placements that indicated certain death in years past could often be mediated by modern medicine or other healing techniques.

Her empathic sense was strong, the woman's pain and despondency over the situation contagious. Many were the times she cried along with clients when they were slogging through a heart-wrenching transit. Like she had with Connie when Sara's mother died.

"Do you have any idea at all if she'll be okay?"

"Hold on. Let me bring up her chart."

To be certain exactly what was going on in the cosmos, she turned to her computer and brought the chart back up. The news she'd been poisoned prompted her to check Neptune, ruler of poison and deception, as well as Uranus, ruler of the unexpected.

Both were considerably stressed. Her hopes diminished when she noticed Sara had two planets at 20 degrees, which had been blasted by that eclipse earlier that month—the one that hit Charlie like a train.

It hadn't done Sara any favors, either. That additional information made things looks worse than ever.

Was it hopeless? So far, it looked like it.

She examined the charts and their dynamics more closely, looking for anything positive. She gasped with cautious optimism. In just under a week, the Sun would go into her ninth house. Then it would be in the house of beliefs and expectations and out of her eighth, the house of death. If she made it until then, that could reflect a turning point as opposed to an ending.

"If she can hold on for another week, things should get better August 2."

"I don't think that will happen."

The sniffling on the other end triggered tears of her own. "I'm afraid she wants to be with her husband," Connie said, sobbing. "I can't blame her. They had to resuscitate her, Patrice. She probably had another NDE. If she saw Bryan, she won't want to come back."

"Do you think he might talk her into returning?"

"No way. He made her come back once already. She's had nothing but pain and misery ever since. Why would she want to?"

Patrice closed her eyes and prayed that Sara's doctors could keep her alive until then. After that, it would be a matter of free will.

INTERSTATE 70 WEST
July 27, Friday
2:44 p.m.

Eddie knew he was toast as soon as that damn video aired again on network TV. Another scathing ass chewing from his mother drove him online to watch the broadcast's recording. He sat at his kitchen table, opened up his laptop, and found the *Today Show* website.

He cussed as he slammed the computer closed. He grabbed it in both hands, lifted it over his head, then stopped.

No. It had good information on it that he still needed.

He set it back down, gradually realizing how badly he'd screwed up.

He lit a cigarette, sucked in a lungful of smoke, then blew it out through clenched teeth. At least the bitch definitely looked bad, showing the effects of his fine work.

Why didn't she come back after the commercial break?

Oh, well. Didn't matter.

The less she talked, the better.

With luck, she was dead.

One thing for sure, he needed to get out of town. Not only to lay low, but for a much-needed break. He'd been working his ass off, all on his own. Going rogue wasn't easy. Yet, he accomplished more the past week than his entire team.

Seemed like he was always the one who did all the work and took all the crap.

Yeah, he deserved a vacation.

Getting some sun and chilling out were well-worth the risk. With his new look, it was doubtful anyone would recognize him.

He hoped he wouldn't have to maintain it for long, however. The fake tan and hair dye smelled funny and rubbed off on his clothes. Putting that crap back on every time he took a shower was a real pain in the butt, too.

Glaring at the laptop one final time, he strode into his bedroom, threw a few essentials in a duffle bag including his .45, then climbed in his truck. He took Highway 6 to I-70, where he set the cruise control for 67 mph. Last thing he needed was to drive his usual speed and attract the freakin' cops.

How would he explain his modified appearance to Aunt Ida? Uncle Sam would understand, but that frizzy haired harpy was another story. She'd probably grill him, wanting to know. His uncle would give him a wink or two, then leave it alone.

Maybe he'd just tell her he was trying to get himself a hot Hispanic chick.

Yeah, that would work.

Meanwhile, he could chill out and not worry about being recognized.

Cheyenne are the greatest horsemen on earth. Their war ponies are swift and when they rode on the side there was no target to shoot.
—*Major Frederick Benteen, 7th Calvary, June 25, 1876*

39. TRAIL RIDE

NORTHERN CHEYENNE RESERVATION
MONTANA
July 27, Friday
3:08 p.m. MDT

Charlie strolled out to the barn with Winter Hawk, *Náhkòhe* dancing in circles of delight. As they stepped inside, his spirit swelled like the Tongue River after a heavy rain. He stood there a moment, savoring the medley of aromas—hay, straw, leather, horseflesh, and of course, the earthy scent of manure—as appetizing to his soul as any powwow feast was to his palate.

"Do you want a saddle, brother?"

Charlie didn't hesitate. "No. I want to connect with her, not treat her like a pack animal."

"I know what you mean. I prefer bareback as well. After all, that is how our ancestors rode."

Winter Hawk handed him a braided buckskin hackamore and set about placing one on his ride, a sorrel tobiano with a red head and white body named Hobo.

"That's an odd name for a mare," Charlie commented.

"She was named after her father. A Cheyenne pony race horse who won lots of races. Maybe they were hoping for a colt instead of a filly."

Charlie chuckled. "It is ironic *vehoe* brought horses to us, is it not?"

"You are teasing, yes?"

Charlie laughed at the teen's squinty-eyed suspicious look. "No. It is true. When *vehoe* came to our land they also brought donkeys, goats, sheep, chickens, pigs, and cattle."

"Wow. I did not know that. Does not make up for killing the buffalo, though."

"True. These are beautiful horses. Have you had them long?"

"We received them at the giveaway during the Busby Christmas PowWow. That was right before my tenth birthday, so five years." He grinned. "I begged my father for a horse for months, so it turned out well. I'm not sure whose prayers *Maheo* answered, mine or his."

Laughing, the pair exited the barn leading their respective rides, *Náhkóhe* still engaged in his canine happy dance. They exited the wooden gate, then mounted up.

"Where would you like to go, brother?"

Charlie couldn't have cared less, just grateful to be astride a horse for the first time in years.

"Your lead. Where's your favorite place?"

The teen smiled. "Eaglefeathers Butte. It has a wonderful view. Makes me feel like a warrior. We will follow our elk hunting trail to the top and I will show you where we sit and wait for the elk to come."

"Perfect. Let's go."

The conversation ebbed as they headed south, Winter Hawk leading the way. The late morning breeze and flawless blue sky clothed Charlie's soul with peace, any landscape vastly improved when viewed from atop a good mount.

Green velvet clung to rolling hills, which in the coming weeks would succumb to brown. Their destination, some three miles away, appeared as an imposing mound, timber ringing its base then following the banks of Eaglefeathers Creek.

His thoughts wandered with the terrain, enjoyment soon marred by his concern for Sara.

Which was why he'd pleaded with White Wolf to let him go for a ride—to escape into nature and think. He smiled, remembering him blowing out a breath and saying without ire, *"É-óetsetanómóho. Náéše-nèhe'xóveotse."*

He'd been pestered to the point he finally agreed—*if* someone went with him.

Winter Hawk quickly volunteered.

Amid the soothing rhythm of hooves on soft ground, his thoughts lingered on Sara. Her face appeared before him, smiling one moment as she had watching the stars, pleading for help the next.

Earlier that day White Wolf sensed his unrest, which led to a conversation on free will. Not only that of individuals, but of interfering with *Maheo's* purposes.

As he'd so recently learned from his accident, sometimes unfortunate events were the catalyst for greater things.

Like bringing him home to his roots and family.

One of the abilities *Maheo* gave a medicine man with grandfather spirit powers of healing was to know when to intervene and when to leave the situation in *Maheo's* hands. No doubt one of those spiritual senses White Wolf told him about.

Wanting a specific outcome, objectivity was impossible.

Another disturbing emotion was his outrage to the point of hating the *vehoe* behind all their misfortune. Everything about that evil man was etched upon his mind in excruciating detail. Wringing his *vehoe* neck and stomping him into the ground had far too much appeal, justified by what he'd done to Bryan and especially Sara, as well as indirectly to himself by killing his white brother.

What a vile human being. A true o'*kòhoméeotse,* a sneaky, stinking coyote. The present day essence of the *vehoes* who stole their land and culture over a century before, murdering his people at will. Relentless fury smoldered, not unlike the borehole's hydrogen sulfide that nearly killed him.

He couldn't remember ever hating anyone this much.

Ever.

He'd sworn to avenge Bryan's death, yet that hadn't happened. He and Sara discovered who killed Bryan and why, but so far no consequences had been dealt to the guilty parties. By him or anyone else.

"You seem troubled, brother. Is there anything you want to talk about?"

Charlie's reverie returned to the present to find Winter Hawk riding beside him. The trail had widened, timber marking Eaglefeathers Creek visible up ahead. He wasn't sure how to respond. If Winter Hawk were older it would be easier, but these were heavy topics for a fifteen year old.

He glanced over at his cousin, startled when instead of a teenager, he saw someone his own age with wise, soulful eyes.

His cousin was an old soul, wise beyond his years. Maybe he would see the situation in a fresh and innocent way that would provide insights he needed. He knew Eaglefeathers was watching over his young cousin since the Prayer Cloth ceremony.

He blinked. Winter Hawk's youth resumed.

"You are right, brother," Charlie answered. "I am troubled."

He proceeded to tell him what had occurred the past three and a half months. His best friend murdered; discovering why; his determination to avenge his death; his job; the accident; and now his concern for Sara.

"Wow," Winter Hawk answered, yet didn't seem shocked or disturbed. "My father never tells us anything about those he helps, so I knew none of that. *Néá ěše,* for sharing with me."

"You were there earlier when your father talked about free will. That is part of what troubles me. Whether to help Sara or not."

"We could use the sacred red pipe to ask *Maheo.*"

Charlie clenched his jaw. As long as he harbored such wrath toward the man who'd caused it all he was not worthy to approach the Creator for direction or answers. *Amasani's* teaching about forgiveness thundered through his conscience as well, reminding him of hate's toxicity.

"I do not feel humble enough. My anger toward the person responsible is very strong. How do you forgive an *ok kliwǔs* who has done horrible things and destroyed so many lives?"

"Like forgiving *vehoe* for what he did to our people."

"Yes."

"There's an old *Tsetsehestaestse* saying, *Oeškēso màxhéxaēsto nevénótse he'poo'o!* When a dog lifts his leg against your tent just smoke! My father said it was advice given to a new chief many years ago, telling him, 'When someone does something bad to you, even as bad as stealing your wife, stay calm.'"

Charlie laughed, but cringed inside, having been in that very position. "That is good advice, but not always easy to follow."

Though he had to admit he hated the man in the video far more than the one who stole his wife, who, like Custer, got what he deserved.

By then they reached a stream running alongside Eaglefeathers Creek. They stopped long enough for everyone to get a cool drink before resuming their trek to climb the massive rock-strewn formation—determined to hold its ground rather than yield to some ancient glacier, even as his people refused to abandon their homeland.

Their excursion resumed, a flash of color in a small tree barely visible up ahead—the prayer cloths. They turned far enough east to avoid the sacred ground, riding toward the ridge that led to the summit. The trail narrowed, forcing them back to single file as they made their way through the heavily timbered base, dodging looming pines as they began their ascent.

Náhkòhe took off in the lead, knowing the way.

Glimpses of Eaglefeathers Butte peeked through the trees, rock layers mimicking sunset hues while reaching for the sky.

Past the trees, the path to the top followed a wash. Steep, uneven, rock-strewn, and treacherous, it required all Charlie's concentration to stay astride the horse as the grade increased. It was apparent Spring Thunder was not as familiar with the trail as Hobo, who was now several yards ahead.

At the summit at last, they dismounted and gazed silently upon the spectacular view. The ranch, miles away, was barely visible, house and barn tiny squares interrupting the flow of the land.

Prairie decorated with imposing rock formations stretched in every direction, slashed by Eaglefeathers and Rosebud Creeks. Stands of timber accented the water's path, fading to a far off misty horizon. While White Wolf's land was his own, along with various other privately owned parcels issued as allotments decades before, the surrounding property comprised a tribal livestock grazing unit.

It was easy to understand why Winter Hawk felt like a warrior up there. It was as if he'd been there centuries before as well, watching for anything that could harm his people, whether bad weather or foreign invader.

They sat down, *Náhkóhe* between them, conversation unnecessary. Two cousins, both bearing the same amount of Eaglefeathers's blood, contemplating the world from the butte that bore his name. The perspective it yielded, of man's insignificance compared to *Maheo* and his creations, blanketed Charlie's soul with peace and hope.

The landscape blurred, prompting him to venture back in time until a large herd of buffalo appeared. The presence of many calves told him they were females, herds separated by gender until the end of summer when mating season began.

The person beside him was no longer his cousin, but a brother from another time. A small heap of shards rested between them. While keeping watch, they were fashioning arrowheads for future battles sure to come.

The buffalo vanished when Winter Hawk spoke. The words came not from a teenage boy whose voice betrayed him by cracking at inopportune times, but strong and confident.

"My father is a great medicine man. He is close to *Maheo*. Kind, wise and caring. He told me that holy men can curse those who do evil. When they do, they are following what *Maheo* tells them to do."

"That is true. There's a curse on Dead Horse Canyon. Where my white brother died."

His cousin turned his way, again appearing in his adult persona. "Then trust the curse to avenge your white brother. If it is

Maheo's will, it will happen. We can make an offering and pray that our Creator honors the curse."

Charlie took the bag of tobacco from his shirt pocket that he now carried for such occasions.

"Yes. We will do that. Let *Maheo* decide."

Charlie sprinkled some tobacco on the ground, each blessed himself with the earth, then knelt as Charlie prayed. He admitted his own faults and weaknesses, then asked *Maheo* to apply the original intent of Black Cloud's curse to the current situation.

By the time he finished, his burden felt much lighter.

"We better head back or we'll be late for our evening meal," Winter Hawk said, prompting both to mount up and head back down the trail.

As was the case earlier, Hobo was sure-footed during their descent while Spring Thunder became a bit spooky. The steep angle prompted Charlie to let the horse lead, hackamore loose in his hand. As the grade increased, he leaned forward, left hand gripping her mane, right arm hugging her neck, knees pressed to her sides.

When they reached a stretch of talus, her hooves slipped, prompting her to falter.

Charlie tightened his grip.

The mare ducked her head.

Next thing he knew he was eating dirt, horse plodding down the trail without him.

Stunned but unhurt, he sat up, hugged his knees to his chest, and hung his head, berating himself for such a stupid stunt. The last time he fell off a horse he was seven years old. He could still hear his father, Little Bear, and Eaglefeathers laughing, one of the most humiliating moments of his young life.

Multiple hooves plodding his way announced his cousin's return, leading what had so recently been his ride. *Náhkôhe* ran up whimpering and licked his face.

Winter Hawk took one look, then bit his lip as his features contorted. Unable to hold back, laughter exploded from his chest.

One hand battled tears of mirth while the other clutched the lead to Charlie's mutinous mare.

Between his cousin's hysterical sniggers and the humiliating situation, Charlie had no choice but to join in. Self-directed humor rumbled in his chest, then morphed into a cough, eventually liberating another glob of phlegm, which he'd been doing since the sweat. He spit it out, then slowly met his cousin's humor-glazed eyes with his own.

"Brother," Winter Hawk stammered, suppressed hilarity rocking his words. "Why are you sitting on the ground? *Tsetsehestaestse* men do not fall off their ponies!"

His cousin lost it again, more laughter following the well-worn trail to the summit of Eaglefeathers's Butte.

Charlie's pride was annihilated. "Yes. You are correct. It is no doubt the fault of my *Diné* mother."

The levity continued until Charlie finally stood up and brushed himself off. As he did, a flash of light caught his eye from the multitude of rocks at his feet. He hunkered down, wondering. Did he lose something during his ego-busting tumble?

Among the thousands of shards reposed a perfectly crafted arrowhead. Had he not landed in that very spot he would have missed it.

He picked it up.

One of his own, perhaps, from another time?

He held it up for his cousin to see, then wrapped his fingers around it, sharp edges biting his palm as he discerned its message.

Their prayer had been heard.

Maheo, our spirits belong to you. Teach us your wisdom of life. We ask not to be fools.
--Pete Risingsun (Northern Cheyenne)

40. VISITORS

MILE HIGH DODGE DEALERSHIP
DENVER
July 28, Saturday
9:15 a.m.

Will strolled through the Dodge showroom, stopping to admire the latest Challenger R/T, a slight distraction from the anxiety searing his heart. He and Connie were booked to fly into LaGuardia the following day, his former colleague due to arrive that afternoon. Meanwhile, he had an idea.

He loved his Benz, but what man could resist such a sleek machine? He owned a Porsche 911, years before, which he loved, but gave up after Sara was born. He'd mostly forgotten how much fun it was to drive a sports car. He opened the door and sat in the driver's seat, checking out the electronic array on the dash.

As expected, it didn't take long before a lanky blond salesman approached.

"Welcome to Mile High Dodge." He flashed a signature car salesman grin as he held out his hand. "She's a gorgeous driving machine, isn't she?"

"Definitely." He took the man's hand, then fought the urge to wipe it on the seat courtesy of the guy's sweaty palm.

While tempted to go for a test drive, he stuck to his real reason for being there.

Regardless of updating the cops the day before regarding Sara's condition, he doubted they'd move as quickly as he'd prefer. He wasn't sure they believed him that her being sick was connected to the break-in without concrete evidence. At least now the case was activated and he had its number, though not the name of the assigned detective.

If Johannsen was even marginally professional, he knew how to disappear.

Probably already had. If he could get more specific information on his vehicle, however, they could put out a more detailed APB.

"Actually, I'm more in the market for a truck. I was talking to some big, Nordic looking guy in the Kroger parking lot the other day who had one. He told me how much he loved it and said I should come by here for the best deal."

"No kidding?" The salesman's grin widened. "We love customer referrals. Did you get his name? We like to send a thank you card along with coupons for special service deals or accessories."

"No, I didn't. But his truck was black, if that helps."

"It does. We don't sell that many. In fact, I heard a former customer of mine came by a week or so ago. He had an unexpected blow-out and came by to check on the tire warranty. He bought it back around May, as I recall. Paid cash." He chuckled. "I remember him joking about getting a black Ram because he was his family's black sheep. Hold on. Let me go check the records."

The man strolled back toward the dealership offices behind the showroom while Will wiped his hand on his pants and indulged in a vengeful grin.

Footsteps sounded from back as the salesman returned, his expression broadcasting he'd hit pay dirt.

"Got it! His name is Glen Smith. Lives in Lakewood."

"Great. Maybe I'll run into him again." He wisely kept quiet regarding what he'd do if he did.

"So what kind of truck are you looking for? Heavy duty? General use? Off-road? Family vehicle?"

"I'm not sure, actually. Just looking for now. I have a few projects going where a pickup would come in handy. Can't haul sheetrock in my Benz." Both laughed. "What do you recommend for general use?"

While he wasn't in the market, the least he could do was feign sincerity by looking at a few.

After wasting close to an hour looking at trucks he couldn't care less about, he shook hands with the salesman and left the showroom. As soon as he got in his car, he wiped his hands on his pants and called Mike.

"Hey, Will.

"How's Sara?"

"Same. Any news from your friend?"

"He's flying in this afternoon. I had a bit of luck otherwise, though. I found out Johannsen's actual, or perhaps assumed, name."

"No kidding? How'd you manage that?"

Will responded with somewhere between a scoff and a snort. "I visited a Dodge dealership, gave them some cockamamie story, and managed to find out he goes by Glen Smith. At least that's the name he used to buy the truck."

"That's great! Are you sure that's the right person?"

"Actually, I am. The salesman said the guy stopped by a week or so ago after having a blowout."

"*Hmmph.* That would be him, alright."

"It's no guarantee we'll find him, but it should be a little easier. If nothing else, the truck should be registered under that name."

"Right. Which means the police can get his address, no problem. Have you called it in yet?"

"I'm waiting on a call back. I left a message on the investigating officer's phone mail. If my CIA buddy finds anything we missed, that should get their attention real fast and provide the evidence they need. Connie and I fly in tomorrow around noon. If you haven't done so already, book a flight home. No reason for all of us to be there."

"Will do."

"Keep me posted if anything changes."

"Of course. Same here."

He started up the car and headed home. The elation faded, replaced by a sick hollow feeling.

He already lost one woman he loved.

What if his baby girl was next?

PERLEMAN EMERGENCY CENTER
NEW YORK CITY
July 28, Saturday
1:06 p.m. EDT

Mike jolted awake when someone touched his shoulder. The floor nurse apologized, a tall, middle-aged woman, hair in a messy knot on top of her head. "I'm sorry to disturb you, Mr. Fernandez, but there's someone here to see your wife."

Confusion beset him. The vigil was familiar. He was in a hospital room with someone, but his wife died under similar conditions years ago.

Had time collapsed?

Then he remembered.

"I'm sorry, I must have dozed off," he said. "Who is it?"

"A Mr. Jenkins. He looks vaguely familiar for some reason."

He took a breath, now established in the proper time and place. "You've probably seen him on TV. Go ahead, send him in."

Mike straightened in the chair as the door whispered closed behind her. Besides the brain fog, sometimes it was hard to breathe, while others he was consciously aware of his heartbeat.

It had to be stress, but he was usually more resistant, being in law enforcement all those years. Maybe he was just getting old.

The rhythmic hiss and alternate beeps of Sara's life-support equipment had a hypnotic effect that often lulled him to sleep. The sense of failure compounded by guilt, however, was far worse.

He'd trade places with her in a moment.

When the door swung open he stood up. Davis Jenkins entered the room wearing a pair of jeans and a pale blue polo shirt. The man's jaw dropped when he saw Sara connected to a miasma of medical paraphernalia.

"Wow," he whispered, then turned to shake hands.

"Yeah," Mike replied. "Not good."

"No progress?"

"Not really, at least in her condition. There was a break-in at her place a week or so back. We're checking for evidence of poison."

"You are? *Whew!* The brass are really sweating down at the station."

"No worries," Mike assured him. "I can all but guarantee she won't be the one to sue you. That guy in the dashcam clip, maybe. But he should be in prison before that happens. He's the one who broke in and the prime suspect."

"They'll definitely be relieved to hear that."

"By the way, I was impressed with your security team. Very professional."

"Thanks. They'll appreciate hearing that. So, do they know what kind of poison?"

"Not yet. The hospital hasn't been able to identify it. If we find anything at her condo, then maybe we can. Hopefully, there's an antidote. Meanwhile, they're doing what they can to get it out of her system."

"Has she woken up since the studio?"

"No."

"I, uh, actually came by to, uh, apologize. I'm so sorry about how things turned out yesterday. My intent, putting her on the spot like that, was to generate public sympathy. So the audience would side with her even more. I expected her to come back with some snappy retort." He chuckled softly. "Then again, maybe she did."

Mike smiled, remembering when he was a Falcon Ridge cop and Sara put him firmly in his place. "Under normal circumstances, I'm sure she would have. She's got a lot of spunk." He cleared his throat, resisting its attempt to close.

A louder, more insistent beep started from the machine on the far side of her bed. Jenkins stiffened, eyes wide.

"It's okay," Mike reassured him. "Time to replace the Ringer's. A nurse will be here shortly."

"So what are they doing to help her?"

He told him the same thing he told Will—various therapies to detoxify her body. Whether or not she'd ever wake up or at what point they'd turn off the life-support had not been mentioned much less discussed.

Furthermore, that was a conversation for Will and Connie, not him.

Jenkins's eyebrows drew together, his expression one of genuine concern.

"Her story deserves to be told," he said. "If it's okay, I'd like to get her interview up on our website. I'd edit out, well, you know, and add an addendum. And her GoFundMe account. She has my support, more so now than ever, with someone determined to keep her quiet."

"She would probably approve, but until she wakes up you should wait, to make sure."

"When she recovers, just say the word. We'll get her back on the show. Everyone at the station is rooting for her. They want to thank her for putting me in my place."

Mike forced a smile. "I'm sure she'd appreciate that. We'll let you know."

The door whooshed as a young LVN with brown curly hair entered to change the spent IV bag.

"I better go. Stay in touch," Jenkins said, shaking his hand again, then stepping out the door.

When the nurse finished checking everything she turned to Mike.

"You look pretty tired yourself. Were you exposed, too?"

"Possibly. Don't know for sure. I feel kind of off, but figure I'll live."

"They should check while you're here. Maybe there's something they can give you to get over it faster."

"What I really need is that nasty concoction my Mexican grandmother used to make out of orange peels or something. God, it was horrible. Had to gag it down. Worse than castor oil. But it worked."

She laughed with knowing agreement. "Some of those old remedies were the best. My mother used to force some garlic-parsley-lemon juice stuff down me. Usually made me throw-up, but then I felt better."

"The good ol' days, right? Well, with that not an option, maybe I will go back to the hotel and take a nap. If I don't feel better tomorrow, I'll think about talking to her doctor."

"Go get some rest, Mr. Fernandez. She's in good hands. We'll call if there's any change."

"Okay. You talked me into it."

WHEELER RESIDENCE
RURAL FALCON RIDGE
July 28, Saturday
12:42 p.m. MDT

Rhonda moved the lace curtains aside to peer out her kitchen window. What sounded like a large truck had just pulled into Barbie's RV park next door. She gasped—there it was again, that shiny black pickup with that huge contraption on the front.

The hair stood up on her arms as she watched the guy get out, looking entirely different than she remembered. If that didn't say he was hiding from someone or something, she didn't know what did.

Determined to do as promised, she tried to remember where she put the business card that former cop, what's-his-name, gave her.

Where was it?

She wandered about the house, checking the usual places she stashed such things—kitchen counter, fireplace mantle, her bedroom dresser—until she finally found it in her top desk drawer, with all the other business cards.

She poked in his number, trying not to hyperventilate while she waited for him to answer. When he did, he sounded different, as if he just woke up or was distracted in some way.

"Mr. Fernandez? This is Rhonda Wheeler, out in Falcon Ridge. We talked when you were fishing. Remember?"

"Yes, of course. How are you today?"

"I'm fine, thank you. I'm calling because you asked me to call if that creepy character in the black pickup showed up again."

"He's back?"

"Yes!"

"When did he get there?"

"I'm not sure. He just pulled in, but went directly into one of the trailers, so he must have checked in earlier, when I was at the grocery store. Maybe even last night."

"What matters is he's there now. Thank you so much."

"He looks entirely different, too. Dyed his hair. If that doesn't mean he's done something wrong and trying to hide, I don't know what does."

"I agree. I appreciate your call, Mrs. Wheeler. Don't be surprised if you see law enforcement over there fairly soon."

"Thank *you*. If anything else comes up, I'll let you know."

"Please do. I appreciate it. Thanks again."

Rhonda hung up, satisfied. Nothing would please her more than to get that guy out of there, once and for all.

What did he do, anyway?

On second thought, maybe she didn't want to know.

GIBSON ARMS HOTEL
NEW YORK
July 28, Saturday
2:48 p.m. EDT

Mike sat on the bed, staring at his phone. The call yanked him up from a dead sleep.

Everything was coming together, almost too quickly. He sucked in a breath then, without further delay, called Will. With luck, that SOB would be behind bars before the day was done.

MONTGOMERY RESIDENCE
BOULDER
July 28, Saturday
12:48 p.m. MDT

Will stared out his den window as distant traffic on the Diagonal flowed unimpeded, people oblivious to other's troubles as they pursued their normal, everyday life.

What exactly was *normal*? He didn't know anymore.

The report he just received from the hospital demolished any enthusiasm generated by his success at the dealership. Whatever poison it was resisted chelation. Dialysis was next. When pressed, the doctor gave her a 50:50 chance if, and only if, she survived being taken off life-support following that treatment.

His cell went off again. Anxiety jump-started his nerves every time it rang, especially when it was Mike.

"Hey, Mike. Is Sara okay?"

"No change. *But* I just got a call from the woman I talked to when Sara and I were out at her cabin. The one who'd seen the black pickup. She said it's back."

"What? Johannsen's there? *Now?"*

"Apparently."

"Fantastic. I still haven't heard back from Denver PD. Handing them the perp's name, alias, picture, and truck description, to say nothing of his real-time location should be enough to nail that SOB. What more evidence do they need than Sara being poisoned?"

"No kidding," Mike agreed. "Maybe they can find hard evidence at his residence. Which they should have checked for when you told them she was sick."

"I should have something after Winnie goes through the place. When you get back, keep things moving on the condo. We may as well seal up the passage between the units. Once Johannsen's arrested, the immediate need is gone."

"Maybe, maybe not. We don't know whether he's working alone."

"True. Thanks, Mike."

The call ended.

If Johannsen wasn't working alone, the threat remained.

Then again, if Sara—

He stopped, refusing to entertain such a thought. The nightmare of losing his first wife years before slammed him again, sending aftershocks through his heart. How ironic that Sara survived two wrecks, only to fall prey to this.

He should have shot the guy.

Right between the eyes.

But that wouldn't help his only child.

His thoughts drifted to her friend, Charlie. He should probably tell him about her condition, likewise the status of finding the guy responsible. He'd want to know.

He couldn't find him in his contacts. It must have been Connie who texted him during Sara's first accident. His wife was at the grocery store, so he called Mike back to get it from Sara's phone.

The number went directly to voice mail. Considering he was on some reservation in rural Montana, it was a good bet he didn't have cell service. He left a message, just in case:

Charlie, this is Will, Sara's father. She's not doing well. My wife and I are headed for New York. The good news is the man responsible should be arrested shortly. Feel free to call when you get this message.

There was some consolation in the fact that Charlie already knew she was sick. Perhaps he was also aware how serious it was.

Not that there was anything he could do about it..

> *Great Spirit, help me never to judge another until I have walked in his moccasins.*
> *—Lakota prayer*

41. EVIDENCE

DENVER INTERNATIONAL AIRPORT
July 28, Saturday
2:09 p.m. MDT

Will sat in his Mercedes in one of Denver International's cell lots, engine and air conditioning running while he waited for a text from Winnie that his flight had arrived.

Winston Ellsworth was in the CIA's special weapons division. They'd worked a few cases together, decades before, when he was in the FBI.

He chuckled, remembering how they took a lot of ribbing as "Winnie and Willie," but they hit it off and worked well together. He never thought he'd call in a favor, but with his daughter's life at stake, there was nothing he wouldn't do. No agency knew more about poison than the one affectionately dubbed *Christians In Action*.

Furthermore, their lab sources were among the best.

The only number he had for him dated back to their last contact, but luckily he wasn't prone to job changes. He was working a case in El Paso, but as soon as Will told him about Sara, he booked a flight while they were still on the phone.

Finding the poison would prove the break-in constituted attempted murder. What more would the police need than that?

Fury raged that anyone would do such a thing to any woman, much less his daughter. Again, he berated himself for not shooting the SOB. On the other hand, death was too good for someone who deserved to rot in prison as someone's bitch.

Around twenty minutes later the text arrived. Will drove to the Frontier Airlines pick-up area, easily spotting him, a medium stature black man. His bristly hair was still cropped short, but sprinkled with more grey.

"Hey, Will. Been a long time," he said, tossing a backpack in back, then sliding into the seat and connecting the seatbelt. "Still a fan of German engineering, I see." He extended his hand for a friendly handshake.

He left the airport on Peña and followed it to I-70 while he explained the situation.

"You're probably not familiar with what Sara's been involved with," he explained. "She's been on the news recently, recounting how she and her husband were targeted after seeing suspicious activity by their vacation home."

"So she's what prompted that State of the Union a month ago?"

"Exactly. We believe this guy was hired to keep her quiet."

"By the *Company*?"

Will shook his head. "No. Some mercenary type. Got her with something bad, though. She's in the hospital in New York City. Tests are inconclusive, symptoms consistent with poisoning."

"Sounds like professionals, all right."

Will described the intrusion during the wee hours of July 22.

Ellsworth's brows lowered. "Didn't you report it to the police?"

Will snorted derisively. "I did. They filed a report, but we didn't find any evidence. I've kept them updated, but haven't heard back. I was suspicious the guy was up to something, though, so I threw out any open containers and put all the kitchenware through the dishwasher."

He recounted how he and Mike went through the place after that and what they'd done to mediate the threat. "We tossed everything else, then sprayed it down with a bleach solution. We must have missed it, though, because she still got sick."

"That should have taken care of anything on those surfaces. Did she experience anything invasive? A needle or anything sharp in the couch or her pillow? Depending on what it is, even a scratch can be lethal."

"She didn't mention anything, but you never know. Unfortunately, she's been unconscious since yesterday."

"So you're certain it's something in her house? When did she leave for New York?"

"Thursday morning."

"*Hmmmm.* That's quite a delay."

Will exited I-70 and wound his way onto I-225 South. "Any ideas what it could be?"

Winnie's eyebrows knit together, as he emitted the *I'm thinking* noises he remembered.

"Most designer poisons act fast. Sarin can be delayed up to forty-eight hours, though. Depends on exposure. If, by chance, it's some old KGB stuff, it could be slightly degraded and work slower. I don't know of any with time-release effects, but no telling. What were her symptoms again?"

"She threw up, had a grand mal seizure, then passed out and stopped breathing. CPR alone didn't work. Had to use an AED. When they got her to the hospital, she was intubated and put on life support."

"Sounds like some sort of nervine. Cuts off electrical signals from the brain so everything stops."

Will eased toward the East Hampden off-ramp, arriving at the condo minutes later.

Once inside, Winnie pulled on a pair of neoprene gloves, then removed a flashlight outfitted with UV LEDs from his backpack. A sweep around the kitchen revealed a variety of iridescent drip and splatter marks along the sink, appliances, and cabinets.

"You say you cleaned out the refrigerator?"

"Yes. Plus all the dishes, silverware, and glasses went through the longest cycle on the dishwasher."

"What about the bathrooms?"

"There was a glass upstairs that I added to the dishwasher. I threw out all her cosmetics and toiletries." He closed his eyes and grimaced. "Did I ever catch holy hell for that. And we sprayed everything down."

"What about the toilet?"

"The toilet? No, didn't do anything with that other than flush a few things. Actually, someone mentioned we should check it."

"Alright. Let's have a look."

Nothing unexpected showed up in the downstairs half-bath, same with the guest bath upstairs. When they got to the master, the UV light didn't show anything anomalous until he lifted the lid. This time the beam revealed a dramatic quarter-inch fluorescent stripe circling the seat, its UV reflective properties making it appear alive.

Will's mouth fell open. Goosebumps tickled his arms as Ellsworth removed a large plastic bag from his backpack. "Here. Hold this."

Will obliged, lost for words. Ellsworth removed the seat and lowered it into the evidence container.

"Wh-what do you think it is?" Will sputtered as Winnie closed and sealed the bag.

"My money's on some organic designer poison. Lab might be able to narrow it down, but it's a longshot. More likely they'll only be able to tell what it's not."

They stepped back into the bedroom where he took out another bag and placed both bed pillows inside. "These and the couch cushions need to be x-rayed, just in case. You said the perp entered through the adjoining unit. Anything disturbed over there?"

"Not that I know of. Didn't check."

"You said your daughter's bodyguard is staying over there. Don't you think he might be on this guy's radar as well?"

"Good point."

Duh. He'd really lost his edge upon leaving his analyst job. Actually it was purposeful, the women in his life forever making cracks about his paranoia.

Back downstairs, bagged evidence by the front door, Will led him through the closets into Mike's condo and switched on the overhead light.

"*Whoa!* Sweet Jesus, whatever happened here?" Winnie asked.

Will sighed. "Foreclosure. Previous owner was cooking meth. We're in the process of putting it back together."

"And your guy's okay living like this?"

He shrugged. "Free rent."

Ellsworth threw back his head and roared with laughter. "He must be one tough *mofo*. You'd have to pay *me* to live in this hole. I had better conditions in bombed-out Iraqi buildings."

Shaking his head, he entered the kitchen and swept around the UV. The sink showed the usual splash signatures, but a coffee mug near the drain went off like fireworks. "So this guy worked for the Bureau at some point, too?"

"Yeah. Out of LA. Years ago."

Winnie bagged it.

"Has he had any symptoms?"

Will's eyebrows pinched together as he took his cell phone out of his jacket. "I'll find out. If he did, they must have been too mild to mention."

"Hey, Mike. I'm at your place. So far it looks like Sara was exposed to some organic designer poison. On her toilet seat, of all places. Your coffee cup was contaminated, too. Have you had any symptoms? "

He switched it to speaker as they headed up the stairs.

"I haven't felt too good. Tired, a little nauseous, some trouble breathing, heartrate a little erratic. But functional."

"How much contact did you have with the mug?" Ellsworth asked while directing UV around the fixtures in the roughed-in guest bathroom.

"Not much," Mike replied. "I came back from my previous apartment the night before. We were leaving early, so I didn't make my usual pot. I made a cup of instant, tasted like crap, so it went down the sink."

By then, they were in the master bath. The light revealed a few drops on the tile floor in front of the toilet. Both men chuckled knowingly. "This guy's in his fifties, right?" Ellsworth commented.

"Yeah, what about it?" issued from the phone.

Ellsworth grinned, but didn't reply as he lowered the seat from its upright position.

UV light resonated from an identical stripe to what they found at Sara's.

He pointed at the phone and Will held it out. "Did you use your upstairs toilet in a sitting position?"

Mike's laugh crackled through the speaker. "No. Never. My daily constitutional is downstairs. Morning coffee gets me going in more ways than one. No reason to go back upstairs for the big one."

"That's one lucky habit," Will stated as that seat got bagged as well. "Your upstairs commode has the same crap, uh, poison, as Sara's."

"No kidding? Wow."

"Your exposure was apparently minimal," Ellsworth stated, "But talk to a doctor, especially if you feel worse over the next twelve hours or so. He might recommend a detox protocol. Meanwhile, drink lots of water. If the lab can identify its chemical composition, the treatment might be more specific. That is, if there's a known antidote."

"Got it. I'll update Sara's doctor with what we know so far."

"Thanks, Mike. We'll talk later."

Will hung up as they proceeded down to the main floor, checked the half-bath, which showed signs of use but no tampering, then returned to Sara's unit where they bagged the couch cushions.

Ellsworth stripped off the gloves and placed them in a Ziploc bag, which he added to the evidence sack before sealing it.

"You mentioned you have other evidence that could identify the perp. What exactly is it?"

"A dashcam clip that shows the guy's face from the wreck that killed my son-in-law. We also know what he drives," he said, explaining their experience driving to Montana.

"They're sure that was the same guy?"

"Reasonably sure, yes." Will sensed Charlie's impression was correct, but didn't think Native American psychic abilities would carry much weight. Ellsworth was solidly rooted in the Sergeant Joe Friday philosophy of, *"The facts, just the facts, ma'am."*

"The break-in occurred that same night, when he knew they were out of town," he explained. "A late model black pickup was spotted around my daughter's cabin last month or so. Circumstantial, I know, but fits the puzzle."

"Is that all?"

"All I can think of. I'll call if I remember anything else."

"I have a plane to catch," Winnie said, checking his watch. "I can't take this stuff with me, plus the lab's in Virginia, anyway. Pack everything up and overnight it with FedEx."

He extracted a pre-printed address label from his backpack, then slapped poison warnings on each of the bags. "Here," he said, handing him a *Hazardous Contents* sticker. "Be sure to put this on the box."

"Any idea how long it'll take the lab?" Will asked as they walked out to his car.

"No sooner than forty-eight hours. Tuesday or Wednesday, maybe. I'll tell them it's urgent because of your daughter's condition and let you know."

They got settled in Will's car and headed back to the airport.

"Text me the GO number from your local police," Winnie stated. "We'll send the results directly to them."

"I assume I'll get a copy. Getting that information to my daughter's doctor is essential."

"Of course."

"What do you think it is?"

"Probably a nervine, like I said before. Attacks the nervous system. Shuts down electrical impulses that drive vital functions— heart, lungs, brain. Indiana Jones running from those poison darts was the real deal. Frogs in South America, blue ringed octopus in Australia, to say nothing of numerous snakes and arachnids. Protection from predators. Survival of the fittest, as with our species, tends to favor the most effectively armed."

"So it could be something derived from poisons like that?"

"Yes. If they've kept her alive this long, that's a positive sign. Death usually comes too quickly for intervention."

He pulled into the loading/unloading lane for Frontier Airlines where they shook hands.

"I don't know how to thank you, Winnie. If I can ever return the favor, let me know."

"Maybe put me up for a weekend skiing with the misses someday. I hope the best for your daughter." His eyes lingered on Will's, the unspoken words discouraging.

On the way back, Will picked up a moving box from a U-Haul place that he used to bundle everything up, then headed for the nearest FedEx depot, arriving just before it closed.

The young female clerk gave him an apologetic smile. "I'm sorry, sir, but that package far exceeds the allowable shipping size."

Will tapped the address.

"Oh!" Her brown eyes widened upon noticing the warning label. "What is it?"

"Sorry. That's classified. But it's nothing liquid, corrosive, or explosive."

"Okay." Her stiff posture radiated suspicion as she handed him the documentation, then wrestled the huge package to the rear.

Having still not heard back from Denver PD, he headed for the local precinct.

After a protracted wait, due to his presence being lost in a shift change, he finally sat in a stuffy office across from the detective assigned to the case. Nigel Muller's thirty years experience was etched in every wrinkle in his jowled face. An equally worn tweed sports jacket shared his chair. His partner, a compact brunette in her forties named Gina, had a hardness about her that could only come from witnessing the worst of humanity.

Nothing in the file had been updated. They listened attentively while he filled them in on Sara's condition, what he discovered at the dealership, as well as the physical evidence on its way to CIA HQ in Virginia for analysis. It took over an hour to provide the entire history of the case which included viewing the dashcam clip, which he still had in his wallet.

"There's no question it was attempted murder," Muller agreed. "We'll issue a BOLO to be on the lookout, an APB, and a temporary warrant until we get hold of a judge. Once I have that and his home address from the DMV we'll send out the crime lab to see what they can find."

42. KARMA

LSO OUTPOST
RURAL FALCON RIDGE
July 29, Sunday
8:15 a.m. MDT

Trey stood outside his office trailer, surveying their progress cleaning up the blowout debris. Fortunately, they'd capped the borehole a few days later, once the bulk of sour gas burned off.

However, to get to the crude that lay below, they needed to set up a new rig—which couldn't be done until they got rid of the blown casing that lay in a twisted heap like a giant, squashed Texas-size tarantula.

The crane and heavy equipment needed were supposed to arrive the day before, but the heavy hauler was delayed in Amarillo by a freak thunderstorm. Thus, the driver only made it as far as Denver the night before. Not wanting to drive the rest of the way through narrow, twisted mountain roads after dark, the big rig's driver promised to get an early start and be there by breakfast.

Trey didn't know what breakfast meant for the driver, but as far as he was concerned, that meal had come and gone hours before. There was only a month or so left before bad weather would set in and there was a helluva lot of work to do before then.

Big Dick joined him moments later, arms extended in a nonverbal "WTF?"

"Yeah, I know," Trey grumbled. "Sure would be nice if something happened on schedule for a change."

Big Dick folded his arms. "Y'all's got that right."

BARBIE'S RV & MARINE
RURAL FALCON RIDGE
July 29, Sunday
8:30 a.m. MDT

Sitting around in what was little more than a tin can was getting on Eddie's nerves. Every time he wanted a smoke, which was often, he had to step outside. Furthermore, he was bored out of his mind.

What was there to do around there, anyway? Maybe rent a jet ski. Zoom around the lake for a while. Sounded good.

Except getting wet might not work too well with his new look.

Fishing, also boring, was another option. His only happy memory of his abusive alcoholic father was the one time they went fly casting. A wide variety of rods, reels, and tackle were kept at the marina for their guests. The more he thought about it, the more it sounded like a mighty fine idea.

He holstered his gun, made sure his shirt covered it, and sauntered over to the office to check out the fishing equipment. After looking over the sagging rods and cheap-ass reels in the side room, he decided fly casting was too damn complicated, anyway. All he needed was a simple pole with a can of worms.

Which he could pick up at that little country store down the road.

While he'd been in there numerous times, surely no one would see through his Tijuana-special appearance. Especially wearing a hat and sunglasses.

Thus, he climbed in his truck and headed out.

His Ram's back tires spewed gravel in all directions, pinging surrounding trailers and RVs as he tore out of the parking lot. A glance in his rearview mirror showed Aunt Ida shaking her fist at him from the office door.

He laughed and gunned it some more.

His confidence soared, liberated from *Eddie the Screw-up* to *Eddie the Omniscient.* He'd proven his worth, taking care of that bitch once and for all, entirely on his own. No doubt Keller would give him his job back. Probably a bonus, too.

But did he want it?

Payment, which he certainly deserved, yes. But maybe being an independent contractor was his destiny.

Why'd he need Keller? After collecting his pay for a job well-done, he'd tell that sorry gimp to go to hell.

Look out, asshole. Meet BKSS's badass competition.

A heady sense of freedom he hadn't felt for decades lifted his spirits higher than a good line of coke.

He loved pushing his Ram 2500 to its limits along the narrow country road. He was a skillful driver, and that was why—practice. His timing, integration with the vehicle as part of himself, and instincts served him well.

He laughed.

Use the Force, Eddie.

He would've loved being a race car driver, but this was close enough. Nothing beat speed, power, and a well-engineered vehicle to blow off some steam.

The hairpin turn where he orchestrated that wreck was a quarter mile down the road. As he drove along the same path their target had taken, he grinned.

That unsuspecting Reynolds bastard had no idea he was about to die.

As he neared the turn, he floored it. Braking was for pussies. Roaring into the bend, he eased the steering wheel to the left.

Far heavier than his previous truck, the Ram's mass conspired with the laws of physics and blatantly refused to change direction.

His foot smashed the brake while both hands fought the wheel. Arm and leg muscles strained as he willed the vehicle to turn. The bed fish-tailed to the right. The back bumper slammed a roadside aspen, rebounding back into a trajectory headed straight for the ledge.

Shit!

He threw all his weight into yanking the wheel hard left. The truck screeched in protest, then whipped around a hundred-eighty degrees as it flew around the blind turn—

—directly into the grill of a Kenworth 953 heavy-hauler pulling a triple axel trailer loaded with LSO's tardy crane.

The rig was stopped, but well into the other lane. Its lack of forward momentum combined with the Ram's grille guard resulted in an elastic collision, pickup bouncing like a billiard ball.

Tires and Eddie both screamed as the truck flew backwards, tipped over the precipice, bounced off the ledge twenty feet below, then tumbled ass over tea kettle into Dead Horse Canyon's yawning depths.

S-h-h-h-h-i-i-i-i-i-t-t-t-t-t-t. . . . .

A stunned trucker climbed down from the Kenworth's cab and looked around. As a seasoned big-rig driver with thousands of hours experience, he'd been in tight situations before. He was concentrating on his mirrors, trying to negotiate the tight curve with his long, over-sized load, when something slammed the grill, hard.

Skid marks slashed the pavement in crazy, impossible patterns that ended abruptly at the edge of a huge drop-off. He stepped over to peer over the side. A crumpled black pickup belching steam lay on its side far below.

"Well, I'll be goddamned," he muttered, shaking his head. He squinted, trying to discern what he could swear was another vehicle down there as well.

"This trip's been a real bitch," he said to himself. "Just one damned, crazy thing after another. You'd think there was a curse on it or somethin'."

**PERLEMAN EMERGENCY CENTER
NEW YORK CITY
July 29, Sunday
2:08 p.m. EDT**

Will stared out the window at the grey steel and glass exterior of the anonymous building across the street, remembering. Another hospital, another time, awaiting tests that delivered the worst possible diagnosis for Sara's mother, Ellen. He'd been terrified then, as he was now.

Connie's meltdown on Friday kept him focused on her. Now she was holding up just fine while his mind and heart raced at similar speeds.

Women had an advantage. Being able to cry and rant and get it out was socially acceptable. While having the same feelings, that option was not available to someone who considered himself a man and tried to act like it.

Now his wife sat beside the bed, calmly watching TV, while the cadre of medical devices keeping Sara alive chirped and wheezed on the other side.

Control was a misnomer.

His emotions were rampant, just contained. A volatile mix that felt as if it might go critical, like enriched plutonium in a nuclear bomb.

As her father he should have insisted—*demanded*—that she not pursue this insanity. Going up against the government was suicide. The dangers were real. He knew this kind of thing happened.

Feared it might.

Nonetheless allowed her to follow her naive and deadly agenda.

Yet, in his defense, he tried.

Multiple times.

She didn't listen.

She was a grown woman.

What the hell was the matter with her?

Didn't she trust him?

Know he had her best interests at heart?

Her very life at stake?

What the hell?

And that stupid husband of hers, snooping around where he didn't belong. Got himself killed, which was bad enough. Then dumps his crap on her to clean up.

What honorable man does that to the woman he loves?

And what happened to the country he also loved? What kind of government did this to their own people?

A corrupt one.

Why he left the FBI.

Then again, this came down to an individual. Probably gone rogue after she showed that video on national TV.

Why didn't he shoot the son of a bitch?

He had the chance, then blew it.

Going to prison would have been worth it. It would have saved Sara's life.

His own fault. His skills were rusty. He hesitated, gave the guy a split second window.

He was the idiot.

His toxic soliloquy halted when the door eased open. He stood up when her doctor entered. Old prejudices fired. The guy was from India. Did he really know what he was doing? Why not some nice Jewish third-generation physician who went to Harvard Medical School?

Connie muted *Let's Make a Deal*.

"Any news?" Will asked.

Dr. Ajay Amavasya responded in soft-spoken but flawless English. "Her symptoms are similar to transdermal contact with sarin, but her acetylcholinesterase levels were too high. So that can be eliminated."

"So what's next?" Connie asked, getting up to stand beside him.

"Dialysis. We'll use the finest possible filters to remove all the toxins we can. It should bring some improvement, combined with an increase in fluid intake to flush her system. The only way to know its effectiveness is to extubate."

"What if. . ."

When he couldn't finish the sentence Connie's hand slipped into his.

"We can restore it, if necessary," the doctor assured him. "If we don't see any improvement after that, we'll try a whole blood exchange transfusion."

The physician stepped over to the bed, lifted Sara's right foot, and ran what looked like a pin-studded pizza cutter along the bottom. His eyes narrowed when there was no reaction. Then he took her limp hand to check her pulse.

"I suspect significant imbalances in her system that I can usually detect with my Ayurvedic training, but not with her on life-support," he said, gently placing her hand back beside her. "Nutritional deficiencies and environmental toxins can exacerbate the poison."

"Why wait for the exchange transfusion if dialysis might not work?" Will asked.

"Sufficient whole blood is not yet available It's not used that much anymore, mainly plasma and platelets. She's A-negative, which is hard to find. I put out a city-wide alert for what's available. I can get her started on dialysis right away."

"How long does it take?"

"Usually about four hours, perhaps a bit longer in this case. I consulted with a nephrologist to prescribe the most effective dialysate for the situation. She's not mobile, so we'll bring the machine to her."

As if on cue, an orderly arrived with the massive device. Hooking her up was relatively simple, IV input and output lines. The doctor stayed long enough to assure everything was functioning properly while a nurse connected the machine to the bedside computer.

Connie sighed, then resumed watching TV. Will paced the floor.

Other than when Sara's mother was in labor, it was the longest wait he could remember. After four hours he started checking his watch every few minutes. It was closer to five when the doctor arrived with a nurse to disconnect the equipment.

"I think her color is better," Connie said, getting up to stand beside him. "Unless it's just wishful thinking."

"Her heart's beating on its own," the doctor reported. "The defibrillator hasn't fired for over an hour. That's a positive indicator. Nurse, extubate the patient. Let's see if her pulmonary function resumes."

Will took Connie's hand, holding his breath.

For a moment, nothing happened. Sara's color started to drain. His eyes burned with tears he refused to shed.

"C'mon, honey," Connie said softly, interlocking her fingers with his. "You can do this."

Moments later, Sara's chest heaved with a huge gasp, then rose and fell in perfect rhythm.

DENVER PD
MAIN PRECINCT
July 30, Monday
1:19 p.m. MDT

DPD detective, Nigel Muller, sat at his computer, checking for status updates on the Montgomery GO. So far no response to either the BOLO or APB, though at this point it was just a matter of time. Crime lab personnel were dispatched to the address on the perp's truck registration to look for evidence. If they found poison that matched what was found on the victim's toilet seat it would be a done deal.

If only all cases demanded so little work. All he'd done so far was update the GO based on meeting with Montgomery, who not only saved him a trip by coming to his office but apologized for calling in a favor from an old spook friend.

He chuckled at the thought.

Did he think they didn't have enough to do?

His phone rang. The 970 area code indicated somewhere in the Colorado boonies but didn't ring a bell.

"Nigel Muller here."

"This is Steve Urbanowski, Falcon Ridge PD," the man said. "Are you the contact for this APB on someone driving a black Dodge Ram? Someone going by the name Eddie Johannsen a.k.a. Glen Smith?"

"Yeah, that's me," Nigel answered. "Is he in custody?"

Urbanowski chuckled. "You could say that. Perp's in a body bag."

Nigel's guffaw exploded from his over-sized belly, causing his partner across the room to spill her coffee. "Best custody I know of. What happened? Did you shoot the bastard?"

"Nope. Big wreck. His own fault. Had a head-on with a eighteen-wheeler that sent him over a cliff. Just recovered the body this morning. Turns out he has family in the area who did a positive ID."

"Well, well. Turns out there's some justice in this world after all. Makes my day." Nigel cracked up again. "Case closed. Thanks."

"Any time."

He hung up, shaking his head. Strangest case ever, solved in a matter of days with minimal effort.

If only his job were always that simple.

"Hey, Gina," he hollered.

She turned her head, eating her usual peanut butter and orange marmalade sandwich after cleaning up the coffee.

"Good news on that poisoning case. Perp's in a body bag."

She grinned as she gave him a thumbs-up. "Good job, Nigel. Do you want to call Montgomery or should I?"

"I'll put it on speaker. I wouldn't miss this for the world."

PERLEMAN EMERGENCY CENTER
NEW YORK CITY
July 30, Monday
3:25 p.m. EDT

Will jumped when his phone vibrated. Denver area code, but unfamiliar number. He met Connie's questioning gaze with one of his own. She muted *Dr. Phil.*

"Will Montgomery."

"Good afternoon, Mr. Montgomery. Nigel Muller, Denver PD on speaker with my partner."

"Oh, hello, detectives. Any news?"

The man on the other end chuckled. "Quite a bit, actually."

"Good news, I hope."

"I would say so. About as good as it gets. First of all, the perp has been found."

"Great! Is he in custody?"

"Even better. Dead."

"*Dead?* Seriously? What happened? Firefight?"

"Nope. Killed in a wreck with an eighteen-wheeler. Came around a tight curve, rig was making a wide turn with a big load, and *ka-boom!* Went over a cliff. Bye-bye, Johannsen." He laughed.

Will's mouth fell open, incredulous. "No kidding? Where?"

"Some mountain road out in the boonies, out by where you said he'd be. Near that little town called Falcon Ridge."

When his second shock cleared enough to speak, he asked sufficient questions to determine it was the same place where Bryan was murdered. The hair on his arms rose to the occasion.

Maybe there was something to this woo-woo stuff after all.

"Wow," he said, stunned. "What goes around definitely comes around."

"There's more," Muller went on. "This just in. The crime lab hit paydirt at his apartment. They found what looks like the substance used to poison your daughter, still in his jacket pocket, no less. Plus his computer's loaded. He was working for some two-bit security firm out of Albuquerque. Same contractor who worked PURF."

"Which we figured from the dashcam videos."

"Right. The job to take out your daughter was a new contract. BKSS got a huge retainer, then paid out a total of $5K in two installments to an account in the Cayman Islands. This was shortly before the break-in. Feds are on it, even as we speak. So, as far as we're concerned, this case is closed."

"Great. Good news is welcome for a change."

"How's your daughter doing?"

He closed his eyes, confronted once more with the fact things were far from resolved. "Not very well. We have our fingers crossed, but that's about all we can do right now. They say her chances are about 50:50. So we're hoping for the best."

"I'm sorry to hear that. But that wouldn't be bad lotto odds."

"That's one way to look at it."

"Yeah, I'd definitely put some money on that. Look, I'll have my wife remember your daughter at her prayer group."

"Thanks. That's probably the one thing that could tip the balance in our favor. I appreciate the call, detective."

"My pleasure. Too bad more of these dirt bags don't do themselves in like that."

"Absolutely. Thanks again for letting me know."

Will's hopes shifted ever so slightly. Maybe the tide was turning in their favor.

Connie looked up expectantly. "Well?" she prompted.

"Johannsen's dead. And you'll never guess how and where."

She, too, was speechless when he explained.

"Personally, I'd rather he rot in prison." That said, he had to admit having that SOB dead was a huge relief.

Knowing Mike would want to know, he called him next to share the news. Will laughed out loud at the man's enthusiastic victory whoop.

He hadn't known anyone that happy since the Broncos won the Super Bowl.

BKSS LLC
ALBUQUERQUE, NM
August 1, Wednesday
07:04 a.m.

Bernie's tiny office in Albuquerque was a stone's throw from the airport and the VA hospital. His desk, chair, water cooler, and a single file cabinet barely fit, a tiny kitchen and bathroom he shared with the other tenants down the hall.

Having a view of the airport and the desert versus the highway and parking lot out front made sense at the time. Facing the back implied a means to escape—except the windows didn't open and with a prosthetic leg it wasn't like he could outrun anyone.

Two other businesses occupied the old, rundown commercial building: An insurance agent, who wasn't doing well enough to afford a better location, and a souvenir shop that specialized in Navajo jewelry.

Those two plus another vacant unit faced the road, while his office, the common areas, and another unoccupied rental space were in back. Neither establishment opened before eleven o'clock, so most of the time it was quiet when he got there, seldom later than 0700.

He made a pot of coffee, then settled into his chair to check his email. Terminator stretched, then assumed his usual position beneath his desk. More often than not, the Rottie was content to sleep there most the day. He usually went out for lunch, then stopped by Phil Chacon park on the way back so the dog could get a good run chasing a few birds.

When the big Rottie stirred he assumed he was just getting comfortable.

Until he let out a low, throaty growl.

The hefty canine didn't do so often, but when he did, he paid attention. Was the dog only dreaming? That theory crashed when the Rottweiler scrambled to all fours and shoved his way past him to stand by the door, hackles raised.

Bernie secured his prosthetic leg. His desert view depreciated to zero, having no way of knowing who or what arrived out front.

The dog's mouth curled back in a saliva-dripping snarl.

He retrieved his Sig Sauer P938 from the top desk drawer, chambered a round, and thumbed off the safety.

He stood up, gun in hand, and listened.

The side door where tenants entered the building to their common hall was always locked. Sometimes he accepted deliveries for his neighbors.

Maybe that was all it was, FedEx or UPS.

But this early?

Furthermore, Terminator knew those guys, his greeting far friendlier.

He jumped when pounding issued from the metal door.

He ordered the dog to stay and stepped into the hall. "Yeah," he yelled back. "Who is it?"

"FBI."

"Hold on a minute."

He relaxed as he returned to his office, reset the gun's safety, and put it back in the drawer. He shut his door behind him, then proceeded down the hall, expecting to see his handler.

Maybe another job had come along, which would be great. The last one seemed all but finished up, thanks to Johannsen's handiwork. Hopefully, they didn't know about that one, which was definitely outside the bounds of legality.

He released the deadbolt and opened the outside door.

It wasn't his handler.

It was an entourage of Kevlar outfitted agents.

His hands raised, more reflex than submission. "Hey, guys. What's going on?"

The one in front held a warrant while the muzzles of an armory of automatic weapons pointed in his direction.

"Bernard Keller, you're under arrest for conspiracy to commit murder for hire in Colorado." The man read him the Miranda while another zip-tied his hands behind his back.

"What are you talking about? I haven't left New Mexico in four years."

"Maybe so, Keller, but one of your employees sure did."

"Johannsen? I fired him, weeks ago. I can't be responsible for anything he did after that."

"Fired, eh? Funny he still had full access to your system."

"No, he didn't. I cut him off myself."

"Tell it to the judge, Keller. You're going away for a long, long time."

Johannsen going rogue was not a surprise. That idiot probably got caught and spilled the beans.

He was screwed.

His first thought, however, was not so much what went wrong as what would happen to Terminator when he went back to prison.

Don't be afraid to cry. It will free your mind of sorrowful thoughts.
                                          —Hopi proverb

43. TIME

PERLEMAN EMERGENCY CENTER
NEW YORK CITY
August 1, Wednesday
9:41 a.m. EDT

Will was disgusted, yet not surprised by the lab report. It told them nothing they hadn't already surmised. Being organic, mass spectroscopy results were useless. Rather than dealing with the relatively manageable number of elements in the periodic table, organics had infinite possibilities.

Numerous plants and animals had lethal defenses commandeered for murderous or defense purposes. Cocktails comprised of such substances were typical in the covert world of espionage, often a combination. Shellfish toxin heart attacks were almost a cliché.

Treatments for unknown poisons were a guessing game. All they could do was try to keep the person alive long enough for the body to eliminate the lethal invader, then heal itself.

Sara's vital signs remained stable following dialysis, but no further improvement had come. Forty-eight hours had passed, during which time the hospital rounded up enough A-negative blood for the exchange transfusion.

If that didn't work he had a very difficult decision to make.

"I'm going to get a snack," Connie said. "Do you want anything?"

"No, thanks." He smiled as she left for the cafeteria, her cell phone on the table next to her chair.

He picked it up and scrolled through her contacts, grateful for the illogical modern practice of listing them by first name. He found who he was looking for, entered the number in his own phone.

Not knowing how long she'd be gone, he'd make the call later. Make a run to the gift shop or something. Maybe he wouldn't even call, depending on circumstances.

As soon as they got back from lunch, that dreadful soap opera, *Days of Our Lives*, came on. Every time Will heard that theme a lump captured his throat. Ellen watched it every day, including the one she died. In fact, she may have passed during it, he wasn't sure. Those were not happy times. Today his lugubrious state was such he just couldn't handle it. No better time to duck out and make that phone call.

"I'm heading down to the gift shop for something to read. Do you want anything?" he asked.

"Yes! Get me a Peanut Butter Cup. I've been craving one since that last ad."

He scoffed. "Woman, you're the ad exec's dream. Anything else?"

"Nope. That'll be great. Thanks."

He checked his pocket for his phone, then left the room. He nodded hello at familiar personnel at the nurses' station, then took the elevator up to the chapel on the 8th floor. He exited the elevator and stepped down the hall where he slowly opened the door a crack to peek inside. A couple sat near the front, the man's arm around a hunched over woman, her shoulders shaking.

Someone else having a hard day, he thought. He eased the door closed and proceeded down the hall, past several small consulting rooms. All were empty. Certainly he could borrow one for a few minutes.

He stepped inside, closed the door, sat down, and got out his phone. He scrolled to the person he wanted, paused to take a deep breath, then pressed *Connect*.

It rang several times, then switched to phone mail.

He debated.

Leave a message? Or not?

The beep sounded.

"Uh, hello. This is Connie Montgomery's husband, Will. I'd like to talk to you about something."

He left his number, then hung up. Fortunately, when he got a call from work, he always stepped into the hall, so that would appear normal. Even better, perhaps.

He'd barely stepped out of the elevator on the third floor when he remembered—Connie's candy. He hit the down button, waiting what seemed forever. He strolled into the gift shop down from the lobby, greeted the women's auxiliary volunteer at the register, then proceeded to consider the paperbacks on a spinner rack.

He cringed at one titled "The Silent Patient." Forget that, he was living it. He selected the latest by Dean Koontz, usually a good bet. The clerk had already rung it up when he remembered the Peanut Butter Cup.

As he stepped into the elevator his phone rang.

He apologized when he bumped into someone as he backed out, then connected the call.

"Hello."

"Mr. Montgomery? This is Patrice Renard returning your call."

"Thank you for calling back." He swallowed hard as he went into the lobby, finding a seat that had a few empty chairs on either side. Now that he had her on the phone he felt foolish, having no idea what to say.

"I understand things are very difficult for your family right now," the woman said. "What can I do to help?"

"Connie told me that you helped her a lot when my wife, Ellen, died. With Sara in a coma, I guess I'm looking for some sort of reassurance."

"What kind of reassurance are you looking for, Mr. Montgomery? I'm afraid I can't promise everything will be okay."

"I understand. It certainly didn't turn out okay with Ellen. But somehow, something you said helped Connie deal with it better. What did you tell her?"

"Well, I don't remember specifically. But what I usually tell my clients is that our lives have a plan. They're not random. We're programmed a certain way and have specific things we're supposed to accomplish so we can learn and progress. It's not random, it's not luck, it's part of a cosmic plan. So when bad things happen, there's a reason. A lesson, either for the person or those close to him or her."

"That's a nice philosophy, I suppose. Why do you believe that's the way things work?"

"I like Einstein's quote: 'God does not play dice with the universe.' There's a plan and a reason. There are no coincidences. I can believe that because I can see a person's cosmic programming, then track what's going on in their life. I can help them understand why."

He had no idea how she derived that from the planets, but as Connie said before, you couldn't argue with something that worked. "Did you know this was going to happen to Sara?"

"No, not specifically. But I could see that she had a rough year ahead. This is certainly worse than I expected, though."

"No kidding. Do you know if she's going to die?"

"I don't. It's a possibility. She's in a transformational cycle. Sometimes that means death, but in most cases it's an important change. Such as being affected at a deep level by some intense experience."

His laugh was tinged with bitterness. "So was I supposed to lose my first wife and now possibly my daughter? Was that the plan for *my* life? I can't say I'm very happy with any cosmic force that would impose that on me or anyone else."

"If your perspective is limited to this life alone, then that can seem unfair, even cruel. An eternal perspective, believing that there's more to life than that, makes it easier to accept."

Some Lalaland woo-woo explanation was not what he was looking for.

"Are you going all religious on me now, Patrice? I was raised a Catholic. By the time I was an adolescent there were too many things I couldn't agree with. Any god who'd condemn an innocent child simply because they weren't sprinkled by some priest was not a god I could believe in. Or that I'd go to hell for missing mass. C'mon."

"Exactly. No, this isn't about a religion. In astrology, religion and spirituality are completely separate. In fact, religion and politics are grouped together as belief systems."

He laughed. "That explains a lot about some of the religious nuts I've know. Definitely not what I would consider spiritual people."

"It does, doesn't it? No, this is about a loving Universe whose plan is far more benevolent. A spiritual realm. There's also the matter of karma. Perhaps people who have a difficult life are learning hard lessons they earned in a previous one. Maybe they were abusive. It would seem only fair if rapists came back as women in some closed society where they're treated badly. I see that as the ultimate justice."

He'd never thought much about karma before, but that made sense. Karma certainly caught up with Johannsen. "So you think it all comes out in the wash, so to speak?"

"Yes. Conversely, someone who's lived a good life—passed all the tests, if you will—may get a 'vacation' life, where things go much better."

"That sounds too good to be true, Patrice. But the fact that you seem to believe it gives me hope. I want Sara to survive. But if she doesn't, at least she'll be with Ellen and Bryan." He ground his teeth. "Even though I blame him for this whole damn mess."

"I can understand that, Mr. Montgomery. But we're with the people we're supposed to be. Our lives are entangled and we teach each other. There was a reason they were together and for all that transpired as a result. We each have our own journey."

"For good or ill. Thank you, Patrice. You've helped more than you know. For now, please don't say anything about this conversation to my wife."

"Of course. All my client interactions are strictly confidential."

"Thank you again. I appreciate your time."

MIKE'S CONDO
DENVER
August 1, Wednesday
2:05 p.m.

Mike stared blankly at the newly hung sheetrock in his bedroom, trying to figure out what to do. The walls were as blank and unfinished as his life. No definition, no color, just a slab of gypsum hiding the framework beneath.

As good as it felt to find out Johannsen got what he deserved, he was still bummed out as a total failure. Will assured him that wasn't the case, but the fact Sara was fighting for her life wasn't much of a testimonial.

It was his careless screw-up that allowed that to happen, something he'd have to live with forever.

When he got back to Colorado he hired a professional cleaning service to decontaminate her condo, top to bottom, and check his as well. To be absolutely safe, her mattress and box springs were replaced, including all the bedding, and the carpet steam-cleaned.

One thing for sure, this bodyguard business wasn't what he expected. For starters he'd gotten too personally involved. Lost all sense of detachment, which boded poorly for sound judgment.

He never had that problem as a cop. He cared about people, but not to the point it was debilitating.

Maybe being a small town policeman wasn't so bad after all. You knew the people for the most part, yet weren't so close it got uncomfortable when something came up.

When he quit the force, Steve told him if he ever changed his mind to let him know. The more he thought about it, the better it sounded.

He took out his phone, Steve's number still in his contact list's top five.

He hit connect.

"Hey, Mike. How you doing these days, buddy? Ready to come back?"

He laughed.

Steve could always read him like a guilty suspect in a line-up.

NORTHERN CHEYENNE RESERVATION
MONTANA
August 1, Wednesday
8:38 p.m.

Charlie sat with *Náhkòhe* beneath the bur oak, sunset an hour away. According to *Diné* teachings, the East pertained to thinking; South to planning; West to life; and North to hope and faith. With Sara on his mind, facing west seemed appropriate.

Maybe if he lost himself in the heavens, answers would come. The others had already eaten, but he was consumed by what White Wolf taught him so far about the art of healing.

It seemed odd that his abilities didn't matter.

The medicine man was not the one who did the healing.

That was strictly the domain of *Maheo*.

If pride or ego got in the way, he'd fail.

While it was important to identify what was wrong, know which plant and even mineral totems could help, and then direct the Creator's healing energy where needed, the power to help directly was not in his hands but in his relationship with *Maheo*.

His stomach wrenched every time he recalled that vision of the snakes in Sara's bathroom. In his mind's eye he saw her in the hospital bed, still unconscious. The cellular damage she suffered came through as angry static versus that of a healthy life force. She was still comatose.

He pondered the time when he was unconscious. Some of the visions were horrifying. Viewing past failures was humiliating. Others, however, were edifying.

Like seeing *amasani*. It meant so much that she came to bid him farewell. Learning the outcome of that vision that haunted him for decades fueled his faith and trust in *Maheo*.

Was Sara having a similar experience? Would she be a different person when she awoke?

What if she didn't?

Was she supposed to cross over to join Bryan?

Was it selfish to want her to live?

The only way he could find answers to such important questions was to fast. At least a day. That would humble him enough to listen beyond his own will. If he started now, by this time tomorrow he might know. If not, he'd fast until he did.

Yes, that was what he should do.

Which explained why he wasn't hungry and skipped dinner.

They could have a special sweat. Pray that she might be healed or peacefully cross over. Like they did for *amasani*.

Being stuck in a stupor of thought, unable to make a decision, was a symptom of not having enough information from *Maheo*.

He didn't move from his cross-legged position until over an hour after the sun disappeared. The evening chill drove him inside to get his blanket, *Náhkòhe* confused when he returned outside.

As much as he loved the tree's sheltering branches during the day, now he sat in the front yard where nothing obstructed his view of the celestial dome.

The sky darkened through shades of blue to black. Stars revealed themselves, one by one. The waning Moon hid beneath the horizon, allowing stars to own the sky. Their brilliance ignited his soul, *Yikáísdáhá's* arch ablaze overhead.

He rose to his feet, slowly turning to absorb the full spectacle presented by the domed sky.

Mars was rising, a red dot just above the eastern horizon. Saturn, brighter than any nearby stars, was slightly more elevated toward the southeast. Jupiter's brilliance was culminating overhead, Venus edging west. Mercury claimed the border between earth and sky, following the sun's late summer demise in the west-northwest.

Nostalgia warmed his heart with memories of such nights, viewing each of Earth's siblings with Bryan, then that last time with Sara.

So much had happened since that carefree evening.

His thoughts shifted to *Diné* constellations. Summer skies were less familiar, being far different from those included in the Winter Stories told by *amasani* during his childhood. Montana was farther north than New Mexico, resulting in minor differences in the night sky. The Coyote Star wasn't visible from up there, barely in Colorado, especially where mountains obstructed the true horizon where Canopus lurked.

This time of year, five of the six stars that comprised the feather of *Iini*, the thunderbird, spanned the celestial dome.

The heliacal rise of the first star heralded the onset of spring, a time of regeneration, with another added each month. Thus, when all were visible, it indicated the end of a season.

His hopes collapsed with its implications.

Just after midnight, a meteor slashed a brilliant path across the sky, just beyond the fifth star.

Signs in the heavens were as valid as those of spirit animals. Did those seen above pertain to eternity while those on earth related to life?

It felt as if that falling star halted the flow of time.

But why?

PERLEMAN EMERGENCY CENTER
NEW YORK CITY
August 2, Thursday
8:38 a.m.

Connie held Will's arm as they settled in the backseat of one of Manhattan's ubiquitous yellow cabs. Like all the others, its interior boasted sagging leather seats that reeked of previous occupants. Olfactory hints of everything from body odor to exotic perfume, even freshly made bagels. Traffic repeatedly surged forward, then stopped. Drivers blasted their horns like competing roosters announcing dawn.

The air was heavy, humidity-drenched exhaust fumes mingled with the briny scent of the East River. Hot, muggy, and oppressive even this early. Nothing like Colorado's dry, thin air.

City ambiance echoed off skyscraper canyons that occulted the sky. A paved wonderland with no grass, an occasional tree. Only sidewalks jammed with unsmiling people intent on reaching their destination while tourists wisely remained in their hotels until the clamor diminished.

The sense of adventure she felt visiting unfamiliar cities in the past was absent. This was no vacation or pleasure trip. Any beauty the city possessed was as invisible as the network of subways somewhere beneath their feet, their presence an anonymous hum.

Upon waking up that morning all she could think of was what Patrice said.

This was the day.

Having that dream a few nights before of the three of them returning to Colorado assured her Sara would wake up. The hope it instilled kept her calm and hopeful.

She shared it with Will. Expecting it would calm his anxiety was to no avail. He simply didn't believe in such things as he'd opined repeatedly with regard to Patrice.

The cab pulled up to the curb in front of the hospital. Will paid with a credit card. They crossed the sprawling lobby and rode the elevator to the third floor.

It wasn't quite forty-eight hours since the exchange transfusion, the point at which they had to decide about long-term care if Sara didn't wake up.

She hoped and prayed that would not be an issue. The fact she survived being taken off life support, albeit still in a coma, fueled her natural *glass-half-full* attitude.

A smile tweaked her lips. Her step-daughter was probably arguing with Bryan about coming back.

She said hello to the knot of people gathered at the nurse's station. Valiant healthcare workers she now knew by name. Some were less talkative than others, but all provided compassionate and professional support. How they did it, day after day, she'd never know.

While she hoped to find Sara awake, she was torn between that and being there for that magic moment. She held her breath as they stepped into her room.

Everything looked the same as when they left the night before.

She doused her disappointment with optimism.

Good. We'll be here to welcome her back.

She stepped to the bed and rested her hand on Sara's arm, as she had every day of their vigil.

"Good morning, honey," she whispered. "Patrice said this could be the day you decide to come back."

What would it do to Will if she didn't? He'd never been so visibly stressed, even when Sara's mother died.

In Ellen's case, however, death was a blessing. A long-expected end to being a prisoner in a paralyzed body, even her ability to speak stolen by atrophied muscles.

Entirely different circumstances than Sara. A beautiful woman in her prime put in this condition by an evil, monstrous man who deserved exactly what he got.

They took their usual seats, Connie in the padded chair next to the bed, Will in a straight-back at the foot, where he opened up his laptop to log into his work.

Thank heaven he has that as a distraction.

Otherwise he would have gone crazy by now.

At home she loved shopping or trying out new recipes to pass the time. Under different conditions, she'd have a grand time exploring the luxurious stores along Fifth Avenue. Or sightseeing. So much to see in such an historic city.

Will encouraged her to do so.

But not wanting to miss anything, she spent endless hours alternating between her tablet and TV. There weren't many channel choices other than local network stations. The usual daytime fare prevailed: Old movies, game shows, and soap operas that were around as long as memory served.

Her mother told her she'd watched *General Hospital* before Connie was even born.

As a teen, she thought they were ridiculously fake. Now she understood why they'd survived since the 1960s.

Far from fake, they reflected the vicissitudes of life in a remarkably accurate manner.

Which was probably why her hard-core realist husband hated them, missing the fact their lives could supply the script for one that would span years.

She settled into checking social media until ten o'clock when tolerable programming began. Will looked up occasionally during *The Price is Right* to put in his bid, which was usually correct. His posture grew stiff when *The Young and the Restless* followed, keyboard strokes noticeably louder.

At noon they strolled down to the cafeteria for something to eat, selections pathetic given the multitude of five-star restaurants mere blocks away. They hadn't even tried any for dinner, too exhausted by the time they left each evening. Fortunately, room service was good, but lacked ambiance.

Maybe when Sara woke up. They could bring her back some takeout, sparing her from bland hospital fare.

She eyed the selections, deciding on spaghetti, which was reasonably good. Will got something that resembled meatloaf with mashed potatoes.

They arrived back in Sara's room just in time for *Days of Our Lives.*

Its iconic theme filled the room.

Like sands through the hourglass, so are the days of our lives...

"Do you really have to watch that drivel every damn day, Connie?" Will grumbled. "I don't care what you watch at home when I'm not stuck listening to it. It's really distracting and grating on my last nerve. I have work to do."

Her sigh was deep and heart-felt. "I'm sorry, Will. I just need something to pass the time. There's really not much on. But I'll see what there is or mute it, if it will make you feel any better."

"Don't you dare change it," Sara whispered, voice barely audible. "Mom loved that show."

Connie sprang from the chair and took her hand. "Oh, honey, I knew you'd come back! Did Bryan talk you into it?"

"No. He knew better," she replied. "It was Mom. She said I had to come back."

Many bluecoats are coming for our blood. We will wear our medicine paint and
fight as one people, strong and brave. Maheo will give us the life of long hair,
he will no longer take our women, children, again, like Washita.
—*Chief Littlewolf, June 1876, Cheyenne Council of 44 Chiefs, "Battle of Long*
Hair" (Custer Massacre)

44. GOING HOME

NORTHERN CHEYENNE RESERVATION
August 2, Thursday
10:04 a.m. MDT

Charlie was a little nervous, but didn't think it would be a problem to drive White Wolf to Billings to get a part for his aging Ford Explorer, which refused to start.

His eyes seemed to be behaving, but up until then the farthest he'd gone was Lame Deer. There was never any need to be in a hurry, so he drove no more than twenty miles per hour. Mostly dirt roads, then a short distance on Highway 212, both typically devoid of traffic.

With the majority of their time together formal in nature, he thought of his uncle almost exclusively as White Wolf. It was confusing to shift between the two personas. This, however, was a simple, mundane errand that felt comfortable. His uncle was relaxed and informal, shedding his traditional buckskin and mantle of authority.

As soon as he left the reservation on Highway 212 heading toward the Little Bighorn battlefield, however, he knew trouble was afoot. Stark visions of the area's past played out before him, so distracting he pulled over and stopped. Fascinated, he turned off the engine and got out to watch, his uncle joining him.

455

The vision of the bloody battle where his Cheyenne and Lakota brothers gave Custer what he deserved played out before him. Like watching a 3-D IMAX movie, except it included all the sounds, odors, and sights of the epic and ultimately successful confrontation.

When at last Charlie spoke, not expecting an answer, he could tell from his uncle's wisdom-saturated expression that it was White Wolf, not Uncle Joe, who stood beside him.

"Why am I seeing this now?"

"It is in your blood. It is our history. Something you must carry within your heart."

"Is this why you asked me to drive you to Billings?"

His uncle laughed. "No. I do need a new alternator. But *Maheo* put the trip to good use as well."

"I understand. However, I need to be able to drive safely. Will I continue to have these distractions wherever I go?"

"It is possible. Areas where there are many spirits with powerful energies will occasionally intrude, whether you are driving or not. You have learned to control your vision, but such places require more effort. Then you will be able to get where you wish without incident. Asking *Maheo* for protection will help you perceive only that which you're supposed to and assure your safe arrival."

Charlie walked a few yards from the road, got the tobacco out of his pocket, made an offering, then closed his eyes and prayed, thanking the Creator for the vision while asking the remainder of their journey be done in safety. He took a deep, cleansing breath, got back in his pickup, restarted the engine, and continued west.

When the onramp for Interstate 90 loomed ahead, a surge of fight-or-flight tingled through him. Any distractions at highway speeds were more serious. He focused on the present and proceeded, again seeking protection from *Maheo*. Peace folded around him like *amasani's* blanket, his mind clear as their journey continued.

Along the way, energy shifts indicated where fatal accidents occurred, appearing in his mind's eye. In some cases he sensed spirits who had not crossed over. On the return trip, White Wolf told him they would stop and sing the Journey Song to assist with their transition.

Gradually, such impressions became no more distracting than eighteen-wheelers thundering past. Confidence swelled within as he realized he was growing not only accustomed, but comfortable in this new world.

When they got to Billings they found a parts dealer on the northeast edge of town to avoid urban traffic, unsettling with or without visions. He never liked city driving, even when his view of the world was welded to the present. His uncle paid for his alternator as well as a new battery, just in case, and the pair left the store.

As soon as he got back behind the wheel, his cell phone rang. The sound was unfamiliar, a figment from the distant past. While he'd used it recently to call Sara, it hadn't rung since his arrival in Montana. He gawked at it in the cup holder as if it had materialized from another dimension, barely remembering that he'd brought it along. He picked it up, mind shifting between lifetimes, trying to remember how to answer. He fumbled with it momentarily, then flipped it open.

"H-hello?"

"Littlewolf! Finally! I's been trying to reach y'all for days. Where've y'all been? Y'all doin' okay?"

He blinked, still disoriented, trying to place the voice that sounded so familiar. Even English sounded strange, *Tsetsehestaestse* his dominant language upon arriving at the reservation. That brief conversation with Fernandez was the only exception.

"Who, uh,. . . is this?"

The words felt like stones tumbling from his mouth.

"This here's Trey. Don't tell me y'all's forgotten us already?"

"Oh! Trey. Right. I've been up in Montana, recuperating. There's not much of a signal up here."

"Right. Out in the Styx, eh? How's y'all doin'?"

"Better. Still have a ways to go."

"I'd sure like y'all to come back. Whenever y'all's ready."

His time working with Trey, Big Dick, and the LSO crew seemed no more than yesterday's dream.

One that ended badly.

"Thanks. I appreciate the offer. We'll see how it goes. If and when I get back to Colorado, I'll let you know. For now I'm just trying to get my strength back and bearings straight again."

"I understand. Just wanted to touch base and let y'all know we's thinkin' of y'all here and would be happier than a pig in shit if y'all'd come back."

He smiled, always entertained by the man's colorful analogies. "Thanks again, Trey. I'll let you know."

"Take care, Littlewolf. We miss y'all."

"Bye, Trey."

He hung up, staring out the windshield as the brief connection with his former life unleashed a flood of dormant thoughts—including Sara's admonition to get a new phone.

A blinking icon caught his eye. A voicemail notification from an unfamiliar number left five days ago. He listened. Sara's father. He and his wife were heading for New York. Sara wasn't doing well.

An instant replay of the vision of scattering her ashes returned. A surge of guilt mingled with panic raised the hair on the back of his neck.

What was the meaning of that shooting star?

Was her spirit leaving? Or coming back?

In his time-warped world, distracted by the trip to Billings, the previous night's urgency slipped away to simmer like a pot of venison stew that demanded no more than an occasional stir.

A stew that was about to burn.

Yanked back to the present, her situation hit like a charging bull elk. The purpose of his current fast was to obtain more information.

Would it be good? Or bad?

He closed his eyes and tuned in to her as he had before, sensing things had changed. Less static. She was still alive. But a sense of dread overshadowed the feeling.

While he had a signal, he had no excuse not to call. Find out directly how she was doing.

He turned to his uncle and said in English, "I apologize, uncle, but I must make another call."

The man's reply came in Cheyenne. "*Ésó-poóta.*" There is plenty of time.

He found Sara's number and hit connect. It rang several times. His concern edged closer to panic. After what seemed like forever, someone answered.

A woman, but not Sara.

"Hello? This is Charlie, Sara's friend. Is she there?"

"Oh! Hello, Charlie. This is Connie. How are you?"

"I'm doing okay, but I'm worried about Sara. How is she?"

The long pause renewed the fearsome jolt of moments before.

"She's struggling, Charlie. She woke up this afternoon, which is a huge relief. But unfortunately, all is not well. She's paralyzed from the hips down."

"Oh, no," he replied, hanging his head.

"The doctor explained that the greatest concentration of poison was where it made contact. There's considerable nerve damage in that area, which explains the paralysis. He said that nerves can sometimes heal, but very slowly. It can take years, in some cases, never. She's really depressed."

It felt as if Spring Thunder kicked him in the stomach. "Can I speak with her?"

"Hold on. I'll see if she's awake."

He held his breath, waiting.

"Charlie?" Her voice was as a feather's touch, soft and distant.

"Sara? How are you?"

It took several long moments before she answered. "I can't walk, Charlie. They don't know if I ever will. I don't want to live like this."

"Sara, listen. Maybe we can help. Do you want us to?"

Silence stretched again. "How?" Her voice was so quiet he could barely hear her.

"I have learned many things. We can help you heal. But it must be what you want. You must not only believe, but know *Maheo* can do anything."

Did her sniffling mean hope?

Or surrender?

"I don't want to live like this, Charlie. I was in a beautiful place. With Bryan and my mom. There was no pain. We were at peace. I was happy. But Mom told me to come back. That I would be glad I did. But I didn't know I'd be crippled. I don't know what to do. I want to go back."

"Sara, do you remember what I was like when you brought me home?"

"Yes. You were not yourself. You were very weak. I was horribly worried about you."

"Yes. But now I am fine. Better than before. I have learned things about myself and my people I never could have known. There's a reason you came back. Maybe it's to learn about *Maheo*. That he can do anything."

"You can make me better?"

"White Wolf knows how to get rid of bad medicine. *Maheo* is the one who heals. It isn't always easy, but it's worth it."

"If I come home will you be there?"

"Yes. I'm still in Montana, but I can drive again. I'll get a new phone, like you told me to. Maybe it will work at White Wolf's. Let me know when you'll be back. I promise to get there as soon as I can."

"Okay. I'll let you know. Bye, Charlie."

"*Ne Stae va' hose vooma'tse.* I will see you again."

Charlie closed the phone, scowled at it a moment, then turned to White Wolf in the seat beside him.

"I'll be right back."

He went back inside the parts outlet where he asked directions to the nearest Verizon store. The sales clerk brought it up on the computer, its location off Highway 90, conveniently on their route back.

Along the way he explained Sara's condition. All his uncle said was that someone put very evil medicine on her. When he made no mention of Charlie's offer to help guilt constricted his stomach.

Such requests were made humbly and formally with an appropriate offering, like when he asked White Wolf to help him. He'd assumed his concern and desire to help would be shared without hesitation. This dual role his uncle played, family on one hand, elder on the other, was as confusing as staying astride the red and white ponies.

"Forgive me," he said, grateful driving provided an excuse to avoid eye contact. "I need your help and did not make the request in the proper manner."

His uncle remained quiet for what seemed a long time. "I understand," he said at last. "You can do that after we get home."

His concerns spiked even more.

What if he didn't accept?

Medicine men reserved that right, particularly if *Maheo* declared it was not the right thing to do.

Was she supposed to remain paralyzed? Was this part of her destiny?

Based on past experience, he knew his uncle could read his thoughts. Reassurance never came, making him feel even more downhearted as they drove in silence for several more miles.

"How are you feeling, Littlewolf?" he finally asked. "Your journey was along a steep path. Your body is still healing. Accepting so many drastic changes and becoming one with your abilities present many challenges. It is too soon for you to take on another's troubles."

Leave it to White Wolf to humble him so pointedly. Riding a wave of over-confidence he made a fool of himself, to say nothing of possibly instilling Sara with vain hopes.

"You have not answered my question," he prompted.

Marcha Fox and Pete Risingsun

He hesitated, not sure of the correct answer. "My strength is returning and I am comfortable with what I have learned. But you are correct. There remains much I do not know."

Seeing his destination ahead on the right, he pushed the dilemma from his mind. Another challenge of a different nature awaited.

An hour later, he sat in his truck in the store's parking lot, trying to figure out his new smart phone. His uncle watched from the passenger seat, wearing another one of his knowing smiles.

Charlie shivered, feeling as if he'd fallen into an icy stream of snow melt. Tripping over the divide between two cultures had always been awkward; now he was even faltering in his own.

His eyes met those of the man beside him. Did he have trouble differentiating between his role as White Wolf versus Uncle Joe?

Unexpectedly, the man's appearance shifted to one bearing unspoken words of encouragement that warmed him like the rising sun.

One he'd seen decades before.

Beyond a doubt White Wolf was Eaglefeathers's son.

PERLEMAN EMERGENCY CENTER
NEW YORK CITY
August 2, Thursday
4:18 p.m. EDT

After talking with Charlie, Sara drifted off again. Somewhere in the shadows of her mind, the murmur of familiar sounds and dialog merged with her dream state. She was herself again, healthy and strong, balanced upon an oscillating beam, its pointed tip approaching a mysterious orb. She leaned into it, edging closer and closer to victory, driven by determination and force of will.

Wakefulness intruded, though the sounds remained. Her eyes cracked open.

Tomb Raider was playing on TV.

Lara Croft would be ashamed of her, not fighting to the last. Whether the conversation with Charlie was real or part of the dream didn't matter. Being defeated by those wicked people was no longer an option.

The screen blurred through a wall of tears.

"I want to go home," she said.

Her father's eyes emanated concern. "Your doctor has some additional treatments he wants to try. He believes he can help your body eliminate any remaining toxins, so your nerves can heal quicker. Then physical therapy can help you walk again."

"How long is that supposed to take?"

"I don't know, Sara. It depends. Probably weeks. Maybe months. Who knows?"

"How can we stay here that long? Besides, I want to go home. Charlie thinks that he and White Wolf can help me."

Will's face clouded like it did when they mentioned Patrice. "Come on, Sara. You trust them more than a qualified medical doctor for something this important?"

"Yes, I do. I've seen enough of hospitals this year. If Charlie can't help me, then I'll find a doctor in Denver."

"Okay, that sounds fair. But are you up to it? It's a long flight, plus all the airport hassle."

"Yes, Dad. I know. But I don't want to be here. It doesn't feel right. I want to go home."

"Okay. Your doctor makes his rounds about this time each day. When he comes by, we'll see how soon he'll release you. Once that's settled, I'll make flight reservations."

He slapped his forehead. "What am I thinking? I'll charter a private jet. It's about time you used some of that insurance money for yourself."

"Good idea, Dad. I like it. But please. Don't wait. Do it now. I don't care what the doctor says. It's time to go home."

WHITE WOLF'S RANCH
NORTHERN CHEYENNE RESERVATION
August 2, Thursday
3:08 p.m. MDT

Upon arriving back home, Charlie wasted no time going down to his room and placing a handful of tobacco in a small pouch. What he kept in his pocket had been used on the way home when he and White Wolf helped those spirits cross over they'd seen on the way into Billings.

As expected, his uncle stood outside beneath the oak, wearing buckskin and his black silk headband.

He set the offering on the ground before him. Then he beseeched him for his help with humility, deep respect, and a fair helping of anxiety.

What would he tell Sara if he failed to pick it up?

White Wolf's scrutiny was one of deep solemnity. His uncle studied him for several seconds, then regarded the pouch at his feet for an equal span of time.

Charlie held his breath, terrified at the prospect of a negative response. What seemed an eternity later, White Wolf stooped down and picked up the small bag.

"Yes, I will help you," he said. "But only because I have met your friend. She is good people. My wife has spoken of her many times. She brought you home. For that I owe her, too."

"*Néá eše*, White Wolf. Yes, she has helped me many times."

"You must understand. This is not simple. It is my responsibility to be home for anyone who requires assistance. I cannot be gone several days without someone equally qualified to take my place. I believe I can do that, but I need to know when and how long we'll be in Colorado. Before we leave, we will have a special sweat for you as well as your friend."

He paused, eyes fixed on Charlie as he shifted to a more imposing stance. "There is another matter we have not discussed. You did not complete your ceremonial fast with Eaglefeathers. To follow the *Tsetsehestaestse* way of life, you must do so before pledging any further rituals."

He folded his arms, emphasizing his message as he continued. "Spiritual preparation requires time and dedication. It is not an easy path. Your commitment and understanding must be as firm and imposing as Eaglefeathers Butte. There is little time and much work ahead. Will you vow that you are not wasting my time?"

White Wolf's eyes drilled into his own.

Charlie held his gaze, absorbing what he said with its many implications. Again he recognized the drilling accident as the wake-up call it was. Years of past failures gnawed at him like a beaver felling a tree.

If he'd obeyed Eaglefeathers years before, he would have been ready for such a crisis. This wasn't a situation where he could easily make up lost time, like cramming for college finals. The responsibilities he failed to assume for nearly two decades thundered around him as if he were caught in the eye of a tornado.

Still searching for who or what he was, at least now he knew where he belonged. There was no reason to straddle the cultural divide. He could walk beside it and "make a new way" as Morning Star declared over a century before.

Determination filled his heart, quieting the storm. No longer shrinking from his uncle's withering look, he met his gaze with one of equal strength.

"Yes. I will make such a vow," he said. "I am ready."

EPILOGUE

ELITE MANAGEMENT PARTNERS INC. (EMPI)
DOWNTOWN DENVER
August 6, Monday
1:42 p.m.

Paul "Mac" McCullough, a.k.a. Jason LaGrange, grinned as his bank balance increased by $1,748,284.30, courtesy of BKSS's offshore account. Now he could set up his own operation.

When Bernie got paid for the PURF job, working for EMPI gave him easy access to his bank information. He kept an eye on it, mostly out of curiosity, startled into action when that massive retainer hit.

Having never met Keller in person, he employed his scruffy-look persona for online meetings. That combined with a Southern Illinois drawl got him in the door, where he found out exactly what he was up to.

He knew that second-rate team would crater sooner or later. Johannsen was a loose cannon from the start. It was just a matter of time before that dimwit blew Keller's operation wide open.

With access to BKSS's surveillance resources, Jason knew Sara Reynolds survived. Otherwise, he would have waited for the second payment. If the cops hadn't traced Johannsen back to Keller, he would have turned him in himself.

He chuckled.

Was that a star performance or what when he delivered the poison? He knew damn well Keller fired Johannsen, just wanted

466

to see how things would play out. He reinstated his access to BKSS's surveillance resources and waited.

He was not disappointed.

Amateurs spying on some unwary target rarely noticed being watched themselves. All it took was a GPS tracker installed when he met Johannsen at the Centennial Airport. He laughed out loud, remembering the map that showed the abrupt stop that bad-ass Ram made at the bottom of a canyon.

Better yet, he knew exactly where that high-dollar retainer originated.

Should he turn them in? Or keep tapping that bottomless resource?

His options were open, one way or another.

We'll "tie another one to it" in Book 3

Revenge of Dead Horse Canyon:
Sweet Medicine Spirits - Novavose

ABOUT THE AUTHORS

Marcha Fox earned a bachelor's degree in physics from Utah State University in 1987, which facilitated a 20+ year career at NASA's Johnson Space Center in Houston, Texas.

Forever fascinated by the heavens, when her attempt to debunk astrology backfired, she pursued knowledge in that field as well. She graduated from the International Academy of Astrology's professional development program in 2012 and created ValkyrieAstrology.com. Much of

the popular website's informational content can be found in "Whobeda's Guide to Basic Astrology."

Her previous fiction work includes five novels in the hard science fiction genre. Her epic Star Trails Tetralogy series has been highly acclaimed for its family-oriented plot as well as its palatable and accurate science content. Directed primarily to teens and young adults with an interest in science or engineering, more information can be found on StarTrailsSaga.com.

Born in Peekskill, New York, she has lived in California, Utah, and Texas in the course of raising her family that comprises six grown children and numerous grandchildren and great-grandchildren. She pampers her indoor and outdoor cats while trying to keep up with her astrology clients, home, yard, garden, friends, family, and of course, writing.

Pete Risingsun is an enrolled member of the Northern Cheyenne Tribe well-versed in their ceremonies and traditions. He has served as a spirit helper to medicine men in ceremonial sweat lodges where traditional procedures are meticulously followed. Born the eighth child of ten in 1950, he was raised on a small ranch east of Busby, Montana. He's a proud fifth generation descendant of Chief Iron Shirt, a lodge keeper and powerful medicine man.

After graduating high school in 1968 he attended Montana State University for four years. When offered a position with Exxon as an employee relations director overseas, he turned it down, instead completing a three-year apprenticeship in plant operations in Billings, Montana. He worked in that capacity for one additional year until he accepted a job as adult education director for the Northern Cheyenne Tribe back home in Lame Deer, grateful to see the refinery fade away in the rear-view mirror.

Back on the reservation, Pete raised black angus cattle and bred championship Quarter horses. He served as a Tribal Council member for six years and was the first Northern Cheyenne elected as a Rosebud County Commissioner, a position he held from January 1, 2007 to December 31, 2012.

He's the proud father of one daughter, Echo Raine, who blessed him with two grandchildren, Sierra Star and Skyler Seven. Pete is currently retired, but stays busy co-writing *The Curse of Dead Horse Canyon* series as well as compiling an accurate history of his tribe from the Northern Cheyenne point of view.

Learn more about the authors, how to contact them
on social media, and news of future works at
Dead-Horse-Canyon.com

www.ingramcontent.com/pod-product-compliance
Lightning Source LLC
LaVergne TN
LVHW042134130425
808565LV00034B/340